Afterdeath

Afterdeath

Benoit Chartier

Copyright © 2017 by Benoit Chartier

All rights reserved. This book or any portion thereof may not be reproduced or used in any manner whatsoever without the express written permission of the publisher except for the use of brief quotations in a book review.

Printed in Canada by Imprimerie Gauvin

First Printing, 2017

ISBN 978-0-9947408-2-3
Trode Publications
Gatineau, Canada
www.trode.ca

MIX
Paper from responsible sources
FSC
www.fsc.org FSC® C100212

Cover Illustration By Cryssy Cheung @ www.cryssycheung.com

I'd like to thank Tierra and Jacqueline Walker, as well as Cory Tibbits and Majid Kafai for their inspiration and hard work. To my precious Beta Readers Lee Ann Farruga, Barbara Florio Graham and Peggy Lehmann, I am in your debt. Thanks to my good friend Pier-Adam Turcotte of P.A.T. Productions for technical support and so much more. Of course, another book would not have been possible without the help of Sylvie Côté and Tony Priftakis and my invaluable of invaluables, Mariko Hara Chartier and Kota Raphael Chartier. I love you all.

Table of Contents

Prologue ············1

Chapter 1: Saying Goodbye ············2

Chapter 2: Last Visit ············12

Chapter 3: Awakening ············26

Chapter 4: Angelina ············38

Chapter 5: Necropolis ············46

Chapter 6: Olivia ············59

Chapter 7: Ferry ············66

Chapter 8: Hunters ············77

Chapter 9: Sunset on Necropolis ············82

Chapter 10: Vikings ············93

Chapter 11: Escape ············114

Chapter 12: Steel Queen ············125

Chapter 13: Wodun ············141

Chapter 14: What We Were ··154

Chapter 15: Break-In ··169

Chapter 16: Return ··181

Chapter 17: Maman Margot ··192

Chapter 18: Getaway ··215

Chapter 19: Middle of Nowhere ····································226

Chapter 20: Choices ···260

Chapter 21: The Wylds ··271

Chapter 22: New Beginning? ···280

Chapter 23: Rescue Effort ··291

Chapter 24: Trapping the Monster ································299

Chapter 25: Reawakening ···304

Chapter 26: Going Home ···313

Chapter 27: Theatre ···316

Chapter 28: The Well ···324

Prologue

There exist worlds.
Universes bordering your own, separated by thin, yet impenetrable veils. Neighbors to your reality. Shifts, forks and bends that split from the original timeline, ages ago. Or merely moments.
There appear worlds.
Places within Universes that occur unseen, nestled within realities, where time and space blur and hiccup. Or are denied.
There become worlds.
That, inherent to your evolving vision of them, shift their meaning, like fresh eyes after a molt. Or remain grey, featureless, immovable walls; purpose and agency denied by those who decry: "I cannot!"
There are an infinity of infinities, all coexisting. Waiting to be explored, experienced, and changed. They are waiting for you to do so.

-The Wahy

Chapter 1

SAYING GOODBYE

No angels showed up at Grandma Rose's funeral. Not a whole lot of actual people, did, either. Apart from the dutifully stern/sad-looking funeral lady, there was me and Olivia. Chloe and Olivia Borders. My twin was presently going from one statuary of God's pigeon-people to another, caressing their stone-like, white pottery feathers with the tips of her mocha-coloured fingers in a not-quite sensual way. Clever lines had been painted on them to make the plaster statuary appear made out of marble. A well done "trompe-l'oeil" unless you happened to be inspecting the thing. Sunlight choked through faux stained-glass, hitting the row of variably sized proto-humans, and I could tell she sat on the verge of some sort of religious epi-phony.

"Hello?" I said to her, trying to wake her out of her sleepwalking trance.

"Think they came down as soon as they saw her pass away, Chloe?" she said, meaning the angels, staring at them still, not having heard me at all.

I think they would have stayed the hell away from our Grandma, I thought. *I think if they knew what was good for them, they'd have known not to tangle with ol'Rose.*

"Yeah, they just rushed down from the Skies and whooshed her away," I said, crossing my arms. I looked over at the copper metal urn containing her ashes, on a central dais that was cleverly lit from above, like a comedian in the spotlight, or police interrogation room. A wreath of white flowers, her namesake, leaned against the Greek (or was it Roman?) column bearing her urn. Her portrait propped up to one side, in case we'd already forgotten what she'd looked like. Her short, curly white hair accented her mischievous grin, smile lines pleating her beautiful brown eyes, deep-set in her cherubic face behind ebony skin.

The faux wood-panelling and dark velvet curtains gave the scene a play-like atmosphere. A dull one. I could imagine our deceased grandmother sitting at the front row, semi-transparent at her own funeral, giving the whole proceedings the slow, cynical clap it deserved. This wasn't her, not by far. I could picture her ghost, irate at all this somber bullshit glaring at the whole proceedings, tisking, while shaking her head in disapproval, in a manner that was proper only to her. She'd turn around and raise an eyebrow at me, asking silently: "Why?" And I wouldn't know what to tell her.

I could have envisioned her body dressed in something nice, crowd-surfing at a Grateful Dead concert. Not this. I couldn't for the life of me comprehend why she would have arranged this as her last wishes. By all appearances, someone'd hijacked her funeral to make a mockery of her death. But there were only the two of us left. I doubt my own sister was responsible.

The same type of music that must have been played while the Titanic sank rang tinny from speakers in the recesses of the room, giving me sparkling shivers every time the frigid waters of the Arctic came to the forefront of my mind.

This sucked. The only oblivious person to the fact was Olivia, who made the rounds from angel to angel, peering into every child-like face as if it could be her own, some day. I sighed. Olivia frowned.

"What?" she said.

I only shrugged and wished I could leave, but of course, that would have been lacking in proper respect. Kind of like the whole present event.

Of course, there could have been no others than Olivia and I to attend. Our mother was her only child, and Grandpa had died years ago. Our great uncle Philbert had been a confirmed bachelor, and, being older than Rose and male, had been only around briefly while we were young.

Mom and dad were a distant memory, kept alive by the pictures we'd squirrelled away in various albums in our rooms.

Simply put, death surrounded us and our family. Distant relatives shunned Rose, because, as they'd told us, she was "hard to handle." That's exactly what I'd loved about her. That's why this was such an unsatisfactory end for me. You'd never expect her to go quietly. Not even at her own funeral.

Crazy how Olivia smiled and looked enchanted by this place, like she'd found her very own personal theme park, and it was even more wonderful than she'd imagined. Maybe she'd start hanging around at other people's funerals and tell them "how wonderful it was," and I couldn't suppress the shudder that came with it.

The imaginary ghost in the front row was getting antsy, and I wanted to leave, so badly.

Afterdeath

'Livia paced around the room, more interested in the trappings of simulated peace than the person we'd come to see, and I felt my neck stiffen. Grandma's ghost had crossed her arms in the front and I had to leave the room.

The warm summer air blasted my face, and the simulacrum of eternal rest was blown away. Here, life *lived.* The busy traffic on Carling Avenue rushed by a few steps away from me, oblivious to the fact that my world had ended. Olivia was still inside, and the heat of the afternoon sun baked the sidewalk I'd planted my feet on. The funeral silence was replaced by twittering birds and the bustling street. No wind blew that day, and so the surrounding trees simply stood guard and watched me put my face in my hands and sit on the steps to the Funeral Home.

I felt an arm around my shoulder.

"Hey you," Olivia said. I don't know how long I'd sat there, lost in my shambling thoughts.

"Hey," I said, feeling nothing.

"You could have stayed a bit longer," she said. Right. And stick around for that whole charade?

"We could have left a lot earlier, too," I replied. I looked over at her, and she shrugged.

"Let's go. We still have to see what's left at our— her house," I said. We hadn't lived there in almost three years, but it still felt like home. We'd done most of our growing up at the brownstone on 31 Gwynne Avenue. Driving back there now reminded me of the empty hole in my heart. Like I'd have to start digging to make it even deeper when I got there. I sighed.

We pulled up to the well-kept house and parked behind Rose's now abandoned 77 Olds 98 Regency Brougham, spotless baby blue save for a touch of rust creeping up on the front grill. I thought of all those times the thing would come to life in the morning when Rose would head out to her nursing job at the Ottawa General Hospital, five minutes away. Her waving her hand at us as we got ready for school in the morning. I'd always waggle my fingers to my nose at her, and she'd mock-scold me as she drove away, the rumble of the car like something you only heard in old movies.

Always the morning shifts, out at 6:30, so that she could be back by evening to spend time with us at night. She'd help us with homework, or whatever crisis we were going through at school. We'd hear the slamming of the door to that beast of a car and her voice calling out as the side door opened:

"I'm home, my little chickens!" and so it went every day until we were sixteen. Until grandma Rose got sick and started forgetting things. Until she started forgetting what things *were.* And then we couldn't stay with grandma anymore.

"You have the key, right?" Olivia asked, as we stepped to the side door. The weeds were starting to show through the cracks wedged between the house and the driveway. Otherwise, it was still pristine, a neighbour having been kind enough to re-asphalt, the previous year. The bottom half was brownstone, and the top a beige stucco. The attic had a dormer sheepishly sticking out from the front of the square house, with old-style six-paned windows that had never been changed. The brown tar-paper roof perfectly matched the skirt, and everything wrapped itself nicely together in warm, earthy tones. Its nicest feature, by far, was the front porch, which had recently been redone, the guardrail resplendent with new pine. The house looked like it had always been a work in progress, but nothing was ever out of synch, as if rejuvenation became it. This is where we'd gone from little girls to teenagers, in a flash. Where *she'd* grown up all her life. She'd stayed in the ancestral home until the last year of her sickness, the last bout coming in hard and fast.

She gave her last breath on the same ward she'd worked at for forty years, which was fitting, I guess. When Olivia and I got word that she was leaving this world for good, we went down to Civic, and had trouble getting to her room; all the staff was there, saying their goodbyes. They loved her as much as we did. Stupid that her family did not. Can't please everybody, I guess.

"Yeah, right here." I put the key in the lock, the old tarnished copper-coloured metal bit slipping in on its own, as if overjoyed to be home, and the clunk of the deadbolt felt like relief. I hadn't been back in a while. Not since Rose had been in the hospital. I'd been busy trying to finish school, and was still adjusting to life at the foster home. So was Olivia, although she'd been placed closer. Yeah, we weren't together. Some sort of cock-up in the system had made it so that we'd been split up, and I was put in a foster home a few hours away, in Renfrew. Not having a car or reliable mode of transportation meant my sister was constantly out of reach. Two hours away, but it might as well have been different planets.

Sure we'd talked on the phone, and met occasionally, but it was a far cry from being constantly together to being eternally apart. I'd missed her terribly. And then I adjusted to my new life. I think it was a lot harder for Olivia. I could tell on the rare occasions that she'd talk about it, that her new foster home wasn't as welcoming as mine was.

We'd applied to be together, but you know bureaucracies.

I turned the door knob, and stepped inside.

I was greeted with emptiness, the likes of which I've never experienced. All her things were gone. *Everything* was gone. All the furniture, books, plants, refrigerator, stove, everything, down to the area rug we'd played on while she read books in her lazy-boy recliner beside us. It was worse than that, though. It was the sucking out of

Afterdeath

life, like being back in the funeral parlour, without the benefit of the mood music. Even the sound of the major thoroughfare, only meters away, was drowned out by the silence. Everything was…

Gone.

"I think they came by yesterday to take everything to the Goodwill," Olivia said, walking past me. I could see the ghost-shadows of drawers that had been against the wall for a hundred years, turning the flower-and-vine wallpaper behind it pale. Or was it simply that it had remained the same while all else changed?

I walked around in a daze, and like at her wake, could picture all those missing items returned, but transparent, their spirits still there even though the physical specimens had been removed. I could run my hand over that lazy boy recliner, and I could trip on that rug like I always did when I was a kid. I could run my hand in the lampshade until I found the little switch that was so hard to turn that I had to ask for help to click it until I was eight. But Rose wasn't here anymore. That I could feel.

It was so—odd. The fact that you knew that love was a tangible thing. That it existed. That you could feel it. And the time that you could weigh it most was when its absence left that hole inside your chest, like a crater that crumbled at the edges, telling you: "I can never be filled."

Olivia's footsteps came to me from somewhere on the other side of the house. Creaky old stairs to the basement I'd been too scared to stay in, but Grandma had shown me the way to beat monsters by showing a fist. How she must have laughed, seeing me go down there with a very serious five year-old face, a white-knuckled, tense little hand in front of me. Our parents were still alive back then, but I remember it being the first time we'd stayed with Rose for a weekend alone. But she hadn't laughed, of course. She'd told me how brave I was and shook my hand. Like an adult.

"I found it!" I heard Olivia say, and wondered what could possibly have been left after this tsunami of departure. She came back up the stairs with a cardboard box, the edges torn and taped, the cover concave from years of abuse. Mostly by us.

The cover was written in a 1970's font that no serious person would ever use today, and the illustration was a photo of two people with their hands on the planchette, supposedly calling forth the spirits of the dead. Or demons. Depending on whose interpretation you ascribed to. Now, for those uninitiated in the use of a Ouija board, it's basically a piece of wood or cardboard, with the alphabet written on it, the words "yes" and "no", as well as "good bye" underneath. There is a small, heart-shaped piece that comes with it, and the participants place their hands on it. The idea is that a "spirit" comes through the players, and directs the planchette to letters, in order to make words. Therefore communicating with the world of the living. Scary fun, huh?

Well, we used to do that when we were teenagers (must have been around twelve or thirteen when we first used it). We'd found this old thing in Uncle Philbert's stuff while rooting around downstairs. Ever since then, we'd hid it behind a fake wooden panel in the basement so that it wouldn't "accidentally" go missing. I sometimes wondered if Rose and Philbert had played with the Ouija board when they were kids, but thought that asking would be attracting attention to the fact that I'd found the thing. Best leave that alone.

"Wow! You found it!" I said. It'd been at least three years, maybe more, since we'd touched the thing. I, of course, no longer believed in that stuff. There was no room in a scientific world for afterlife nonsense.

"I wonder if it still works." Olivia said. She, on the other hand, was still a firm believer of nonsense and spirituality.

"Of course it doesn't 'work', 'Livia. It's just a toy." I felt exasperation at even having to say it.

"You want to try it anyhow?" She wanted to contact Rose. That much was clear. As much as my wishful thinking wanted the same thing, I knew it was stupid to take part in that fantasy world. Then again, maybe if I could prove that none of it existed, perhaps I could prove to Olivia that what she believed was false, and even damaging.

"Well, okay I guess."

"Tonight. We'll do it properly. Like we used to," she said, and I could see the excitement in her eyes. Is that why she'd wanted to come back to the old house? Or did she just want to be where we'd been safe for so long?

I looked outside and the sun was low on the horizon. I could feel a craving growing in my stomach, and nothing in this house would fill it.

"You want to go for supper?" Olivia asked, mirroring my thoughts.

"Sure," I said, and she placed the battered box on the separator that divided the open kitchen from the living room. I made one more round around the house, basking in our old room, and taking a minute of silence in Rose's, and we left through the same side entrance we'd come in. Crickets had started their leg-rubbing in the tall grasses behind the house, and the pillowy clouds had taken on a purplish-orange hue.

Davey's on Carling was an old haunt of ours, ever since Rose'd taken us there our first day back from the lake trip. The one that hadn't gone so well for us.

"I'll have the Reuben," I told Carla, the half-owner, half-server there. Her husband Dave was in the kitchen with his son and daughter, cooking up the food. Dave had gone to grade school with Rose, and she'd been one of his very first customers, way back in the day. She'd been a regular since.

"Just the house salad for me," Olivia said.

"Have you gone vegetarian?" I asked.

Afterdeath

"Just not hungry, Chlo," she said, attempting a smile. I explained to Carla we'd just lost Rose, and she patted us on the hands, saying how sorry she was, that she'd heard it from Dave. They were warm, calloused and sincere, but sorry wouldn't bring her back, would it.

I thought of leaving the city of my discontent for a while. Just going. It felt like the pall had fallen on the entire place, and it wasn't just localized to the house. The whole city was under it, making it reek of death.

Choking me.

We used to escape it at times, to go camping, and cross-country, but it'd been years since we'd done it.

"You feel like going on a road trip, Olivia?" It just came out, without thinking about it. Spontaneous, but right. Olivia looked at me, rocking from side to side, as if considering her options, her fingers intertwined and elbows on the table. It was almost mid-summer, and I knew she was working all the time.

"Well, I would like to, but I would have to ask my boss. Summertime is usually pretty slow, but I still have to ask." So a definite maybe.

I wasn't working at the moment, but still stayed with my foster parents. Olivia had a place of her own in Vanier, and worked for a small furniture store with a silly name. "Sofa So Good" was the worst name I'd ever heard, but she did well there anyhow, taking orders and working in the office. The owner was a French Canadian with an appalling sense of humour.

We finished eating, and Olivia asked for the cheque. She must have known I was broke. Carla told us that Dave was waiving it this time. We looked over at the kitchen area, and Dave's face could be seen at the hot-line, giving us a stiff upper lip and two thumbs up. We both thanked them profusely, and Olivia still left a ten dollar bill on the table for tip.

"Why'd you do that?" I asked

"It's not because you get a free meal that you don't leave a tip. You leave even more, then." I'd forgotten that she'd worked as a waitress a few years ago, right here, nonetheless.

We stopped by the dollar store while the sun was now throwing its last rays of light over the rooftops, and we picked up the necessary items for tonight's ritual. We did this with the kind of girlish glee that we'd had on the first tries of the Ouija board; a kind of transgressional trepidation of doing something definitely not right, but mighty fun.

It was dark out when we got back to the house on Gwynne Street, and the orange fluorescents cast short shadows beneath them. This time, the deadbolt made it harder for us to get in, and I had to give the whining door a bit of a push while turning the key for it to give.

It was dark inside, of course, and with no lamps or light sources other than the outside street lamps shining through the front window, the empty house looked downright creepy. I rustled inside one of my dollar store bags and found a box of white candles. I slipped it open and tapped one out. I rustled some more and found the lighter I'd bought. The red plastic kind with the long neck and the childproof push-lock used to light barbecues. The kind you just loved twirling like a six-shooter before clicking on and blowing out.

I lifted the wick from my candle and lit it. The flickering yellow light shone on the emptiness inside, making the shadows dance devilishly. Olivia fiddled around with one of her bags and found a small black metal candle holder. She took my candle and set it near a corner. I would light candles, and she would put them down. There was nothing strategic about it; just as many candles as we could light to make the night leave us alone for a while.

She picked up the box she had left on the separator. She set it down in the middle of the room and lifted the old cover. Inside smelled of mildew and old glue, and I screwed up my nose as the wooden plank came out with a cloud of paper dust from the typewritten instructions. It was a thick board, with the letters and symbols singed into it, not printed, as more recent games might have been. I set it on the floor, and she found the planchette, which had fallen out.

She took a deep breath, and I looked nervously about. Nothing would happen. That much was certain. This was a game for the superstitious. I'd stopped believing in that crap. So why had I agreed to play this again? Oh right, for her to stop being superstitious.

The silence in the house was deadly. I'm sure that in horror movies, they'd have evil, nasty sounds and music playing in the background to make your skin crawl. All we had was nothingness, and the sound of our breathing, which made it worse. Once in a while, a candle would make a flickering, fizzing noise, perhaps from a draft in the house.

"Are you ready?" she said, as we both knelt in front of the board. Might as well have gone upstairs and called Bloody Mary in front of the mirror for all we were doing now; it was just as dumb.

"Sure," I said, rolling my eyes mentally. Of course we'd loved this game when we were kids, but now it was just silly, and I'd prove to her just how silly it was.

We both placed our hands on the planchette, and I felt my throat dry up.

"We are calling upon the spirits and the ghouls of the other plane. We are calling upon you to reach our grandmother Rose," she said, and I thought: *knew it*.

Afterdeath

"Think of her," Olivia told me, "think of her as hard as you possibly can, so that she will come back to us. Think of her now, so that we may communicate with our grandmother." Don't ask me why, but I did. I thought deep and hard about my grandmother, the woman who'd raised us for so many years. The lovely person she'd been, sometimes stern, but always loving. I thought of her and wanting her to be with us. I thought of her and wanting to say goodbye, one last time.

The candles flickered. Hard.

My heart skipped a beat.

Olivia looked up and smiled.

"She's here," she whispered to me, and that might have been the scariest thing I'd ever heard. My skin began to crawl, my stomach lurching. But then something bad started to happen. My fingers moved. Olivia's fingers moved. The planchette moved under them. I wanted to take back my fingers, but they were glued to the piece of heart-shaped wood. Olivia stared at her moving fingers with fascination, and I did so with horror. I strained to take my hands back, but still they moved without my control.

The planchette moved up to a letter. The letter was "I". And Olivia would sound the letter under her breath. The planchette moved again, this time to the letter "F", then "O", then "U", then "N", then "D", and every time, Olivia would sound the letter, and in my head, all I could think was: *nonononononono!*

It was wrong. It was all wrong, and this wasn't a game. More than that, whatever it was, wasn't Rose. The planchette kept moving, all on its own, as if our fingers were only riders on a boat, and it knew where it was going, taking us along for the ride. "Y", then "O", then finally, "U". I screamed, and pulled as hard as I could, and finally, the planchette let go of my hand.

I found you. But what?

I found you. But how?

"We—we made contact," Olivia said, breathlessly. Not terrified, but also not as enthusiastic as she'd been a few moments ago. Her eyes as wide as dinner plates, and her mouth dipping into disbelief. On the board, the planchette moved *on its own*, to the words "Good Bye", which were inscribed at the bottom.

Then the candles snuffed out, all at the same time, letting out an exhalation of white smoke that twirled about like the longing caress of the Dead.

We ran.

We ran to the car, leaving everything behind, save the car keys and our purses. Olivia jumped into the driver's seat and started up her old beater. She screeched out of the driveway, and we booked it down the street. It wasn't until we were a lot farther down Carling Avenue that she turned to me and said:

"I'll—I'll see what I can do about getting that time off tomorrow, okay?" she said, and she smiled at me, but her eyes were an off-colour shade of shit-scared.

"Yeah, yeah, you do that," I said, running the night's events through my head, not quite comprehending the complete picture. She invited me to stay at her place, telling me she didn't feel like driving me all the way back to Renfrew. I agreed, even though it felt more like she needed me close after that weird incident, and to be honest, I felt the same way.

We never did go back to that house, and I think it was just as well. All good memories of it lived in the past, now.

Chapter 2

LAST VISIT

The next day greeted me from the un-draped window of her apartment's living room. I'd fallen asleep on her couch, as I'd done on so many other occasions when visiting. The place was squeaky clean, the total opposite of how I kept my room, because, echoing Rose as she did: "You never knew who might come visit." Not that anyone ever did, as far as I knew. Olivia was shy. Not terminally so, but she didn't go out of her way to invite people over, that at least I was painfully aware of. Apart from the Crosstian Youth group she was a part of, I had no idea if she had any other friends. Across from me was a cheap TV stand with gold trim, the kind you could pick up by the curb-side any given garbage day. The couch had been a gift from the Ministry. A statue of Jesus looked at me forlornly from the top of the stand, between a family portrait of Rose, Olivia and I, and a ceramic white book with some sort of inspirational quote written in silver lettering across its glossy, white, open pages. I felt as if I was visiting an ailing spinster aunt at the retirement home, once again.

"Morning," I heard her say, as I got up to stretch. A kink in the neck was the usual payback for my restless nights on the rough sofa. I was happy to notice that the neck-pain was absent, but I'd inherited the uneven waffle pattern imprinted on the side of my reddened face. So laughed the mirror on the dining room wall.

"Morning," I said, rubbing blood back into my cheek. She was already dressed and ready for work. What time was it?

"Help yourself to whatever. I have to run," she said, and waved goodbye as she went to the door, closing it behind her. We'd come to the agreement that I could stay an extra day at her place. It was Sunday, after all, and I had nowhere to go but back to my place in the sticks. Instead, I'd spend the day in Oddawa and wander about town. Maybe do a bit of window shopping. Have a nice coffee. In short, enjoy all the amenities that were in short supply in a small town. Besides, I could save a bit of gas by taking the bus around town.

I dressed and ate, putting the pyjamas Olivia had lent me in the basket, then headed out the door.

It was a gorgeous day, and I took the number fourteen bus all the way downtown. I'd save money on parking that way. Oddawa was a bureaucratic town, and to be honest, there wasn't that much to do apart from museums and gawking at the Parliament Buildings, but one place I loved was the Bytown Market. Located in the centre of town, behind a mall that straddled Riddell Street, the Market had a great many things to offer. A central building which had at some point been a warehouse been transformed into a cornucopia of shops and restaurants, whose doors all stood open to the sidewalk, on all sides. Curries and teas, spices and chocolates, divine odors to a starving girl in need of lunch, all wafted temptingly out of the building like a cornucopia. Surrounding this two-story rectangular brown brick building were merchants and hawkers under white awnings, selling fruit and vegetables as well as jewelry and hand-crafted items, plants and maple syrup. It was two blocks away from the Parliament Buildings, separated by the Canal and a hotel styled after a European castle, as well as a few city blocks of two hundred year old heritage buildings.

Today the place was hopping. Being the Capital of the country meant that tourism was a must. Bus-loads of tourists poured out of the long, sleek vehicles, cameras clicking at a frenetic pace as they were shepherded to the next point of interest by loud, flag-waving guides. Asians and Europeans, from what I could tell, wandered the sidewalks of the Market, admiring the merchandise and pointing to places that they, for lack of having the equivalent in their home countries, found interesting.

I'd never been off the continent. I wondered what it would be like for me to go to China, or France, or Spain, and be the one who didn't speak the language. I thought they were pretty brave, tour group notwithstanding, to leave their comfort zones, to see how others lived.

The sun beat down on the cracked pavement, and the smell of coffee, hot dogs, as well as fresh asphalt came on the wind. It would be a hot day, and I stepped under the Market's awning, walking slowly among the stands, watching the tourists turn objects over in their hands and ask questions of the shop-owners. It seemed like an interesting life, to be outside all day, selling your wares to visitors from far away, who would take the things you made back to their far-flung countries to use or display in their homes. A lot different from the nine-to-five grind.

What did I want to be?

This looked like a fun life, but what did these people do in the winter time? Did they migrate down south like the geese? Was it their full-time work, or simply retirement projects?

People drank steeped tea, on long-legged stools around tiny circular tables painted fire-engine red. The babble of voices and laughter flowing from the restaurants was constant, but reassuring. I was alone, but not. A little brown girl carried by her white father was eating an ice cream cone with long, concentrated licks, and some of it dripped down the side, onto his navy-blue shirt, and I smiled. He was talking to his gorgeously wavy-haired black wife, who was pushing a stroller. The baby inside looked as big as a hand, but the love in her mother's eyes could have filled the Market itself.

All of a sudden I caught myself feeling happy. And for that I felt guilty.

I spent some of my remaining money on a sandwich outside the Market (touristy places always jack up the prices, naturally), and went back to the apartment, staring out the window of the bus to this city which until recently had been the friendliest place on earth. But back then there had been an anchor that kept it that way, and she had drifted off to somewhere else. Into nothingness.

Olivia, thankfully, had her cable television account paid up, and I watched my favourite afternoon shows. I also updated my social media accounts, explaining to friends what was going on in my life, and of course got the regulatory amount of sad faces and condolences for our loss.

When Olivia came back around five, she seemed pretty upbeat.

"Hey, why don't we leave tomorrow?" she said, as she sat down next to me on the couch. That got my attention right quick, and I turned the TV off.

"Are you serious? I thought you had to get time off from work?" I said, stunned. She kind of squirmed and said:

"Well, I asked, and Jean-Charles says I can go for three weeks. It is the dead season after all. Things usually pick up around the fall when we start having end-of-the-line sales. Now would be a perfect time to go. What about you? Do you want to leave tomorrow?" she said, with a smile. I was torn. This sounded too good to be true. Ever since our grandma's passing, I'd wanted to refresh my thoughts in some other part of the country. After last night, I most definitely wanted to go. But tomorrow? That felt like a jump off the diving board.

"Listen, I gave it a lot of thought last night before going to bed. I do want to go, and soon. It's been a long time since we took an actual road trip. This will remind me of the good times we used to have with her. That's how I see it," she said. I did see her point. For her it was a way to reconnect with the past.

"Like when she rented that Winnebago when we were twelve, remember that?" I said.

"...and got a flat tire outside of Wawa?" she said, grinning.

"Haha, yeah, and it took two hours for the tow truck to get there, so you chased frogs, and she kept saying..."

"Olivia! Get out of that ditch! You're going to get dirty!' God, it's been so long," she answered, putting a hand on her cheek. "That was what, a hundred years ago?"

"Surely my dear, you do exaggerate!" I said, shaking her gently, laughing.

"I miss her, Chlo," she said, her hand still on her cheek, which had reddened. I could tell what was coming. I put my arm around her shoulder, hugging her close.

"Me too, Liv," I said. She trembled slightly under my embrace.

"I... I miss her so much, Chlo!" I put her head against my shoulder and held her.

"I know. I know. Shh, it's okay," I said into her ear.

"Do you think she's in heaven?" she said. God, the question that killed. My heart popped a few rungs down the ladder.

"I don't know where she is, Liv, but wherever it is, it has to be better than what she was going through." I pulled her away and looked into her down-turned face. "Hey, look at me," and I squeezed a smile onto my face. She looked up, let one corner of her mouth lift, gave a nod, and asked:

"Where do you want to go?"

I shook my head and shrugged my shoulders, letting out a sound as a shorthand for *I have no idea.*

"How about all the way, this time?" she said. We'd never managed to make it to Vancouver. It had been our dream, but somehow, we had always stopped short. This seemed like great idea. We'd get to travel again together, as we hadn't since we were kids.

"Yeah! Let's do it! And if we can't, we'll just let the Winnebago die in Wawa!" I said.

She giggle-sobbed, and ran her sleeve across her face.

"Or hitch-hike the rest of the way," she said.

"Or hitch-hike the rest of the way, yes," I replied. I made some mental calculations.

"How about I go home tonight and you can get packed. We can meet up in Kanada tomorrow, almost halfway, and then we could go on to Toronto, taking it by the Great Lakes." I said. This seemed the most sensible way, plus, if we were going to do this trip, I wanted the option of not being stuck in the forest for three days, guaranteed if we took the Trans-Canada Highway. Besides, I had a friend in Kanada who would

Afterdeath

watch over my car for the duration. She agreed, and I headed back to Renfrew before the sun began to set.

***

It was six a.m. when I got to Travis' house in Kanada. Travis had said he'd wake up early. His parents didn't mind my parking my hunk of junk in the driveway, off to the side. It was just a tad chilly when I got there, but the sun was starting to peak over the houses in this modern suburban development, and Travis' mom had been incredible enough to make me a hot cup of coffee.

"He's still asleep," she said, as we stood out front on the driveway, me leaning on my old dilapidated orange Sunfire, and she holding her cup with both hands.

"I guess I'll see him when we get back," I grinned.

"That child of mine was never a morning person." That's the least you could say about him, but he was kind, and he was usually dependable.

"Unlike his mum," I said.

"Oh, his mother is amazing, I'll give you that," she said, lifting her mug in a toast. Olivia pulled in then with her grey Sonata. It was the old kind, before they modelled it after the Mercedes. It was round, and beautiful in its own rights, and a lot more dependable than my rust-bucket.

"Hi there, I'm Olivia," she said, holding out her hand, after getting out.

"My, you two do look alike," she said, shaking it.

"Only superficially," I said. "Olivia is the brains of this operation."

"I am. I just don't brag about it," my sister answered, staring at the ground.

"Well, you both be careful on the roads, okay? Drive in shifts and try not to do it after dark, if you can avoid it. It's fatigue that can be the most dangerous," Travis' mother said.

"No worries there. We plan on taking our time. Thanks for the advice, though," I told her. Not mentioning Rose made me feel slightly better. If she had offered her condolences, it would have started this trip on an odd foot. Leaving her out of this for now made the whole enterprise a different story. One of adventure instead of grieving.

This was, to my mind, the perfect time to go. Our hectic schedules and personal lives had kept potential long-term relationships at bay, so there was nobody on either of our sides to say goodbye to. Neither one of us had a boyfriend. I had left mine a few months previous and was soured to the idea of meeting anyone new in the near-future. I just needed time to recuperate before launching myself into anything. Since I was to go off on a trip, no point in attempting the scene before leaving. I didn't know what Olivia's deal was, but as far as I knew, she had pretty much stayed away from relationships all her life. Another point where we differed. I saw the way those boys at school looked at me, and thought I chose wisely. I guess she just stayed away, period.

Of both our cars, hers was considered the most road-worthy, and this, just by looking at them. Besides, I think my engine had accumulated a hundred thousand kilometres more than hers had. The previous owner had been a tad bit of a skater and hippie, and had taken it out West a few times for cherry picking during the summer. I'd left some of the skateboard company stickers on the dashboard. I thought they gave my ride some style. I'd added my own, of course. My car had travelled more than I had. I tried to keep my jealousy at bay.

As much as we had enjoyed the camper so many years ago, we thought we'd enjoy staying in motels and hotels more. Besides, renting was expensive, and there was something about having to find a campsite before six pm that I didn't like. I thought, if we want to go further, we should be able to go further, and the idea of parking this huge thing in a shopping mall parking lot kind of creeped me out. No, Liv and I agreed that driving the car would be both safer and more comfortable. Rose had left us a bit of money in her estate, having no other family to speak of (she had some, but she didn't like to talk about them. Ba-doom-ching!). We wouldn't stay in the lap of luxury, of course, but there would be no garbage rummaging, either.

I started pulling my luggage out of my trunk, and she opened hers. The exhaust sputtered from her car's tail pipe as I lifted my big plastic suitcase and inserted it among the various odds and ends she had packed, very neatly, of course.

I gave Mrs. Dirkson the key to my car and a big hug, asking her to send it to her son when he would become conscious, and she replied that it would be a miracle if he ever did, and we both laughed.

I got in the car on the passenger's side, and Olivia put down her phone, which she'd been fiddling with, checking her messages, no doubt.

"Aren't you freezing?" I said, rubbing my shoulders.

"They're announcing thirty degrees later on," she said, but I noticed the goosebumps on her bare shoulders.

"Suit yourself," I said, and she started the engine and we left. Liv popped in some Shania Twain. Not really my type of music, but we had a rule: drivers got to choose, no matter what the other thought. I wondered if she had picked this because she knew it was going to get on my nerves, as punishment for having made her get up so early. She was the organized one, punctual and exact. I was the opposite. I'd made an effort to be there on time, of course, but it was still an early morning for most mortals.

Afterdeath

It was weird being the sibling to someone so different, even though we were so similar in many other respects. When we were very young, we had been like one. But then mom and dad had died, and that's when things began to change. Liv had turned to religion shortly afterward. Something about a counsellor at school that had turned her on to all that crap. I'd dealt with things my own way. I can't say either of us got much happier, but at least we had each other and Gran, so that made it survivable.

We stopped by a fast food place, picked up some basic morning items to go, and did so. My head was full of the past few years: of Gran, and Liv, and the funeral, and all the other stuff. It was weird, like when you look up in the sky and see a plane, and you wish you were on it, heading for whatever direction. Then you end up doing just that, but concentrating on what's bothering you instead of being one of those people you'd wished you could be when you were looking up. That's how I felt now: I was at lift-off, but instead of seeing this trip as a new beginning, it was just an extension of my problems.

"Look in the centre console," Liv said, and smiled. I tilted my head and opened the hatch between us. Inside were two clear plastic re-sealable bags, each one full to the brim with candies of all sorts.

"No. You didn't," I said, opening one of them. I must have made quite a face, because Olivia started roaring laughter.

"Of course! You can't have a trip without farewell candy!" The memories of us sitting in the back seat of our family car with our mom and dad at the front came rushing back. Every summer, we would take a vacation, and farewell candy was a tradition that had to be observed religiously. I opened a bag and asked: "Which?"

"Gummy worm," she said, and I rummaged around, found an orange and green striped one, which I popped into her mouth. I myself chose a coke bottle. The big, flat ones that almost took out a tooth, you had to chew so hard to get through it. There were all kinds in there: sour gummies, sharks, neon ones, berries, cherries, cola bottles, spiders, frogs, and all of them gave off that smell of pure sugar and gelatin. Unlike when I was a kid, though, I'd try to make them last until the halfway point of our trip, something Liv alone had been able to do so far. This time I would beat her.

Our plan was fairly simple: We'd go from Oddawa to Toronto, then follow the Great Lakes. We hadn't been to Toronto in two years, and it would give us the chance to go back to Young St. and Bloor, to those districts we had escaped to, once, on a dare when we were old enough to go there alone, but not of legal drinking age. I doubted we would go nuts like we did that long weekend, but it was worth the detour to rekindle old, great memories. We needed to make new ones, to help all this angst and sadness along. Of course we grieved, but technically, we'd been grieving since Gran's disease reared its memory-destroying head. This was more like a return to life for us, I think. It was for me, anyhow. Besides, I also wanted to get to know Liv a bit better. As I have said before, even though we were both taking care of the same person, it was in alternating shifts, and we seldom crossed paths outside of the changing of the guard. At that time, what could we share with each other outside of what we were living at that moment?

For now I was happy to munch on the candy she had so thoughtfully brought along. Heat was coming, now, and we both opened our windows a crack. I watched as cars sped past us, reminded once again how my sister was a stickler to rules and limits. A few of the other drivers gawked at us, as many do when they see twins.

We aren't freaks of nature, folks, just issued from very similar genetic material! I felt like telling them sometimes. I knew it would bring on all the same questions as usual, though, and kept my lips sealed tight, lest I have to repeat myself for the millionth time about something so simple they could have looked it up themselves. Things like: "Have your boyfriends ever mistaken you for one another", or even, "have you ever switched classes without anyone knowing?" Classic stuff that got older every time I heard it. People just weren't ready to see us. Maybe it confronted them with the idea of what *they* would do if they switched places with Olivia and I. Whatever the reasons, it remained obnoxious to be stared at like circus sideshow freaks. I had nothing but admiration for conjoined twins, who brought what my sister and I lived one notch higher, attracting even more problems unto themselves, through no fault of their own.

We branched off the Number One Highway onto the 416, and a bit of a quieter drive. We headed South and a bit West, to Brockville and then onto the adjacent 401 Highway, also known as the MacDonald-Cartier Highway, which we would take all the way to Toronto. On our left, the St-Lawrence River snaked on, and we followed the current to its origins, the Great Lakes. On the other side of the river was the State of New York, to Syracuse where grandma sold recreated hand-made dresses from a hundred years ago at summer fairs and historical society re-enactments. We had always loved these as girls. Imagine being a kid surrounded by grownups who were very serious about playing dress-up. We had always had a hoot when we had gone down there. That's what Rose called it: "Having a hoot". I loved that expression. Olivia looked at me knowingly. I don't know if you could call it telepathy, but there was something about knowing someone so well that no words were needed to transfer the notion that you were thinking the exact same thing. It might be easier as a twin, but I was pretty sure you could do it with just about anyone you got to know thoroughly. That'd kill the mystique around my sister and I, though, wouldn't it? Would it be better to let people think that we could listen in on each other's thoughts? Sometimes we did, and that was good for a laugh as well.

Afterdeath

On the highway for a while, now, I'd tried to block out Shania's mewling with little success. We both had our windows open a crack (saved a bit of money on the air conditioning). Ahead of us was an eighteen wheeler tractor-trailer, dirty white, with a sticker asking: "How's my driving? 1-800-DON'T-CARE." We passed him on the left, as he wasn't going quite the speed limit. As we did, a cigarette butt came hurtling out of the cab, hitting our windshield straight in the centre, shooting sparks out in every direction. The stench of the offending cancer-cause filled the car briefly, and I coughed.

"Shoot!" Olivia swore. I was thinking much worse thoughts. As we passed, I looked up at the driver, who harboured a big, fat, evil grin, and was in the process of lighting another one of his fiery projectiles.

"Jerk!" I yelled at him from my open window. He must have heard, because his brows came together and he looked down at me, pointing a finger of innocence at himself. We passed him as fast as we could, and I gave him the finger. This, I have to admit, might have been a mistake.

We finished climbing the hill, and Olivia took the right lane again, staying at her usual speed.

That's when I noticed the rumble of the engine behind us, and turned around to see the grill of the semi-trailer. Burnt-orange cab, menacing, with a lot of chrome. The flat-nosed kind that had probably been more popular twenty years ago. It was so close, you could see all the little personal touches the driver had lovingly done himself. Like a Rainbow Kid plushy, mutilated and tied with bungies to the front grill. I shuddered. The fact remained that he was right up our butts and didn't want to back off. I kept glancing back, a constant shiver developing in my neck. Maybe I should have been nicer to him?

On this road, there were only two lanes, so if it wanted to pass, it would have to do so onto oncoming traffic, just as we had done. In front of us was a line of cars, longer than I could see. It made me uncomfortable to have this guy behind us, and Olivia was biting her lip, her eyes flicking back and forth from the road to her rear-view mirror. This area was rolling hills and dips and turns. I'm certain Olivia hadn't driven outside the city in quite some time, and wondered how she would react if the unpredictable happened. I kept my demeanour cool, but my feet were pressed against the floor mat as hard as I could push it. The semi grunted and groaned behind us, close enough to touch our bumper. I thought my sister would swallow her own face she was chewing on her lip so hard. We began to climb a hill again, and both were driving at a hundred. Well, we were doing a hundred, but the jerk-off behind us was going a slight bit faster, trying to gather steam and pass us while we were climbing. At least, I hoped that's what he was trying to do, because I certainly didn't want him to try to ram us off the road. The rumbling behind us got louder, and the semi changed lanes while no traffic was coming. It barely clipped the edge of our bumper, and Olivia said:

"Shit!" and began to swerve in our lane, while this monster grumbled past us to the left. The cab was at the height of the front of our car, and Olivia spotted it first: a delivery van, coming the other way, around the other side of the hill, straight for this bastard's truck which was having trouble passing us on our left. Things decelerated for a moment. I glanced up, and the brown delivery truck was almost upon the semi. The semi hit the brakes, reeling, then accelerated again, changing lanes to get back behind us. "Shitshitshitshitshit!" she said, and I felt my face contort and go numb. I didn't know what to grab onto, my seat, or the handle above me, so I settled on holding the front console with both hands, bracing for impact. I looked back in time to see the rear of the semi swerve, and the brown delivery truck hitting the back end of it, sending it flying into the side of the hill, it bouncing off, and falling sideways onto the road, taking the cab with it a few seconds later.

"Ohmygodohmygodohmygod!" Olivia said, her rapid-fire breathing, face covered in sweat, as we rounded the corner and lost sight of what had just happened.

"Did you see that?" I finally said.

"Uh, yeah!?" she said, "Are we still alive?"

I patted myself down and gave two weak thumbs up.

"For now, I think."

"I need a drink," she said, and I concurred with her wholeheartedly. It was all I could do to calm my beating heart at this point. I was shaken to my core and just needed to stop, anywhere, and recuperate. I thought of calling the police right then and there, but wasn't sure just where my 911 call would be transferred.

Luckily, Olivia saw something called the Misty Mornings Motel on our right, and turned in. It had the prerequisite restaurant/bar/gas station/sleeping quarters that all these little stops along the way always had.

"Good driving," I told her, my shaking legs having grown stiff over the two hours we had driven.

"Thanks. No thanks to that guy back there," she said, and we walked into the greasy spoon, which was still fairly quiet before the lunch crowd would start coming in. I went straight for the counter and told them to call the police about the accident we'd witnessed, then went to sit down at a booth with my sister, soft padded seat squishing under me. It reminded me we'd be getting back in the car shortly, and I should at least try to enjoy the comfort while it lasted.

"What can I get you ladies?" a kindly looking waitress asked us over bifocals tied behind her neck by a plastic-jewelled cord, smile wrinkles stretching just for us.

Afterdeath

"Scotch rocks, double," I said, and the woman, whose nametag professed her to be Margaret gave me an odd look, while scratching the hip of her pale orange uniform with a long, red nail.

"Same," Olivia said. She looked at us both with a suspicious look, waggling her pen at us.

"Yes," I said, nodding, meaning: *Yes, Margaret, we do look the same. We were born that way.*

"So what are you celebrating so early?" she asked, almost in a motherly scold. I let it slide; she meant well.

"Still being alive," Olivia said, matter-of-factly, and I smiled at our waitress, over-angelically. Margaret shook her head.

"You young ladies do have IDs, right?" she said, putting her palms on our table, hovering over us. We both smiled and took out our university cards. Both looked so real, we'd used them since our trip to Toronto, and had never had problems with them. Margaret held both in one hand, eyes slits, darting from the cards to our smiling faces, back to the cards, and said:

"Here you go girls. I'm not one to judge. Be right back with your drinks." And handed us our fake IDs back. We thanked her and put them back in our purses. I always found it funny that in Ontario, I had to be nineteen to imbibe legally, but if I went over to Quebec, it was okay, and I'd been doing so for months now with my proper driver's license. Go figure rules and regulations.

I realized that that quick brush with annihilation had made me deathly hungry, and picked up the lunch menu. A death-defying drink was one thing, but an empty stomach was entirely another. I wanted to get to Toronto before the sun set tonight, find a hotel and get to go out while I still had the energy.

"You remember those guys who wanted to pick us up at Faze?" I said to Olivia, putting my hand on top of hers, reminding her about our previous experience in the Big City. She put her hand over her mouth and suppressed a laugh.

"How could I forget? 'Hey girls, how's you like to get to know the most eligible bachelors…"

"…bastards…" I added.

"…bachelors in TO,'" she said, in her smarmiest accent. What a night that had been.

"The little one was cute, though, wasn't he?" I said in a dreamy voice, batting my doe eyes at her, and she slapped my hands as I gave her lovelorn look with my head nestled in my cupped hands.

"Stop teasing me. That was years ago, you dork," she said.

"There is no moratorium on using your own words against you!" I said.

22

"Well there should be," she added, as our early-morning pick-me-ups arrived. We thanked Margaret and grabbed our rock glasses, smelling the amber liquid inside. We had Grandma to thank for our choice in poisons. She had been a strong believer in not letting first experiences with alcohol be at the legal age, but a gradual education. She had her 12 year old single malt every night before bed. An ounce, for those of you who might starting crying: "alcoholic!" Over time, Olivia and I had grown fond of Scotch whiskey and it earthy tones. It did well in soothing raw nerves, as it did now. As well as surprising the crap out of middle-aged waitresses at road-sided diners who never in a millions years would have believed that kids our ages would be drinking atypical old-man drinks. That would make a nice story for her return home tonight.

"That's going to hurt," Olivia said, and we clinked our glasses before taking sips. It was warm going down, and took the edge off our fear, but boy was it awful. Olivia choked on hers as I grimaced from mine. No Bunnahabhain, this was some third-rate bar-rail stuff. I looked outside and saw two police cars, an ambulance and a trio of fire trucks rush off to where we had come from.

"Poor guy," Olivia said.

"Which one?"

"The truck driver, of course," she said.

"How can you have pity on that idiot? He was the cause of his own misfortune!"

"I know, I know. You know what, though, he made a mistake. He made a mistake and he may have paid for it with his life. I hope God forgives him."

Not this again.

"Nope, I'm pretty sure he's going to hell. He also almost killed us, or had you forgotten about that?" I said, putting my glass down on the table, a little too hard. Someone at another table turned around, raised an eyebrow, shrugged, and went back to his meal.

Olivia didn't say anything. She knew me too well to do so. This is why I didn't like talking to her, about *anything* anymore. It always revolved around the one thing. That one thing that she thought defined her, and it drove me nuts. I tried to keep my frown to myself, not wanting to see the pity I knew I'd find in her eyes. We swished our scotches around in their glasses, taking slow sips. We decided to order lunch, breakfast feeling far behind us. The food made my nerves calm, and I felt bad for having been like that with her. I looked at her with what I thought might be my most piteous look, and she replied with a smile. Apology accepted.

I heard the jarring whine before I saw it, then the blurred flash of a white ambulance heading toward town, fresh from the accident, and hopefully carrying only survivors.

Afterdeath

It was noon by the time we left, and the parking lot was filling up with all sorts of semi-trailers and cars, making me glad we had stopped earlier. Families filed in with kids in tow, and I gave a wink to a little girl who stuck out her tongue. I answered in kind and saw her pulling on her mom's shirt, pointing at me as they walked inside. *Mommy, that lady was rude!* she'd say, and mommy would answer: *What did you do?* to which, of course, she would answer: *Nothing!* We'd all been there at some point in time, and been entirely innocent of all wrongdoing. When did we start taking the blame for things that we did? When did we think: *Oh, I did do that. I guess it is my fault.* This line of thinking always led me back to our parents. Always.

I shook my head, walked onto the freshly asphalted parking lot. The ground smelled of that fresh tar, and it had a bit of give, like a fudge brownie that had just cooled down a bit before you pushed the top with your thumb. Fresh tar always reminded me of vacations, because we'd get stuck for kilometres on end on the highway during construction season. That's when we'd play "I spy" (I spy, with my little eye, something… red!), and dad would always lose because he was driving and had to keep an eye in front of him. Mom was pretty good, but Liv was always aces.

She sat on the trunk of the car; I followed her gaze to the left, where a white monster tow truck was carrying the semi, scraped beyond recognition on its left side, the driver's side almost entirely gone. Some weird part of my brain associated it for me to that character, Two-Face, from Batman, only its vehicular counterpart. The one side fine, the other destroyed, mangled and torn, bits of the interior hanging flaccidly out the gaping hole.

Olivia crossed her arms. There was no way anyone could have survived that. Ever. I felt my stomach growing smaller, and it was as if a ringing were taking over my hearing. I took a deep, long breath, and let it out as a series of short spasms. No, of course he hadn't deserved that. I saw Liv do a sign of the cross, and it did nothing to me, this time. Let him rest in peace.

On the other side of the road, the tree branches began to sway, leaves flitting with a sigh and rustle. My sister jumped off the hood of the car, as a stronger wind pushed some strewn garbage across the pristine black asphalt, from the direction we meant to go. Sand particles flung themselves at us from neighbouring fields and lots, stinging my face.

"You're driving!" she said, in a voice that tried to rival the winds. Of course, she would never drive in bad weather. I rolled my eyes and jumped to the driver's side.

Pulling out of the parking lot, we saw it, clear as day: a straight line of black clouds, cutting the horizon from left to right, roiling and immense, blocking the sun where the darkness had overtaken.

This is going to be fun, I thought, as I looked into the heart of the storm, sheets of rain blurring the scenery far ahead. Small twigs and insect kept thwacking against the windshield, and the radio squawked about a "severe weather warning".

"Are you sure you want to keep going?" Liv asked, but I only had contempt for her cowardice.

"Little rain never killed anybody, Olivia Borders," with that adult tone she hated so much. This wasn't so bad. Soon the blackness enveloped us, though, and my intestines began to tweak a little bit inside me. Olivia held the door handle loosely, but I knew she'd be gripping that thing tight if things got screwy.

We passed a corrugated steel garage on our left, where the fateful semi had been deposited. That would be the last we would see of that machine, or so we thought.

Fields to our right, and the St-Lawrence to our left, when we would get close enough to see it. Jagged lightning blades lit up the sky far, far away, and then a sheet of sky burst, spilling itself like a solid pool of water onto the car. I could see virtually nothing, but kept my cool and speed. I'd get us to Toronto before supper. It wasn't a little bit of rain that would slow us down. The radio was a mass of static now. Voices could be overheard, but nothing clear. Not music, at least. At some point, I thought I heard: "Get you," between bouts of shrill noise, and even Olivia turned around, frowning, but then the radio sizzled and popped again, and I ignored it from then on. I clicked on the CD player and chose Queens of the Stone Age to listen to. Not Liv's favourite. Tough titties. I drive: my choice.

The winds kept getting stronger, the car veering left and right, but I held it under control. It looked as if we were going through the longest car wash ever invented, there was so much water coming down on us. I had turned on the front headlights, yet managed to see nothing. The wind-shield wipers worked as hard as they could, but it was as if we travelled through the bottom of the ocean. I gritted my teeth and drove on.

All of a sudden, the rain stopped. I almost let out a sigh, but then saw I was in the wrong lane, heading straight for another car. I veered left, already almost on the left shoulder anyhow, it veered to my right, scraping each other's paint on our respective passenger's sides. Side-view mirror popping off with a bang as they collided, like a high-five that ripped off your hands. I saw the terrified couple's faces as they veered away from us, then ditch, coming fast. We dropped, driving down into a culvert, then up the side, getting airborne. I started to scream, and noticed Olivia had been all this time. Upside down, holding onto the ceiling, we both saw the line of trees.

Chapter 3

Awakening

I was in bed. Had to be. I hadn't left home yet. How did I know I was in bed? The birds chirping. Olivia would be coming to pick me up in a little while. What a nightmare. There was a soft whoosh of wind. Left my window open again. That explained the birds so close. So comfy. Just wanted to keep my eyes closed and forget that crazy-ass dream. I'd tell her all about it when she got here. In the meantime I could enjoy my... strangely... hard bed, and lack of pillow, apparently. My nightmare faded away.

"Chloe, where are we?" I heard from close by. *What do you mean, where are we?* I thought. *I'm at home. Where else should I be?*

"Chloe, for God's sakes, get up! How long are you going to lie in the grass?"

Grass? I put my hand down and felt the long, rugged stems of grasses that had never been cut. I opened my eyes and found Olivia standing over me, hands on her hips, but looking more concerned than angry.

"Whoa! Where are we?" I said, sitting up. I picked a ladybug from my cheek and tossed it away, watching it deploy its wings and fly off, as if it hadn't minded. There stood a chickadee on a wooden post, a few meters away. It looked at us both with curiosity, and let out a chirrup, cocking its little black and white head. Overhead, the sky was radiant. The few clouds that sauntered by looked harmless in every way. A noon sun bore down on us, but not unpleasantly. I noticed that everything was bluer than before. Not that it was *all blue*. Someone had taken the colour palette and just upped the blue in there, giving the world this subtle, barely noticeable shift.

I looked over at my sister, who was climbing the embankment of the highway, and called after her: "Hey! Liv! What are you doing?"

"Looking for the car!" she said. This was true. Where was her car? I looked behind me, but only saw a stand of blue spruces, big and old. A deep breath brought me their Christmas tree smell. The car should have been right around where I was sitting. I stood up and looked around, batting down the wild grass like an idiot, as if it could have been hiding underneath. Neither high nor low. The car had vanished.

I walked after Liv and got up onto the road as well.

"Couldn't find your car," I said, by way of explanation. She closed her eyes shut and looked up at the sky, taking a deep breath. I stared down the road, one way, then, the other. Nothing. Nothing moved. There was only us, and the sky, and the gently waving grasses by the side of the road, and probably that bird down there on the post by the ditch.

Clouds moved in straight lines, I thought, *not like this.*

Various shapes of cumulus, nimbus, et al., compressed, as though through straws, before regaining their shapes, or swirled in place, like whirling dervishes, then continued on their way. I rubbed my eyes and looked again. They kept on doing just that, regardless of what I might think of them.

I patted myself down, looking for my cell phone. My blue arm-banded watch was dead, the hands holding onto 1:07, no matter how much I tapped it. Without a frame of reference, time was officially a non-issue. Gone like the car. Sure I could look at the sun, but how would that tell me any precise instant of the day? I'd never gone to girl-scouts, which would have made that particular skill rather useful right about now. This was the moment that I first felt any real sense of loss. I'd lived by the clock all my life. It gave order to everything.

It had stopped.

"Wonder where everybody went?" I said, trying to distract myself from that horrible realization, shaking my watch impotently.

"Chlo, what's going on?" she asked me, turning me toward her and holding me, her hands on my shoulders, her eyes wide and accusatory. Like this was somehow my fault, and I was hiding the truth.

"I'm not sure. We were… driving. Then, something happened. It's fuzzy, though."

"I don't remember, either. I just woke up next to you a few minutes before you did. Do you think someone stole the car and left us there?" she said.

"I… don't see how that could have happened. I don't quite recall the last part. We… we had a meal, I know that for sure, then we started driving. Then… I don't know. It's this blur." I rubbed my fist on the top of my head, searching for a memory that should have been there, but had simply melted away. Maybe if I rubbed hard enough, I could extrude it, I thought, like a splinter.

"You drove. I know that because there was this terrible music playing," she said, and walked to the centre lane of the highway, her index on her lips.

"Hey! I happen to like that music!" I frowned, hands on my hips. The gravel by the road crunched as I walked.

She put her hand on her forehead, pinching it with thumb and index, ignoring me.

"...but then what happened? Ack! I hate this! I hate it! There's some kind of fog in my mind and I can't lift it!" she said, turning to look at me. "Are you sure you don't have anything else?" There was a pleading look in her eyes.

"No, I'm sorry," I said, and shrugged. I looked up and down the road again, and there stood a long pause between us.

"Well..." I said.

"Well what?" she retorted, anger in her voice.

"We should decide what to do next. We can't just stay on the road all day. Maybe we should get walking or something." I stared off into the direction we had wanted to go before the car had vanished. Or what I thought was the right direction. Hard to tell.

"Where do you think we should go?" she said, raising her arms high. She had a point. Would it be easier to go home, or to keep going? I wanted to go on. It was ridiculous, I knew, to wish to push on, but the idea of going back did not appeal at all. Even if we'd lost all our gear. My inner compass pulled me like a magnet toward our destination, not our departure point.

"I— I feel like we should go on," I said, feeling sheepish. Olivia put both her hands over her face and dragged them down, as if pulling her face off provided some modicum of relief.

"You— want to go on. You want to go on when we have, what? Nothing? Have you checked your pockets? Is there anything you have to barter with, any phone I should know about, a wallet, or even your purse? Just look, will you?" she said, her voice getting shrill. Pockets were patted, and of course, she was right, there was nothing in any of them. Purse? Forget it. That must have been in the car as well, like the rest.

"I just have this feeling that we have to go on, that way," I said, in a soft voice, pointing toward Toronto. Maybe. Why there? Why did I want to go so bad? Not even I could tell you, but that's what I knew in my core to be the right thing to do, logic be damned.

Olivia started to laugh, a high, desperate sound. I'd never seen her react that way before. As she stamped her foot and guffawed, she became choked, and her laughing turned to sobs. It was a horrible cacophony of coughing, laughing and sobbing, and I grabbed her by each side of her face and yelled:

"Stop that right now!" I noticed that I held her face a few inches below mine, though, and wondered if she was sagging to the ground. I looked at her feet, though, and realized that she was sinking into the spotless road.

"Hehehe, I am going to stay here, okay Chlo? I am going to stay. You go on. You go wherever the heck you want. I am just going to-- stay. I am not going anywhere," and with those words, she began to lower into the highway as if it were her very own personal quicksand. She went down to knee height, and she kept looking at the road as if it were the most interesting thing that had ever happened to her. She chuckled, ignoring me now. I stared in horror, and grabbed her under her armpits, but it was as if she'd become one with the road. I pulled harder and harder, but she just wouldn't budge.

"Olivia, what the hell is going on?" I screamed, digging my heels in.

"Just seems like a waste of energy to fight, you know?" she said, slipping in a bit more.

"No, don't say that! What am I going to do without you? Olivia, stop! Just stop! Come back to me!" Hot tears like acid blurred my vision, but both my hands were stuck under her armpits, trying to pull her out. "I'm sorry, okay? I didn't mean to!"

The sinking stopped, and she just stayed there.

"Chloe, what is going on?" she asked me, as if she had just woken up on the scene, unaware of the last five minutes. I felt as if she was growing lighter and began to drag her out of the road. Her legs kicked, helping me in the effort. We pulled and kicked, with me bawling my eyes out and her encouraging me on, and in the end, the tip of her left foot came out, then the right. We both tumbled to the ground and held each other. We got up and dusted ourselves off, looking at the spot where she had almost drowned, for lack of a better word.

"I just..." she began

"Lost hope?" I finished for her, and she nodded, round eyed. "No more losing hope, okay? Now we stick together."

"Forever," she said.

"Forever."

***

The sun never got hotter, but it did start to dip, after a while. I had no idea what time it was. I did think we were not where we were supposed to be, however. This place had subtle and not so subtle differences from that hence we'd come. All things

Afterdeath

pointed to some sort of alternate universe where the physics were different from that of what we were used to. Olivia's sinking into a solid being a fairly straightforward example. I'd read enough of grandma's brother's pulp magazines to know what that was, at least. My great uncle Philbert had been a consummate sci-fi reader before it was even cool. Call him the proto-nerd, if you will. A scientist, he'd taught physics at the Oddawa University for many years. Sadly, he'd passed away when we were babies. He'd left behind his neat-o collection of Asimov's and Starlogs and all sorts of amazing stuff in the basement. I preferred going down there in the storage room to open a long-box and grab one of those gems instead of turning on the boob-tube or spending my nights on the internet. I imagine his room must have been either mine or Liv's. Grandma had redecorated before we'd moved in, so I guess we'd never know. I could only imagine, though, this skinny kid in the 1950's, lying on his single bed with a pile of pulp magazines, with the sunshine coming into the window, a metal rocket hanging from a string on the ceiling, our great uncle growing up to be this brilliant scientist. It made you wonder. I liked them because they were so full of possibilities. Actual, real possibilities, not the empty promises Olivia believed in. I'd dust one off carefully, then take it to grandma's room where she lay, and I'd read her a story or two. I never got a reaction, but I liked to imagine that inside the prison of her mind, there was one of those amazing tales unfolding, just for her, and I was the one narrating it. It gave me comfort.

"Shall we get walking?" I said, tilting my head and pursing my lips.

"Yeah," she whispered, and I put my arm around her shoulder. She slid her arm around my waist and gave me a quick squeeze, then let me go. I knew she had a lot on her mind. So did I. We'd have to figure out what this place was, eventually.

"Hey Chlo, do you recall how she would read us bedtime stories?" Olivia asked.

Maybe I should believe in telepathy, after all, I thought. "Uh-huh. What about it?" I said.

"I don't know. It just feels like we're stuck inside one of those stories. Like we're supposed to *do* things. Fight dragons. Rescue princes. You know, like the stuff she'd tell us before we fell asleep," she said, scratching her head.

"You know, grandma did turn those stories on their heads. Usually it was the princes who would rescue the princesses."

"Princes are dinks. They wouldn't know how to rescue anything," she said, and I laughed out loud.

"Some princes are dinks. Not all of them," I said.

"No: all of them," she said, with a frown. We walked on in silence for a while. The road was sloping downward, and veering to the left toward what I could only assume was the St-Lawrence again. Then again, not knowing where we physically were, guaranteed nothing. The fields'd been replaced by blue spruces on either side of the road, still deserted, still quiet. Their tall, slender shapes stood immobile, no wind swaying them at all, and beyond them, more, a forest of them, deep, and dark. The heat had not changed at all, and we still felt no discomfort at the sun's lowering rays.

Further still, the shadows of the trees, gold outlining black, draped themselves across our path, and night bugs furtively prepared for their concerts by tuning their instruments. I heard crickets and the peep-squawk of starlings in the undergrowth. Rounding the corner, we stopped. By now, neither of us kept to the shoulder; there was just no point. We hadn't spotted a single vehicle since we had woken up. A dark shape, on the side of the road, darker than the surrounding shadows, still and silent: waiting? It absorbed light, it seemed, an oblong black hole, near the line of trees. We walked again, slower this time, keeping to the opposite side, wondering if this thing was alive, and would come for us. A chill ran through me, but not from cold.

"What do you think that is?" Olivia asked, and I looked at her, unsure how to answer. I felt just as uneasy in its presence as she. Even from this distance, as we walked parallel to it, there was an immovable stony quality to it, like an alien megalith left by an ancient people, in a weird place. The last rays of sunshine flashed overhead, illuminating the Thing, and we both fell down laughing. It was a car. A big, old Cadillac. Black as night, almost matte, with silver accents, tail fins, and a drop down roof. It was, by any standards, huge.

Liv was the first to get up and yell at it, giggling: "You scared me, you dope!" The car, of course, did not reply. We crossed the road and looked through the windows. A sparkling white interior, and immaculate at that. It looked as if the owner had just dropped it off there a moment ago, since no pine needles littered its convertible roof, but that was impossible, since we would have seen the car go by, coming from the direction we'd been walking.

"It's gorgeous, isn't it?" I said.

"Yeah, a real classic. This thing must just drink gas like a monster, though, don't you think?"

"Yup, I'm sure it gets thirsty. Let's check to see if we can drive it." Just then a movement caught my eye, as I raised my hand to touch the door handle. From where we had come, something paced up the road. It was human, I thought, by the height and width of it. Liv caught my sleeve and peered over my shoulder. It must have been ten meters away, hobbling closer. It was thin, emaciated. There was a jerky quality to its movements that made me nervous.

"Hey! Can I help you?" I called out. Maybe he had come out of the forest. There was no way he could have come down the road. Like the car, this was some pretty spooky stuff. The thin man did not answer. He wore a suit, I could see, but it was threadbare, hanging off his frame, and strands floated about him, grey and wispy.

Afterdeath

Light dimmed when it hit him. Still the man came forward, without answering our calls. He said nothing, and Olivia was gripping my arm as if she was going to tear it off and run away with it. When he was three meters from the car, we both saw the long, horizontal gash that ran across his neck, like a tree that someone had begun chopping down with an axe. No blood, but now I heard a sucking sound, and no mistake, it came from the visible windpipe through his slit neck. The reason for his strange walk became apparent as well: his left leg was broken at a strange angle, and he half-walked, half dragged it along, the foot making no sound on the road. He was coming straight for us, bleached white eyes wide, the rims bloodshot and pink, his mouth open, teeth bared.

Olivia screamed, and time accelerated.

I panicked and looked around. There was nowhere to run. I grabbed the door handle of the car and pulled. Nothing happened. The man was near the rear of the car, raising his hands, broken grey fingers reaching for me, and I turned to run, grabbing Olivia's hand as I did so. I took her to the other side of the car, and tried to pull the other door. What an idiot I was. In my fear and panic, I had forgotten to push the button that unlatched the door! As the man walked around the front of the car, that sick sucking sound gurgling from his throat, the car door finally opened wide, and I pushed Olivia inside, jumped in, and closed the door behind me. He put his face against the window, squishing it tight against the glass, and in some surreal fashion, it pressed entirely against it, as if he had no bones. A deep sigh rose from outside, as his gaping windpipe pressed against the window as well, hands pressed hard on the side of the car. His face slid right, and I followed his empty bloodshot gaze to the door handle. As his sliding hand reached for it, I slammed down the silver lock that protruded from the top of the door with a "Clack!"

The man put both his hands on the window and began to hit it, slowly at first, with his head. Olivia cowered by the driver's side, her feet under her on the vinyl seat. I gritted my teeth and watched this psycho smash his face into the glass, but every hit was like being struck by a pillow. I saw him stand back and cock his head, staring straight at me. He glanced around him, to the ground. I peeked over the side of the window and saw him bend down to pick up a rock.

"Look for keys!" I yelled at Olivia, "Now!" I opened the glove compartment and rifled through it, but found nothing. Olivia went straight for the classic hiding spot and lowered the sun visor: bingo. One set of Cadillac keys. The man was hissing through his neck at us, and raised the rock over his head. Olivia fumbled with the key and with a trembling hand stuck it into the starter. The rock came flying at the windshield and hit with a loud "tock!"

Rumbling, satisfying and huge, roared out from the engine. The man picked up his rock again, and I saw the chip in the side window where the first blow had struck. Olivia grabbed the shift lever and put it in drive. The tires threw shreds of gravel behind us as the Caddy leapt forward like a drag race champion. I had time to look back and see the man throw the rock, ineffectually, onto the road, before we rounded that corner and left him behind for good.

"What was he doing there?" she said. Good question.

"What *was* he, you mean? Did you see that cut across his throat? How could he walk around with something like that?" Further off, I saw that the line of trees ended, and light still shone onto the road.

"Maybe… maybe this is like some sort of zombie apocalypse?" she said.

"Oh, come on! You don't believe *that*, do you?" I said, with a forced laugh. The forest had led off to more fields, and in the distance, the sun was getting ready to approach its final descent. We had maybe an hour, maximum, of sunlight before we had to drive in the dark.

"Well, why not? How else would you explain that we haven't seen a single solitary living human being since we woke up? It does make some kind of sense, though, don't you think?" Golden rays of light gave the clouds pink and purplish hues, and the fields swayed like fire.

"Well it's not a 'zombie apocalypse', I can tell you that for sure," I said, not willing to give credence to her theory. Next she'd lay into me about the religious implications, and I didn't want to hear any of it.

"Whatever it is that we're living right now, is not what we know. Are we agreed on that, at least?" she said.

"I'll go that far, yes," I said.

"Good, at least you'll meet me half-way. I just think we should watch out from now on. Things have changed somehow, in a very real, very tangible way. It scares the heck out of me," she said, and turned to look at me, a frown lining her brow.

"What are you proposing?" I said.

"Just to stay on our toes, is all."

The car's engine, though loud, was soothing. We at least had wheels, no matter how unlikely a source, and had been saved by them. I hoped it would be the last time. I wanted to figure out what had happened to us, and what fundamental laws of nature had changed for my sister to sink into a road, and for some weird creep who looked like he should have been dead to come and attack us. Zombie apocalypse indeed. I was starting to regret my decision to go on.

As the orb of the sun began to touch the horizon, I saw a neon sign on black metal post, with an arrow pointing to the right, and a single word in red, enticed: "Repose", surrounded by flashing yellow bulbs. Olivia slowed down and came to a stop before it. The buzzing of the neons came to me, as I had lowered my window about half way.

"What do you want to do?" she said.

"'Repose' sounds good to me," I said, imagining the prospect of encountering more strange people on the road in the middle of the night. I looked to the right in the direction where the sign pointed, down a sandy road and over a small hill, into a distance I couldn't fathom. She nodded her head once and pressed on the gas, taking us down the slim road. We kicked up dust, and the car rumbled and shook over uneven terrain. We went over the tiny hill and found ourselves with a breathtaking view: a valley of rolling terrain and tended vegetable gardens before us, and further off a single, white house. The sun was partially occluded now, and long, slender shadows lengthened and splayed along the valley floor. To the right of the house, the path continued, and off in the distance, another forest began. The path was swallowed up within it.

Flaking white paint covered the old two-story farmhouse, which had no decorations to speak of. Cracked concrete steps led up to the plain screen door, which opened when we drove up to the side of it. I'd been expecting a motel of some sort. This looked more like a family-owned camp-ground or farm.

Three little men walked out of the house. Each one bald, and each one identical to the other. Triplets! They looked both young and old, all three of them reaching four feet tall. They all smiled at us as we pulled up, and Olivia turned off the car and stepped outside. They all stood side by side, dressed in olive-green pants, white muscle shirts and brown suspenders.

"Hello," the first one said.

"It's nice," the second one added.

"To see you!" the third one said.

"I'm Olivia, and this is Chloe," my sister said, pointing at me.

"We're the guardians," they said, smiling broadly.

"Of what?" I asked, curious.

"Of those who rest," they said, turning to me.

"Well that's good to know. At least someone will look after us." Olivia said, smiling at me.

"So where can we go set up, do you think?" I said, peering around. Light was fading, and I didn't want to have to park the car in the darkness of the campground, even if I did have to sleep in the car.

All three turned toward the forest and pointed, saying: "Over yonder. Just beyond the trees. You will find the place. You cannot miss it."

"Sounds great!" Olivia said. "Do you want us to pay you now or…?"

"No, no…" the first one said.

"Accounts will be settled…" the second one continued.

"Later…" the third one finished. "Pleasant stay, ladies."

"Thanks!" We both answered, and looked at each other, realizing we'd just done what they did naturally, and almost guffawed.

"You drive," Olivia said, walking over to the passenger's side. I looked over to say goodbye to the 'guardians', as they'd dubbed themselves, but they were nowhere to be found. I shrugged and went to take the wheel.

"How about we take in some of this country air before settling in for the night?" I asked Liv, and she shot me an inquisitive eyebrow. I unclasped the hook for the roof on my side, and she did the same. We folded the cloth back until it rested in its hold. "Don't worry, I'll pull it back up before we go to sleep; I'm not that fond of bugs."

"I like country air as long as it isn't mostly cow poop smell," she said, getting in the car.

"But that's the best part!" I said, and she snort-laughed. The sun was almost gone when we arrived at the bottom of the hill, bumping along the sandy path and its many divots. I turned on the headlights as we drove into the copse of trees, lighting the thin path ahead. The dark trunks of maples absorbed the light, yet the leaves were still. Many offshoots went left and right, stopping soon thereafter. I heard the soft hooting of an owl, and the forlorn chirping of crickets, in a kind of endless echo. I decided that any of these spots would do, and took a left down one of the paths long enough to accommodate the Cadillac. There was space around it as well, so we could get out without having to jump over the doors into brush. The forest was thick, but mostly trunks, as the branches began well above our heads. I turned off the headlights, thinking the dashboard was enough for me to see, and to close the roof. In the gloom, however, I noticed a blue glow, in the underbrush. I turned off the interior lights as well, to see what was going on around us. A thin fog hung above the ground, and small patches in the soil glowed a luminescent blue, giving the entire forest floor an eerie hue.

"What are those? Olivia said, standing up in the passenger's seat, peering over the front windshield. Whatever they were, they were everywhere. I got out of the car and walked into the forest, toward a bluish patch on the ground.

"Don't go too far!" Olivia called out, and an echo called back: "Too far! Too far!"

"Don't worry," I said. "Worry. Worry," my echo answered. I shivered and walked on toward the glow, branches cracking and snapping underfoot. I got on my knees and stared in amazement. A clump of mushrooms, the size of a half-watermelon,

Afterdeath

grew out of the soil. The strange thing was, though, that each had the shape of a plump, white cross.

"Chloe!" I heard from behind me, and turned around. The echo that accompanied it was repeated a lot more than it should have been. The mist beyond our car swirled gently, rising and falling, yet no wind animated it. It coalesced, taking definite shapes, though of what, I wasn't sure.

"Chloe, look out!" Olivia pointed behind me, and I turned around to see a wispy, see-through hand rise from the "mushrooms" and attempt to grab mine. I fell on my back, and watched as an arm followed the hand, and a figure, transparent, came after that.

I scrambled backwards on my butt, kicking up leaves and sticks.

"Start the car!" I yelled, and heard the engine turn and rev. I turned, jumped onto the hood and into the driver's seat as I felt something cold slip along my leg, freezing me to the core. I pulled the lever for reverse, and drove the Caddy into a squealing turn, then booked it through the now animated forest. "Mist" and "fog" crowded the sides of the car, reaching tendrils of smoke into the open vehicle.

"Country air?" I heard Olivia say, a panicked laugh in her throat.

"Now's not the time, Liv," I said, my arm around her seat rest, furiously trying to remain on the path while driving backwards. The fog charged us from the front, an occasional face appearing on it, leering, tendrils grasping at the hood. I had no time to pay attention to it as I kept my eyes behind us, avoiding the sloughing fog that ran over the back of the car and tried to grab us as it drifted over us.

"Ah!" Olivia screamed, as something snatched at her hair.

"Duck down!" I yelled, and she cowered on the floor in front of the seat.

We burst out of the forest into the valley, and the mist spilled out after us, becoming one single entity, with many faces and limbs, like a bloated, jumbled blob monster. The full moon lit the way, bathing the valley in pale calico light. I gave a swift turn of the wheel, and we did a 180 degree turn on the path, so that I could drive forward. I kicked it in gear, and the sand that the car spewed back rose in the air to meet the fog.

"It's stopping!" Olivia said.

"I'm not!" I replied. From the farmhouse door, I saw the three men exit, jumping off the concrete steps and into our path, raising their hands as if to halt us. I clamped my jaw shut and jammed my foot against the accelerator. A look of surprise crossed their faces, and they all jumped out of the way, avoiding getting flattened by sheer luck. There was no way I would have slowed down after what I had gone through. I turned the headlights on and drove to the highway, crossing the "Rest" sign on the way out.

"That was *bullshit*!" I yelled to no one in particular. "Rest, my ass!" I felt a hot tear start to run down my cheek. The wind blew through my hair, and I remembered that I hadn't had time to close the roof. Even though it was now night, the air remained warm and pleasant, as if no temperature drop had occurred.

"Well, it depends on what kind of rest you were looking for," a voice said from behind me, and I slammed the brakes.

Chapter 4

ANGELINA

The car spun once, but miraculously stayed on the road. Smoke and the smell of burnt tires filled my nostrils as I turned around and saw a blonde white woman sitting on the back seat, smiling at me. She wore what looked like an ancient dress, made of some rough-looking brown tartan material, and leather leggings. Next to her sat a little white, black and brown terrier, wagging its tail.

"Who the heck are you?" Olivia asked, eyes bugging out.

"My name is Angelina. I really have to thank you for getting me out of there. But please, let me tell you all about it while you drive; it's not safe to stay in one place for too long," she said, her gaze darting around outside the car. I made a judgement call and turned the car around, continuing in the direction we'd been going. Whatever was out there was probably worse than her. We'd just gone through something that proved that.

"And you are?" she said.

"Olivia and Chloe Borders, from Oddawa," Olivia said. "We were going on vacation."

"Huh," she said. "Vacation not panning out like you planned it, then, I take it?"

"How did you get in the car?" I asked, looking at the open road.

"I must admit, I jumped in while you were in the Garden of Lost Souls," she said.

"The Garden of Lost Souls? What the heck is that?" Olivia said, looking at her with a frown.

"For a lot of folks, it's their final resting place," she said.

"But the guardians said it was a place to *rest*! That they were there to make sure nothing would happen to us," I said.

"Yes! It is! But you have it wrong about the guardians," Angelina said, and laughed.

"What's so funny?" Liv said.

"The guardians are there to make sure that whatever is in the garden *stays* there. They guard the outside world from greevers, ghosts that have no place to go. Nuisances, really," she said.

"Ghosts?" Liv and I said, and laughed.

"What do you think you saw in there?" Angelina asked. The terrier stared at the moon, its tongue lolling. I noticed for the first time that the moon had a strange look to it. Not the one I was used to. As if the man-in-the-moon was a bit... off.

"I have no idea what happened, but ghosts? Come on. You really want me to believe in *that*?" I said, and smirked at her. She just smiled and crossed her arms, in a way I found extremely annoying.

"All right," she said, "What is a ghost?" and tilted her head sideways.

"Myth. The spirit of someone who's stuck in the physical realm," I answered.

"Right. Well, partially, anyhow. It's someone who is stuck between planes of existence. It usually happens to those who do not know they are dead," she said.

"How can someone not know they're dead?" Olivia asked, turning around fully in her seat and staring at our guest.

"Easily. You two obviously don't," she said, and grinned.

"What?" we both yelled in unison.

"Impossible!" Olivia said.

"Yeah, there's nothing after death!" I said, peaking in the rear-view mirror at Angelina, who continued to smile beatifically at both of us.

"Well, no, but there's a heaven, right?" Olivia said.

"Who says?" Angelina replied, leaning forward.

"All the... all the books, all the holy books: they say it!" Olivia stuttered.

"Right, because all those people that wrote them died, then, came back to tell you all about it, is that it? Ever noticed how all of those accounts are contradictory, from the earliest on. Oh wait, are you basing your knowledge on just one book in particular? Some people do that, you know. They think that theirs is the only one in existence; that all the others were never written or don't count. Now that's hubris, if you ask me." There was something unpleasant about her superior smirk that I wanted to wipe off, right then and there.

Afterdeath

"So how did you find out you were dead, Miss Smarty Pants?" Olivia said.

"The hard way," and at this, Angelina turned her head to look outside, "I almost became a greever myself. I went after this little guy and became trapped in the Garden. I would have been there for eternity if you guys hadn't come along. Word to the wise: never despair."

"Why's that? There seems to be lots to be desperate about, these days," I said.

"Yeah, that's the catch. If you do, you'll turn into one of those desperate and lost souls you find along the way. Once you become fixated on the negative, the world just swallows you up and will never let you go. You have to have a reason to, well, live, for want of a better term," Angelina said, her lips becoming a tight line.

My thoughts returned to when we first woke up and I almost lost my sister to the quicksand that had become the highway. This also explained the man on the highway and the Garden, but didn't make it any easier to swallow.

"So what are we supposed to do now?" Olivia said, raising her hands.

"Whatever you want, really. You're dead: enjoy it. There's nothing to tie you down, and you can go anywhere you like. Nice car, by the way. Where'd you get it?"

"It was by the side of the road, lurking," I said.

"Yeah, that'll happen too. Listen, you know I say "souls", but I have no idea what we're made of. I could call it energies, and it would come down to the same thing. The point is, objects have the same energies as we do, to a certain degree, and it seems to work by age. You won't see a lot of new cars, but ones like these, they appear once in a while. Honestly, I don't know how it works, but they're wheels," Angelina said, running her hand along the door, almost lovingly.

"What about new technology?" I asked.

"Such as?" she said.

"Well, cell phones, for instance," Olivia said.

"Never heard of them," she said.

"You've never heard of cell phones?" Olivia said, frowning.

"Jeez, give me a break! I died a long time ago. As far as I can tell, anyhow. New stuff takes a while to get here. You'll get used to it."

"How long have you been dead?" I asked.

"Bit of advice: don't ask the deceased how long they've been toes up. It's bad manners," she replied, winking.

"How do you even communicate?" Olivia said.

"Séances," Angelina said.

"I really hate death," I said.

"Give it a while, it grows on you. Look, we should find a place to sleep. Yes, you still get to do that. Something about recharging your batteries. If we can find a rest stop in the next few kilometres, just turn in, okay?" she said, and I nodded slightly.

We kept going for a good long time. Every time I looked back, Angelina was staring at the moon, as if she was seeing it for the first time. Who knew how long she'd been in that Garden, with those… greevers? Was it so hard to believe we were dead, all of us? It took some time for me to wrap my head around it, that was for sure. Was I even driving to Toronto? What would it look like in this place, I wondered. If this car was any indication, we'd be heading into a cheesy 1950s replica of the city. Was that the truth of it? What about this concept of objects with souls, how was I supposed to take that, as well? Some cultures buried their dead with their favourite objects, pets, even servants (I'm looking at you, ancient Egyptians), does that mean that all that was passed on to this side, or isn't that how it worked?

Angelina whistled and pointed to our right. A turnoff was coming up, and no lights shone down the path.

"Are you sure," I said, turning around.

"Sure I'm sure. I've been through here before. Trust me," she said. As I opened my mouth in protest, she answered my unvoiced concern: "What choice do you have?" Good point. I turned off the highway onto a paved road that led to shelters under which picnic tables could be seen. An expansive parking lot with angled spots, and no other cars in sight came into view.

"Anywhere is fine," Angelina said, seeing my questioning look. I parked the car, but left the headlights on, and the motor running.

"Don't worry, it's perfectly safe," she said, hopping over the side. "Here Barkley!" and the dog bounced over, following suit. With long strides, she walked up to a fire pit between picnic tables and extended her arm, palm toward the pit. She grasped her elbow with her free hand, and I heard her say a few words. A reddish flame burst from the heap, and a fire began to rise in the night. Somewhere, a dog or wolf whined, and was silent.

She rummaged around near the fire pit and picked up a long, thick stick. She grasped the end with one hand, and plunged that end into the fire. When she retrieved it, it was glowing red hot. She sauntered by us with her glowing stick in her hand, flashing us that knowing smile, and stopped a few meters from the car. She inscribed something on the ground, which glowed briefly and returned to nothing afterward. She did the same thing four more times, at regular intervals, with us in the middle of her work.

Afterwards, the stick was discarded into the fire, which had gone down a bit in intensity.

Afterdeath

"You can come out, now. We're perfectly safe," she said.

"What did you do?" Olivia asked. Looking around to where there she had put her marks on the ground.

"Just protecting us for the night. Better safe than sorry, I always say."

Having been dead a long time gave her a leg up. I'd have to ask her a few questions in some future alone time. I turned off the car and the lights, walked out, and put the top back onto it. Might as well. If we were going to sleep in there, creepy crawlies were the last thing I wanted to worry about. Liv looked spent. With one trembling hand, she pushed her door open. I took a deep breath and let it out. She shut her door carefully, leaving her hand against the door for what seemed a very long time, then walked with hesitant steps to where Angelina was already sitting with Barkley.

The moon was huge, hovering so near I felt I could have touched it. It too was bluer than it should have been. The man in the moon looked a bit like a grinning skull, if you looked at it sideways, and squinted your eyes. Questions crowded in, as they tended to when I found myself in a strange situation. Couldn't get stranger than this. Ever. I walked to Olivia. Picked her up by her shoulders. Walked her the rest of the way, like a nurse would an invalid. Or a granddaughter her ailing grandma.

Thoughts of Gran came rushing back, and then I too walked more slowly, one foot after the other, the universe becoming heavier. My heart following suit. Angelina's head whipped toward me.

"Don't let it happen. I can smell it on you. On both of you. I still need you both, so stay with me, okay? Remember why you're still here. Remember why you fight." Barkley barked, and I felt lighter. Thoughts of Olivia came to me, and I was okay again. I sat her by the fire, next to me, on the opposite side of Angelina and her dog.

"You said desperation turns you into a greever. We saw a man earlier. When we found the car. He tried to attack us. Could he have hurt us?" I said. I looked at her over the dancing flames. I noticed there was no wood apart from the single stick she had put in there before. The fire itself burned, free from kindling or wood to feed it. It just was. I was too tired to question it. The physics of this place certainly took some getting used to.

"Yup. Could have absorbed you both. Then you would have made him stronger," she said, not looking at me. Her eyes glazed, searching in the heart of the white-hot blaze, like a star.

"How could he not have known he was dead? He had a giant gash in his neck. His head was practically falling off!" And I made a slicing motion over my own neck with my hand to illustrate the point, recalling the event, and shivering.

"It's called denial. You have to go through the steps of grieving to realize, fully, that you have passed away. If you're still in denial, how can you have that 'Ah-ha!'

moment? Add to that some heavy despair, anger and confusion, and you have yourself the perfect recipe for a greever, whose only will is to feed on others it can prey upon. That's how it works." She was looking at me now, her mouth set in a line. She was stroking Barkley's fur, who had curled up on her lap and was looking at her lovingly, on his back. So that might explain Olivia's sinking, as well. Despair had taken over, and she had begun to be absorbed, somehow. I shook my head, laughing derisively, thinking about the truth of the expression 'sinking feeling'. On my shoulder, Olivia's head was resting. I heard a soft snoring sound and rested my own head against hers. The temperature never changed, so my worries about throwing a blanket around her evaporated as soon as it came.

"Who are you, Angelina?" I said, leaning a fraction of a hair forward. She squinted and tilted her head.

"Wouldn't you like to know? I'm not what you think, if that can help," she said.

"I don't know what to think, honestly," I said, and put my arm around my sister.

"Good, that'll make things easier for all of us, I'd say." This woman was no help at all. I sighed, loud enough that she could hear me.

"What comes next?" I said, my mouth screwing up at the corners, and I had to fight the urge to bite the inside of my cheeks, like I used to when I was young.

"Well, for starters, we'll sleep a bit, then tomorrow, it would be nice if you could drop me off in Necropolis. I've some business to attend to, if I'm not too late." And she leaned her head back, staring up at the sky. "Then you can be off to do whatever it is you want to do."

"But I don't know what we're supposed to do!" I said in a harsh whisper.

"Bully for you, sister. I'm just along for the ride. It's up to you to figure out your eternity, not me. I've got other souls to fry, if you know what I mean?" Still looking up.

"No, no I don't know what you mean. You haven't been very forthcoming about your situation so far," I said.

"Whatever," she said, and let Barkley off her lap, got up, walked away, and disappeared into the darkness of the forest. Her little dog followed her, tail wagging, and vanished, too.

I decided then and there that I didn't like her. I didn't like her one bit. The fire was dying, as if its non-existent fuel was becoming spent. I shook Olivia gently, wanting to get back in the car before the lights went out. Even though I could navigate by moonlight, I preferred not to. She moaned and her eyes fluttered. I got up, holding her as best I could, and stumbled to the car. I rested her against its side and opened the passenger's side door. I pushed the front seat forward and half-dragged, half-pushed Olivia in after me. I ended up with her on top of me in the back seat. I sighed.

Afterdeath

I wiggled myself out from under her and crawled over the top of the seat, pushing it back in place. I then pulled the door shut. I sat behind the wheel and looked at the spot where the fire was going out, all that was left the size of a lighter flame. Leaning back into the seat, I watched the treetops and the visible stars, washed out by that enormous, leering moon. How many were the same ones I knew? I had woken up alive and grieving this morning, and tonight I was dead and grieved for. I would not cry over my fate, though. That was the best way to wander around aimlessly, trying to devour others. I took a long, shuddering breath and thought of grandma, and where she might be. Was she somewhere around here? What about our parents? Would we encounter them as well? The thoughts gave me hope. We hadn't seen them since we were seven. If not for the pictures Gran had given us to keep in our wallets, I'm sure I would have forgotten their faces by now, I'm ashamed to say.

I looked for my purse, for the reassurance that I'd find within. Those faded, happy people with their two young girls, so long ago. Those Kodak moments taken mere months before their demise. I stopped my hands from wandering when I realized that those material things were on the other side, where the living would be picking them up, along with our bodies, in the remains of Olivia's trashed car. Our foster parents'd be alerted to our terrible accident. From what Liv had told me, I don't think hers would have cared that much. They had too many under their care already. It'd been more of a mill than a family, if what she'd told me was true, and I had no reason to doubt her words. I closed my eyes in the dark and put my hands by my sides, taking a deep breath. I could barely remember how we'd gotten here now. It truly was like a dream, or nightmare, the kind you had to forget in order to stay sane in the waking world. The only thing left, flashes, every so often, then nothing to tie them together. Deep breath. Calm. I opened my eyes and lowered a window. The night sounds refreshed me. Birds and insects. A gentle rush of wind, enough to make the treetops sway, just so, then be still. What was this place called, apart from the land of the dead? Strange to think of it that way when the trees, and animals, even we, were so alive. When it came to the greevers that attacked us, they were just as dangerous as feral animals, and I considered them as such.

A movement caught my eye, and a gray shape moved in the rear-view mirror. My breathing came in faster, and I turned my head as slowly as I could. From directly behind the car, something shambled toward the direction we'd come from, going onto the highway off-ramp we'd taken to get here. It never turned its head. It looked like an old woman, with all the colour drained from her body and clothes, with just drab grey remaining. A dirty ghost, wandering the night. Footsteps crunched on gravel. She never turned in my direction. Just walked, without pause. Oblivious.

Whatever spell Angelina had woven around us was effective, and I was glad for that at least.

I sat back down, feeling the vinyl stretch under me, making a pleasant sound as I shifted. I'd have to name this car. I'd talk to Olivia about it in the morning. Grandma had told me that when she was a girl, her parents had named their cars. Newer cars had no personalities, she'd said. This one was chock-full of personality. I ran a hand along the seat and grinned. This beast had saved our lives twice in one day.

I thought about what Olivia had said, about us having to fight dragons and saving princes. I think I knew what she meant. When you were in unfamiliar territory, going against unknown forces in ways you were totally unprepared for, there was just improvisation. Action and reaction, and that was it. The mundane world was repetition after repetition, and so left little in the ways of imagination. This was an adventure, in all the senses of the word. No safety net. It was more dangerous, I felt, to be dead than alive. Or maybe that was the "me" who was out of her depth speaking. Angelina did okay, perhaps. I had no idea about all the other people who might live on this plane of existence. Not all of them were of the roaming, soul-sucking kind, at least. Perhaps there were those who'd be more agreeable than our temporary companion, yet I had no way of knowing until I experienced it.

The smells of nature, with the bittersweet tang of conifers, as well as powdery gravel and charred woods came floating to my nostrils. Some things weren't so different. Olivia's snoring interrupted my thoughts, and I turned back to see her curled up in a ball. She stiffened and her brow furrowed. She mumbled in her sleep: "No. no, don't." and covered her face with her free hand, and spoke no more.

I lay down and thought of the coming day, anticipating what a Necropolis built over one of Canada's largest cities might look like.

Chapter 5

NECROPOLIS

Knocking on the car window startled me awake. I lowered it and rubbed the crust out of my eyes, as Angelina grinned at me gleefully. Crick in my neck. Of course. The sun was risen, and I'd missed the dawn. I'd wondered what it was like, but now I'd have to wait to see. Olivia stirred behind me and sat up, yawning.

"Where did you go last night?" I asked Angelina.

"Had to go make some money," she said, and held up a leather purse that looked half-full. She shook it, and a musical tinkling of coins sounded.

"How... how did you make money in the bush?" Olivia said, leaning over the front seat and looking at her out the window.

"That's for me to know, and... just for me to know." She threw the pouch in the air and caught it, putting it onto her belt. I didn't remember her having such an item yesterday, and wondered where she might have procured it. Barkley trotted out of the forest and looked up at us from the front of the car, panting. I leaned over and turned the clip for the roof, and Angelina did the same on the driver's side. She then pushed it back, over Olivia's head and into its resting place. I lowered the side windows, and started the engine.

"Shotgun!" Angelina declared, and jumped over the door, landing on the passenger's seat. Barkley came over to her side and began jumping on his little legs.

She swept him up into her arms and put him down next to her. Olivia crossed her arms and looked out the side.

"You'll get a turn later," I said, turning to look at her, but she merely looked further away.

Great, now I have a pouting twin on my hands, I thought. I put the beast in reverse and got satisfaction out of the great rumble of the engine. I put it in gear and headed for the exit. What a beautiful day. There was not a cloud in the sky. The sun was climbing, reaching the tops of the trees, and shadows cast on the highway.

"Why is there no one out here?" Olivia asked, voicing a question I'd had dancing inside my head since we'd gotten here. I looked over at Angelina, who was comfortably sitting with her back to the door. No worries about falling out and getting killed in the afterlife. Seatbelts were a tad superfluous as well, I supposed.

"It's dangerous. You girls saw it yourselves. Those things are everywhere. You can't even call them human anymore. They're "its", and they're out to get you. Mostly bounty hunters and ferrymen and women who brave the outside. Regular folk live inside the cities," she said, her hand dancing as she explained.

Olivia and I both spoke at the same time:

"Bounty hunters?" I said.

"Ferrymen?" she said.

Angelina laughed. "Well, yeah. People have to work, you know. Of course, there are many things one can do to earn their keep, but the real money resides in those two areas. Everybody wants to make coin. Although, the main difference is that here, you don't need to eat. You do have to pay for lodgings and other minor expenses: clothes, gadgets, weapons, etc.

Bounty hunters: they're the ones who get rid of the unending supply of lost souls that wander the countryside. Some you have to destroy, and some you can mercifully take to prison, places like the Garden where you found me," she said, looking at her nails. The trees had once again gone away, and a sloping hill had begun. A cliff rose to our right, and descended on the left, beyond the guardrail. A vast expanse of water shimmered in the early morning light like chrome.

"And ferry woman?" Olivia asked.

"That's easy. Well, sort of. A ferryman or woman takes the newly deceased from the world of the living to this side," she said, turning to face Olivia and smiling at her.

"And you get paid for this?" I said, keeping my eyes on the road. Stumpy pines partially obstructed the view of the water on the right, but occasional clearings gave us glimpses.

Afterdeath

"Sure do. From time immemorial, people have put coins on people's eyes to pay for their crossing. That's what they give to the ferrymen."

"But what about bounty hunters? How do they get money for a job? Do they get those coins as well?" I said, tapping the wheel with my thumbs.

"Bounty hunters *take* the coins. Everyone has them, whether they realize it or not. When a bounty hunter either destroys a soul or takes it to some guardians, he or she gets a share of the deceased's loot," she said, grinning widely. The idea of obliterating that thing that had threatened Olivia and I was appealing, I had to admit. Much more than taking it to any "prison".

"You know, I think I heard about that tradition. The one where they put the coins on your eyes and you pay them to death's ferryman. He was called Charon, I think, and he took people across the Styx. This is Greek mythology, if I'm not mistaken," Olivia said. She beamed at having remembered something from history class. I myself was terrible at all things requiring mental effort, and had more often than not counted on my sister to do my homework or even go into class for me when we could trade, so that she could take the test. Another one of those twin tricks that people asked about all the time. This one was true.

"Give a star to the bright kid!" Angelina said, pointing an index at Olivia and pretending to cock her thumb to shoot off an imaginary gun. "Except for one small detail: can you imagine the backlog if there were only one ferryman? You'd be on the earthly plane forever! No, they made things more efficient with the population boom. Now there are hundreds of ferrymen (and women) taking fresh souls across. Those greevers, though, boy, they find their way over here without having gone the proper route, not having been briefed about their situations. That's how they get created in the first place. It's a logistical nightmare, I imagine," she said, and spread her arms wide. "How did you guys cross over?" she added.

"We... we just appeared in a field," Olivia said, almost in a whisper.

"Then you two are supremely lucky. You could have turned out like a lot of those things roaming the wasteland. I think it's because it was the two of you. Yeah, that makes sense," she said, turning serious for a moment, and looking from myself to my sister in wonderment. She nodded her head several times in thought, silent during that time. She crossed her leg onto the seat. The only sound was that of the wind rushing over our heads. Barkley was fast asleep between Angelina and I.

"Hey Liv, what do you want to name our ride?" I said, breaking the awful silence.

"Name our— ," she started, and smiled. "Yeah, she needs a name, doesn't she?"

"Oh, it's a she, is it?" I said. "I saw it more as a he."

She shrugged and said: "Whatever you prefer, Chlo." Angelina watched our exchange with amusement.

"Flip for it," she said, looking down at her waist and opening the bag of coins. She shoved her hand in, tongue sticking out the side of her mouth. "Heads or tails?" she said.

"Heads!" Olivia said.

"Tails!" I said, and we both laughed. Angelina balanced a lumpy-looking coin on her thumb and flicked it. It fell into her upturned palm and she flipped that onto the back of her wrist. The image of snake was topmost. It seemed as if a simple piece of metal had been stamped, but the excess had not been removed.

"Tails it is," she said, seeing the snake.

"Where is that coin from?" I asked, noticing the strange design. Angelina turned it in her hand, and showed the other side, which was just as crude, but had the profile of what looked like some sort of emperor, with laurels crowning his head.

"Ancient Roman, by the looks of it," she said, and handed it to me. I pinched it between thumb and forefinger, holding it up above the steering wheel so I could both drive and gawk. This coin was rough in the grooves, but the embossed areas were worn shiny. I imagined it had been in circulation for an inordinately long time. The coiled snake was especially curious, and I wondered what it might mean. I made a head gesture toward my sister, and Angelina nodded. I passed the thing back to her by bending my arm over the seat.

"No paper money, huh?" I said, and Angelina laughed with all her heart.

"No, no paper money. Not until they start stuffing people's eyes with hundred dollar bills, that is."

"Isn't it weird," Olivia said, "that we haven't done that practise of placing coins on people's eyes in a very long time, yet they still have them?"

"To a certain degree, yes. Some cultures still do it, albeit few. But you're right, though. Somehow the idea of worth has been incorporated with the soul, and you can't get stuck on the earthly plane: everyone has their coins when they die," Angelina said.

"That means there's a God!" Olivia said, clapping her hands. I half-expected her to razz me and stick out her tongue, but none of that came to pass. We steadily climbed higher, and all we could see on the left was water, all the way to the horizon. I doubted we were still in Canada, even an afterlife version of it. There bore no resemblance in any way.

"How so?" Angelina said, cocking her head.

"Well, ah, because of the coins, and the ferrymen and all that. That proves it, doesn't it?" her joy had evaporated as fast as it had come.

"I hate to rain on your parade, but our philosophers have been discussing that for years on end. If God exists, he hasn't shown up here, either, hon. I'm sorry." And

Afterdeath

Angelina truly did look contrite. Olivia looked as if her sails could not take another knock. Seeing what was going on, I said:

"Hey, Olivia, we still have to name the car. I think it should be a she," I said, looking at her downcast face in the rear-view mirror. "Come on, Liv, Angelina just said that they don't know. Doesn't mean the guy doesn't exist! Cheer up!"

"Philomena," Angelina said.

"I'm sorry?" I replied.

"The car, you should name it Philomena," she said, nudging toward Olivia.

"That's a terrible name. What do you think, Liv? Philomena?" I said, trying hard to laugh.

My sister looked up and passed a hand over her red eyes.

"Bertha," she said.

"Bertha? Why Bertha?" I said, stunned.

"Because she's a tough mother," was her reply, followed by a meek smile. Angelina and I both burst out laughing, repeating "Bertha", in tough-gal accents. "Big Bad Bertha" became her nickname, and I was glad I let Olivia choose it after all. The road began to descend, lower and lower, getting dangerously close to the water.

"We're getting there," Angelina said.

We followed a road that hugged the cliffs, but water lapped and frothed over the guard-rail, washing the road in waves, then retreating. It came up a few centimetres, then receded, rushing under the car and touching the cliffs. Ahead, a bigger wave crashed over the railing and splashed all over the cliff wall.

"Don't worry, it's just a measure of protection," Angelina said, her arm over the side of the car door, getting some wet spray on it and enjoying the sun's drying rays. The road wound up again, going inland, and the ground dropped down a hundred meters or so, where the ocean continued its eternal assault. We slipped onto a bridge, white support pillars extending down into a hellish pit of roughly circular pools filled with clear, bubbling waters. Concentric circles of rainbow colour reached to their brims. Thin vapours steamed from their centres, emanating from the bubbling spots. I thought I saw people, arms extended, within those roiling furnaces, but decided for my own sanity that I had only imagined them.

For the first time, I spotted traffic. Angelina'd been right. This reminded me of Cuba: all the cars and trucks I spied dated from the 1950's or about. It was weird to think that the afterlife was so retrograde. The road branched off to make a proper four lane highway, and more traffic joined us from criss-crossing off-ramps. On each side of the road, but with a healthy separation, houses stood in several rows, parallel to it, the row behind in slightly higher, as if in a stadium. Many of them harboured barn-style roofs, and were enormous. Further off, we passed one that had a jetliner incorporated into the structure of the house, and Olivia gaped at it. In the distance, the high-rises and office towers loomed. There wasn't a single style to speak of. Perhaps, once again, my assumptions about this place were terribly misplaced. Olivia stared out the side of the car, her chin in her cupped hand, taking it all in. Angelina sat with her bare feet on the dash, arms behind her head, smiling as if she'd come home from a long vacation.

Once I'd come to the conclusion that the afterlife wasn't the complete evaporation of consciousness, had I fallen into the trap of the Emerald City, where we'd drive up to some Pearly Gates and be let in by an angel of some sort? I guess I had, as some sort of default. The city ahead was nothing like that. There rose spires from all different epochs, from Egyptian stone-masonry to... yep, there they were: the Twin Towers. All these different peoples cohabitated in their beliefs, and brought the flavor of their architecture along with them. I had to ask myself: was this Heaven? Why should I have resorted to that single-minded vision for all humans?

Traffic slowed down a bit as we approached the core area, an hour after reaching civilization. The bright reds, blues, lime greens and blacks of Chevrolets and Fords, as well as a few Packards was astonishing. I never tired of looking around to discover one more car I'd seen and loved at classic rallies. Monumental buildings towered above, the streets packed with people of all epochs and mode of dress. It was almost a carnival atmosphere. To a certain degree, it was like your uncle Bernie who grew up in the seventies and refused to be current, except people from every single era were doing it, from the animal-skin wearing tough guys on the corner of the street to the dandies in tights and voluminous collars, sporting thick moustaches and wide-brimmed hats. Women in Victorian dress wandered down the streets with majestic poodles on leashes, followed by their maidservants in plain clothes and headdresses. I spotted a pair of Australian aboriginal warriors with their elaborate facial tattoos, apparently talking business to some Huns in leather coats and pants. I had trouble keeping my eyes on the road as they darted everywhere, trying to take in everyone and everything at once.

"Pull up here," Angelina said, when we grew nearer a grey stone skyscraper with several sets of stairs leading to the brass front doors. I turned into the first available parking between a Ford Model T and a horse. She jumped out and then opened the door for Barkley.

"Where are you going?" I yelled, as she climbed the stairs, three by three.

"To make a deposit. I'll be right back," she said, pointing at the building, with only a small break in strides. The sign above the door was an immense bronze plaque that read: "CBA", in big, block letters. Olivia and I looked up, and up and up to the top of the skyscraper, wondering where it ended. 150 stories at least, I thought. I got out

Afterdeath

of the car and checked for a parking meter but there were none. What a relief. I had no money to speak of anyhow, so this saved me the trouble.

Ten minutes went by, and Angelina was nowhere to be seen. Ten minutes later, I went into the building to find her. Long lineups wound around red ropes hung on silver posts, like the queues at fancy movie theatres or government buildings. The fancy grey marble everywhere, though, hollered: "Bank!" I squinted to see where the lines ended, and rolled my eyes. Wickets lined the far wall. No sign of Angelina, but at least now I knew why she was here: to deposit her loot. I walked back outside and Olivia was sitting on the hood of the car, chatting with a couple of big guys. Both were fairly stacked. The short one was bulkier, but the tall one had a more defined musculature. My heart started beating a bit faster when I saw them. I ran down the stairs as fast as I could, yelling:

"Hey! Can I help you?" They both turned around, smiling.

"You sure can! Are you the other beautiful woman related to the one posting guard on this vehicle?" the tall one said, with what I thought must be a Scottish accent. He had deep, pale blue eyes, and his blond hair looked like a short chuck of mown wheat. His features were thinner than the shorter man's.

The other man mock-punched him on the shoulder, berating him: "Of course she is," he said, with an Irish accent, opening his arms wide in mock consternation, "she is obviously this fair maiden's twin." He looked like a brawler, with a nose that seemed to have received a few knocks, but they gave his face character. His shaven brown hair looked as if it was so for practicality. The stockier man wore a sleeveless black muscle shirt and army-style olive-drab pants, while his taller counterpart a thin, short-sleeved cotton shirt and shorts, revealing intricate tattoos all over his arms, which ran all the way to both wrists.

"It's okay, Chloe, Brock and Carson only wanted to keep me company until you or Angelina came back," Olivia said, throwing her legs over the side of the car, leaning back on the hood.

"Thank you so much. I'm back now. Goodbye!" I said, waving at them.

"Strange people about. Can never be too careful. Wait, did you say Angelina?" the shorter man named Brock said, cocking an eyebrow.

"I believe she did say Angelina, cousin," the taller man named Carson said, smiling.

"Do you know her?" I asked, cocking my head sideways and frowning.

"That depends, you see," Carson said.

"Yes, it really does," his cousin said.

"Depends on what?" Olivia said, leaning forward, intrigued.

"Is this Angelina about, oh, yay tall?" Brock said, lifting his hand to about five feet something, his palm toward the ground.

"Maybe," I said.

"Is this Angelina, say, blonde, with striking blue eyes?" Carson said, opening his eyes wide, holding them both with thumb and indexes, batting his eyelashes. Olivia giggled.

"Perhaps," she said, feigning seriousness.

"Is she accompanied by a seven foot tall giant of a man with long, brown hair?" Brock said, pretending to straighten invisible hair with his fingers and flicking it over his shoulder like some sort of diva. I covered my mouth to laugh, then regained my composure.

"Definitely not. Our Angelina has a little dog. A terrier. Sorry guys, you've got the wrong girl. If you don't mind, we'll wait for our friend alone," I said, and Olivia shrugged, as if thinking: too bad! I wondered what had gotten into her, but it was true these two were fairly cute in their own way. I personally didn't go for the mountain of muscle type, but maybe Olivia did. There was so much I didn't know about her anymore. Just then, I heard a voice calling from the top of the stairs:

"Brock! Carson! What the blazes are you two doing here?" It was Angelina, skipping down the stairs, followed closely by Barkley, who wagged his tail excitedly.

"Well what do you know? Your Angelina is our Angelina!" Brock said in a mock-surprised voice, right before she jumped into his arms and gave him a hug. She let go and jumped into Carson's.

"I am so sorry for making you girls wait so long! I had to have a personal interview with one of the bank managers since I was gone for so long: they'd put a freeze on my account. Everything should be back to normal tomorrow," she said, beaming at Brock and Carson, putting her arms around their biceps.

"What does CBA stand for, anyhow," I said, sticking a thumb out to the sign.

"Charon Bank of the Afterlife," Brock said.

"Man's done well for himself," Carson added, nodding approvingly.

"I see that," I said, putting my hands on my hips, glancing back at the mammoth building.

"So, uh, where's Barkley?" Brock asked, looking around. I frowned, thinking: does he really not see him?

Angelina crossed her arms and started biting her lip. Barkley barked at her.

"I will, just a second, will ya?" she said to the dog.

"Just a second what?" Carson said, not understanding. Frankly, none of us were in the loop at the moment.

"The thing is, about Barkley..." she paused, pinching her temples, then licked her lips. I grew slightly uncomfortable, looking at her. It was as if she were about to admit that someone had died, and didn't know how to express it properly. "The thing

Afterdeath

about Barkley," she repeated, "Is that he came back as a dog." And she looked up at the sky, gritting her teeth.

We all just stood there staring at her. Olivia and I still didn't understand a thing. Of course he was a dog! That was plainly obvious.

"Your man. Is a terrier," Brock said, dumbfounded. Then he started to snort. He covered his mouth. Carson turned around, and I could see his shoulders rising and falling. Brock broke out in a full, heart-felt laugh. "Barkley is a dog. For real. He's a dog. I'll be doggone," he said, and Carson broke out laughing, too, hysterically at that.

"It's not funny you guys! That's what he came back as, we had no choice!" Angelina said, anger flashing in her voice, her fists clenched. The hilarity died almost at once. Brock regained his sober composure and knelt down on the ground.

"Nice to see you again, man," he said, and put out his hand. Barkley looked up at him, panting, and licked his fingers. I just looked at the whole scene as if watching something entirely too surreal to be true. Carson just stared at Barkley, arms crossed, a small smile on the corner of his lips. Olivia had jumped down from the hood, and looked as if her mind was furiously working things out.

"Does this have anything to do with reincarnation?" she asked.

"Yeah, and punishment," Angelina said, staring her down, daring her to ask more. Olivia lifted her hands in a defensive gesture, and I took a step forward in case things took a turn for the worse.

"Relax, Angel, ain't no one attacking you. I'm sorry for laughing at your misfortune. That was très uncool of me," Brock said, bowing low, not a trace of humour in his voice.

"Ditto," said Carson, bowing deep as well.

"Apology not accepted, jerks. You should know better than to mock a woman in pain," Angelina said, punching them both in the gut, getting a bit of a reaction from them, but you could tell she hadn't hit as hard as she could, and that they were only reacting to humour her.

"So how do you know each other?" Olivia said, looking from Angelina to the two men.

"Oh, he's my cousin," Carson said, playing dumb, pointing at Brock.

"No, dork, how do you two know Angelina," I said, realizing full well that he was joking.

The shadows were getting longer on the street, and I looked up at the sun, which was playing peek-a-boo with the high-rises and skyscrapers.

"Oh, we went to bounty hunter school together, Angel and I, back when Barkley was human, I guess. Carson's been my roommate forever. He's a ferryman on the banks of ol' Styx over there," Brock said, pointing in the direction of the water.

"So, uh, you two, um…" Olivia said, looking at both men and crossing her fingers.

"I'm not that kind of fairy man," Carson said in a feminine voice, putting one hand on his hip and jutting out his other arm with a limp wrist.

"Could've fooled me!" Angelina said.

"Bitch," Carson replied, rolling his eyes, in a huff.

"Gay jokes stopped being funny a while ago," I said to Carson, who looked at his hand as if surprised, then put it down and hid it behind his back.

"Why don't we all go back to my place for the night? I don't like the streets after dark," Angelina said.

"You still living in Crosstown?" Carson said, turning his head to where we'd come from.

"Hell ya! Rent is cheap. You guys want to come and hang for a while?" she said, and both men put up a fist above their heads, holding an invisible noose, letting their heads roll around on their shoulders and sticking their tongues out.

"Sure," they both said, as if their larynxes were constricted, and walked on tiptoes around the car and got in the back. Olivia and I both stared at them for a moment and then both started laughing: come back and *hang* with us for a while. Ha. Olivia got in the back and sat next to Carson. She kept her head down and her colours were more on the pink side, especially every time he looked her way and smiled. Methought my little minx of a sister was developing a crush on a manly man. I didn't say a word, just got behind the wheel and took instructions from my guide, Angelina.

We turned back a few blocks from where we'd previously been parked, then headed north, left down a wide avenue lined with tall, black street-lamps topped with ornate lanterns. A man in dusty black trousers and a worn top hat stood at the apex of a ladder, a box in one hand. He held a tiny flame in his hand, which danced and swayed. The closer I looked, though, I realized that that flame had a person in it. A tiny naked being carouseled in his open palm, and he gently placed it inside the glass house of the street lamp. I noticed that half the street was already lit this way, the flame dancers gyrating joyfully in the dusk.

The streets were becoming less and less populated as we got further away from the downtown area. I don't know when it happened, but at some point, all the architecture changed, and the buildings became white, with fluffy blue painted clouds on them, covering the stucco walls. There was an eerie uniformity to the whole place: white walls, red doors, people on the street dressed in identical white robes and black boots.

"Turn right here," Angelina said, and I did, down Halo St.

Afterdeath

Small, well-manicured bushes lined the roads. Row-houses, all identical, ran parallel up and down the street. The only way to tell them apart was by the numbers next to the doors.

"Aaand... 312. You can stop right here in front of the place," she said. I pulled up, and as per her annoying habit, she jumped out of the car, then let Barkley out. She ran up to the door and knocked, standing on her tip-toes to look through the magic eye on the door. No answer for a few moments, then someone opened. The man looked at her, shrugged, and seemed to be pointing further up the street, but when Angelina said something again, he only shrugged once more. Angelina's shoulders fell, and she came back to the car.

She looked crestfallen as she let Barkley back in and sat down. The engine was running and I was wondering where to go. It was fully dark now, and I wondered why they were so nervous to be outside, and if it had anything to do with greevers.

Please, I thought, *please don't let it have anything to do with greevers.* I don't care if I was surrounded by bounty hunters and ferrymen, I didn't want to have to deal with those things.

"Ronny doesn't live there anymore," she said, pouting. "Hasn't been there in years. How long have I been gone?"

"Years," Carson said, unhelpfully. Angelina turned around and glared at him. He smiled weakly and shrugged. "You'll need to find Ronny if you want to retrieve your immaterial possessions."

"Meh. It's just stuff. I have all I need right here."

"Come to our place," Brock said. "We've got a garage you can stick the car in for the night. You can try to get a new place tomorrow," spreading his hands.

"You got a new place?" Angelina said, curious.

"In a manner of speaking," Brock said.

"We're squatting in an old garage in Dis," Carson said, leaning forward.

"What happened to...?" Angelina started.

"Evicted," Brock and Carson answered together.

"You two and your parties. I should have known," and Angelina sighed. "Dis District. Couldn't find a more dangerous area, could you?" she said, flashing them a coy grin.

"No town like Low Town," Carson said, in a showman's demeanour.

Dis, or Low Town, nicknamed The Pit, or so I overheard as I was directed to turn around. My confidence in this expedition was deflating faster than a hot air balloon that had caught fire. I glanced at Olivia who was palling around with Carson, and smiled. She, at least, was having a good time. Brock threw a muscular arm over the seat, pointing down the street, and said:

"Onward, mighty…"

"Bertha," Olivia said, and giggled.

"Onward, mighty Bertha! Good name," Brock said, nodding gravely in agreement.

"Thanks, I chose it," Olivia said, a sheepish grin rising on her lips. Carson gave her a little nudge with his elbow and her face lit up bright red. I rolled my eyes and put Bertha in drive. We kept going north, then turned west. The white homes gave way to regular, simple red brick ones, then to a semi-industrial area, where a run-down factory squatted, heavy and unlit, then on to a light industrial area; garages with corrugated metal walls filled with rust spots and covered in faded signs. Further away, I thought I spotted the early warning signs of a port; a large crane swaying above some long, low buildings.

"This is us," Brock said, pointing at a two-story business with a double-garage and large windows on the second floor. I stopped the car, and Brock jumped over the side, walked over to the garage door and opened a panel by removing the padlock with a key. The door revealed a long double chain, which, after he had pulled on it, made the door inch up a few centimetres.

"Weakling!" Carson taunted. Brock turned around and smiled. He grabbed hold of the chain, and gave it a massive heave. The door almost went flying up into the ceiling, and the interior of the garage was revealed. It was empty, yet had all the equipment necessary to fix most any four-wheeled vehicle. The far right side was taken up by a long work bench that went all the way to the stairs at the back, with rows of drawers beneath, as well as cupboards above. The left side wall was covered in swords, knives, and various types of hand weapons. The floor on that side was covered in blue mats, and a few pairs of boxing gloves lay on the floor near the mat.

"I take it back, O, giant bear of a man!" Carson said, and Brock smiled, flipping him the bird. He then proceeded to bow, throwing his hands out to invite us, and the car, inside. I drove to the far wall, near the stairs, in case someone else needed to park their car behind us at some point. It was only common courtesy. Brock went outside to close and lock the access panel, then came back inside.

As soon as we were in, he pulled the chains, which were openly accessible on the inside of the building, and the door closed behind us. He flipped a light switch, and we all got out of the car. Carson led the way, climbing the wooden stairs in big strides, followed by Angelina and Olivia, then myself. Barkley hopped from one to the other, and looked at me with concern in his eyes. Brock was last.

The smell of machine oil in the garage gave way to a thin incense smell. Nothing cloying, just an aftertaste that lingered on the senses. I was surprised at how clean the place was. I'd seen a few boys' apartments and knew how they could be. It looked to be partially under construction, with some walls unfinished. The far wall was all windows, with a view on the port a few hundred meters away. Lights reflected and danced on the water, and above them, that eerie moon, looking less than benevolent, as always. There was a semi-circle of three comfortable-looking mismatched sofas before the windows, and Olivia threw herself on the first she could find. I sat opposite her, Angelina took up residence on the one facing the windows, and the guys went off down a corridor on the right.

"Angelina," I said, "I was wondering about Barkley." I looked at the dog, which she was stroking behind the ears.

"What do you want to know?" she said, looking as if she might regret answering.

"Well, I mean, you two used to be lovers, right?" I said, feeling a bit squeamish.

"We were, yes," she answered, matter-of-factly.

"Since he's a dog now, you two can't, I mean, it would be gross if you... you know..." I had no idea where I was taking this conversation, but Angelina just looked at me, round-eyed, and barked out laughing, looking at me as if my brain had fallen out of my head.

"You *are* young. You don't even know the difference between love and *making* love. Of course we can't *do* it. You know what, though? I love him so much that I went through *hell* to get him back. I don't care what he looks like. It just doesn't matter. He could be a tree and I'd still love the energy that animates him," she said, with a force of conviction that I can't say I'd ever heard anyone use before. Olivia was lying on her back, eyes closed. Maybe sleeping, maybe not. I wondered if visions of Carson were dancing in her head. The men came back, changed into karate *gi*, whose belts were both black.

"We're going to go spar downstairs if anyone wants to join," Brock said, and Angelina answered in the affirmative. They headed down the stairs and I got up to get a better look outside. It was dark out there, but the occasional streetlamp illuminated the area in patches, giving the whole place an old, worn-out feel. The moon was losing quarters, but still shone brightly enough so that I could see silver reflections over the water.

A movement caught my eye outside. A grey thing shambled into view, from around an adjacent building. Then, another, larger shade. I looked down directly below, and saw that three had gathered in front of the garage doors.

Greevers.

"Guys, we have a problem!" I yelled.

Chapter 6

OLIVIA

I got up with a start as soon as I heard Chloe's yell. I'd only closed my eyes for a fraction of a second, long enough to wonder if my dream was reality or vice versa. She stood by the window, fear in her eyes. I sat up on the old sofa.

"What's the matter?" I said, the anxious expression in her eyes contagious. I got up and joined her. Oh God. They were down there. Six, at least, and more joining by the minute. Some flitted along the ground, without even touching it. Others walked, but they all headed to the garage, pushing and jostling to get in. They hit the door with their hands and heads, making a soft padding noise from up here. The chains rattled. My heart and throat constricted, and I thought I might stop breathing. I might have, if I didn't remind myself that I was already dead.

"Don't open the door!" I screamed. Chloe took off for the stairs, and I just stood there, immobile with dread. My eyes were riveted at the window, unable to do anything but watch the patch of light grow longer and longer as the rustle of the chain increased. As if I'd turned into one of the things down there, I headed back to the stairs, teetering from side to side, wondering if I was in my right mind. Nope. I wasn't. Not one bit. I held the guardrail and slumped down, sitting on the top stair. Chloe was halfway down the stairs, holding on to the ceiling, frozen in place. Angelina and the men stood in a line, in the middle of the garage, as the shades shambled in, arms outstretched and mouths gaping open at impossible sizes. I then noticed the swords in their hands, upraised and falling on each new assailant. A thin fog lay on

Afterdeath

the floor, around the three. The lost souls they slashed fell, cut through and through, the yells of our friends renting the air as they took aim and let the swords fall. I looked at Carson's muscular body move like that of a dancer's with every stroke. And he was a ferryman?

"Damn," Carson said, "Sure are a lot of them," as he cut off the head of a woman who tried to jump him from the side. The cut was clean, and her shocked expression was almost comical, as her cranium bounced once on the floor, and then began to melt.

"Some powerful attracting force at work here. You wouldn't know anything about that, would you, Angel?" Brock said, turning to Angelina, a thin sweat lining his brow.

"Me? How the hell should I know?" she said, taking a step forward and cutting an evil-looking little girl from shoulder to opposite hip. The sword got stuck, and half the girl hung off at an odd angle. Angelina pulled her sword out, and the girl jerked toward her. She kicked her, then chopped the rest off, letting her fall to the ground where she began to disintegrate. "Requiescat in pace," she said.

The fighting went on, with blow after blow landing on ghosts that were substantial until cut down, then would fall into a heap and begin to melt and deliquesce into nothingness.

The crowd of souls began to thin, and soon, no more of the demented shades were presenting themselves at the door to meet their doom. A grey fog rolled gently where their "bodies" had fallen. I sat still, my head resting on the guardrail, frowning. Chloe took some tentative steps toward our friends, who were rummaging in the fog, picking up coins. Brock went to close the garage door, and the fog thinned until the floor was all that could be seen anymore, as if the ground had absorbed those souls like water. Carson wiped his brow and turned back to look at me and smiled. I felt myself turn several shades of crimson, and I couldn't meet his gaze.

"All right," Brock said, "What the heck was that all about? We haven't had an infestation like that since both those airliners crashed on the same day. You remember that, right?" Hands on his knees, sword leaning on the workbench.

"Yeah, mighty peculiar if you ask me. 'Sides, they were headed for here, not just shambling out of the water. We were a target, man," Carson said, his sword above his head, held between thumb and forefinger of his other hand. Brock went to the middle of the garage and got down on his hands and knees, putting both forearms together, with his hands flat, in a symbol of prayer. With his eyes closed, he bowed his head slightly and began to mumble under his breath. The light dimmed, as if photons were being expelled backwards away from the kneeling figure. That was when I noticed a strange shimmer on Bertha. Heat lines coming off of her, growing hazier. A few moments later the car burst into black flames, casting a purplish aura.

A five pointed star shone, singed into the hood in those same black flames. Chloe gasped, and Angelina slapped her forehead. Carson, catching the gesture, turned to her.

"What do you know about this?" he said, pointing at the car bathed in dark flames. At first, all we heard was a low mumble come from Angelina, barely audible.

"I'm sorry, I didn't catch that?" Chloe said, walking down the steps, irritation in her voice.

"I did that, okay? Are you happy now?" Angelina said, turning away from us, arms crossed. Brock stopped chanting and got up. The flames were dissipating, as was the star on the hood. He surveyed all, scratching his head once.

I got up, waffling between the idea of coming down the steps and stopping Chloe, or letting her loose and seeing what she would do. As much as I hated the idea of seeing her getting into a fight, I was too afraid of getting involved.

"No, you don't get to avoid this by pretending to be the aggrieved party, lady. What the hell did you do to our car?" Chloe said, teeth bared, and pushed her from behind. I was glad at that moment that Angelina had put down her sword, because things really could have taken a turn for the worst. Angelina got up, turned around, fists balled, and sent one toward Chloe's face. Brock caught it in his hand, and closed it upon Angelina, who struggled to get loose.

"Let go of me! She attacked me first!" Angelina said.

"There'll be no fighting amongst ourselves," he said, raising Angelina's fist high, so that they were face to face. Barkley danced nervously around Brock's feet, letting out little yips of uncertainty.

"It's okay, Barkley," she said, and Brock let her go.

"Now, why don't you come upstairs and explain to us what you did to these ladies' car for them to have the Baphomet's star on it," Brock said, in a calm tone.

"The Baphomet's star?" I said, my heart speeding up. Great, our car was possessed by Satan now.

"Nothing to worry about, except if you don't like the company of unrested spirits, that is," Carson said, winking. I turned red again, and walked stiffly up the few steps, and then to the sofa where I'd lay before. Angelina sat next to me, and I squeezed as far away from her as I could. She gave me a glance and sniffed, turning her nose up. Chloe, still furious, sat opposite us, and Brock as well. Carson stood by the window, after having turned the lights down low.

"Last night, I made the sigil around the car. I bolstered it with a hiding spell, though," Angelina said, staring at the floor. Chloe glanced at Brock, who pursed his lips in Angelina's direction.

Afterdeath

"What does it do, this Baphomet's star?" I asked, my arms extended around my knees. Carson kept an eye on the proceedings as well as one outside. As far as I could tell, there was no trouble brewing. He looked calm, his arms crossed. His karate gi had slipped a bit and I could see a bit of his muscular chest… I turned back to Angelina, feeling heat in my cheeks. Had Chloe noticed?

"It… it attracts the spirits of the dead. It has many uses, but I used it to call in all the wandering greevers in the area," she said.

"You said you were putting a protection around us! What the hell kind of protection is that!" Chloe practically yelled.

"I did though! I put a hiding spell! They were attracted, but they had no idea by what! Those things could have wandered around the car for hours and never, ever spotted you two! I just stayed out of range and took them out as they approached," she said, and looked up, straight into Chloe's eyes, which made her want to flare up even more, I saw.

"Why would you do such a thing? Who in their right mind blows on a whistle to call the dead?" Chloe said, her hands slashing the air.

"Bounty hunter," Brock and Carson said at the same time. Then it all became clear to me: Angelina had used us as bait to attract the nasties, so that she could destroy them for their coin. It made sense, in a twisted sort of way. With the right kind of perverse mindset, I could see why she'd done it.

"It'll fade away, I swear! I totally forgot it was there!" she said, pleading.

"Oh, you're still a bad girl, aren't you Angel. That's why we love you," Brock said, smiling, as he ruffled her hair. Of course he would, he had the same job description. That kind of move should be in a playbook, he'd think. Not so much fun for those who weren't in on the joke, though.

"Speak for yourself, cousin. Just be glad there were three of us defending the homestead. That kind of dumbass move is what gets people absorbed," Carson said from the window. Is that what happened when a lost soul took possession of you? Chloe got up and started to pace back and forth in the wide open space of the living room. Did they call it that here? A living room? No matter.

"So what happens to those things on the floor? I mean, they're dead already, obviously, so where do they go?" she said, pausing and looking back at us. I hadn't thought of that. Where do the deceased go in the land of the dead? Another world, deeper still than this one? What if you died again there? The possibility for depth seemed endless.

"As far as we know, they're absorbed by the earth. Their particles lose cohesion and they become one with the 'universe', if you will," Carson said, his palms pointing toward the ground, making a pushing motion. "Only their coin is left after they go."

"Does anyone else feel like this is some sort of bad video game? You kill the bad guy and he or she disappears, leaving some tokens for you to pick up?" Chloe said, tittering nervously. She walked over to the window, to get a better view of her surroundings as well. Barkley got off Angelina's lap and trundled up to her, licking her fingertips. Chloe looked down at him and smiled sadly.

"We didn't make the rules, love. It is the way it is," Carson said, his eyebrows raised.

"What about us? You said we could get absorbed. How does that work?" she asked, looking at Carson. He looked at the ground, lips going taut. Brock cleared his throat and we all turned to see what he had to say.

"That's pretty much the worst that can happen here. If you get absorbed by a lost soul, you become one with it. End of story. It takes your energy and uses it to grow more powerful. There are some pretty twisted creatures in the wild. Some ancient ones that you could never take out on your own, so malignant they've become. But the bounty on them, and in them. That would be something," Brock said, and in his eyes, I could see he had a particular one in mind. If I thought it was bad to be here, never mind that Chloe was, too, what it would be to have your mind, and your particles taken from you by some mindless creature bent on the absorption of victims, never to return as yourself. I shuddered at the thought.

"It's getting late. I don't know about you folks, but I have to go to work in the morning," Carson said. What did we have to do? Decide what our place was in this world? "You can have the couches. We'll wake you up bright and early. Angel, what are you going to do about that curse on their motor vehicle?"

"It should fade within a day or so," she mumbled. "I have to go see about a place and what my new assignment is."

"Good, I'll go with you," Brock said. "I'm between jobs at the moment as well. Might as well team up, no?"

"Sure, why not," Angelina said, raising her hands in the air in a gesture of giving up. I felt sorry for her, I think. She just made everything harder for herself. Carson closed the drapes in front of the bay windows, and I wondered how many more lost souls wandered out there, attracted by an invisible force that dragged them inexorably to… us. The two men walked out of the room, and I gave a nod to my sister, who shook her head. She glanced at Angelina, who intercepted her look.

"What?" she said, with splayed hands. She lay down, facing away from the window, and Barkley sat on the floor at her feet. Carson came back and handed us each a comfy blanket, but tossed Angelina's at her, which she caught one-handed without looking. I'd have to ask how she did that at some point. The lights got turned off, but the moonlight streaming from the cracks in the drapes still illuminated mine and Chloe's face.

Afterdeath

I lay down and thought about where we were, and what we were. I'd never thought I'd be dead at eighteen. I don't think anyone ever does. You hear about kids with terminal diseases, of course, but us so-called "healthy ones" never have to worry about kicking the bucket. Or so I thought. I was going to graduate this year. They'd put an obituary in the yearbook, probably. Some girls I neither knew nor liked would say nice things about me, without ever having known me. I'd never have a baby. I'd never grow old and... well, that part was done. The dying, I mean.

Dead. Dead. Dead.

I was dead. No matter how many times I repeated it, it never felt real. I'd never go to university. I'd never go travelling the world, discover new and interesting cultures. I must have worn a weird look on my face, because Chloe looked at me with a frown, as she lay down on her sofa. I gave her a weak smile. I didn't want to talk to her about it, not with Angelina so close, and potentially listening in. That was just one of the things I kept from her. I couldn't help it. I would never see my foster family again, thank God, or my so-called friends from High School. All of them would be mourning me. I kept the despair at bay. It wasn't despair, per se, just a longing sadness that there were so many things I wish I could have accomplished, but hadn't, and now it was too late, forever. I sighed and heard Chloe say:

"Are you okay?"

"Yeah, yeah. I'm fine. You should sleep," I said, and turned my head the other way so that she wouldn't worry about me.

Because she put herself on trial every day. Except it was a show trial, where the verdict was always decided in advance, and she invariably found herself guilty.

She was a light, but then mom and dad died. For a while, I saw her waver, and thought: she'll pull through. But then it went out, too, and I never saw it come back as bright as it used to be, if at all.

I closed my eyes and thought again about where we were, and what we were supposed to do. What do we do about the road trip? I thought. Is that as dead as we are? Might as well be. There would be no Vancouver Island at the end of this world. Might as well stick around the city where things might be relatively safe. After tonight, did I still believe that? Let's face it: there was just as much danger, if not more in the afterlife as there was in life. What could possibly have made me believe otherwise? The Bible I knew had said nothing about a place like this. I was curious about Crosstown, though. What kind of people lived there, and what their beliefs were. I'd have to ask Carson tomorrow.

If he was a Believer, I could definitely see myself putting a ring on that man. What a specimen. Every other man I'd encountered so far came nowhere close to the gallantry that he'd shown me. Chloe hadn't been there when he'd introduced himself and offered his services as my personal bodyguard. I'm sorry, but any man does that, you have to say yes, don't you? Without expressly admitting so, I had. Of course I wasn't dumb enough to run away with a complete stranger, but he was the kind of cutie that I could see myself doing so with.

I drifted into sleep, and a woman's voice came back to me, from far away and long ago. It said:

"It's okay, honey, you can let go." But I couldn't. If I let go, I'd never see the owner of that voice again. It was murky in my dreams, and I felt myself floating, waves pushing me up, then down, and I felt as if I'd drown.

"Just let go, honey, just let go," a different voice said, a man's this time. I cried. I bawled my eyes out. I gripped a thick sleeve with all the force I could muster, but it was nowhere near enough. The sleeve was pulling me down, into the water, under it, and I had to let go or be dragged down as well. Screaming. Letting go against my will. Kicking for dear life.

Chapter 7

PERRY

Morning glowed through the half-opened curtains, making my aches and pains come through in waves as if I had struggled all night long. The sound of brawling came to my ears and I sat up as fast as I could. Angelina was gone. Chloe perked up her head from under her blanket, and I got up and ran to the stairs, wondering if another raid was taking place on the garage. I padded down the stairs, and saw Carson and Angelina sparring one-on-one. My heart clenched. He gave her a long-legged kick, aimed at her shoulder, which she caught in her arm, ducked down, and swept his foot from under him, sending him to the mat. Brock looked on, impassive, arms crossed. Carson sprang back, taking a defensive position. Angelina began to give him short jabs, which he swatted away, looking for an in. I felt a presence at my shoulder, and Chloe whispered:

"I hope he kicks her ass." I smiled and watched the proceedings, as Chloe walked down the stairs and went to stand by Brock. She crossed her arms as he did, and said something close to his ear, and I didn't catch it. Brock smiled and raised a hand. Both fighters on the mat paused for a moment. Barkley sat near the mats, enjoying the show.

"We have a new contender," Brock said, and Angelina began to walk off. "For you, Angel." Angelina paused, looking at Brock curiously, as Chloe slipped on some sparring gloves and head protection. Carson removed his equipment and joined his cousin. As my sister put on the last of the padded equipment, she looked up at me and smiled. That was when Angelina decided to attack, pushing her from the side, sending her to the mat.

"That's for yesterday," she said, shaking her head and bouncing in place a bit to loosen up. Chloe pushed herself up, her smile evaporated. She sent a kick straight at Angelina, which she caught with both hands, lifting straight up, spinning Chloe like a wheel, so that she fell, face down onto the mat. Brock was checking things out with a smirk, his hand framing his face. Chloe got up, or rather, bounced up, went straight for her opponent, lashing out with kicks and punches, her face red, teeth clenched. Angelina, serious in her defence, deflected what she could and blocked the rest. She was not getting angry or upset. This was a joust, not a personal vendetta. I admired her cool in combat. I don't think I could ever fight in the first place. I'd be the one between fighters trying to make them give up on the idea of violence. I'd been in that position many a times in school when Chloe went picking a fight. I thought that she'd gone beyond all that. By her face, I could tell she was getting tired. Sweat flew, and her movements didn't have the same speed as they did a few minutes ago.

"Put up your hands," I yelled, as I saw her guard go lower and lower. Her rib cage heaved longer and larger, and I knew she'd have to give up soon. Angelina looked tired as well, but you could tell she knew how to conserve her energy. A moment after I told Chloe to protect herself, a surprise left came barrelling toward her and smashed her, right in the face, sending her flying backward onto her back with a thud. I waited a moment, but when I saw that she wasn't getting up, I rushed to her. Of course she couldn't die now, but who knew what the results of such a blow could be. I knelt down beside her, putting a hand on her face. There was no heat coming from her, but I assumed that was normal. It was a weird sight, though, as her face was a bit flattened, I could only assume by the blow. Her face inflated like a balloon, and I have to admit it was one of the weirdest sights I'd ever seen.

"Anyone else want to have a go?" Angelina said from behind me. I shook my head in the negatory, and held my sister's head in my hands. How could I tell if she was okay if she had no pulse?

"Just give her a sec, she'll come to," Brock said.

"How do you know?" I said, feeling dumb for asking.

"She hasn't disappeared, has she?" he said, and I thought that was a strange thing to say, and wholly unsatisfying at that. Her eyes opened, and there was a blank expression on her face, as if she had just woken up and had no clue where she was. She turned her head toward me and asked:

"Who won?"

Afterdeath

"Not you," I said, and smiled. She extended her hand, and I pulled her up.

"I thought I'd take some of my anger out on her, seemed like the right time to do it," she said, pointing her chin at her opponent, who was removing her padding and gloves.

"Perhaps you should have picked someone with no martial arts expertise. You would have fared better," Angelina said, a grin on her lips. A numb silence fell on the garage, and I could see the plethora of replies that crowded at the forefront of Chloe's mind. After such a trouncing, though, I think she knew better to mouth off at the person who'd handed her her own ass.

"Sorry to interrupt such a pleasant family moment, ladies, but we should start thinking about our daily tasks. Carson and I have to head downtown to attend to our duties. We, at the moment, find ourselves without a motor vehicle except for the ones the city is kind enough to provide as common transportation. Do you think you could find it in your heart to give two broke gentlemen a lift?" Brock said, the last sentence growing more sheepish.

"What did you do with the last ride you had?" Angelina said, eyeing them suspiciously.

"Sold it for the gas money," Carson said, inspecting his nails.

"Ha. Classic. Let me guess, you lent it to someone who never brought it back?" Angelina said, hands on her hips. Brock looked to the ceiling for aid, and when none was forthcoming, he smirked at Angelina.

"When did you get to know us so well, Angel?" he said, jutting out his chin.

"Pff, you guys are like open books with pages made of clear plastic, is what you are," she said.

"So what do you say," Carson said, looking at me. I felt myself flush, and I hoped to God he couldn't see it.

"Sure, why not?" I said, hoping for approval from Chloe. I looked at her with a raised eyebrow, and she answered back with a look of curiosity.

"Sure, why not," she said in a flat tone. Brock pulled the chains to open the garage door, but not before checking outside through a tiny slit to see if there would be a greeting committee on the other side. As the door rose, the sun flooded the garage, and I lifted a hand to shade my eyes. What a glorious day. Even in this run-down area of town, there was a magic time of the day when all things were made beautiful, and that time was now.

"You drive," Chloe said, and gave me a wink. It was then that I noticed Carson sitting in the passenger's seat. I froze for a moment, keys in hand, not knowing where to go or what to do. I think I made a slight turn where I stood, brain on complete lockdown until Chloe gave me a friendly tap on the shoulder. I got in as if buzzed. The motor rumbled and I backed up out of the garage.

There was still a bit of dew on the tar-paper roofs of the ramshackle buildings as I drove among them in the early morning. These weren't streets as much as crooked, pockmarked dirt alleyways where I had to be told where to turn ever so often lest I become lost forever in the maze of rusted sheet-metal and porous-looking wood structures. Dis had the look of a place that had grown organically, not been built. Of course, it also looked like it was in the process of going back to earth. Sloping roofs and slanted shacks leaned on each other, like drunks trying to get home after a late night binge. Grimy windows hid what might have transpired inside their shadows, and frankly, I was glad for it.

"Ugh, how did you guys fall so low?" Angelina said, voicing my thoughts.

"How do angels fall, Angel?" Brock said, turning to stare at her with a pointed look. She simply crossed her arms and ignored him. Carson pointed to the beginning of an actual road, and the bumpy ride gave way to pavement and the red-brick row houses I remembered from the night previous. From then on, the way was clear to me: I knew where to turn, and brought us back to the general downtown area where the bank was. I was still curious about Crosstown, though, and asked Carson about it.

"Oh, I know some people there. I could introduce you, if you'd like," he said. "You'll want to pull up over there, next to that line of people." I slowed down and stared, hard. Line of people, he said? There must have been a kilometre long waiting line heading into a building five stories tall, but massive. This one was entirely made of brown bricks, and squatted menacingly. I didn't feel comfortable in its shadow, let alone so near the rows upon rows of dangerous-looking people, most of them armed, waiting around for God-knew-what. Carson saw my look of horror and smiled.

"Would you like to come visit my work, today? You might like it better than being surrounded by trained killers. I promise you, it doesn't get all that exciting. What do you say?" he said. I looked back at Chloe, and barely glanced in the rear-view mirror, but saw her nod. I reddened.

"I'd love that," I said, biting my lip.

"Everybody out," Brock said, jumping over the side of the car. Chloe looked as if she was torn between following me and going with Brock. I knew how she felt about Angelina, but I realized that sort of thing was more her style. If she could be trained into the art of bounty hunting, she might be a happier person than if she drove a boat, at least I surmised so.

She furrowed her brow at me, and I nodded and smiled. So far, the men had been nothing but perfect gentlemen, as they'd promised. Being dead meant not having to be afraid about certain aspects that living women might have been leery of. There was that to be thankful for, at least. She gave me a tight-lipped smile and put a finger to her lips and kissed it. I smiled broadly and put the car in gear.

Carson explained how the city had expanded throughout the years he'd been there. He told me he couldn't recall exactly how long that was, because time was something people didn't really worry about all that much. It's not like he had to be on time for his job every day, he just did it out of courtesy for the souls that waited for him on the other side. I saw some pretty strange characters, the city a perpetual carnival, somewhat like the re-enactments grandma had taken us to, save that there was nothing inauthentic here. The fact was that no one was dragging the past back to pretend it was still that time period: these people actually came from then, and these were their clothes and tastes. A few period re-enactors would have blushed in jealousy, I'm sure. We drove on a downward slope, reminding me of San Francisco, but I noticed the buildings were changing as we went. Then, two lanes cut in and the road became slimmer. Higher up might have been considered turn-of the century European or North-American: tall brick buildings with fancy curves toward the tops, rectangular drop-down windows and large entrances at the bottom. We regressed in time, the further down the hill we went. I saw what could very well have been considered palaces: three or four story edifice, salmon pink, with silver accents on every corniche. Bull's eye windows at the corner dormers, with rounded dome roofs. There were a few more horse-drawn carriages than higher up, saloon-types, covered and black. Hearse-like, but without the tassels. Then we went through a stone walled archway into an even older part: stark castles with parapets and brown stone walls, ramparts and slits along the walls. Blockish and angular, they ran along a certain level, then different types of constructions, houses with thatched roofs and wooden timber frames. I saw that further down spread the marina, as wide as the city was, with glistening white boats all along polished quays of floating wood. The final buildings toward the water's edge looked as if they'd been put together by a giant with a surplus of icing: all white, with blue capped domes, reaching up perhaps six or seven stories. Carson pointed to a parking lot on the right, already half-full. There were all manner of vehicles, from horse-drawn chariots to cars only a hair more modern than what we had inherited.

Bertha safely ensconced between a Buick and a Bel Air, we walked the hundred meters or so to the marina, the stone blocks cool under our feet. The marina itself was surrounded by a chain-link fence, which we walked along for a while before coming to a small white wooden guard house. Carson flashed a smile at the lady behind the window, who let us into the grounds. Carson explained to me that Charon had built this place mostly on his own when he'd seen the influx of people coming in in the past several centuries.

"What about before him?" I asked.

"What do you mean? Carson said, turning to me as we walked down the wooden pier.

"Well, how did people cross before Charon came along and had the idea of ferrying them with a boat? Must have been quite a few that wanted to get here, no?" I said, waving my arm toward the silvery, glistening water.

"They're the reason we have to be careful crossing. If we do it right, you won't have anything to worry about," he said, but that made me worry, a lot. Our steps made a delightful hollow sound along the pier, and I enjoyed the whoosh of the waves on the sides in the perpetual motion of the sea. Seagulls danced above the water in groups, and I wondered what they were doing there. It's not as if they needed to eat or anything. Maybe they obeyed some primordial lizard-brain imperative. Down every pier we passed were rows upon rows of identical boats: long, thin and white. The front and back had raised pieces that came up higher that myself or even Carson. They were smooth on the exterior, as if made of one piece of wood, but the interior was unfinished, and smelled of cherry wood, mixed with salt water.

Many of these crafts were gone from their spots, and I imagined others liked to get to work early as well. Carson turned a pier and walked to what I thought was his very own boat. He stepped inside, and it rocked a bit from side to side.

For a moment I was gripped with anxiety, as memories of terrible times came flooding back. But there was nothing to be afraid of now, just the memories. I pushed them down with a deep breath.

"Step into my office," he said, and I giggled nervously. He handed me a long, white paddle, and grabbed one for himself. He offered me a hand and I took it, stepping into the boat as well. It was smooth and warm, and I felt a pang as I let it go. I sat on one of the three seats on offer: two on each side and one in the middle. I thought I'd be less in the way if I stayed toward the front. From what I remembered about gondolas, which this resembled, it was steered from the back. Carson jumped back onto the pier for a moment, and I had a sudden panic attack, thinking that he would unmoor me and send me off to drift with the currents. No, he did unlatch the boat, but hopped right back in, holding the rope in his hand, and his paddle in the other. He pushed the boat off the pier with one deft stroke of the paddle, and we headed for the open water.

What an incredible day. Few clouds marred the bluer than blue sky. The sun was gaining altitude, but the temperature, as always, was perfect. I was inside the picture of an incredible Mediterranean vacation. I sat facing Carson, who paddled expertly,

71

Afterdeath

standing at the back, looking at the horizon. He was almost angelic, which made me think of how Angelina was not. How had she possibly acquired a name like that with a personality that was the polar opposite? It made one wonder. Had her parents named her in irony? I hoped Chloe was all right, but I felt that Brock was a reasonable man, and would watch over her, especially since Angelina would not.

The piers were now tiny, the boats mere toys. The city was a layer cake of colors and shapes incongruous, growing tinier, at an inordinate rate. How fast were we going, anyhow?

Carson pointed ahead, and I turned around to see a bank of fog rolling in. The sounds of seagulls and lapping water died as we entered the thick, moist vapour. I turned to Carson, about to say something, but he put his index finger to his lips, and I paused, my mouth half-open. The mist thinned, but it got darker, and then I saw other boats heading back from where we had come from. My captain raised a hand in greeting, and a few others smiled and waved, not a one uttering a single word. They each carried a single passenger, who sat or stood, depending on their will and personal preferences. I saw a point of light in the water, a few hundred meters away, and motioned toward it. Carson nodded, and paddled a bit faster. I wondered what it could be, but with his admonishment to stay silent, I did not want to put us at risk by saying anything.

The gondolas slipped past, and soon we were alone again, heading into another thick blanket of fog. As we crossed, the waves became steadily choppier, and a thin rain began to fall on my head. Carson looked up and frowned. Neither of us felt the cold of the rain, but we knew had we been alive, we'd have been soaked and chilled to the bone.

The waves rose and fell, higher and lower, the rain a heavy drizzle now, and then a storm. I was having second thoughts about having come with him, and I could tell Carson felt the same way.

"Sorry about this!" he said, and lightning slashed the sky, four hundred meters away. Thunder followed immediately, deafening us both. My heart beat so fast I thought it would jump out of my chest and drown in the green waves that raged around us.

But I have no heartbeat, so how is that possible? I thought, touching my still chest, the fear fluttering beneath my hand.

I grasped the sides of the boat, which listed heavily from side to side. I saw a dark expanse in the distance, and as we bobbed and weaved over the waves, it became apparent that there was land ahead. A sheer cliff wall, with a tiny strip of beach, and a shipwreck against its side. The boat, a tiny fisherman's vessel, rocked against black rocks in the roiling waters twice, and fell asunder, swallowed whole by the sea in one crushing blow. Its last words a crushing of wood and agonizing wrench as it was sucked in violently.

Winds howled like the damned, and I saw on that beach a lone bearded man, dressed in a yellow rain slicker, pacing with great angry strides. Carson aimed our skiff straight for him and the front where I was sitting hit the gritty sand of the beach with a shriek. Carson told me to sit on the other side, and I got up, stepping over the middle bench, sitting where the boat still bathed in the ocean, flowing from right to left, as well as up and down, in this ungodly weather.

"About time you showed up!" The portly man yelled at Carson over the howl of the wind. "The rest of the crew is dead; I'm the only one left. I've been here for hours, was starting to think I'd never get rescued." He held his rain-battered hat with one hand, squinting at Carson.

"I'm sorry. You didn't survive. You went down with your ship, Captain. What's your name, sailor?" Carson said, himself hollering.

"Howard Henry, pleased to make your acquaintance. What do you mean, I didn't make it? I'm here, aren't I?" the man said, and stuck out his hand for Carson to shake, which he did, vigorously. I looked back, and could see further off to my right a giant squall beginning to form, and in the middle of that storm, a typhoon, of epic proportions.

"I want you to think real hard about the circumstances of your boat's accident, Captain. With all due respect, if you recall, you went down with it. There's no way you could have survived. Do you feel cold? I suspect if you search your feelings, you'll realize that any living person would be freezing to death at the moment, whereas you might only be bothered by the rain. In any event, I'd like to invite you to join us on our boat, and I'll get you out of here. I'll have to ask you to remain silent for the duration of the trip, though, as there are certain aspects of the crossing that are considered dangerous," Carson said, smiling. How many times had he explained to his passengers the precautionary steps to follow when going into the afterlife? It reminded me of the safety procedures on an airplane before take-off: "Please remain seated at all times and keep your hands inside the boat. Thank you for sailing Charon seaway transports, and enjoy your death!"

The captain went from one foot to the other, contemplating his options, staring up at the heavens which had opened up and offered a deluge of rain and winds for an answer. He stared off into the distance where the typhoon had decided that it wanted to make landfall: somewhere not too far from where we were now, making me wonder if we were safe, dead as we might be.

"I'll follow you, but I'll make my own rules, thank you," he said, and lifted his chin, walking past Carson and onto his boat. Carson scratched his head and looked like he

Afterdeath

was sighing. Being a taxi driver for the dead seemed to have just as many asshole customers as the living kind. Some people just didn't improve with death, I supposed. The captain sat on the middle seat, and Carson signalled for me to stand up. I did so, with my paddle in hand, and pushed off where I could feel the sandy beach below the boat. The Captain turned around once to give me a glimpse, was unimpressed by what he saw, and turned around again, hands on his knees. Carson pushed off as well, and we headed out onto the swelling crests of the sea, the typhoon coming closer, whipping winds and bullet-fast droplets into our faces. The fog bank reappeared out of nowhere, and once again, calm asserted itself.

Carson gave me a sign to sit down, and the sound of his paddle stroking gently through the waters became the only one. I once again saw a light off to our port side, but our passenger got up, and the boat rocked dangerously from side to side.

"What's that?" Captain Henry said, and the light changed direction, making a tiny wake, heading toward us. Carson put his finger to his lips, irritated, and made a sign for the man to sit down.

"I will not, sir, be quiet and sit at your command. I am also a ship captain, and you owe me respect!" he said, insulted. I looked over the side, and there were more than one light now. I counted about ten of them, all heading our way, and speedily, at that. I made the mistake of looking on the starboard side, and the captain, who had turned around to look at me for reasons unknown, followed my gaze.

"By God! There are dozens of these... lights, what are they man, tell me!" Carson held his lips closed, having given up on telling the man to be quiet. They grew larger, and closer, as if someone were swimming with light bulbs underwater. I peered overboard into the green waters, and saw a human shape, but with long, trailing fins. In front of it was the glow, attached to its scaly, fishlike head, inset with two, huge, dead eyes like bottomless wells. The captain held the side of the boat with both hands, and things went askew from then on. One of the things jumped out of the water and opened its large, sharp-toothed mouth, and latched itself onto the captain's chest, who screamed out in pain and surprise. The light, I saw, was at the end of a stalk, like a lamprey, a creature of the deep. It grabbed the captain around the waist with palmed, long-clawed hands, and attempted to drag him out of the boat while he screamed and screamed, its light whipping madly from its forehead. From every direction, I saw lights, lights, lights, converging, all at once. I held on to the side of the boat, wanting to scream myself, tears running down my cheeks, as I kept my teeth clenched.

I turned to Carson, who stood over the Captain, his paddle raised. He brought it down in one wide, circular arc, and the screeching man fell into the festering waters. The water bubbled and frittered, as the creatures devoured the captain right then and there. I lay down into the boat as low as I could go, and Carson waited, silent and barely breathing, as the trauma subsided.

A cold, dead head lifted from the now still waters, giant eyes peering around the side of the boat. I cowered at the fore section, back pressing into the post with all my might. If Chloe had been here, she'd have fought. She'd have found a way to get out of this mess. She would have done something, at least. I watched as a clawed hand reached for the side, pulling the boat over. It was going to capsize us! On the other side, a long-haired head rose from the water, blank, bulging eyes roving around the boat. It opened its maw, and three rows of shark teeth adorned its upper and lower jaw, tongue flicking wetly this way and that. A hiss came from the first creature, and the second answered with a clacking sound of its tongue.

They were half a meter away from either one of us, unable to see us, but pulling themselves into our boat. Something rubbery and wet slipped over my hand, and I jerked it away. Long claws, greenish black, clicked onto the very spot where my hand had been a second ago. The boat teetered toward the new arrival, and another large, unkempt head peered over the side, directly into my face. Huge eyes, glassy and deep as the sea, stared blindly, a few centimetres from me. Wet snuffles came from tiny slits where its nose should have been, sending bit of spray on my arm covering my mouth. A scream, jammed down my throat, desperately fought to get out. I tried to avert my gaze, but the horror drew me, like hypnosis, to want to be with it.

In the depth.

Far from worry.

No!

I shook myself awake, knowing that those weren't and never could be my feelings.

Carson took his long paddle and extended it over the water, as far as he could, then let it fall with a whack and took it out just as fast. The sound startled the things climbing aboard, their heads turning to see where it had come from, and as the frenzy began in the water where the paddle had been, they dove in. He pointed at my paddle, giving me the "come here" signal with his fingers, and I pushed myself away from my post and stepped on the tip of my toes all the way over, making sure that it never touched the boat. He took the paddle and lifted it over his head. In one thrust, he sent it flipping end over end, as far as he could throw. It landed with a splash, and the lights left the vicinity of our boat, to careen like glowing piranha where the paddle had landed. I went back to my seat, padding with the flat of my feet on the boat deck. Carson paddled as slowly as he could, soundless and without waves. A fight ensued over the wooden paddle in the distance, water boiling, shrieks of outrage rending the stillness. As we got further from the scene, Carson accelerated, and we entered the

Afterdeath

fog wall. I kept looking back over the side for sinewy lights, but the waters had gone silent again.

Chapter 8

HUNTERS

Olivia departed with a wave and I was left with Brock, Angelina and Barkley. I wondered what was up with my sister, but if anything was going to make her happy, I'd of course let it happen. Carson appeared to be doing just that. I hoped he'd be the kind of guy my sister deserved. Even though they'd met the day previous, sometimes you got a feeling about a person that you just couldn't deny. That didn't mean that they'd be dating in a few hours, I knew, but it did leave the door open for something to happen in the future. Even though I trusted Angelina as far as I could lob her, there was no denying that these friends of hers were okay. I didn't know what had happened to Liv to make her dislike men in general, which was sad, as we used to share everything. She'd told me about everything since we were babies, and I her, of course. Her first kiss from a boy named Ken at recess in grade seven. I'd called her Barbie for a few weeks after that until she took her revenge by making a guy think I liked him, and he me. She'd always been the sly one, my Liv. Our first periods, which I had had first, and she a week later. That was normal, since I was the older sister by a good half an hour. Since grandma had gotten sick, our friendship had grown... colder somehow. Not to the point of enmity, mind you, but there was that camaraderie that we'd had, which had slid off the map. I took a deep breath, and wondered why I still needed to breathe.

I looked around at the peaks of the skyscrapers, the tops almost a blur at their heights, framing the sky in brilliant blue all around. Wide, three-lane Acheron Avenue bustled with old cars, bringing me once again to the images of Havana, but set in 1970's Manhattan. It was still odd to see different generations of cars all on

Afterdeath

the same roads, and I wondered if I would get used to it. Trolleys on rails went up and down the streets as well, their green wooden frames curved and elegant.

On the other side of the street, a block away, a construction crew stood around an empty hole the size of a skyscraper. The men and women in hard hats came together in a rectangular shape on the outside of the gaping crater, hands held tight.

That was weird.

An enormous building appeared, slowly, taking up the space that had a moment ago been vacant, the workers lifting their hands to the sky, as if in prayer. The building coalesced, as I stared, bug-eyed at the event. It felt like a reverse disappearing trick, one far more magical than anyone had ever perpetrated before.

"Did you—did you see that?" I said, pointing at the miracle.

"Mmmm? You mean the building?" Brock said, barely turning around.

"It just—appeared out of nowhere!" I said.

"Yup. Pretty cool." He said, before continuing his chat with Angelina.

They discussed away on the sidewalk, and behind us was a lineup the likes of which I'd never seen in any amusement park, let alone a city street. It was almost like being at a comic convention, one of my sister and I's favourite activities, except instead of *superheroes*, people dressed up as their favourite *eras*. I noticed a lot of what could've been considered "barbarians" standing in line, with leather pants and moccasin-like shoes, battle-axes and double-handed long-swords slung over their backs in long, tan scabbards.

I watched as a line of men and women wearing stylized skull masks walked by, and I must have been staring, because Brock was smirking. The men wore tuxedos with red silk cravats, and the women frilly dresses in all manners of colour.

"The Dia de Los Muertos people. Everybody's got their thing here, you'll notice," he said, jutting his chin out at the colourful group that kept walking down the street. "Death takes on a life of its own in this place, if you'll pardon the pun."

"I always figured that mythology stuff was fake. A big, dark void, that's what was awaiting me, in my mind," I said, and he pointed to the end of the line, which had gotten shorter in the span of time we'd been standing there. "Are we really going to have to wait in line?"

"What, you think new assignments just fall out of the sky? You're a special kind of ignorant, new girl," Angelina said, walking faster than Brock and I, and slipping into the line just as a group of five arrived. They gave each other glances of disapproval, grumbling about Angelina, and accepted her presence. I think I'd have enjoyed tossing her out of the line, personally. Brock and I got behind a few more people, and I was thankful for the respite from the attitude.

"Yeah, we have to wait. Fear not, it goes faster than you'd believe, you'll see. To answer your question, though, imagine you have a door in front of you. The old, wooden kind, and below the doorknob, there is a keyhole. Let's say you wanted to see what was happening, and all you could see was what transpired through the keyhole-- what then? You'd have to extrapolate everything else that you didn't see, wouldn't you? Well, to some larger degree, death is the same thing. People might have caught occasional glimpses of what happened here, but without the bigger picture, all they could do was fill in the blank," he said, and we walked at a decent pace around the rope barricades that snaked around the front of the building. It reminded me of the line at the bank the day previous, but without the interminable wait. I could tell where Angelina was, because on the outside of the line a tiny tail wagged, just up ahead. It was around eight, a clock on the wall of the brown building told me, but I felt no pressing urgency of it. It wasn't the same as when I woke up and hurried to get ready for school, rushing a breakfast into my stomach before jumping on my old bicycle to get to class on time. It was, how should I say? Abstract. A relic that you kept around to remind you that somewhere, there was this thing called time that others were slaves to. Here it told you the cycle of the sun, and that was about it.

I fell to wondering about Olivia, and her personal beliefs.

"My sister was of the 'poofy clouds and man with a long beard' persuasion. I can only imagine the shock she's feeling right now at seeing that there is none of that," I said, spotting men and women in orange robes and shaved heads across the street, hanging off a cable car and smiling. I judged that we had gone halfway to the building. Strange, quick was not the word I'd have used to describe this waiting line when I first got here. Brock had been right in his assessment.

"Weeeell, everybody kind of gets jolted when they get here, but as you can see, everyone adapts to their surroundings," he said.

"But they all still believe what they did when they were still alive, don't they? Even in the face of evidence against it?"

Brock rubbed his face with one hand and glanced around, then said: "It's comforting, though, isn't it? It's not because you died that you stop believing what you do. Besides, there's no proof *against* their beliefs, by and large, just that the afterlife is not this tailor-made place to one specific subset of people's personal idea of heaven. It's communal, like the living world," Brock said, and we entered the building. I guessed it was silly to think that only one group of people would be right about what this place would look like. Why should it? Everybody died, after all. Why should some be condemned to an eternity of torment for not believing the same set of stringent rules as others? I nodded in satisfaction, taking in the new information. I'd go to sleep less stupid tonight, as my grandma used to say.

Afterdeath

Grandma.

"My grandma died a little while ago. Do you think I'll find her here?" I asked, as we walked down a hall of purple granite, two stories tall, and sombre. Voices echoed, barely muffled by the grey carpeting. Further down the hall, slits in the walls disgorged lengths of white paper. Without stopping, Brock walked along the wall and tore a strip of paper with a deft move. He kept on walking, and as he did, typewritten words began to show on the paper. He frowned, crumpled the paper and tossed it in a small metal door along the same wall, which opened like a post office box, from the top.

"Depends. How did she die?" he said, searching the crowd for a moment, then heading for Angelina, who waited a few meters away, beaming at us.

"In her sleep, from Alzheimer's."

"I don't think so, then. Only people who died of violent or traumatizing deaths usually end up here, as far as I can tell," he said. "Hey Angel, what's up?" as we exited the other side of the building, into an enormous courtyard filled with picnic tables and a gigantic fountain in the centre. In a circular basin kneeled a giant stone statue, its arms extended, and from its chest protruded a long, shining sword, most probably silver. Water spurted from the wound being inflicted on it as well as cascading from its open mouth, down to its knees. My neck twitched from a weird spasm, not unpleasant, mind you, and I forced myself to look away from it.

"Great news!" she said, over-enthusiastically, "I'm sticking with you ladies for a while."

I eyed her suspiciously.

"Is that your assignment?" I asked. I didn't want to have to stick with this woman for any longer than I had to.

"Sure is. I'm supposed to watch over you and make sure nothing happens to you. First ever body guard duty. Aren't you happy?" she said, arms on her hips, a giant smile plastered on her face. Various groups of mercenaries and swords for hire stood around, chatting and laughing, their weapons gleaming in the sunshine, much like the fountain's. The building itself surrounded the area, and we were in what I would describe as a "donut hole", with an exit off to the right, leading to the street. The edifice was brown brick and tall, slim windows, going up about five stories, but sprawled over a large expanse of the downtown area. I wondered what people did inside? Keep track of the deceased?

"Thrilled," I said, trying to get as much of the cold I felt in my heart into my words. Five minutes ago, she couldn't wait to get away from us, and now she couldn't wait to pal around with us. It felt more and more like High School around here, with two-faced people saying one thing in your back and another in front of you. "You'll excuse me if I don't entirely trust you motives, won't you?" I said, straight to her face.

"Ooh, you still sore because I kicked your butt? Don't be! Not a lot of people can take me on. That's just the way it is. Come on." She turned around and walked away. Brock looked at me and shrugged, following Angelina and Barkley, who'd been leaving his mark on the side of the fountain.

I turned around one last time to see a mainly empty corridor, where few papers now exited their slots, and grudgingly followed the only people I knew here, apart from my sister who was out gallivanting with some hot beau on the Dead Riviera. This sucked.

I ran after my party, which was ahead a ways. A big, burly someone bumped into me, and I was knocked back from his sweaty chest.

"Hey! Watch where you're—" I said, looking up into the scowling face of a mountain of a man, "going there." I finished, weakly, as he reached for his sword over his shoulder. I backed away, a step at a time, and bumped into something just as unyielding, yet sharp, behind me. I peered over my shoulder and came face-to-cheek with a dress-clad woman with a dagger. Pointy end in my back.

"Guys! Help!" I yelled, before having a hand clapped over my mouth.

Chapter 9

SUNSET ON NECROPOLIS

I heard the gulls wailing in the breeze as we exited the fog, and I never thought I'd find that to be the most beautiful music I'd ever heard. Carson steered gently, and I exhaled for what felt like an eternity. I didn't even realize I'd been holding my breath. I let go of the sides of the boat, and felt something underneath my nails and looked: white paint. I hugged myself from a chill that was entirely imaginary, but wholly felt.

"I want to go home," I said, looking up to Carson, who tightened his lips and mumbled under his breath.

"I want to go home, you hear me?" I screamed, giving me a jolt of surprise. He nodded, and I sat on the middle bench for the rest of the trip back to the mainland, facing the front, away from him. The calm seas gave off a briny scent, soothing to anyone who hadn't gone through what I had, I was sure. I bent over the side of the boat and peered into the depths, but there was nothing. Nothing but murky green water, as it should have been.

Carson steered the boat to its mooring-place and jumped out, securing it to a post. He then held out his hand for me, which I did not take it, pulling myself out on my own, refusing to look at him. I stalked off without a word, heading straight for the exit. The beauty of the day was lost on me now. Just this sinking feeling of having escaped a fate worse than death remained, anchored in the very core of my being. The girl at the guard booth saw me coming, with Carson trying to catch up, and barely said a word before I had gone. I heard her say something to the effect of "Where's your charge?" to Carson, but I was beyond the reach of his words when he answered. There were a few people driving into the parking lot, and I hit one car on the hood as it tried to turn into the same aisle I was crossing. The driver gave me a weird look and I flipped him the bird.

Our Bertha waited for me, and I felt like Angelina for a moment: not giving two shits, and jumping in the driver's seat. Carson appeared on the passenger's side, both hands on the door.

"Hey, are you leaving without me?" he said, attempting a smile. His eyes showed fear, though, and I only wanted to leave this jerk behind.

"What do you think? After something like that? Do I look like I want to be with a guy like you?" I said, gripping the steering wheel and staring straight ahead.

"I'm sorry! I don't know what happened! Even when the customers make noise, the ranfirar don't attack, or at least not in such huge numbers." He said, looking despondent. I started the car and put it in reverse. He ran in front of it. "Olivia, wait, please!" I gritted my teeth and looked into his face. His palms were pressed in Bertha's hood.

"Don't scuff the paint-job, jerk!" I said, revving the engine.

"Do you even know where you're going?" he said, putting his hands up in the air, stepping away from the car. I pressed the accelerator and passed him, his arms dangling by his side. I turned the corner and slammed the brakes. He was right. I had no idea how to find Chloe again. They might have left the building in front of which we'd left them earlier. Without Carson, I might not find them again. Damn.

"Are you getting in or what?" I said, turning around to yell at him. He seemed to wake up from a stupor and ran to the passenger's side. I grinned inwardly.

"It's a big city. I get lost here sometimes," he said.

"What are the ranfirar? You mentioned the name earlier. You meant those fish-people. What are they?" I said, as we pulled out of the parking lot and began tracing back our steps. The steep incline was slow going. Cars seemed to be crawling up the avenue. I never thought the afterlife would get traffic jams, but then again, I was wrong about a lot of things. I sighed. At least the view was nice. Those tall, white and blue buildings reminiscent of Greek islands glowed in the afternoon sun.

"It means People of Ran, in Old Norse. She was a kind of sea deity back in the day. Here she's in charge of all those who drowned. Usually, they don't attack our skiffs. We tend to be careful anyway, but it was just… odd. I've never seen them swarm before," he said, contemplative. Cars were slow moving, so I guessed we had time to discuss the finer points of mythology. Maybe that would get my mind off things a bit.

"Does that mean that there are gods here?" I said, peering higher above the windshield, trying to glimpse what might be slowing down traffic. Carson shifted uneasily in his seat.

"I wouldn't call them gods or goddesses per se. Just people who've amassed spectacular amounts of power. I mean, to be a god, you have to gain your power from people's worship. They're more like rulers, really. Although, if you ask them, they might think they're gods. People are pretty vain that way," he said, looking at me.

"They? As in there are more than one?"

"Well, yeah, of course! Think of all the different cultures throughout history, and all the beings they worshipped. Some of that stuff was based in reality. Not everything can be true, of course, but there are a lot of them, each with his or her own domain, and their adepts and followers, just like any religion," he said.

"But no One God?"

"How can you know an unknowable being?"

"Point taken. But Necropolis is full of all sorts of different people. Are you telling me they all worship just the one god, person, whatever?" I asked, screwing my eyebrows into a knot.

"No, no, Necropolis is neutral ground. There's a truce in effect over the city. There's all sorts of influence peddling going on at the Soul Management Bureau, but that's the extent of the others' power inside Charon's sphere of influence," he said. "Pull over to one of the side streets, will you?"

"Why? What's going on?" I said, but as we finally went over the hump that led into the more modern area of the city, I saw. It took me a minute, and much honking from the truck behind me, but I turned right and kept on gaping at the odd scene before me.

Dozens of men and women fought, their swords and axes, pikes and various other weapons swinging wildly, clashing against those of others, near the building where we'd left the other half of our party.

"Oh my goodness! What's going on?" I yelled, over the din of the combatants' screams and interlocking weapons.

"I have no idea," Carson retorted, as we both began to head for the carnage. I kept my eyes peeled for my sister, Brock, Angelina and Barkley, but there was so much going on that I could not spot them. It was like trying to find specific ants within the frenzy of a hive: it just couldn't be done.

As we drove down the street, a tremor pushed down on the pavement around us with a low, deafening sound. Everything slowed on the other side. Then it all stopped.

They all stood frozen, faces twisted in battle cries, no words emanating from their mouths. On the streets, and the sidewalks, ready to destroy each other, the moment the spell that had been cast over them vanished. I lost sight of the battle as I passed the brick building on the corner. Carson kept staring, his neck twisting to see what was happening.

An open spot offered itself and I parked. We jumped out of the car, stopping at the corner to peer at this impossible open-air wax museum. To the left was the building where we'd dropped them off, and further up the street was where all these warriors stood. Passersby came up to the statues, intrigued, but no one dared touch them in case they came to life and began to smash things as they must have been doing before being glued to their spots.

The doors of the building opened, and brown-robed monks, (or so I thought they resembled,) came out in droves. They carried their gold-hilted longswords by their sides, faces hidden under long cowls. Carson tapped me on the shoulder and began to walk in the direction of the new arrivals. I gripped the side of the building more tightly, doing a little dance of indecision, my heart rapping fast. I chased after Carson and followed a few steps behind him, keeping an eye on the "monks". They ignored us and went to the warring factions, removing their weapons carefully, taking them out of reach, and waiting.

The closer I got, the more I realized that they weren't so much frozen as very, very slow. Almost imperceptibly so, yet their movements continued in the arc they had begun them, like a pantomime measured in years instead of seconds.

Other monks came up to the fighting figures and carefully picked them up, and lay them on the ground, on their backs. Movements quickened, and the robed figures backed away, as did the gawkers. Fighting began in earnest, but the assailants found themselves thrashing on the ground for a few seconds before getting their bearings. Most sprang up, at least those who were not too wounded to do so, and searched for their weapons about them. The monks drew their swords and took a step in the direction of the nearest fighters, holding the points at throat level.

Two of the brawlers decided to rush the intruders, perhaps thinking they'd take their weapons, or some such nonsense, and in both cases the monk attending to them took a step back, whirled their sword and slashed them in half. The offending parties disappeared as they hit the ground. All others put their hands in the air.

As one, the monks sheathed their weapons and took a step back. They turned to the building and in single file returned inside.

"Come on!" Carson said, grabbing my arm and running after the robed figures. I was tempted to pull away from him, but then I noticed Chloe, Angelina and Brock being led away inside the building as well, by the last of the robed monks. Carson

Afterdeath

pulled a door open and I spied a long corridor, lined with pedestals. Stone statues identical to the monks stood on each one, and I that down the corridor, those monks were getting back up on their pedestal and turning back to stone.

My sister and our friends, however, were headed to a bank of elevators further away. I pulled away from Carson and ran as fast as he did, rushing to see where they would go. Up ahead, two of the monks turned around and drew their weapons, pointing them straight at us. We stopped, and they asked:

"Why do you follow us?" the tip of their swords held steady before our faces.

"You have our friends," Carson said.

"And... and my sister," I added.

"You wish to suffer the same fate?" one of them said.

"I... guess so," Carson said, but I stayed mute. The wording made me think that survival was not part of the deal. A set of stone guards animated behind us and walked off their pillars, unsheathing their swords as well. The ones before us turned around and walked away, and we followed, the ones behind keeping pace. The others had already taken the elevators, and we stepped inside a different one.

"The Master," one guard said, and the elevator doors closed, a sensation of lifting, rather than rising took a hold of me. I had never taken a spacewalk, but I imagined it would feel somewhat similar. I felt myself becoming much lighter than I should have, and might begin to float at any time. The walls of the elevator began to evaporate, and a large room took its place. The feeling of weightlessness dissipated, as did the elevator. We found ourselves in a large office. Walls of expensive woods, with libraries full of thickly-bound books in earthy browns and greens lined most visible surfaces. Angelina, Barkley, Brock and Chloe stood before a desk a certain distance away, and I peered over the motionless guard's shoulder to see who or what they were standing in front of. I had the urge to shove one out of the way to run to my sister, but thought better of it. The man holding a cutting blade mere steps behind me probably would have relished nothing better than to use it. After what felt like forever, the guards moved, and I followed eagerly. I raised my hand and was about to shout my sister's name, but Carson pulled down my arm and put an index to his lips, shaking his head.

A large wooden desk separated our compatriots from someone with a loud voice, berating them in no uncertain terms. Behind this man, on the wall, hung an enormous painted scene. It depicted a cowled figure standing at the stern of a small skiff, exactly like the one we had so recently taken, pushing through murky waters, a few huddled, sulky-looking ghosts sitting at the fore.

"...have any idea the trouble you've brought on me and this city? Do you?" I heard the contempt eviscerating the four, and I wondered even more strongly what this person looked like. We rounded the corner of the desk and I saw him. Tall, gaunt, even, wearing a tailored suit of shimmering grey, a small, blood-red handkerchief in his breast pocket. His large eyes bulged as he spoke, peering down the length of his crook of a nose. Slender fingers danced in the air, punctuating his remarks. He peered sideways at me, then did a double-take, his gaze flitting back to Chloe.

"You two are never far apart, are you?" he said, jutting his chin out to Carson, who looked uncomfortable.

"We tend to stick together, Uncle," Carson said, puffing out his lower lip. Uncle? The guards took a step back, and somehow blended into the background, so that I stopped noticing them, or they did the same trick as the elevator and disappeared. I'm not sure which.

"I'm Olivia," I said, with a nervous smile, putting out my hand for him to shake. His furious gaze fell on my hand and a smile broke his lips into a horrible shape, and he did not take it. I almost wished he had continued scowling. I put my hand by my side, wiping sweat onto my skirt.

"Are you really, now. I'm Charon, young lady. All of you, take a seat. We have important matters to discuss," he said, splaying his hands. I hadn't noticed any chairs on my way in, but as I furrowed my brow and turned around, I noticed that five comfortable-looking red leather armchairs had appeared behind us. I threw a glance at my sister, and she nodded, chewing slightly on her lower lip. Angelina crossed her arms and stared at the man, and Brock leaned back on his chair, staring at the ceiling. I noticed for the first time the gold-embossed decorative friezes at the peaks of the pillars that separated the libraries, connected to the squares of gilded relief flowers and vines that covered the entire area of the room like a French palace.

"You are all lucky to have been within distance of my influence when they attacked you," Charon said. "It turns out orders were put out by several very influential people for you. As per the rules, I can't say who it was, or for what. Suffice it to say, you're all in danger. You're also threatening the order I've worked so hard to build in my city," Charon said, his elbows on his desk, his fingers clasped together in a wiry ball.

Brock's head snapped forward, a sneer on his face.

"It's not your city. It doesn't only belong to you. You just reap the rewards of everyone else's hard work," he spat.

"Silence!" Charon roared, standing up. "You might be my son, but I will not be insulted so! Have you not caused enough trouble already? Are you so enjoying your exile that you wish to extend it?" he passed a hand over his forehead and regained his composure. "I do not like this… thing… you are going through, but you know the laws. If you had been anyone else, we would not be here speaking of this." He

Afterdeath

turned to look at Brock, who held his gaze defiantly. Brock was Charon's son, then? What could he possibly have done?

"What I did, I did out of love! You have done the same!" Brock said, slamming his fists on the desk.

"You are not, and never will be the ruler of *any* land of the dead! You wrecked the balance, you unconscious maniac! Nothing can go back unless by our say-so!" Charon howled.

"Screw your balance! Who resurrected and made you Emperor of the Underworld?" Brock flung back, and as he was about to get up and pounce on the tall man, a hand came slamming down on his shoulders, and he whipped his head around to see a guard standing there, impossible. Charon gave a dismissive wave of his hand, and the monk receded into shadow, eclipsed my some trick of the light. Brock crossed his arms and brooded. I looked over to Carson, who probably wanted to melt into the carpet, so incredibly uncomfortable he looked.

Barkley barked and jumped from his chair onto Angelina's lap, who smiled at him and scratched him behind the ear. Charon shook his head, pursing his lips when his gaze fell upon Angelina and Barkley. He held his hands behind his back, as an old sage would, and began pacing under his portrait.

"Do you have any idea who you've crossed, son? No you don't, and you don't even know the people with whom you keep company. But I do," he said, flashing an angry glance over all of us. "And they'll get you annihilated," he said, his voice having turned to sadness, as he took a deep, searching look into all the faces that were present before me. When his eyes fell upon mine, it felt as if a well, dark and cold, absorbed my mind. It told me: "I know you," and for a moment, I was not myself, but some other, who had somehow been ripped asunder. His eyes continued on to Carson and I felt a shiver pierce me. I had stood naked before the crosser of souls, and a light had been lit, but stood beyond my reach to grasp.

"I can't help you without putting our peace in peril. What happened today was ordered today. That means that whoever wants you, wants you so badly that they don't care about it. I'm sorry to be the bearer of bad news. I can't risk having all this torn asunder because of a few renegades, no matter who they are," Charon said, pacing back and forth behind his desk, and Brock turned his head, scoffing loudly.

"What happens to us?" Angelina said, ruffling Barkley's neck fur.

Charon paused. "Obey your orders. If balance is to be restored, it's by satisfying those who have given out assignments. I wash my hands of all involvement," and he threw Brock a sharp glance before he could say anything. "Perhaps one day you'll be forgiven. For now you remain outcasts. There is only so much I can do for you once you have left the city. Now go," he said.

Chloe got up and said, "But this has nothing to do with my sister and I. What are we being punished for?" Charon put both hands on his desk and looked at my sister with the most intense stare I have ever seen in my life.

"One day, you will know yourself. On that day, you will no longer wonder. Guards!" Out of the surrounding darkness, ten armed monks shimmered becoming solid. Carson tapped me on the arm, and I rose to my feet, unsure as to where to go. Angelina put Barkley down and got up, as did the others. We turned to where we'd come from, and the guards made way to let us pass. As I walked away, I turned around to see that Charon had evaporated into thin air.

***

On the street before the building, it felt as if no time had passed at all. I ran to Chloe and gave her a great big hug, not knowing whether I should laugh or cry. I think I ended up doing both.

Carson, Brock and Angelina were discussing what had just transpired in hushed voices, and Barkley sat at Angelina's foot, wagging his tail. All those assailants had retreated. Calm had returned.

"So what happened?" I asked Chloe. She slowly shook her head, as if trying to get her marbles in order.

"As far as I can tell? One group attacked us, and one tried to defend us. That's the short form. We'd just left the hall where Brock and Angelina'd gotten their assignments, when some woman grabbed me from behind. I yelled for the others, and they came to my rescue, but then fighting just started on the street. A lot of people got cut down, and I just saw them vanish into thin air." She put her hand up in a fist and opened her fingers, mimicking an evaporating assailant. "Everything stopped, and then those guards came out of the building. I think you know the rest." She went to the curb and sat down, putting her elbows on her knees. I'd seen this pose often enough, and knew that Chloe was deep in thought, trying to figure out a conundrum. I sat next to her and put an arm around her shoulder. She turned to me and smiled weakly, then stared at the ground, her smile gone.

"How went your day with Carson?" she said, forcibly half-smiling.

"Pretty horribly, actually. Some captain guy we picked up from the other side started making a racket while we were in dangerous waters and these— creatures came out, tried to attack us," I said, shivering at the memory.

"Holy crap! Are you okay?" she said, putting her hand on my shoulder.

"I'll... live? I made it out of there, but it gave me such a jolt. I'm usually okay on the water now, but that was just intense," I said. Our past was swimming back into

Afterdeath

view, and as always, I pushed it down into its watery grave. I was not ready to face it. Not now. There were other things pushing up at our feet, below the surface. I wanted to stay as together as possible.

"What about Carson?" she said.

What about him? I thought.

"Just another Prince," I said, and she knew exactly what I meant. She put her hands behind her back and leaned backward, grimacing. It wasn't her fault things never worked out for me, that was just my luck. She'd inherited all the good traits, and I the bad. We were like a battery, with her as the positive.

"What are we supposed to do now?" she asked, and I laughed. "What's so funny?"

"That's my line. I'm the one who's always confused, remember? You're the strong one," I said, jostling her amicably. She put her head against mine and said:

"I'm never as strong as I look. I just fake it until I convince myself." I felt a squeeze in my heart. Is that how she did it, or was she just trying to make me feel better? I don't think she'd joke about that, but it still felt weird hearing it from her. I felt a presence behind me, and turned to see Carson standing there. My insides squeezed a bit.

"We should go. I think we'll be okay inside city limits for about a day, but we have to make a plan to leave," he said, extending a hand to Chloe and I. We returned the hand, and he lifted us to our feet. "Let's get back to the car," he suggested. I nodded and started walking in its direction, wary of any potential attackers. The people on the street looked nothing like those who had been in suspended animation when we had happened on the scene previously. I knew that that was no guarantee, but still, it made me feel a tad safer. Where had the survivors gone? To regroup and plan a different attack? Possibly. Only time would tell.

I heard Angelina say something along the lines of: "So *that's* what got you kicked out of your cushy place?" I turned around just in time to see Brock throw her a truly ugly look.

"Shall we talk about the reasons why that happened?" he tossed at her, and she walked faster, catching up to us. Chloe dropped back, and I heard her talking to Brock.

"Why didn't you tell us you were Charon's son?" she said, looking at him.

"If you were the son of the Devil, would you tell anyone?" he replied, staring straight ahead.

"Is he? The Devil, I mean." I asked, turning around.

"The man takes bribes from all the Rulers surrounding Necropolis, in their own little fiefdoms so that they can put hits on people they don't like. Usually, the City is the one safe place for all. That seems to no longer hold true, doesn't it," Brock said, waving his hands. A few people turned to look at him, but his scowl made them step a bit faster to get out of his way.

"How can we tell who's after us?" I asked, worried about being jumped at from the shadows.

"That's the beauty, pardon the pun, of the system. It's set up so that all requests are made anonymously, and no one knows who gets them. If you want to, you might turn on your best friend if the bounty is big enough," Carson said.

"How do you know who you're working for, then?" Chloe said, intrigued.

"You don't, not directly. It's a double blind. All transactions are dealt through the Charon bank, sent through the distribution service, and even those who place the bounties are left in the dark, even after the hunter comes forward with the hunt to claim their bounty," Brock said. He stared at the sidewalk while walking. This whole situation bugged him, I could tell. "Of course, there's always educated guessing, but you might never know for sure. Usually, you never even get to find out. It prevents retaliation against all parties. Fairly clever, in a Machiavellian sort of way."

"Why didn't you become a ferryman, then?" I asked.

"Because I hate water," he answered bluntly, shrugging. I found that ironic, somehow. The son of the greatest boatman in history was afraid of water. My amused look must have betrayed me, because his anger was palpable. I didn't press the matter.

Where should we go then, if not here? Danger for danger, what advantage did the outside of this metropolis hold? What should we do? The others had their orders, but we were free agents. Our only goal now was to stay with our body parts attached. Without training, or experience, how far could we possibly go, and for how long? There was also the time factor involved. Even if, say, we did go on for months in the wilderness, following roads into unknown territories, exploring this new world, what then? We had forever. What purpose was to be had in meandering the afterlife without some sort of *raison d'être*? Wouldn't it be better to find something, anything we might be good at? I'd have to talk to Chloe about all this, of course, but I for one did not want to be wandering with no plan for all eternity. It reminded me too much of people who took a year off of school to get "life experience", but then never went back. I had seen them, some of the seniors from High School, still behind the counter at some menial job, two years after graduation. I just wanted to shake them and tell them to find their purpose! That wasn't going to be me, though, alive or dead. Or just dead, I guessed.

We crossed the street and turned the corner, the car still waiting where we had left it. One of the advantages of the Afterlife was no visible parking meters. Thank God for small favours. As Chloe went for the driver's seat, I called shotgun and opened

Afterdeath

the door so that the others could get in. Carson got between Angelina and Brock, who looked like they were no longer on speaking terms. That was fine with me. If I could get Angelina from speaking entirely, that would have been a profound relief.

Chloe started the car, gripped the wheel, let it go, then, turned the engine off.

"Does anybody have any idea of what we're supposed to do now?" she said, staring the three in the back in the eyes, each one in turn. She left Barkley alone, because he didn't have any bearing on the situation. "Because I have no idea. I've been dead for a few days now, and I thought I had a pretty good grasp on what was going on over here, but so help me, I'm at a loss. I'm half tempted to leave all of you behind save my sister, and just take off. You wouldn't be our problems anymore. I'm kinda liking that idea. What about you, Olivia?" she said, turning to me. Burning intensity shone in her eyes, and I was half-afraid to answer.

"Sure, I guess. Question is, where would we go?" I answered, turning my palms up.

"I have to go with you, whether you like it or not," Angelina said, leaning forward.

"Why is that, huh? Why should we let you even near us? After putting a curse on our car, and getting the local contingent of greevers to attack your friends' home? Give us one good reason we should have you along for the ride?" Chloe said, bitterly.

"Easy: I know how to get you out of the Afterlife. I'll even take you there."

Chapter 10

VIKINGS

"What?" I said, and Olivia stared at her, gape-mouthed.

"I can get you out of the Afterlife. You don't have to stay here," Angelina said. After all the lies that this woman had said, I would have liked nothing better than to see her evaporate before my eyes. Was she lying still?

"Is this your assignment?" Olivia said. Would that explain her willingness to stay with us after having shown such disdain only a short time ago? Angelina's changing moods irritated me beyond belief. You'd think that someone you'd yanked out of prison would have the decency of showing gratitude for more than a day. No, this was her personality. I'd hated her kind when I was alive, and I'd be hard-pressed to endure her in my death. What if she was telling the truth, though? What if? What if? What if my head sprouted wings and I could fly away?

"No, you're lying. I don't know what you're playing at, but we don't need you, Angelina. You've brought us nothing but trouble since we met you. Why should now be any different?" I said. Carson raised an eyebrow beside her, and I interpreted that as meaning "she's got a point."

"Listen, I can see how you'd feel that way, but I'm serious, I do know how to get you out of here, the both of you. I just have to take you to see someone," she said, and there was the beginning of panic appearing in her eyes.

Afterdeath

"Who?" Olivia said, softly. I knew what she was thinking: perhaps if we knew, then we might be able to make a better decision. The thing was, I was enjoying seeing the cracks in Angelina's devil-may-care attitude.

"I... I can't tell. I don't know," she said.

"Get out," I told her. "Get out of the car. You make empty promises for reasons I can't fathom, for people you don't want to talk about. The hot air you blow out stinks, lady. Take it with you, somewhere else," and I turned around, to stare at the empty street before us, arms crossed.

"Are you sure?" Olivia asked, touching my elbow. My lips tightened. Olivia reached for the door handle, and pulled it inward with a click. I took a peak back in the rear-view mirror, and saw that Angelina was staring at Olivia in agitation.

"Come on! Don't you want to leave this place? I understand how hard it must be. You were so young, so full of promise, then all of a sudden, bam! You're dead, and there's nothing you can do about it. But think about it: you could go back! You could live that life that was stolen from you. You have one chance, and I am *it*. Do you really want to throw it away?" she said, waving her hands at me.

"What do you get out of this?" I asked.

"I can't..." she pleaded.

"Then leave," I said. I was done being nice to her. She might be stronger than I, but I was holding the baseball bat this time.

"Okay, all right, you know what I get? I get forgiveness. That's what I'm hoping for, anyhow. I pissed off some pretty powerful people, and if I get you to go home, I can go on with my afterlife without having a price on my head. Satisfied?" she said, angrily.

"Barely," I replied. "Who's this person you want to take us to, and how do we know it isn't some sort of trap for either or all of us?" I said, turning around to stare her in the face again.

"I wasn't lying when I said I didn't know. I'm not supposed to tell you this, but yes, it is my assignment. You're making me break my vow by telling you," she said, gripping the front seat.

"You won't see me shedding tears for you, Angelina. You do realize you've been a pain in the ass since we rescued you, don't you? Maybe if you spent less time thinking about yourself, and more thinking about others, I might have been more willing to help you," I said. Should I allow her to stay? The idea of going home certainly was appealing, if it was the truth, of course. I desperately wanted to trust her, her recent history notwithstanding.

"Does that mean you will?" she said. There was that light of hope in her eyes. Maybe with a tight leash on her, we'd get somewhere.

Before I could reply, Brock said: "If she says it's her assignment, I'm fairly certain you can be sure it is. Not a lot of bounty hunters would break their oath on any account. If it makes you feel any better, I can come along with you, to make sure everything is aboveboard. I have some time off coming up anyhow."

I looked at Olivia, and she gave me a weak smile. I grunted. Any poor soul walking by would have wondered why two men, two women and a dog were having an argument in a parked car on the side of the street. I massaged my temples and glanced upward, finding no guidance in the clear blue sky. Not that I'd expected any, but one could hope. I could feel my resolve shaking. What if? What if?

"I think we should decide democratically," Olivia said, startling me out of my waffling. Without waiting for my reply, she continued: "All those in favour of Angelina's plan to take us back to the Living, raise your hand," and she did so, as well as everyone else in the car except for me and Barkley, who merely barked his assent. It wasn't that simple, though, I wanted to yell to her: You can't just go on a hunch! You can't just trust these people to do right by us. But it was too late, it had been decided without me, it seemed, against my better judgement. I glared at Olivia, who put her hand down and shrugged "sorry". I sighed.

"So, now that we are agreed," she said in a clear voice, bolstering her courage, "where do we go?"

"I recommend we get ready for the trip," Angelina said, giving me a sly grin. She wouldn't get away with this, I swore to myself, and threw sharp objects at her face in my mind.

"How so?" Olivia said.

"Well, I may not know who ordered the assignment, but I do know where we have to go. The Deadwoods to the Northeast of the City. The Lady of the Cottage is our contact," she said. "If we have to go there, we have to stock up on protective spells, amulets and such."

Protective spells? Amulets? What the heck was she talking about? Then I remembered the fuel-less fire she had made that night at the rest stop, and the "protective circle" she'd made around Bertha. I shouldn't sniff so quickly at this idea of magic. Perhaps in this world it was the norm.

"Okay, where to?" I said, turning the car on.

"Forward, and to the right," she said, which would take us to an older part of the city, judging by the buildings on that side of the street. I drove until the first intersection, then turned down the street to my right. I'd been correct: it was like taking a trip through history, in reverse.

I was still miffed with Olivia for having gone over my head. It was insulting to me, I felt, that she would have done such a thing without consulting me. I don't know if it was this place, but she seemed to be developing this streak of independence that I hadn't seen in her before. So far I couldn't exactly say I liked it, either.

Palatial, expansive constructions gave way to brick, fort-like edifices with vertical slits for windows. Within their walls, two-story, thatched-roof homes, arranged pell-mell around a frenzy of slim streets and alleys, as if those had been built as an afterthought.

"Stop here," Angelina said, and I shot her an annoyed glance.

"I'm not a taxi driver," I said.

"So sorry, love. Please, do stop here if you could? You're a *dear*, darling," she said, bowing low behind the car seat. I gave the brakes a tap, and she smacked her head against the back of the seat.

"Oops!" I said, bringing the car to a complete stop by the curb. We all exited, Angelina rubbing her head, and I throwing her my most angelic smile, flapping my eyelashes extravagantly.

"It's this way," she said, pointing, and we meandered down dirty alleys whose broken cobblestones were covered in filth and garbage. An odour of moist catacombs floated, like a basement that had suffered water damage and been left to rot. Shadows lengthened on the streets, lanterns hung from medieval homes giving us a bit of respite from the growing darkness. Most of these homes followed a similar pattern: Tall, pinnacle thatched roofing reaching almost all the way to the ground, with the base of the house made of field stones, turning to weather-beaten planks of wood at waist height. Three or four steps led up to wooden doors, almost hidden under the roofs. Windows like lidded eyes, tall and gaunt, all blind to the outside at this hour, cutting through the thatching like a knife. Once in a while, a sign hung above the street, and I guessed by the noise from inside that these were drinking houses. Many had a post jutting out onto the alley that were carved dragon's head, or monsters of some sort, like the prows of old ships with their mermaids attached under them to bring them good luck. An owl hooted nearby, and Olivia jumped, coming over to clutch my arm.

Angelina turned left and walked up three steps. The sign above the door was wood-carved, with a small vial painted on it in fading green paint. She knocked four times and entered. I wasn't going to be left out on the street, so I followed her in, my sister and our other companions following behind.

"Good evening," an old man's wavery voice came from behind a counter on the far wall.

"Don't touch anything," Carson said to Olivia and I. Temptation was everywhere, though. There were jewels, trinkets and hats, baubles and glasses full of orange liquids. *Things* floated in vials; some dead, others that looked alive and trapped. It had the aura of a bazaar you might have tripped over in some forgotten part of Europe, I supposed. There, in a dark corner, stood a horse from a merry-go round, its mouth half-open in flight. Cabinets and shelves, all filled to the brim with coins, strings, pendants and arcane instruments, no two of which were the same. I approached a Bridal Gown made of some shimmery material, glowing with perfection. Intricate patterns hand-stitched in this whiter-than-white dress. It looked ancient, yet brand new, and it called me from the rack where it was held. I could feel my eyes grow wide as I reached out to it, my index pulled toward a pearl on the collar, hanging like a nacre tear-drop. A hand fell on mine, and Brock yanked me back. I shook my head, wondering what had come over me. Where the beautiful dress had been was a horrid rag, falling apart in places, worn by a corpse whose grey flesh flaked, and grizzled hair fell over empty eye sockets and gaping mouth. I recoiled in horror, almost falling, save for Brock holding me up.

"You *really* don't want to touch anything," he said, and let go of my hand. I looked again at the mummy in its dress and walked away, fast. The others were looking around the store, with the short older gentleman assisting as he could. Angelina already had a small pile of objects on the counter, and was asking about another when I caught up to them.

"What do you think, Asmodeus? Can I make it to the Deadwoods and back with all this?" Angelina said, not looking at the little man. He stroked his wispy-haired, balding pate, and readjusted his spectacles. His small nose offset his large eyes, made even more enormous by his glasses.

"Oh, that's not for me to say, young mistress. I've others go with more, and never come back. I've seen some go with nary the clothes on their backs and return triumphant from adventuring. It's all in the skills, I reckon," he said, smiling, "Or luck."

"A big help, as always," Angelina said, frowning, reaching for a higher shelf and making a gesture before picking up a phial with a greenish liquid inside. In it floated a severed finger, bone protruding from one end, a long, jagged nail from the other. She inspected it closely, and the thing tapped against the glass, as if to be let out. She nodded, satisfied, and lobbed it gently at the old man, who ran toward it with cupped hands. He caught it, but just, and carried it like he might have a live land mine to the counter, grumbling under his breath.

"Do be careful, milady. These things are not to be trifled with, as you know," he cautioned.

"Write me a receipt for the lot of this stuff, Azzy. We'll see if I can't get reimbursed by my client, when all is said and done."

Afterdeath

I walked to where Brock was peering at some odd mirrors. Strange images swam in every one of them, none reflecting *him* in any true sense of the word. I saw one with a cemetery, a marker faded by years of neglect the focal point. Another showed a woman, smiling, walking down a narrow brick road in an old city. Still yet another showed him, or some likeness of him, in full medieval armour, swinging his sword at vaporous enemies from atop a pile of fallen soldiers.

"Hey," I said, and I saw by his sudden tremor that I'd made him jump. "What are you looking at?" I said, nodding at the apparitions in the surfaces.

"This one," he said, pointing at the battle-hardened hero version of him, "is my one true desire. Or so this thing thinks. I think it's broken. Perhaps it's supposed to show what you want it to, to make you believe that this is what you want. Anyway, I can tell you that I don't want *that*."

"What about this one?" I said, pointing at the grave marker.

"It's supposed to show how you'll die. It's a bit late for that, so it shows where my body is interred. I can't even remember where that is, or what my name used to be. That was a long time ago," he said. I thought about how we'd gotten here, and still the memory felt fuzzed, dreamlike. I could only imagine what spending several millennia here might do to my memories.

"Who's that?" I said, pointing to the pretty woman in the last mirror.

"Nobody," he replied gruffly, and walked away. I frowned and followed him.

"Hey wait! I'm sorry. I don't know what I said, but I didn't want to offend you. I was just wondering; how does all this work?" I said, extending my arms to encompass all that was held within the store. He stopped and turned around. The look on his face told me it was safe to keep talking to him.

"How so?" he said.

"All this stuff, it feels like magic. Is that what it is? I mean, I saw Angelina use what I can only term as magic a few days ago, but this is… overwhelming, you know? There's just so much of all of these different kinds of… of powerful things, just lying around here. How is this possible?" I said. I glanced around, taking all this capharnaum in. Like an evil sorcerer's garage sale, or magician's storage locker, there were objects hanging from the rafters, a mezzanine, which I only now noticed, which was accessible by ladder, from behind the counter. For some odd reason, the room now looked bigger than I had first thought, as if it extended in ways that were not apparent from the outside.

"Well, for starters, we're all energy, or residual energy, if you will. Some people, throughout the ages, have been able to store their energy in objects. This, however, does not help them live longer, as they get to find out when they get here. It just makes them completely vulnerable to others who would harness their concentrated energy. Call it magic, if you will. Their negative energy is great help when it comes to things that are even worse than they were, because, let's face it: anyone who wanted to trap their life essence into an object of power in the first place, probably wasn't that good of a person," he said.

I guess it made sense. I'd heard about alchemists and magicians who'd done stuff like that on popular (albeit fictional) TV shows. I just thought it was weird that that's how things really worked over here, as a matter of course.

Angelina was wrapping up her bag of goodies at the counter, and the shopkeeper writing up her bill with an old quill pen that was made out of an extravagant feather, quite possibly ostrich.

Once the gang was back out on the street the sun had vanished, and the only light remaining came from vacillating candles on houses' doorsteps. Our feet on wet sand-covered stone were the only sound for a while, and Carson led the way. We turned a few times down the meanders, and most of the homes started to look too similar for comfort. Down a stretch of narrow, straight road, I spotted over the tall man's shoulder a house larger and more illuminated than the others. It was in the middle of a square, or at least, further away from the other homes to appear shunned. The reason became clear as we approached. Loud laughter and music came ringing out of the opening and shutting front door, as people entered or left. A strong light poured from the tall windows, threatening the night with blindness. Raucous cries and singing began, and I looked around me, wondering if everyone else thought this a normal place to be headed to after dark. Olivia came closer to me, and I was thankful for her company. I relaxed, though, when I saw our companions striding forward without fear. Olivia, however, held my arm as we drew closer.

Above the door hung a wooden sign representing a large man sitting in a rocking chair, with the words: "The Relaxing Barbarian" written in golden letters on his protruding gut.

Carson pushed the door open, and the sound became deafening. As soon as we were inside, a great greeting came to our ears, men and women dressed in earth-toned clothes, beer mugs in hand, raising them high around long wooden tables. A band playing instruments I barely recognized were high up on a stage, and the bar took up almost the whole length of the room, to the right. A tall blond man with braids came striding up to us, mug in hand.

"Brock, Carson! How are you, my friends! Wilf and I were starting to wonder if you'd been annihilated, or worse!" He said, beaming. He was a whole head taller than Carson, and was more on the stout side. His tan leather shirt seemed to stress under the weight of the big man's gut.

Afterdeath

"Hail, Sigurd! And how is your brother, nowadays?" Carson said, grabbing the man by the forearm.

"Hahaha! You know Wilf. He's still got the same old problems plaguing him." As he said this, a tall, thin man came walking out of a side room, followed closely by a voluptuous woman, who was in the middle of explaining something to him, which he was trying hard to ignore.

"...and I'll tell you one more thing, you good-for-nothing lout, if I catch you looking at Karina like that once more, I'm through with you. I should have married Sigurd— who is here," she said, noticing him for the first time and stopping. She grabbed the thinner man by the arm and twirled him around like a marionette. "Not so fast, where do you think you're— Carson? Brock?" They both nodded, smiling covertly. The woman grabbed them both in her expansive embrace and held them, squeezing the life out of them. "My goodness, it's been so long!"

"It has, Aetta. I see you haven't lost your vigour," Brock said, regaining his breath after she had let him go.

"You have to stay on your toes, with a man like Wilf as your husband," she said, her eyes slits, as she stared the culprit down. "Who are your friends?" she said in a soothing voice, looking me, Olivia and Angelina over. Barkley made himself noticed by standing up on two legs onto one of hers.

"What's this?" Aetta said, bending over and picking up the tiny dog. "Ooo, you've been cursed, haven't you? Who's the little dog who used to be someone else?" she said in a baby voice.

"You're holding Barkley. These are the twins, Olivia and Chloe," Carson said, presenting us. "And Angelina." At this, her smile turned down into a fresh new frown.

"I've heard of you. You're trouble. Stolen anything valuable lately?" she said, then realizing something, she lifted the dog again and looked at Angelina. "He's the reason you did it, isn't he?" she added. Angelina nodded silently. Aetta bit her lip and put Barkley down.

"Let's go somewhere a bit quieter. I'm sure we have a lot to discuss," she said, and led the way toward the back, where a door on the far wall gave way to a staircase that wound itself to the second floor, and a long hallway to their left. The din of the revellers downstairs still made the floor thump, but it was at least muted. Aetta opened the second door on the left and invited them in.

"Sit, please," she said, spreading her arms as invitation to take one of the large, brown, leather sofas arranged around the room. A small, tough-looking wooden coffee table took up the centre of the room, and various animal trophies decorated the walls. Antlers of various sizes circled the tent-shaped ceiling-space, making it look like some bizarre type of coral reef growing upside down.

Aetta had been staring at me for a few moments. I must have been staring without blinking around the room.

"You may have noticed, by now, that death wasn't the banquets and epic battles advertised," she said, in a motherly tone. This took me slightly aback.

"Why would it have been?"

"Oh, I'm sorry. What religion were you again?"

"I'm non-religious, actually," I said, rubbing my arm, not really knowing how to answer, but feeling a bit foolish for not having altered my world-views in the past few days. The large woman smiled.

"Ah! Then this is a happy surprise for you, isn't it!" Then, conspiringly: "Might be better off that way. Most folks who end up here get... disappointed, if you know what I mean." I turned to Olivia, who looked just as lost as always, but for different reasons.

I noticed Sigurd must have stayed downstairs, because he was nowhere to be seen.

"How long has it been, Wilf?" Brock said, smiling at the man who sat next to his wife. She held one of his hands lovingly, and I realized that all the bluster was for show. She really did look as if she loved her husband, and he returned it.

"Not since our Royal Guard days, my friend."

"The bad old days, you mean," Carson rebutted, crossing his arms.

"Who are the Royal Guards?" my sister asked, leaning forward, and I remembered her passion for all things fairy-taleish. Aetta licked her lips.

"I don't think the girls—" Brock began, his hand in the air.

"Well. A long time ago, there was a plague. In the living world." Aetta said, cutting him off. "A terrible plague that cut down the living by the millions. The monarchs at the time had too many souls coming over to be able to handle the flow on their own. Everywhere, greevers and souls would appear, and without proper guidance, the greevers would tear into the souls, turning them into more greevers. We all retreated to the cities for protection. That's when Charon formed the Royal Guard to defend what could be from this menace. He also instituted the Ferryman program so that we could fetch more souls to join in the fight."

"We were all Guardsmen—" Carson said.

"And women," Angelina added.

"I came after all that, but believe me, I've heard all the stories. Should come by sometime and I'll pull your ear with the tall tales I heard from this lot. You'd never believe it!" Aetta said, accompanied by Wilf's slumped shoulders, which she did not see.

Olivia came to my rescue.

Afterdeath

"Oh, I think we believe you right off the bat. So they were all part of the same group, then?"

"We were," Carson said. "Those were grim times indeed. They are the reason for the Bounty Hunters and the heavy defences around cities. You never know if something like that could happen again." For a moment I pictured all those present dressed in full, shining armour, on some bloody battlefield, slashing their way through hundreds of leering, pustulant monsters trying to devour them, and shuddered. Could they be talking about the Black Plague? That was over seven-hundred years ago!

Wilf cleared his throat to end the uncomfortable silence that had settled on the room. Even the strident yells of revellers below us blanched for a moment as we all were lost in our thoughts.

"I hear you got into some trouble a while back?" the tall man asked, cocking his head.

"I'm in trouble now, Wilf: we all are. Someone's put a price on our heads. We're not safe inside the city and will have to leave as soon as possible," Brock said, his fingers interlocked, elbows resting on his knees.

"What about the pact of non-interference? Doesn't Charon have any control over incursions?" Aetta said, putting her hands together in what looked like a gesture of prayer before her face, her brow furrowed. Brock frowned, shaking his head sadly.

"This is why I'm calling on you tonight. You are the only ones who don't get mixed up in these affairs anymore. Whatever tenuous control Charon has, it's being stressed to the limits by the Monarchs, it would seem. They're the only ones who would be powerful enough to get so much manpower lined up against us," Brock said.

I turned to Carson and whispered "Who are the Monarchs?"

"They're the rulers of the other nations of the afterlife. There are a great many, and they are all extremely strong, with hundreds, or even thousands of followers and slaves under their command. Brock figures if we are hunted like this, it is because some have decided that they want us taken out," he whispered back.

"Why inside the city, though? And in broad daylight?" I said. Angelina leaned in and said:

"Someone's in a hurry to dispatch us. They couldn't rightly send an invading army into the city without declaring civil war, so they decided to hire Hunters instead. Sneaky. Anyhow, that's why we can't go back to Brock's and Carson's tonight. I'm certain we will have a welcoming committee there if we show up. The place is as good as toast." She leaned back and crossed her arms, listening to what Aetta had to say.

"And I had just finished remodelling the living room," Carson mumbled.

"This is indeed grave news. You are of course welcome to stay in the tavern tonight. I cannot promise you would be safer than anywhere else in the city, but the Vikings are people of their word. Besides, how could I leave Wilf's friends in a lurch?" she said and smiled.

Wilf rose to his feet, and I saw that even though he was thin, he was wiry as well, his muscles lean as a greyhounds'. His eyes became slits and he said, with a clear, high voice:

"No one will set foot in our establishment who has the intention of harming our guests. Aetta is right. We will set up the first floor as our command post and wait for any would-be intruders."

"Right, everybody out," Aetta said, clapping her knees, and I was about to leave, but she rose, and Angelina put her hand on my arm. I sat down, curious, and saw the large woman head out the door. For a minute, we sat there, and I wondered what I should expect, but then the din downstairs ceased, and the music died, as if cut in half by a battle-axe. There came a huge bellow that I scarcely understood, and a rumble like a stampede.

"Shall we?" Wilf said, grinning, and we headed downstairs. Walking through the door, I was stunned. No one save Sigurd and Aetta were left in the entire room. Mugs of beer lay spilled on tables and the ground. I looked to the bar, and the barmaid, Karina, lifted her head from behind it, wide-eyed and shocked.

"You can go home, Karina," Wilf said, and Aetta gave her a toothy grin. "I was not looking at her, dear," he started to say to his wife, but I walked away without listening to the rest of the conversation. Sigurd sauntered over to the door and locked it after Karina had said goodbye. He lifted his hand and pinched his fingers, and the lights began to dim, until we could barely see each other. Aetta walked over to a window and looked outside, peering this way and that.

"Does anyone know you were coming here?" she said.

"We've told no one," Angelina said, her hands on her hips. Barkley was lapping up a spilled beer, and Olivia found a dry corner of a bench to sit. Wilf came through the far door with a collection of weapons in hand. Mostly blunt, one-handed swords, but there was also a mace and bow and arrows. He deposited his trove on one of the tables, and Brock, Carson, Wilf and Sigurd each picked up a sword. Olivia and I just stared, not really sure what to do. I had never touched anything like that in my life. I wasn't sure what I'd even do if I did have one. Maybe give myself a nasty cut, but that was about it. Forget Olivia, she couldn't even lift one. Aetta walked over and picked up the mace, which was a stick with a metal ball on the end, with long strips of iron soldered on vertically. She inspected it for a moment, then hefted it over her head, bringing it down onto an empty bench, which broke in half.

Afterdeath

"That'll do nicely," she said.

"Don't break all the furniture, honey," I heard Wilf say from afar.

"Sorry dear!" she replied absent-mindedly, swinging her weapon in an arc.

Left with the choice of sword or bow and arrows, Angelina picked up the bow, stretched the cord as far as it would go, then brought it back slowly. She inspected the arrows, looking down the length of the shafts. She took a seat on one of the bar stools, after having pushed some mugs and garbage out of the way, and crossed her legs.

All I could do was fidget. Somewhere out there, in the dark, were enemies massing against us. It felt as if we were inside a bubble, silent save for my pacing back and forth on the creaking planks. The dim light gave a haunting glow to each of our faces, and I had a hard time with the other's calmness. They were warriors, and I was not. Brock and Wilf were joking quietly in one corner, no doubt reliving some exploit from long ago.

I saw Carson walk over and sit next to Olivia, who turned away from him.

"I'm sorry," he said.

With head bowed, she answered: "Why? What do you have to be sorry for?"

He sighed, and tried to find her eyes, but she only looked away.

"I shouldn't have taken you to work today. I understand that must have been terrifying. Ran's children are a vicious bunch. It was wrong of me, and I'm sorry," he said, and got up to leave. I felt my heart sink for her as well as him.

"Wait," she said, and Carson paused. "Please, sit down." Carson threw his leg back over the bench and leaned on one elbow on the table. "My... our parents died in a drowning. I've been terrified of water for the longest time. I thought it'd be okay, now that I... well... now that I couldn't die. I was wrong. More than the horror, the thing that ran through my mind were the memories of my mom and dad trying to save us from going under. It's... it's not your fault, Carson."

Just like that, a rush came over me and I was seven years old again, going on a canoe trip with Olivia and mom and dad, a bright day announced overhead and prospective calm weather on the horizon. We'd never gone canoeing before, and Olivia and I were over-excited by the prospect, to the point of fatherly irritation. The drive to the lake and the canoe-rental place had taken less than an hour in the dark of the morning, and the grizzled man at the dock pushed our boat into the water with a practised hand and uncaring attitude as the sky began to lighten. Olivia and I had jumped at the splash coming over the pier, and dad had traded angry words with the man for his carelessness. Nevertheless, we were out on the lake within ten minutes, Olivia and I in the middle, with my father steering at the back, and mom in the front.

Dad hadn't told the man we'd never done this before. I think out of pride. Maybe he should have. Probably he should have.

How peaceful it was, so early in the morning on a calm lake. I heard what must have been loons cry out from the banks of tiny islets in the distance as mom navigated, holding a newly unfolded glossy map, which she held with one hand, pointing with the other. We took turns at paddling, but as we were too young to be effective, we got tired pretty quickly. Mom handled a paddle fairly well, and we watched the sky brighten among the pines, a burnt umber glow on the water around us. It smelled of conifers and strangeness, yet naturally so. The water had a certain smell to it I could not yet describe, and the opaque blackish hues broke with whitish foam. Mom and dad spent half the time paddling, the other resting, and the boat coasted silently, ripples gently forming an inverted "V" away from our craft, behind us. One of those small islands drew nearer and Olivia spotted movement on the flat-pebbled beach. Something scrambled ponderously over fallen trunks whose upper branches now dipped in the water. I giggled nervously as we veered off a bit. A small brown bear, followed by two cubs, made its way along the outer edge of the island. I pointed, practically bouncing in my seat. I looked at my father, who smiled, and put his index to his lips.

Look, and listen, he was telling me. I had a hard time containing myself. The mother bear paused, looking at us go by equanimously, and its cubs never noticed us at all. They just kept on climbing, trying to catch up to mom, little squeaks of effort coming from them every so often.

"Wait, momma, wait!" they were saying, and I giggle-snorted at their efforts. We passed by them, and Olivia and I waved goodbye.

The sun rose higher, and we found an island that had been equipped with a picnic table. Olivia and I argued as to how someone might have brought it there. After long deliberation, I settled on helicopter, and she by submarine. I kept pointing at sticks poking out of the water near to us, telling her that the submarine had come back, and she would whip her head comically around to spy it, mouth full of sandwich. I'd then fall back on my side of the bench laughing. Mom and dad stood by the water's edge with the map between them, and they looked like they were pondering something of strategic importance. I imagined they were forming a plan of attack for out little army to get the better of the enemy. Who was the enemy? Mystery.

We packed up what was left of our lunch and took a right at the next island. An enormous, long-needled tree stood almost alone on it, peaks much higher than any other in the region. Its closest companions must have been its children, but they stood tiny and stunted in comparison. By this time the sun was fully up. I don't think I had a watch, but I guessed it must have been close to noon, because it beat down

Afterdeath

on us pretty hard. I was glad mom had thought of lathering us with sunscreen before we left the marina. We would have been cooked by now. I noticed that dad was paddling a lot less energetically, and that the pauses were getting longer than before. Off in the distance, a small house had been built on a rocky outcropping on an island slightly bigger than the others. An old couple sat on the protruding pier in front of it, both holding books, next to a small motor boat tied to it. The closer we got, the more I noticed their age. I remember thinking that they looked older than grandma, but just as kind. They waved as we paddled by, and we, of course, returned the kindness.

It was only after we had gone a few hundred meters beyond their home that we had a problem. The canoe came to a halt, after making a terrible screeching noise and raising slightly at the front. Dad said we'd hit rocks, but mom held up the map and told us that there shouldn't be any. Whatever was true, we were now stuck. The boat did a queasy side to side motion as dad tried to go to the front to see if he could un-jam us. We leaned out of his way, and mom tried to duck so he could go over her, but somehow he lost his balance, and the canoe capsized, sending us all overboard. The icy water took my breath, and I fought the reflex of inhaling as I went under. All sound disappeared save that of the bubbling underwater world's. For a moment, all notion of direction was lost, and I fought to find the surface. The silty blackness of the lake stopped light and therefore made it impossible for me to find my way back. I panicked, gripped by the cold, thrashing about in this alien world, fighting the urge to open my mouth to scream and gulp air I knew I wouldn't find.

A hand grabbed my arm, and I was pulled sideways. As my head broke the surface, I took in a giant gulp into my burning lungs. My father's strong hand clasped my upper arm, and I heard crying nearby, as well as my mother trying to reassure Olivia.

"Are you okay?" dad asked, and I wiped water and hair out of my eyes. I finally opened them to see his look of concern. I nodded, and he brought me closer to our capsized boat. Strangely, I did not feel the rocks that should have been under our overturned boat. My father disappeared under the water and returned shortly with two lifejackets.

"That's all there was," he said, and threw one at mom, who put it on Olivia. I tried for a smile, but I could tell it was forced. He put the other lifejacket on me, and I said:

"What about you, dad?"

"I can swim just fine, bedbug," he said, and put his hand on my cheek, swimming in place.

Bedbug. That was his nickname for me. Rugrat was Olivia's. I'd always hated it. Hated bugs of all kinds, really. After that day, though, I would have given anything to be called "bedbug" again. Mom and dad pushed us both to the boat and we clung to it for dear life.

Olivia saw something in the distance, and I heard a whining sound coming from far away. From the direction of the house on the island, a blue motorboat was coming. The elderly couple must have seen what happened and were on their way to help.

When I yelled, "Look dad, someone's coming!" and turned around to show him, but he was gone, and so was mom. Frantic, I told Olivia, and we both searched for them, letting go of the boat to peer underwater. Impossible. There was no way we could either see or feel them. They had just... disappeared. We screamed and screamed for them, even after the old couple got there and helped us into the boat. We both fought to stay in the water to find them, but it wouldn't have helped anyhow. The police rescue boats came an hour later, and searched until dark. Olivia and I stayed at the window of Frank and Janet's island house, staring at the searchlights roving the waters, until finally they left.

That was eleven years ago. Grandma Rose took us in a few days later and we lived with her until she got too sick to take care of us.

I looked at Olivia and Carson, and she was whispering to him in the penumbra. I can only assume she told him the same story I had just recalled, as he nodded gravely every time she punctuated her words with a hand gesture.

From somewhere at the back, a low hum began. It was guttural, and raw, with high notes toward the end of each stanza. I assume it was Sigurd who began, but eventually, all the men and Aetta were humming that vibrating dirge. It reminded me of musty graves, the smoke rising from a funeral drakkar and the dried, bloody aftermath of battlefields. Of the forever loss of family and friends. It rose around the room, like an uncoiling snake made of wind, choking the hope out of me, and I felt a hiccough in my heart where the last of my joy used to be.

It changed. The low rumbles heightened to clear tones, raising the dead from their mausoleums with a tap on the shoulder, shaking off the dust. Like a match that's been extinguished, re-lit by touching fire to its smoke. There was strength in their voices, and I felt as if the tavern could have shaken if they had *really* tried. My heart pounded as their voices soared, but then, somewhere out in the dark, a voice called, and the humming stopped.

"You in there, come out, or face another death!" a woman's voice said, high and clear. Aetta opened her window a crack and yelled out to the voice.

"No, come in here and we shall discuss it face to face. Unless it is your own dissolution you fear." I could not see her face, but I was certain it would have been fearsome to look at.

Afterdeath

"We are many. You are few. Are you sure you want us to come in?" and there was much laughter from the camp outside.

"Get to the point: what do you want?" Aetta said.

"The woman, Angelina. Give her to us, and we will leave you all in peace. Otherwise, we extinguish you all. Does that not sound fair?"

"I'll tell you what. You have five minutes, all of you, to leave. After that, whoever I find will suffer terribly for having taken us on. I promise you that." Aetta replied. I then noticed that Angelina had moved from her spot by a table and was standing on an upper dais or counter, and had opened a window of her own, bow drawn.

Aetta turned to her.

"What do you think, girl? Should we give you up to the mercenaries?" Laughing from all our friends.

"I'd rather you not, if at all possible," she said, peering down her arrow. "Do make her talk again, will you?"

"You're being unreasonable," the woman's voice came again.

"Never mind," Angelina said.

"We will get her…aaaah!" the woman's voice came, and the screaming ended after a loud thump. Angelina pulled in her bow and closed the window, one arrow gone.

"They're on the opposite roof. I have no clue how many. Too dark to tell. That won't stop her for long."

All got to their feet and brought their weapons to the ready. For an interminable time, there was silence, and only the faint flicker of the lamps over our heads. I thought I heard a noise from outside and twitched. I looked at Olivia and we both silently agreed that we'd be better off with a weapon than without. We picked up the remaining swords, which were surprisingly light. I waved mine a bit to get a handle on it, and I saw Olivia grit her teeth at the thought of having to use such a thing.

A window broke, and a torch landed on the floor beside me. Wilf jumped on it and stamped it out. Soon, one window after another broke, and torches flew into the wooden building, landing on the floor, on the counter and on the tables. A tapestry caught fire. It spread to the ceiling. Even though we didn't need to breathe, having smoke in our eyes did affect us. The walls were catching fire, and still the enemy outside had made no move to come in. They were waiting for us.

Angelina pulled something out from a satchel, and turned to Aetta.

"Create a diversion. I'll meet you all at the car," she said.

"If there's still a car." I told her.

"You worry too much," she replied, as the floors around us began to burn. She tossed whatever she had been holding at the wall behind the bar, making it disintegrate outward in a concussive explosion. Aetta grabbed a table, and was followed by Sigurd, Wilf and Carson. I stayed with Brock, Olivia, Barkley and Angelina. Aetta hefted the massive table over her head and ran out the hole in the wall with it, the rest of her group underneath it, all of them screaming bloody murder. I saw arrows rain down on the table before turning back and running after my group. Brock and Angelina peered from the corner of one of the windows, all of them smashed to bits by now. A face appeared in one of them, and Brock sprung up, grabbing the man by the neck, and pulling him inside.

"Hello. How many are you out there?" he asked, his bicep crushing the man's neck, as he held him down on the floor.

"I don't answer to you," the young bearded man answered. Brock punched him in the face. We would have to leave soon if we wanted to escape the fire, but Brock took his time as if nothing was troubling him.

"Hello. How many?" he repeated, scowling at the young man. The youth only glared at him silently. Brock raised his fist and the man winced.

"How many," Brock said in a calm voice.

"More than you could handle," he said. Brock's face took on a look of annoyance I had seen once before: at his father's office. This time, though, there were no guards to prevent him from destroying this poor guy. Hit after hit rained down on his face, and eventually, there was not much left of it to speak of. Brock stopped.

"Shall we try again, boy?" he said. The young man's face took a few moments to coalesce, and when it did, the look of utter fear on it told me he was done trying to play brave.

"About thirty. We just want Angelina, why do you have to make this so difficult?" he whined.

"She's not yours to have," Brock said, and with one slice of his sword, cut the man's head clean off. He once again got up to the window and peeked outside. Whoever had been ambushed on the roof across the street were now running after the other half of our party. He looked at us and gave us the all clear signal. We came in low to the window and he slipped outside, keeping watch as we did the same. Just in time, as well. The fire was consuming everything in sight, and had begun to spread to other buildings. The strange part was that it was neither red nor yellow, as it should have been, but a bluish green. I guess even fire burned differently in the afterlife.

We ran over the open ground that lay between us and the neighbouring buildings, and as I thought we had made it safely, I heard a whistle, and saw a figure pointing at me and yelling as I rounded the corner.

"We've been spotted!" I yelled, and we accelerated down the meanders of the Viking town, steps resounding like the sound of my beating heart in my ears.

Afterdeath

I heard another yell, and someone appeared before us, turning the corner. Angelina pulled out an arrow and shot him as he raised his sword at us, and we kept on running. The sound of heavy footsteps came from behind us, and Brock slowed down to let us go before him. Angelina kept looking around her, trying to get her bearing. We paused for a moment, and she turned right. A dead end. As we stopped to turn around, three men and a woman, all dressed in armour, came at us, weapons drawn. Angelina and Brock got in front of us, but I didn't want them to have to defend us without our at least trying to help. I raised my sword with trembling hands and Olivia looked at me with terror in her eyes. In front of us, our friends were defending us, and here I was cowering behind them. I didn't have to wait long until more attackers showed up and went around Brock to come at me and my sister. Sword raised, the woman charged me, a look of rage transfiguring her into some sort of nightmarish figure. I brought my sword lower and thrust it into her throat. I don't think she was expecting that. Her look turned to one of utter surprise, as if she'd accidentally swallowed a fish bone. A mighty big one at that. She gasped a bit, and I pulled my sword sideways, tearing out the side of her neck. She grabbed at it with her free hand, all the while looking at me with that look of utter amazement. She began to dissipate as she hit the ground. Olivia couldn't seem to quite believe it. I jumped into the fray, attempting to help Brock out, and Angelina took a step back to more easily nock an arrow. I couldn't see what Olivia was doing behind us, but I had no time to wonder. There were three assailants in front of us. An arrow flew over my shoulder and into a large-jawed man's cheek. It stuck there by the feathers and he screamed, pulling at it while we fought. The jagged head of the arrow tore his cheek and he tossed the arrow back at us. The man came at us with his sword and Brock gave a feint, running him through as he tried to pass. The woman tried to take advantage of Brock's opening to strike him, but I jumped in, raising my sword to block her. As we struggled, an arrow appeared in her chest. She clutched at it and fell to the ground. I finished her by slicing her down the middle, and she evaporated into the ground. The lone man tried to run, but was hit in the back with yet another arrow from Angelina, and he fell flat on his face while trying to run away. Brock advanced on him and chopped him across the head, and he melted to nothingness.

I turned to see that Olivia was back against the far wall, face in a rictus of fear, sword held in front of her, limply. I ran to her and grabbed her hand, and we all ran back to where Angelina thought we might have taken a wrong turn.

The sky was ablaze. The fire that had been set on The Relaxing Barbarian now ran rampant through the wooden city, jumping from house to house, with no signs of stopping. The only difference now was that the inhabitants of those homes were in the streets, in their nightwear, fighting off the fires, as well as those who looked to be the culprits. Whenever we turned a corner and were confronted by armed men and women, pyjama-clad denizens of the city would arrive and begin to attack them.

"Angel, do you remember where we parked?" Brock yelled, as a broad man in long striped jammies ran toward his home with a bucket of water. The thatch roof had begun to crackle, and threatened to ignite. Bright turquoise cinders floated lazily on the winds, latching onto nearby homes, setting them ablaze. The sound of sirens came to me from somewhere too far away, and I wondered what good it would do now that the whole town was on fire. I looked at her, and her face was covered in soot and sweat, as would mine be, I realized. Olivia looked like she was about to collapse from fatigue, and Barkley held his head low and tail between his legs. Angelina looked around her, craning her neck this way and that. It was dangerous for us to stay in one place for too long, but running blindly through the maze of Viking Town was not a better option. The fires raged on surrounding roofs, and the smell of burning hay filled the air to the choking point. Angelina's face was a mask of calm. I couldn't fathom how she could stay that way. With all the chaos flaring around us, she had no expression to betray how she felt. Olivia practically leaned on me for support, and Brock tapped his foot, his hands on his hips.

Angelina closed her eyes. She took an arrow out of the quiver and extended her index vertically, then placed the arrow on it by its mid-section. It stayed perfectly still, balanced on her digit. She closed her eyes and whispered to the arrow, and it began to revolve, like the needle of a compass. It spun a bit, then settled, its point directly toward a house that stood in our way, in the direction we had come from originally.

"There," she said, and Brock harrumphed, shaking his head. Angelina ran down the alley from which we had come, turning left and right, following the approximate direction the arrow had been pointing in. We followed as best we could, Barkley nudging Olivia on by the tip of his muzzle. The ground became wet as we ran, and we passed firefighters in long black rubber trench-coats, spraying water from hoses snaking along the ground. From then on it was easy. All we did was follow the hoses back to the main road.

The main thoroughfare was choked with emergency vehicles, many turn-of-the-century fire trucks pulled by horses. We popped out right in the middle of them, and doubled back, up the street, to where Bertha was still parked.

I heard a war cry coming from somewhere behind us and cursed.

"They're still coming!" I yelled to the others, and Olivia gave a weak groan. We ran faster and hopped into the car.

"What do we do about Carson and the others?" I said, as I started the car. No response.

"Well?"

Afterdeath

"We can't wait for them, love. We have to get going. They'll catch up," Angelina said, from the passenger's seat. The enemy was drawing closer behind us. I clenched my jaw and put Bertha in gear, then stepped on the gas. Our assailants slowed down, discouraged. I went up the hill, watching the eras change as we drove. Most of the other constructions were safe from the ravages of fire, being made of either brick or stone. I would have loved to have a nice chat alone with the genius who'd had the bright idea of setting fire to a city made of wood and thatch. From the rear-view mirror, I watched the blue flames dance in the night, consuming everything in its wake. We would not be there to see the aftermath.

The city was converging on the disaster area. Pedestrians amassed in droves, walking toward the place we were now escaping. I hoped this would slow down our pursuers.

"Where are we going?" I asked.

"We're leaving. Tonight," Angelina said.

"What about the others?" I said.

"Worry about yourself," she said. I gave her a hard stare, wanting to slap the egoism out of her. I didn't care that we were wanted. I didn't want anything to happen to those who had put their souls on the line to help us out.

"Carson and the other can take care of themselves. He might not look like it, but he's an accomplished fighter," Brock said from the back seat. The street lamps, tiny burning figures inside, watched us drive north. Bertha's engine rumbled with satisfaction, but I was not made to feel any better about Brock's assurance at his cousin's and friend's safety.

"He's a ferryman! How can he possibly survive against all those bounty hunters?" Olivia said, a tremulous strain in her voice.

"He didn't always used to be that," Brock said, and left it at that.

"What's our destination, then?" I said, watching the high-rises go by, their towering heights obscure in the inky night. The moon had all but gone, leaving stars too weak to shine above the city's lights. There was no traffic and no people now. The streets had become silent, save our car, attempting to wake the dead. It comforted me.

"We have to go to Domum. Larunda is the ruler of that northern country, bordering that of Charon's," Angelina said. "Take the turnpike." Pointing at an on-ramp on my right. The large, white on green sign announced cities by the names of Mistry, Almo, and a larger one underneath that said Domum, with a flag I'd never seen before, of course. I took it, and soon we were two stories above the city, flying down an abandoned highway that bisected it, on arched trestles. On each side were tiny dwellings, lights in the windows lit by candle.

"What are those candles for?" Olivia said, voicing my own question.

"To help the recently deceased find the rest of their family in Necropolis," Brock said. Olivia put an elbow on the edge of the door and fell in contemplation of the thousands upon thousands of tiny lights, perhaps wondering if one of them might have been our parents' house. As much as I wanted to find them, myself, I had no inkling if they would be in the city or not.

"How would you know if your family is here?" I asked.

"You would know," Angelina said, turning toward me and smiling. I blushed and turned back to the road. No, they weren't here then. I'd felt no such pull while in the city. Perhaps they were in some other universe. The rules for entry here seemed somewhat random, to me. I knew I should let it go before it dragged me down, but it was hard letting go of the prospect of seeing my mother and father again after so long. What would I say to them?

"Hi mom and dad! Good news! We're dead!" That, as weird as it sounded, probably would have been the most realistic thing to say. No, I really had to concentrate on what was coming instead of this. The smooth ride down cantilevered roads continued on until we crossed a wide river, heading to future unknown.

Chapter 11

ESCAPE

I was exhausted, and only wanted to curl up on the back seat and sleep. Chloe, thankfully, was driving. Brock looked out the side of the car at the last sliver of moon above us. Already, there were more stars in the sky, pinpoints of light no longer repressed by the city's glare. Funny, I thought it had been full, the night before. Was my memory playing tricks?

Barkley lay between us, curled up and sleeping. The events of the night must have been hard on him; I could sympathize. No matter my desire for sleep, I don't think I could have achieved it. I was worried. Worried for the others. Worried for Carson. I wished I could have helped, somehow. Was I a coward for having left him behind against so many? It certainly felt that way. What had he been in a previous life that made Brock so sure he'd be able to survive the onslaught of so many assailants? Had he, himself, been a bounty hunter? That was what he appeared to imply, but I was not sure. I didn't have the energy to ask, and so leaned on the side of the car, letting the wind rush through my hair.

Had I fallen for Carson? I did feel some sort of attraction for the tall man, but I'd be damned if I gave my heart away to the first good looking guy in the afterlife. That was a dummy move I'd never permit myself again. The falling part. Not the afterlife. I'd suffered too much at the hands of one such bastard while living with an adoptive family. I shivered. No one noticed. Chloe was the lucky one. She'd gotten the great family with the perfect kids after Grandma became ill. Me, not so much. I'd had to change foster homes twice, until I'd been placed with decent people, finally. The first had been bad. The second, worse. I wondered sometimes what the criteria for adopting were? "Must have dysfunctional family operated by abusive parents. Violent children a prerequisite." Fortunately, God had been there for me. I at least could count on him while everything else was falling apart. That's something Chloe would never understand, of course. I loved her nonetheless. She was like my other half. I sometimes thought my better half, as some married couples liked to joke. I don't know where she got her courage, or resolve. I wish I did. I'd go there and get some of my own. In the meantime I had someone watching out for me from above, I knew.

The metal bridge that brought us over the wide river descended toward land. I looked back at the city, and thought I could still see the remnants of tiny fires burning blue in the far distance. I felt horrible for Wilf, Aetta and Sigurd. They'd paid a heavy price for helping us. I offered them a prayer of safety and looked ahead. The clean, black pavement was perfect. One would expect that in a wealthy city. On each side of the road, long grasses swayed in the soft summer night's breeze, as far as the eye could see. Tall, it was higher than the car itself. It was as if the road cut a direct swath through it. I felt an inner chill that had nothing to do with the ambient temperature. The tall, thin grasses susurrated words in the dark, and I felt them tell me the level of my worthlessness.

"Hey. Don't listen to them. They're lying," Brock said. I started at his voice. He was right next to me, his face only a foot from mine. "They're here to discourage greevers from going on. They attract you off the road, and then you're done for. Look." I stared at where his finger pointed, and thought I could discern a man's figure by the road, sitting cross-legged, its whole upper body rocking back and forth in inconsolable sadness. The grasses nearest him twisted about, harsh words lacerating him into immobility. "It's just another defence mechanism for the city."

"Speaking of which," Angelina said, "if we don't want to find ourselves in the company of our pursuers anytime soon, I might want to do something about that." She pulled out her satchel and rooted around inside it with both hands. She removed a silver lighter and uncapped it, flicking the wheel. A green torch soon burned in her hands, illuminating the inside of the car, blinding me. I looked away, and saw that in the fields, an army of lost souls stood in place, rocking back and forth, sobbing silently, all in the light of her torch, all standing facing the city. Horror gripped me, and a prickling sensation ran down my back. I wanted to duck and hide between seats, but knew that would have served no purpose save make me look ridiculous. Brock also saw them, his eyes going wide for a moment as I looked at him. For a second he almost didn't look human. There was also a mountain of a bearded man with us, whom I'd never seen before. I glanced to the front of the car and I almost jumped out as I saw that Chloe's head and body had radically changed as well. She more closely resembled a giant snake with a wolf's head than my sister, and I held back a scream by putting my hands over my mouth.

Angelina blew on the flame, and it changed colour, turning from green to purplish red. At the moment it did, Chloe was back to her usual self, but I saw that she was staring at me with wide eyes as well.

"What happened to you?" she said to me in the mirror.

"Me? What happened to you?" I said.

"For a second, you were some kind of monster."

"Same with you!" I said.

"Side effects," Angelina said, and closed the cap on the lighter. "We should be okay from now on. I put a field over the car. The Bounty Hunters can't pinpoint our location with any certainty." And she put the lighter back in her leather satchel.

My heart was still pumping wildly from the vision I'd just processed. It had given me the jolt I'd needed to have some energy back, it appeared.

"Who is Larunda?" I asked. The name had felt both familiar and strange when I'd heard it. I was curious to know the person we'd be going to meet.

"She is also called Muta. She had her tongue cut out a long time ago. She's the goddess of House Ghosts. She, like Charon, is one of the older rulers of the Afterlife," Angelina said.

"Tongue cut out? That's disgusting! Why would anyone do such a thing?" Chloe said, glancing over at Angelina, her mouth in a pout of disapproval. Angelina leaned back in her seat and crossed her legs.

"She couldn't keep a secret. That was her punishment. She lives in the forest, hidden in a cottage, because the gods that wanted to take her life are still trying to find her: to finish her," Angelina said. I felt my stomach hollow out when I heard this. "That's the legend that's been circulating, lovies."

"And she will help us return to the land of the living," I said, not as a question, but a reinforcement of my own wishes. I still did not know how much I could trust Angelina, let alone this Larunda person. One thing was certain, it was better to head for help than stay put and wait for the Bounty Hunters to come for us.

"That's the hope," Angelina said, sternly. Nope, definitely didn't trust her.

We'd only been driving for half an hour when I heard a rumble from behind us. The fields had ended, and rocky terrain had begun. In shallow marshes in the recesses of the land, dead trees stuck out like unfinished telephone poles, branches sticking out, leafless. The sound got louder and I turned around to see what it was. Two large headlights shone, from far away, yet getting closer.

"Anybody you know?" Brock said, turning around to see the vehicle better.

"I just got here. I haven't had much time to make a lot of friends," Chloe said. The headlights approached rapidly, the sound of the engine growing louder and louder. Whoever was behind us was in an awfully big hurry. I had to cover my eyes to block out some of the light. This jerk, whoever he was, had his high beams on. As he got closer though, I had to rub my eyes to make sure I wasn't seeing things. The right side of the orange cab was destroyed, some of the truck's innards spilling out of it. It was fast approaching. It was driverless.

"It's that semi we almost crashed with!" I screamed at Chloe over the sound of its enormous engine.

"What?" she said.

"The truck! The truck in the accident! It's here!" I yelled, and just as I did, it hit us, making Bertha skid sideways. Chloe took control of her and with a squealing of tires got her back onto the middle of the road. The giant truck honked at us, and sped up again, bashing the rear of the car. The air smelled of burnt tires and electrical fire, and the deafening sound of the semi's engine threatened to drive me insane. I put my hands together in prayer, calling on all the powers that be to come to our rescue, and the truck hit us again.

"Go away!" I yelled at it, while Barkley made a threatening display of tiny teeth. The terrain began to climb and veer to the left. I barely noticed our surroundings as the semi kept up with us and tried to run us off the road.

"Any great ideas?" Chloe yelled to Angelina. She rummaged madly through her bag, her lip curled in disgust, bumped sideways every time the truck hit is full-force in the back.

"I got nothing," she said.

"Hit a tire with an arrow or something!" I said. She picked up the bow from the front seat and jumped to the back, narrowly missing Barkley, who scrambled out of the way. As she drew her bow and aimed for a front tire, the semi accelerated and bashed the car once again, sending Angelina flying backwards, her arrow unleashed vertically, wildly off the mark. The road continued to climb leftward, and on the right a great plain could barely be seen in the darkness. The road straightened out, and it felt as if a new plateau stretched out before us.

The truck stuck to us, coming at all different angles, trying to ram us off the road.

"What the hell is that?" Chloe yelled, and I whipped my head around to see some kind of giant humanoid creature stepping onto the road before us, towering maybe three stories high. Chloe narrowly missed one of its feet and legs, roaring around it at the last second. I heard a mighty screech, and I turned around to see the giant rush the semi-trailer, bashing it with both fists, toppling it sideways. For a few seconds more, I stared at the enormous creature hitting the truck over and over again with its giant fists before it was lost in a curve.

"Did I just see what I thought I saw?" I said, wide-eyed.

"I didn't know giants wandered out of Domum," Brock said, crossing his arms and smiling, "we were lucky."

"This was *normal?*" Chloe said, turning around to look at him for a moment. I felt the same way. Giants? What next?

"Not at all. Giants never cross out of Larunda's country unless they have good reason to," Brock said.

"What would that reason be, do you think?" Chloe said, looking at him in the mirror.

"Care to go back and ask it?" Angelina said.

"No stopping, please," I said. "Any idea why a truck that had an accident we nearly got wiped out in would be over on this side trying to ram us to pieces? Without its driver, no less."

"Sometimes, people who are on the cusp of dying will call on a higher power to save them. The problem is, you never know who you're really calling upon," Brock said. The terrain began to go down again, and I noticed the road was no longer as smooth as it had been a few moments ago. Cracks and potholes formed here and there along the way.

"You mean like, you're calling to God, but it's not God who answers. Like the Devil?" I frowned, pondering.

"Not exactly. There are a great many who could answer, not only Satan or his cohorts," Angelina said.

"So this guy made a deal with something that answered his call," Chloe said.

"Precisely. You probably did something to annoy him, and his grandest desire was to get revenge on you two," Angelina said.

"But there was no one driving! It was just the truck! How could a truck want to destroy us?" I asked. This was starting to become more and more absurd.

"Well, sometimes, when you invest a lot of time and energy into something, your soul might become fused with it. Apparently this person loved his vehicle so much that he became a part of it in death. That happens too," Brock said.

"Unbelievable," Chloe said, rolling her eyes.

"Believe it. There are things that happen in this world that defy comprehension. You better be ready to accept some pretty outlandish things if you want to survive," Angelina said, and to prove a point, a man who was now a little dog jumped from the back seat to her on the front seat and curled up in her lap.

I took the opportunity to let myself fall into a deep sleep, the sound of Bertha's engine a soothing lullaby for me this night, and tried not to dream dreams of death. Before I fell asleep, the concrete form of Satan planted itself in my mind, and I fell into a well of souls filled with grasping, ghostly arms, trying to reach me as I fell. A cavern the size of which was unimaginable yawned before me and I landed with a thud on hard-packed earth near an enormous lake filled with magma. In the gloom surrounding the stalagmites, shadows moved menacingly.

***

Not much time must have passed when I finally awoke. The crooked needle of a moon still shone, if but a little lower on the horizon. If I had had to judge, I'd have said it might be two in the morning. Bertha's engine had just been shut off and I could hear the soft *toc-toc-toc* of it cooling down. Crickets chittered in the thickets, and we were parked at a motel somewhere off the main road. A sign above the plate glass window read: "Foreverest" in cursive, and I hope that wouldn't be our case. I heard someone's foot scrape on sand and dirt, and opened my eyes fully to take in a thick forest surrounding the tiny resting place. I could barely see the sky above. I stretched and got out of the car, limbering my cramped body. No light in the office, but when Angelina knocked, a voice came from behind the door.

"What do you want?" the man said, rusty with age.

"Two rooms for the night, old man. I pay in coin," Angelina said. I thought it would be a wonder if anyone opened to one as rude as her, but I guessed the attraction of coin made it worth the elder gentleman's while.

"Good, we don't accept souls anymore. Too many problems with strange provenance. Counterfeits are hell to get rid of. Come in. I'll have you sign the register," he said, opening the door and turning on the porch light, as well as the offices'. He was of average build, dressed in a plaid flannel shirt and jeans, with a tuft of white hair floating around a bald spot on his head. It looked as if a particularly industrious bird had buried a pink, flesh-coloured egg almost to the top, leaving breathing room for its bulbous nose and grey eyes. The man stepped behind a counter and grabbed a big, musty guest book from underneath. He opened it toward the end, a small cloud of dust rising as he did.

He leaned forward and confided to me: "We don't have many visitors. Don't worry, I still keep the rooms clean." It did nothing to quell my anxiety. The man looked about, absent-mindedly, and then patted his shirt-pocket. He slipped a pair of reading glasses out and put them on his nose. He patted his pocket again, and started looking around again, this time peaking under the counter and behind him. A look of frustration crossed his features for a moment, and he put his fingers to his lips and blew. The shrill whistle that issued from him surprised me, and I felt my ears ringing for a bit.

"I'm sorry, this might take a bit," he said, and crossed his arms, sitting on a stool that I hadn't noticed was behind him. A cuckoo clock could be heard ticking on the wall. A few moments later, I saw a hairy leg, the length of a pencil, claw its way onto the counter from the opposite side of where we were. Another appeared, striped black and brown, and then a gorgeous pen, covered in nacre was tossed onto the counter. Another leg, then another, and then a large, furry body climbed on top. An extremely large spider made its appearance, bowing to the man.

"That'll be all, Gorgolu. You can go," the man said, waving the enormous arachnid away with a shoo of his hand as he picked up the writing implement. The spider bowed again and skittered off the counter. I turned around to see Chloe hiding behind Brock, holding his shoulders in a vice-like grip, throwing glances at the creature.

"Do you uh, have a lot of servants like that?" I asked him.

"Like what?" he asked, looking up from his writing in the ledger for a moment. I thrust my chin in the direction the spider had fled in.

"Oh, him! Yes, tons! It's so hard to get good help nowadays, especially when you consider we're a bit far off the beaten track. Why, you're not afraid, are you?" The way he said that, almost with a leer, made me regret having asked the question.

"No," Angelina said, "we're just wondering if you'll miss them if we get hungry." The expression on the man's face fell, turning away from Angelina's lip-smacking. He scribbled furiously in the ledger, taking down our names, which we falsified in case the bounty hunters got the idea of looking for us in such an out-of-the way place. He gave us four sets of keys, for two separate rooms. I of course stayed with my sister, and Brock, Angelina and Barkley would share another.

As we walked outside to the tiny cottages situated a bit further from the main building, Angelina said: "There's probably some sort of protection on this place. Just to be careful though, don't open any doors or blinds during the night. I think it's supposed to look abandoned unless you know what you're looking for." We both nodded and took the first tiny shack. The key slid in easily, and I turned on the lights. Despite the decrepit look on the outside, the inside was perfectly clean, if a little dated. Patterns that would have felt comfortable in a 1960's Las Vegas motel zig-zagged across a thin carpet, both brown and yellow. The desk and lamps could have easily been pilfered from a Salvation Army, save the fact that they looked brand-new.

The small brass lamps cast short shadows, leaving most of the room's corners in darkness. I hoped the man's helpers were nowhere near.

"What a day!" Chloe said, and let herself fall backward on one of the two double beds. The covers were a brownish burgundy, and looked scratchy to the touch.

"You've got the gift of understatement, Chlo," I said. "If I had known I'd be running for my afterlife from a gang of mercenaries bent on burning a city down just to apprehend a runaway criminal that we're now harbouring, not to mention chased by a possessed undead truck that we miraculously escaped because a giant with a bone to pick happened to shamble by, I might have tried harder to stay alive." I looked over at her, and saw her lying on the bed, holding her thumb in one hand. Not saying a word. She looked away from me.

"What's wrong?" I said. I went over to her bed and sat next to her. I noticed her shoulders shaking and put my hand on her upper arm. "You okay?" Tears ran to the ugly brownish covers, and she turned over, away from me.

"It's my fault," she said, sobbing, covering her face with both her hands.

"Oh Chloe, no! No it's not! It was just our time, that's all! I was just kidding about all that! I don't think there is *anything* we could have done to prevent all this!" I said, rubbing her arm gently.

"There is no God, Liv! Get it in your skull! No God would have done this to us, no benevolent one anyhow. This is all fluke, accident, but it's still mine and I'm so sorry for everything! I killed us both," she said, and I felt suddenly very sad for her. I got up and walked to the bathroom.

"Angelina said we'd go back to the living world. Will that help you feel redemption, do you think?" I said. If we did get back, how could we go back to a normal life? Everyone who'd known us until now, knew we were dead. We'd have to move to a new place, build new lives with new identities. Not impossible, just very difficult, I felt. More difficult than coming back to life after who knew how long. What bodies would we inhabit? Our old, decayed ones? What state would they be in anyhow? The prospect frightened me. There was still a very big question before all that could come to fruition.

"Do you trust that woman?" Chloe said, and there it was, once again, out in the open. The giant 'IF' that loomed over us like a nuclear bomb ready to drop. I don't think I'd ever trusted anyone less, but...

"What choice do we have?" I said, washing my face in the sink. I hadn't felt the rush of water on my skin in what felt like months, and even though I knew I didn't need it, it still felt refreshing nonetheless. I poked my head around the corner to see Chloe wipe her sleeve across her face.

Afterdeath

"None. We're doomed," she said, and I giggled, glad to see my sister was back to her old self. I hated seeing her lose control. She was my rock, and I needed her to be steady for me. I hated myself for it, but I didn't know any other way of operating when she was there. It was ingrained in me since I was born. Sometimes beyond the womb, I thought. I rubbed a soft white towel on my face and pushed the wet strands of long hair out of my eyes. She stood up and walked to me, held me by my shoulders.

"We're going to survive," she said, looking me in the eyes.

"No we aren't," I said, making her realize the absurdity of her statement. She twisted her mouth in a strange contortion, then said:

"I'm serious. We'll make it out of this." Then she gave me a hug. I held her intensely, glad to have her in my life.

"Thanks," I said.

"For what?" she asked, looking in my eyes.

"For just—being there. I would *not* still be here if it wasn't for you. My big sister."

"Oh, you're such a softie, Olivia," she said, but she hugged me tighter still. That moment was the happiest I'd been in a long time, but like all happiness, I knew it was only temporary.

We let each other go and headed to bed. The fatigue I'd felt in the car returned, and I was glad we were holed up in a safe place for the night. I turned out the light and drifted to my pillow, this time feeling as if I was drifting upwards out of my body, or whatever you wanted to consider the envelope I wore in this universe.

***

A sound, like snorting, woke me from slumber. All the lights were off in the room, the curtains drawn, but the light from outside was blocked. I heard it again, and my blood ran cold, frozen in my veins. Chloe was on her elbows in her bed, closest to the door. She pulled the covers from her and I wanted to yell at her not to, that this wasn't the time to be brave! Snuffling, like an elephant might have, directly outside the door. The sound came under the half-inch crack, loud and unnerving. Chloe crept out of her bed, and I pulled the covers up to my eyes, sitting in mine. She bent over, trying to spy whatever was going on, on the other side. She got up and looked at me, shrugged. I batted my hand at her, telling her silently to come back. She turned her head left and right, tiptoeing to the drapes. I felt all the muscles in my neck trying to snap, and my hands were icy claws clutching the rough covers. With one hand on the wall, she slowly pulled a drape open. I couldn't see anything. Everything was dark out there. She pulled again, making the slit a bit bigger, but still no light came in from outside. Then, as she went to pull a bit more, she tripped, and her hand went up the wall, flicking the light switch. In the open window, a giant grey saucer looked at us, with a rapidly widening black pupil.

I screamed, and the giant outside rose to its full height, emitting a roar like no wild animal I've ever heard before. I jumped out of bed and ran for the door. This wasn't like the movies where you could take the back window of the motel and run. No such exit was extant in this place. We had to take our chances through the front. How the hell had this thing found us? It was like the bounty hunters all over again. A giant bull's eye had been painted on our backs, and giants were coming in for the kill. We burst through the door, and Angelina and Brock were already outside, attacking the lumbering beast.

The motel owner came out of his office, furious at having been woken up in such a rude manner.

"What's going…" he started, but stopped at the sight of the giant, words caught in his throat, and a look of having swallowed something altogether out of the ordinary spread over his features. The giant turned around, squinted, and swung a tree-trunk arm in his direction, snatching him into the air.

He had only the time to yell: "Let me go!" before being popped into the giant's mouth, screaming, until a 'crunch' cut him out.

"Whatever happened to leaving the drapes closed?" Angelina said in our general direction, Barkley jumping around the thing, barking madly.

"I don't think this thing would have cared much," Chloe answered, trying to stay out of its reach. Brock gave it a good slice of his sword in the leg, sending a clear spurt flying, and the giant reeled back, angered.

"Let's run into the woods, we can split up and attack it by surprise then," Brock said. I doubted the sanity of heading into dark, unknown forests in the middle of the night, but perhaps Brock knew something I did not, and we all ran into the murky underbrush, pursued by a hulking giant bent on our destruction.

Undergrowth and dead trees littered our path, not so much that it slowed us down, but thick enough that our pursuer had trouble keeping up. A small path had opened up in front of us, behind the main building that housed the owner's office. Barkley led the way, finding the easiest path for us. The giant crashed its way through the woods, making so much noise that dark birds flew into the sky to escape the frightening racket. Soon it was out of sight, and we paused for breath, barely a moment.

"Chloe, I want you to go back to the hotel and start the car. We'll lead it away for a moment, then we'll come around and find you. It shouldn't take more than five or ten minutes. Agreed?" Brock said, and my sister nodded, veering off to the right

Afterdeath

down an alternate path. The giant came back into view and we ran once again, taking it with us. It paused for a moment and sniffed the air, then came after us.

We made great headway. After two solid minutes of running at our top speeds, we barely heard it behind us. I had to stop to catch my breath. My sides ached, and I don't think I'd ran this much since phys. Ed. Classes had ended for me in grade eleven.

Angelina had her hands on her knees and tried to catch her breath. For reasons I didn't understand at the time, Brock said: "Sorry!" and raised his hand, holding what looked like a stamp. He brought it down swiftly onto Angelina's neck, and she fell to the forest floor, becoming transparent, evaporating. He then did the same to Barkley's neck, who began to dissolve. He walked toward me and I screamed.

"I very much wish I didn't have to do this love. Good luck," and he grabbed my arm and twisted me around, planting something burning on the back of my neck, making me dizzy and ethereal.

Chapter 12

STEEL QUEEN

I'd run as fast as my legs could take me back to the car and started it, swinging it around in an arc of flying gravel and sand, to help in our escape. From the dense forest behind me, I heard the crashing of trees and the howling of the monster as it chased my sister and the others. I sat, tense, my hands on the wheel, jumping at every noise. I could feel the cords of my neck tighten as I wiped the sweat from my brow. The shrill sound of a scream rent the night, and I gripped the wheel even harder. A few moments later, from around the corner of the motel office, Brock came running, his eyes huge.

"Where are the others?" I asked him as he jumped into the car. His eyes were wild and he stammered:

"The giant got them! We have to go!" In the distance, I could hear the bashing of trees, and the immense figure came, towering above the office, searching.

"What the hell happened?" I yelled at him, banging the steering wheel with my fist.

"It caught up to us and swallowed them! It just grabbed them and threw them down its gullet! We have to go, Chloe! We can't save them! They're gone!" I couldn't believe my ears. Had I really lost my sister again? The giant stared at us and raised its arms, throwing its mouth open and letting out a holler of despair. It charged through the office, making wood beams explode, the roof caving in around it. I slammed the accelerator and sped out of there. I bit my lip, trying to hold back the tears, the immensity of the situation stabbing me in the chest. I'd lost my sister. I was alone in the afterlife.

As the car skittered down the dirt track, I could see the monster chasing us as fast as it could, shrieking the whole way. Why had it followed us? Did we look like easy

Afterdeath

prey? Apparently so. A hard ball was lodged in my throat, impossible to dislodge. Brock kept looking back, until the creature had vanished around too many bends to be of a threat anymore. I slowed down, barely, concentrating on not skidding off the path, sand and dust kicking up into the air behind us as we made another getaway.

The highway, now down to two lanes, made itself known a few kilometres later. Beside the road stood a wooden sign covered in peeling paint announcing the "Foreverest Motel". Turning that corner left felt like severing a cord that I had had all my life, and now I would be doomed to float: free and tetherless.

I didn't want to stop.

I had to.

I drove for ten kilometres, enough to put some distance between the giant and ourselves, and pulled the car over. I only noticed then that I'd been clenching my teeth so hard that my brain hurt. I took a deep breath, unclenching my aching mouth, and the first salty drops began to drop onto my cheeks. I wouldn't stay for long, but driving with this feeling was too hard to bear. We would have had an accident before long. I opened the door, letting the engine run, headlights illuminating the dark road before us. Ancient trees loomed above us, and I noticed that the way to ahead seemed wilder than what had come before. More challenges. More heartache. I leaned on the car's driver-side door and put my hands on my hips. Everything that had come to pass reminded me that it was my fault. The accident, Olivia getting…getting…getting devoured. I cried now. Harder than I had in a long time. I don't remember having had this much pain in my chest since mom and dad had vanished. Since grandma had died. I was a moon, knocked out of its orbit for good. What good would it do to go back to the land of the living?

"We should go," Brock said. I swung around to look at him, tears still streaming down my face.

"I'm just about done listening to you, Brock. Who gives up so easily on his family and friends? Carson was your cousin. Angelina was your friend. How can you just…leave them? I don't get it!" At these last words, my voice had risen to a fever pitch. I wanted to rip off the car door and throw it at him.

Coward.

I wanted for him to go back and gut the giant to get everyone back.

Traitor.

I wasn't willing to just give up on them on the say-so of this almost-stranger. I owed it to Liv.

"Because there is *nothing* you can possibly *do* that will bring them *back*. Do you think it gives me pleasure to see them gone? Let me answer that: no! If you only knew how many people I've lost, you wouldn't be standing there, accusing me!" It was his turn to be angry. He practically stood in the car, his hand on the backrest.

"Can't we kill the giant? Isn't there a way to stop it and get them out?"

He shook his head no. He held up his hand, two fingers extended.

"Two reasons: one, we are only two, and you are nowhere near experienced enough to fight a wild giant. Two, they've been absorbed. That means that even if we "kill" the giant, they are now a part of it. They. Are. Gone." My arms dropped by my sides and I looked up at the sky. Was that it, the extent of my fight? If there was a flaw to his logic, I couldn't see it. With a long shudder, I wiped the last of my tears from my eyes and got back into the car. No point sticking around long enough for the thing to show up, or have other, weirder ones come along, either. Brock relaxed, and I put Bertha in drive. It suddenly felt so lonely in the car. It hadn't been a pleasure cruise, of course, but this made it that much more awkward.

"Shall we finish this?" I said, nudging in the direction where were heading to.

"Only if you want to leave the afterlife," he replied. With Angelina gone, though, there was no longer any reason to run away from Necropolis. There was also no clear reason to stay. I was sure Brock was a good guy, but not enough of one to justify staying in this strange world. I nodded in agreement. We were off to Larunda's, the Ghost Queen.

***

I let Brock drive for a bit. Exhaustion and sadness got the better of me. Thankfully, he had enough energy to keep going all night. When I woke up, the sun was beginning to climb. It was hard to spot, though, because the tree canopy was hundreds of meters above us, throwing deep shade onto the forest floor. Tree-trunks the circumference of large swimming pools thrust out of the ground to incredible heights, with branches only spreading out from those enormous heights. A cacophony of birds and other, unknown animals resounded through the forest, and I was reminded of videos I'd seen when I was a kid, about trekking through jungles. The forest floor was covered in verdant, healthy ferns, and bees hovered about a variety of wild flowers that grew on vines, clinging to the giant trees, as lazy pollen floating, thick and hazy, among them.

The road was no longer paved, and Brock drove more slowly, the dirt path treacherous at any speed above fifty. I looked at him, and the dark circles around his eyes told me it was my turn to drive. We stopped for a bit by the side of the road to switch.

A darting movement in the ferns made me hurry to my driver's seat.

Afterdeath

As I drove, Brock slept. It was a gorgeous day, and there was a magical quality to the forest, as if you would expect a unicorn to trot by at any moment. The green canopy of leaves, so high up above, cooled the forest floor, which proffered sweet scents of exotic plants. This changed nothing about my loss. Olivia was permanently ingrained in my thoughts, and my heart threatened to follow the emotion at every turn. All of them churned, making me feel physically ill.

Brock woke several hours later when I tapped him on the shoulder. On our left was a bisection of the road with a wooden sign on a post that indicated a rest stop. Brock nodded in agreement and I turned down that road. A few minutes later we crossed a wooden bridge over a small, clear stream. On the other side, in a clearing overshadowed by the trees stood a small brick cottage with rounded windows. A smoking chimney topped it off, red wooden shingles artistically arranged all around the two story building. There were a few vehicles parked in front of the cottage, and we pulled up beside a red pickup truck with rounded fenders, the kind you would have seen on an old farm.

Inside, what might have been someone's home or cottage beforehand had been transformed into a quaint Bed and Breakfast. A small wooden counter stood on the left of the door, and a waist-height fireplace lay unlit a bit further to its right, when facing it. In the centre of the room, a long staircase led up to the second floor. It was then that I was struck by the improbability of the construction. Further up was a third floor, as well, which could also be reached by stairs. I was tempted to go back outside and count the floors, but knew I hadn't been mistaken: this place was an impossible structure.

The slim lady with the short chestnut-colored hair at the desk greeted us with a coy smile, and asked us if we were expected, to which Brock replied:

"We are on our way to find the dwelling of Larunda. We are not expected, no." I wondered how safe it was to mention the Ruler's name in this place. Who knew what kind of spies she had working for her.

"I see. You have some ways to go, then. Did you want to take a room to rest? You do seem tired," she said, smiling sympathetically. I looked at myself in the mirror behind her station and couldn't help but agree. Those few hours might have done some good, but a few more would be more than welcome. I felt myself grow sleepy as I stood, and Brock agreed that it would be a logical idea to take a room for a few hours to rest up before we went on to the Ruler's domain. The lady took a key from behind the desk and invited us to follow her. After ensuring that we had no bags with us, she climbed the steps to the second floor and walked down the lavishly-carpeted hallway to a door on the right side of the building. She led us into a room with two queen-sized sleigh beds. Unlike the motel we had left a few hours ago, the taste of the designer of this room was exquisite. The lamps were porcelain, shaped like statues of young, mostly nude men, holding candelabra in their uplifted hands. They reminded me of Greek marathon runners as they might have been a few thousand years ago during the Olympics. I don't know if they had relay races back then, but if you replaced the candelabra with batons, they would have been in the perfect positions to race.

The curtains were delicate, see-through lamé and lace, the carpet thick, and light beige. Two chairs stood in either corner of the room, both of them a pale blue with white star-like patterns on their fabrics. They were rounded and plush, the legs made of some dark, claw-footed wood. Behind the white marble-topped dresser hung an immaculate mirror bordered in ormolu relief. I felt as if I had been given a room in a French chateau, albeit a small one. The beds were high, leather-headboard affairs with immaculate white linen and duvets. I didn't even wonder why we'd only been offered one room and went to lay down on the second bed. As I put my head on the pillow, I saw that Brock only made it as far as the first chair and was passed out cold. My eyes fluttered and I let sleep take me, above and beyond my control.

***

When I regained consciousness, I was still lying down, but nowhere near the place where I'd gone to sleep. I jerked my head up, and I scanned the surrounding room furtively.

I noticed fire-lit lanterns hung around the periphery of the wide room. Was I in a dungeon? A low ceiling made me feel small and crushed. Stone walls, clean, yet dark, did make it look like an oubliette of sorts. I got up and grabbed the sides of the simple cot where I'd been left. The floors were a pale cream colour, completely smooth, like concrete, but reflective, as if stained and polished. Brock lay asleep next to me, in another cot. I got up, and when my feet touched the floor, I felt as if it was made of a slow fluid, like supple glass. I felt it ripple under my feet as I walked to Brock. I tapped him on the shoulder, and his eyes opened.

"Where are we?" he said, wide-eyed, looking around the room, groping his side, as if looking for something that wasn't there.

"I just woke up. I have no idea," I said, and started walking around it carefully. Toward the wall in which our cots pointed, there was a large wooden chair with no backing, just a big red padded velour seat. It was on an elevated dais, three steps up, like the throne of a conquering Roman general. On its right, and a bit further back sat a huge royal blue pillow, on the ground. On the wall behind both the chair and pillow hung an enormous painting in a gilded frame, much like the one Charon had

Afterdeath

behind his desk in his office. This one, however, depicted a woman of maybe fifty years of age, in long, flowing gossamer white robes, sitting on a tree trunk with her arm around an enormous snake with a very strange head. There were other animals in the image, such as a large brown horse and several birds. I couldn't keep my eyes off that snake though. I'd seen something similar not so long ago. Someone had rent a deep slash through the painting with a sharp object, right through the animal she held. It reminded me of old, Italian paintings in museums, dark tones and almost true-to-life illustrations. Everything save that malignant gash, slit with malicious intent, testimony to a fury on an undeserving object.

As I stared intently at it, I heard Brock inhale sharply behind me and turned around. The floor was rising, a geyser of liquid sand. He backed away, but I was drawn by curiosity. A shape began to form. First, the face, then the shoulders, all the way to her shapely feet, which were adorned with slim golden sandals. It was the lady from the painting. Yet not. She had aged. Not so much that you would call her old, but a streak of white ran through her hair, and eyes that must have been joyous and innocent when the painting was drawn were now steely and wizened. A black satin dress flowed over her body, tight collar raised to her fierce chin, a colourful, flowery mandala its only decoration around her midriff. Then I noticed the smell, of heavy perfume, permeating the air as she formed. Under it, though, was a stench like baskets of mouldy fruit, left unattended for weeks, the fuzzy spores ripe and pregnant. The flowery perfume overpowered, but it was that undertone of decay that made me queasy.

A door opened on the far wall, which I'd not noticed before, and the young woman from the reception desk entered.

"Please kneel in the presence of Larunda: Steel Queen, Ghost Mother, ruler of Domum, and the Deadwoods," her hand extended to the apparition. The now fully-formed woman motioned to dispense with the formalities.

The younger woman walked to the elder and kneeled beside her, face to the floor. The robed woman put her hand gently on the kneeling woman's head, and the younger woman spoke, but in a tone a few octaves lower than she previously had.

"I see you are awake. Good. It is rare I get visitors. I'm sorry I brought you down here without your knowledge. If you will allow me, I will speak through my interpreter, Iuturna," the young lady said. "I am Larunda, as my servant so eloquently put. Why do you seek me out?" I stared almost in disbelief. We had found her.

"We've been told..." I started, but Brock cut me off.

"I was to bring this woman and her sister to you, but unfortunately her twin has been lost," he said. Larunda looked at me, frowning. She gave me a look of curiosity and raised her hand to draw me closer. I nibbled my lip, unsure as to how to proceed, her odour ever-more stomach-churning the closer I got, but she smiled then and all my fears evaporated. I held my breath and told myself this was like being near a dear relative who didn't know how to hold back on the Chamelle no. 5. I walked to her, and she peered at me, inspecting me, this way and that.

Why had Brock lied? I was tempted to confront him then and there, but it might turn out to be a foolish idea. Larunda, if she had the power of giving me my life back, might decide not to if she felt we might be cheating her somehow.

"You did well, young man. I see your father's prowess in you," the young interpreter said, head bowed, and Brock repressed a frown. "Antonia, it is good to see you, even in your diminished form."

I looked behind me, wondering who she was speaking to, but realized it was me after all. I pointed at myself and Larunda nodded sweetly.

"My name is Chloe. I'm sorry to disappoint you. I've never met an Antonia," I said, hoping not to make her angry. She raised a hand, palm toward me.

"You do not understand," Iuturna sighed for her, "This is normal. You've lost your memory since your last incarnation. I can assure you, though. You are Antonia. Half of her, at least. You were split in two at birth, I am assuming. Look upon who you once were, Antonia. Would you like to be yourself again?" She pointed at the serpent of the painting, and a dread I'd never felt before coursed through my body. That was me? Or rather, us? Olivia and I used to be some sort of wolf-headed serpent *thing*?

"Listen, I have no idea what you're talking about. Obviously, you have some issues. I don't look like a crazy snake beast, right? I'm here because we were told you could help us. Now I'm having second thoughts, Mrs. Larunda," I said. I knew my mouth would get me in trouble someday, but honestly, what did I have to lose at this point?

Her smile buckled, and my insides twisted for a moment. She tapped Iuturna's shoulder, who rose to her feet. Larunda walked Iuturna to me, deliberately, and the young woman's vague stare bore straight into mine, not a foot away from my face, the older woman's smell so strong I had trouble keeping my composure. I could feel a chill churning in my belly and wondered what could possibly happen next, as I stared into the slackened gaze of the woman named Iuturna.

"I. Found. You," she said, slowly. I looked over the interpreter's shoulder to see the widening smile of the Lady who manipulated her. "I was the one who spoke to you that night, when you called out. Weren't you looking for an answer?" Larunda tilted her head, still smiling, and walked the younger woman back to the dais, where she sat on her chair. Iuturna was made to sit on the cushion, within touching distance.

"That was you?" I practically yelled, pointing at her. She nodded, a strange smile spreading over her features. "You scared the crap out of us, lady!" So she knew who

Afterdeath

we were. Was she responsible for our demise as well? No, I didn't think so. I was the sole guilty party on that count.

So if she knew about that, and she knew about Olivia and I, then—

I looked over at the slashed painting on the wall, walking toward it in a daze. Scales and whiskers and teeth, oh my!

"You've got to be joking. How could I possibly have ever been that?" I said, tittering nervously. Gave a whole new twist to reincarnation: that was certain. And she was offering me the chance to be that thing. Again. If it were even remotely possible, becoming that monstrosity was the last thing I wanted to do.

"We live in a world of possibilities, Antonia. How was your other half lost?" the interpreter, Iuturna, said.

"A giant killed her, at the same time as two other companions," Brock said, shaking his head.

"Ah, but we only need to find her energy, then. It will be possible to retrieve your other half, dearest disciple," the young woman said in my direction. Olivia could be saved? Is that what she was implying? For a moment I wondered if Brock knew about it. No, obviously not, or he would have suggested it in the first place. This whole Antonia situation made me very uncomfortable.

"Please, call me Chloe. That's my name. Who was this Antonia, anyhow? Tell me about her," I said, my curiosity piqued at finding out about a past life. It wasn't every day that the opportunity presented itself.

"Ah, Antonia. She was a favoured adopted child. I had her since she was only this big," Larunda spread her hands the length of a forearm, "saved from the jaws of something much larger, she was. I always kept her by my side, as my daughter and companion," she said.

Sounds like a nice relationship, I thought, *despite being a giant snake-monster*. Brock stood apart from us. He kept looking around the room, as if judging the distance between himself and the exit. I wondered what was eating him. Perhaps he felt guilt for having given up so easily on Angelina and the others. I know I did.

"Let us find this giant," the interpreter said, and Larunda made a horizontal swirling motion, as if she were washing a countertop. I was smiling at the movement when I noticed the watery sand-like substance at our feet begin to swirl. Larunda put a hand on my shoulder, and an image began to clear in the sand, as if a pool had formed and a vision materialized within it. I drew in a quick breath when I saw who it was. Olivia, Angelina and Barkley. All three, walking along a dark road, bordered by stunted trees covered in moss and long lianas clinging from one tree to the next. I gaped open-mouthed, emotions tripping over themselves in my heart. They were existing! The giant hadn't killed them. Which meant…

I whipped my head up to find Brock, but he was gone. Larunda as well was searching for him. Iuturna began to speak in low, threatening tones, and the sandy substance under my feet began to writhe and shift, like quicksand. With Larunda's hand on my shoulder, I did not sink. I half-hoped she did catch Brock. I wanted to do things to that man that would leave him less than one. My feelings of betrayal only grew as I thought of all the things he'd said to me the previous night. The pool at my feet closed, and the sand rushed downward. Larunda, Iuturna and I walked to the dais, stepping onto hard stone as the liquid sand departed. Once it was gone, I asked Larunda,

"What will you do to him if you catch him?"

Larunda once again put her hand on Iuturna's head, and spoke through her.

"It is a question of when, not if. In my domain, it is rare for anything to escape without my say-so. It also depends on what he has to say. I have no love of liars and deceivers." A hard demeanour had taken her, and she no longer looked like a kindly aunt, as she had when I'd arrived. A churning, sucking sound came from the deep pool that housed the sand, and it began to fill once again. Once full, Brock was ejected vertically from it, to land on his back, screaming. He tried to get up, and I could tell he strained with all his might, but he was unable to move a muscle. The smell of fresh-cut grass filled the air around him, like some primal shriek. The sand had its grips in him and refused to let go. Larunda walked down from the dais toward him. She removed one of her sandals and put her foot on the side of Brock's face, and Iuturna placed herself by her side.

"Where are they, little man?" Iuturna said, in a chilling voice, face close to Brock's ear. Brock only stared at Iuturna, teeth bared. Larunda expected no response. The sands began to churn once again, and a clear, water-filled pool formed beside Brock. The image of Olivia, Angelina and Barkley appeared again. This time, they were talking to a wizened-looking African man who sat on the driver's seat of a wooden cart, on a dirt track.

"Why are they in Wodun?" Iuturna said. Larunda's foot pressed harder on Brock's face, his head sinking under the sand for a moment. He came back up, sputtering sand and trying to shake it out of his eyes. I almost felt sorry for the bastard. He struggled with all his might, but still the sand held him fast.

"I don't know. My job was to dispatch the other woman, Angelina. I don't know who hired me. You know the rules," he said.

"Indeed, as I helped to set them. You will help me. Get Chloe's twin back. I want them both here. I do not care about this other. But bring back... what is her name?" Iuturna said, and Larunda turned to me.

Afterdeath

"Olivia," I said. I felt a shiver as I said her name, glad she was alive, but coming to terms with the fact that now powerful forces were being put into action to retrieve her, wherever she may be.

Brock became still. He looked at Iuturna, unable to turn his head further.

"A beautiful name, Olivia. Go, wretched little man. Go fetch Olivia for me. Perhaps I will spare you in return for your service. It is hard to be forgiven in this world once you have committed the unthinkable, is it not?" the interpreter said knowingly. The hint was not lost on Brock, and his cheeks became red. Rage boiled inside him.

"With my assignment done, I have been forgiven. It was promised me! You have no sway over me! My father…" he said, before sand filled his mouth, and I was astonished that he would invoke the man, so much hatred for him he had displayed before. Sputtering and spitting, he no longer spoke.

"Your father is very, very far away, boy. As for forgiveness, *I* have not forgiven you. You have just now betrayed your friends, and for what? Your own selfish gain. I've heard of you, Brendanus of Heraklion. Let me see what she looks like," Iuturna said, and at these words, Brock began to struggle anew, almost ripping his skin from the morass that held him immobile. The pool deepened, and a street in an old-looking European city began to materialize before our eyes.

"Stop. I beg of you," Brock said, tears welling up in his eyes, and he pulled with all his strength at the restraining molasses.

"Oh, little one, I won't hurt her. That's the point. Look at her. So young, so vibrant. A jewel. Yes, it would be a shame if anything were to happen to her. Not from your perspective though, correct?" A shark's grin stretched onto Larunda's now horrid visage. Brock watched the young woman in the pool helplessly. I recognized her. She was the same person who'd been in one of those magic mirrors in Asmodeus's shop, in the Viking city.

"Who is she?" I whispered.

"Just another poor unfortunate soul living among the fleshlings," Iuturna said in my direction while Larunda looked at me, stifling a yawn. She turned back to Brock.

"You will get me Olivia. You will bring her here, unscathed. You will do this, or I promise you that this young lady will never suffer a terrible end. She will die peacefully, and you will never see her again," Iuturna said. So that was it. It struck me as a bizarre threat, but then it dawned on me that only those who died horribly gained access to this place. Brock looked at the smiling woman walking down the street and closed his eyes. He stopped struggling and the pool dried up, the images gone. He slowly, shakily got to his knees and bent his head forward toward Larunda. "You are not so unreasonable as all that, young man. I promise you, that in return for Olivia, I will let you off the hook, and you shall be free to pursue this woman whichever way you want." Brock nodded. "You will need a vehicle. Take the first one you find outside," Larunda said, and stepped off the sand, back onto the dais. The sand once again began to descend, enveloping Brock, taking him to who knew where.

It took me a moment to know what to say. A deep silence hung in the air, and neither of us cared to break it, unsure as to how to proceed.

"Are you satisfied with my decision?" Iuturna said, Larunda with an eyebrow raised.

"I was expecting something a bit more…bloody, I guess," I said. It was true. I thought she would bring him back and tear him to shreds. Wasn't that what gods usually did with those deserving punishment? Apart from the threats to his one true love, of course, I thought he'd gotten off fairly easily.

"Ah, but he is much more useful in one piece. I have turned an enemy into an ally, no matter the fact it is against his will. Your sister will soon be returned to us," Iuturna said, and Larunda smiled warmly. "In the meantime, you are to be my guest. Iuturna will return you to your room for now. Feel free to wander the cottage as well as the grounds. Do try to stay within the confines of the property. Even after all these centuries, I am still sought after. I thank you for your understanding," the younger woman said. I felt as comfortable as could be expected after finding out that my companion was a traitor, of course. I was in a strange place, but I had been in strange places before. As that went, this wasn't so bad.

Larunda turned around and Iuturna rose to her feet, indicating the heavy wooden door on the far wall. I let her lead me up a set of circular steps, up to the first floor, after what must have been a solid five minutes of climbing. I felt depleted as I reached the main floor, and Iuturna turned to steady me.

"Larunda must hide deep underground. She has enemies everywhere. It takes some getting used to," she said, in a soft voice which was completely unlike that which Larunda had used through her. I saw that we had exited under the main stairwell that led upstairs, through a tiny, almost closet-like door, and we kept on going up, but only after I had let out a sigh. She led me to my room, which until so recently I'd shared with Brock. She bowed after opening the door, and I gave her a weak wave before entering.

"If you need anything, please feel free to ask. I will be at the front desk," she said. I nodded, and she closed the door. I went to the window and tried the latch. It opened easily, and I looked through the many-hued flower garden and into the forest. A moment of doubt gripped me, and I walked back to the chamber door, putting my hand on it. I held my breath and turned the knob. It opened onto the silent, deserted corridor. I started to close the door again, but paused. I once again opened it, and padded to the next room down the hall. I hope to heck that Larunda wasn't spying on me at this very moment, as I was about to attempt something very un-guest-like.

Afterdeath

I put my hand against the door and expected it not to budge, but to my surprise, it turned, just as easily as mine had. I pulled it open and crept inside. I was curious to see who her other guests might be. There weren't many vehicles downstairs, so perhaps this room would be empty.

From the edge of the room, I saw four pairs of legs, resting on the beds, each side-by-side. Four pairs of high, black leather boots rested at the foot of the beds, one for each person lying there, straight and stiff as boards on their backs. For a microsecond I thought I'd been caught, and my heart raced, wondering if I could scramble back to my room without getting noticed. As I vaulted around, my foot slipped on the carpeting and I fell to the ground, on my hip. It made a terrible thump, and I thought for sure whoever was lying there would get up to find me, sprawled like a drunk on their bedroom's floor. I didn't dare look, closing my eyes as tight as I could, like a kid who thinks you can't see her because she can't see you.

Ridiculous.

I opened my eyes and turned around. Not a sound. Not a movement. I got up, putting a hand on the wall to support myself. My hip hurt like a son-of-a-bitch. I rubbed it, gritting my teeth, and hopped as slowly as I could to investigate further the immobile people on their beds. As I drew closer, I saw that their neatly-pressed pants were all a deep navy blue, as were their cotton socks. They all wore the same coloured jackets, in an army style that reminded me of toy soldiers I'd once seen in uncle Philbert's collection, from an era where wars were fought with pomp and ceremony, supposedly. They'd held long guns with bayonets at their sides, all hand-painted lovingly in red. These men had black epaulets ornamented with crimson rope, their arms held at attention by their sides, hands in white gloves. Brass buttons kept their jackets shut, all the way to white collars. If they slept, I couldn't tell, because there was no sign of breathing from under their trim moustaches and beards. Apart from their facial hair, they all seemed identical.

I crept closer, and noticed that the guns I'd remembered from my uncle's "toys" were neatly resting against the wall nearest me as I passed it. The long silver knives at their ends gleamed in the sunlight of the unobstructed window. I shuddered and walked backwards toward the door, my hip still hurting from the brutal landing. I gave the soldier's feet a last glance before closing the door as carefully as I could, and bumped up against something.

"You could have asked," Iuturna said, and I screamed, almost pushing her down.

She put up a hand in a defensive gesture, and I slapped mine onto my mouth, wild-eyed.

"You scared the shit out of me!" I said.

"That's what you deserve for sneaking around like that. Listen, she doesn't mind if you want to explore, but you might want to ask permission before you go snooping around," Iuturna said. I felt embarrassed for having done so, of course.

"Who are those men?" I asked, nodding my head toward the soldiers in the room.

"Those are Larunda's guards, of course. You don't get to survive for so long without having adequate protection."

"Why are they like that? Sleeping, I mean." There was something a bit more than creepy about a retinue of sleeping soldiers lying about the bedrooms of your mansion.

"They're not sleeping. Think suspended animation. They're not needed at the moment, that's why she keeps them that way," Iuturna said simply.

"Are there a lot more like them?"

"Yes. Much, much more. You have to understand, Larunda's country is on the border of the Wyld Lands. The things that can come out of there are monstrous! That's why there are so many that have given their lives to the mistress; to protect the border lands. If they were to go unchecked, so much chaos would be unleashed on the world that nothing we know now would survive."

I'd heard about the Wyld Lands. Who was it? Carson or Brock had mentioned something about them. Creatures so old that they were practically indestructible lived there. Had the giant come down from that place?

"Iuturna, why would Brock deceive us?"

"I do not know such things. I am fairly recently in Larunda's service. I came here to be with my father. I called out to her in my previous life and she granted me her aid. Those things she discussed with you are foreign to me."

"Who is your father?" I asked.

"He is one of her soldiers now. He lies but a few rooms away." I felt sad for this woman. I couldn't say why.

"Do you have a few minutes? I mean, do you have anything to do apart from stand behind that desk of yours?" I wanted someone to talk to, I think. Someone who might know about this place and could help me make up my mind. I don't know if it was from having listened to too many fairy tales when I was a kid, but I couldn't put my mind at ease. I felt like Gretel when she first discovered the Gingerbread House. Of course, the witch was *super* nice, but when would I get sacrificed? Larunda had already demonstrated how ruthless she could be, so it was not a matter of if. Who was I to her? The image of the wolf-headed serpent swam up to greet me, and I shook my head.

"Are you okay?" Iuturna said, putting her hand on my shoulder. "I don't need to stay there, if you need something..."

"I'm fine. Let's go for a walk. That's what I need more than anything right now," I said. The mansion did feel oppressive in its deathly silence. Knowing that there were potentially hundreds of soldiers in suspended animation did nothing to appease my discomfort.

We headed out the front door and around the side of the cottage. I marvelled once again at how tiny it looked, now knowing all the secrets it held inside, like a nut filled with infinity. It reminded me of the kind of painting you ran across at garage sales and flea markets, appealing to people of a certain age who hung it behind rose-patterned sofas. Well-tended flower gardens appeared off to the side as we rounded the left of the building. Those must have been the ones I'd seen from my window. I tried to reconcile how it was possible to have hundreds of rooms with views on the garden within, and only two from without, and gave up. Serious mumbo-jumbo operated here, no mystery I could pierce anytime soon.

Lush green grasses plied underfoot as we walked toward the bushels of rhododendron, camellias, roses and lilacs, all artfully displayed. At their feet, mulched redwood bark gave a pleasant conifer scent, mixing with theirs. Beyond that, I noticed a path heading into the forest.

"What's down there?" I said.

"I'm not sure. I'm not allowed to go there," she said, a look of worry crossing her features. Now, nothing in the world piques my interest more than the words: 'don't do that' or 'don't go there'. 'You're not allowed' runs a close third. I engraved a giant mental note to myself to go exploring as soon as I had the opportunity.

"That's alright. Let's stay in the garden. It's very pretty. Do you tend it?" I said, with my most reassuring smile. So far, I'd noticed no one on Larunda's staff resembling anything remotely like a gardener or maid, so I had trouble resolving how so much could get done by only one person.

"No, no!" she laughed, relieved. "Mistress has assistants that do those things for her." I made a show of looking around, then asked, laughing:

"Where are they? I mean, apart from you and the soldiers, I haven't seen any of the staff yet."

"They only work at night, so as not to disturb the quiet of the cottage," she said. Odd for a place where the owner hid in the subbasement, I thought.

"I see. Tell me, what is Larunda like, Iuturna," I said. She looked around in the flower beds, biting her lip.

"Oh, she is very kind, and generous. I am happy to be in her employ," she said. I frowned and tried to see what she might have been looking at. The subject of her mistress caused her some distress, obviously.

"Where do you come from? Before you died, I mean," I said, changing the subject. As much as possible, I wanted her on my side. I wouldn't achieve this if I freaked her out by grilling her about the company she kept. She had a look of innocence about her that I wanted to be careful about. It was not my place to shatter that in any way.

Prussian. That took me by surprise. She was a Prussian citizen before the state had been abolished, living in the capital, Konigsberg. Her father had been a military man, and had decided to continue service after death, unbeknownst to her. Made sense, I guess. I had no qualms with soldiering. It was a job like anything else. The only problem came when they were used for disloyal means, which happened way too often. In any event, Herr Franz Ehrlichmann had left his family in poverty when he'd had the terrible idea of shuffling off his mortal coil during one of the Prussian Empire's expansionary forays into Poland. Military widow pay not being what they were today, and with five children to feed, Mrs. Ehrlichmann had had to force her eldest daughter out of school to marry a rich, albeit violent nobleman when she turned sixteen. On her twenty-fifth birthday, she'd implored the Heavens to help her, and Larunda had answered, taking her across the veil to her lands in the aftermath of a particularly horrid beating which centered around her inability to conceive a child. I shuddered to think about it.

Iuturna was not her original name, of course. Larunda stripped all in her service of their previous incarnations and saw to it that they became hers in name and spirit as well. The warmth of the afternoon did nothing to stop a terrible chill from shrieking down my spine. Whether it was from Iuturna's story or the end result of her pleading to a higher power, I was not sure. Had I made such a call during our transfer? It didn't sound like something I'd do. Olivia, on the other hand, might have. I wondered if one of these rulers would pop up and ask for his or her due for having "saved" us at some point in time. Just another thing to worry about in a hostile land.

"What exactly is that sand that she controls?" I said.

"The land itself, in its most basic form," she said, and then I knew I was scared. "She can make it do what she likes, and can make it see what she wants, anywhere. That is how she knew that your twin was alive. Through the vibration of people's energies, she can sense things, the earth as her amplifier."

So that was it. Everything around me was her spy, basically. My paranoia had jumped to unknown heights now, and I wondered what, if anything, I would be able to do if I wanted to escape? What could I hope to achieve now that I knew that the Gingerbread House was alive, and that the witch had super-powers? I had no choice but to sit tight and wait until Olivia was brought back to me. I'd be dead meat (even more so) the minute I tried to run from this place.

Afterdeath

Try enjoying a wonderful garden when you knew it was made of eyes and ears, and I think you understood what Iuturna dreaded. I remembered her worried glances around the area just a few moments ago and realized they were fully justified.

"This is a beautiful area. How far do Larunda's lands stretch to, do you know?" I said, peering into the depths of the woods.

"I have never left the cottage. I do not know," she said, and my heart sank once again. I nodded silently and told her I wanted to return to my room. Once there I lay on my bed, wondering if my thoughts were safe. What could a woman like Larunda do to me if I got on her bad side? I knew what a dark path that line of thought could take on, so I pushed it aside for now. All I hoped was that Olivia was safe. I wondered how she'd gotten to wherever she was, and how long it would take to get her back. Perhaps I could warn them somehow, of Brock's treachery, before they came in contact with him.

I was so lost in my own thoughts that I almost didn't hear the bird chirping on my windowsill. That is, until it started talking to me.

Bother.

Chapter 13

WODUN

Mosquitoes, buzzing around my ears and landing on them. Loud. Biting me everywhere exposed skin was available. That's what I woke up to. Face down in muck, some wet embankment in the dark. I felt my arm tugged, and I groaned. A dog barked around my ear, competing with the blood-suckers for my attention.

What do mosquitoes drink in the afterlife? I wondered mindlessly while being pulled upward by the arm.

"Get up, Olivia! We can't stay here!" I heard Angelina's voice coming from above me, and I put my spare hand on the slippery ground, pushing myself upward, getting a knee under myself, then slipping down a bit. It was so dark, but I saw lazy lights flitting about in the distance. Lightning bugs, perhaps? I'd never seen any in real life. My other hand was grabbed and pulled on, and I gave a great big push with my legs to extricate myself from where I was. Three, four steps up the steep incline, and I was out, hands and knees pressing on wet grass.

"You're a mess." Angelina said, a look of disgust on her face. I saw that I was covered in mud, so I could only imagine what my face must have looked like. I looked around me to get my bearings, but there wasn't much to be seen. A thick penumbra covered all, making everything save my immediate vicinity visible. A symphony of frogs croaked nearby, and a few feet away from me was the incline up which I'd just been pulled. What parts of my nose weren't filled with mud smelled something sweet, rotten and putrid. Like vegetation going back to the soil, releasing all kinds of noxious fumes as they did so.

"Where are we?" I asked, then, remembering, "Why did Brock 'kill' us?"

"I don't know, to answer your first question, and because he's a traitorous bastard, for your second. He didn't kill us. He branded us. That sent us... somewhere. Now be quiet. I have to concentrate," she said. That didn't help much at all. Branded? I touched the back of my neck and felt the bumpy ridges of a design, the flesh smoothed like a scar in a convoluted pattern.

The sound of a stream gurgled in the background. Barkley sat next to Angelina, looking up expectantly. She looked as confused as I did, slapping away the occasional bug, which just flew away, annoyed. Darker shadows where the greenish lights flickered called to me, and I stepped carefully over what sounded like dead twigs and dry, cracked clay. The stuff I was coated in was drying, and made my skirt stiff and hard to walk in. I ran my hand over my face and flecks of the gunk fell off. I tried rolling the tips of my dirty hair to remove the excess. If I hadn't looked like a ghost before, now would be a good time to compare myself to one.

I was curious about the bugs, though. They acted as one of the only light sources in the area. If there was a moon up there, roiling cloud cover made it impossible to see. One of the little green lights rested on a tree, about chest height, unmoving, and I came close to observe it. It illuminated the bark, and I surmised there was a forest back there, where its entire family danced around. It was a tiny little crab insect, like a spiny scarab, with long eye stalks. I moved my hand toward the glowing thing, but before I could, my wrist was grabbed and pulled back.

"Don't touch that, or we are in serious trouble." I did a double-take. I looked at her, and she dropped my hand.

"Ss—sorry," I said, shaking my head.

"It's a kind of hypnosis. This thing is a kiopteryx. Nasty little bugger. It's practically indestructible. You touch it, it'll latch on to you and suck you dry. But before it does, it'll call all its little friends to come and feast with it. Yeah, they love to swarm," and I saw her smile in the green glow of the miserable little creature's light. I took a step back, and saw how the undergrowth where I guessed the forest was, teemed with luminescent green lights.

"Bad news, then. We're in Wodun." She looked around, and Barkley sat near her leg, expectantly.

"What's Wodun?" I asked, getting a bad feeling.

"The last place we want to be," she said.

She sighed and knelt down beside Barkley. I heard her whisper something, and the dog gave one short bark. I heard sniffing from below, as Barkley took samples from four or five directions.

"Try to keep up, okay?" Angelina said, and Barkley began to trot through the undergrowth, followed by his master. I stood stunned for a second, but my mind started working when I realized she'd leave me here if I didn't do as she said. I really disliked this woman.

"What are kiopteryx? I've never seen anything like them," I asked, as I tried to keep a bead on her moving back.

"Quiet," she said, whispering harshly. "Another kind of lost soul. They're harmless, unless they swarm. Fortunately, I stopped you before you could touch any of them. Before you ask, we're in Wodun because that's the only place you can find the little buggers. Damn 'Zâmes sans repos', the restless spirits. Now keep quiet."

My real question, of course, was how the heck had we survived being "branded", evaporated and left for dead by that butthole Brock? Where was Chloe? Had she been dispatched by that double-dealing traitor as well? If not, why? My questioning brought me dangerously close to one of the little horrid glowing insects, and I swerved past it, not wanting to bring on what Angelina had warned about. It was difficult to avoid the little buggers, because they flitted about among the trees, and Barkley made a bee-line straight through them, albeit too low to the ground to be a bother to them. Fortunately, they lit the gnarled trunks well enough that it was possible for me to walk around them instead of straight into them.

The forest had a strange, greenish glow, but so dim it was difficult to see properly. Still, I knew Angelina was in front of me from the swishing sound her feet made through the underbrush.

We must have walked for twenty minutes, following the jumping terrier through the low-lying plants, avoiding the "Zâmes san repos", as she called them, slapping myself to get rid of virtually indestructible insects trying to suck blood I did not have. Is this where they all ended up when we killed them in life? As the hellish nightmares surrounding us now? If I ever went back to life, I'd think twice about killing one again, just to avoid sending them here to be someone else's bane. That seemed like a very big if, and I felt a sagging lack of energy at the thought.

Off in the distance, I spied an orange light, moving from the left toward the right, and Angelina put up a hand. I froze. Barkley stopped and turned his head, questioning. Angelina walked without a sound toward it, lifting her feet carefully, and hid behind the trunk of a tree when she came to the edge of the light. I could hear a musical tinkling in the distance, like pieces of metal knocking together. The little

Afterdeath

dancing lights had disappeared, but this more powerful one had replaced them. I heard Angelina call out, and the light stopped. Barkley barked twice.

Silence.

"Olivia, come out, it's okay," I heard Angelina say from afar. I noticed I'd been holding onto the trunk of a tree with my hand, and let it go, bits of bark sticking under my nails. My heart beat a tad bit faster as I approached, but I noticed a large vehicle of some sort, entirely made of light-coloured wood. It looked like an old-fashioned caravan, the kind gypsies (or Roma, as they are officially called) lived in over a hundred years ago. It was entirely covered, and an old black man with a wise demeanour and white goatee sat on the passenger's seat, holding the reins to something I couldn't see. As I got closer, I saw the lamp he had hung on a curved pole above his cart. The little man inside the lamp squatted, shining brilliantly over the animal that pulled his owner's home and business: an enormous grey-green alligator.

To say the thing was huge was an understatement. It was at least one-and-a-half times the length of the cart it pulled, with jaws that went on forever. It could have readily eaten all of us in one snap. For now, it rested, one eye open, staring at what I hoped it didn't consider snacks, head tilted our way, resting on the dirt path.

"Toussaint says he can give us a ride. Ever been on an alligator cart before?" she said, grinning at the driver. The old man smiled and said:

"Girl, you look like the ghost of a ghost. You go in da back my home and get cleaned up, okay?" he said, his thumb pointing to the back of the cart. I nodded sheepishly, walking back there followed by Angelina and Barkley.

There was a back porch with a few steps leading into the cart, and around the door hung several blackened pots and pans. I wondered where he kept the barbecue, before going inside. Then I wondered what he ate, if it wasn't necessary in the afterlife. I took one last look at the bleak road behind us, faintly illuminated from the front of the cart, before closing the door with a shiver.

A fine smell of frankincense, pleasant, tickled my nose when I entered. Angelina closed the door after letting Barkley in, and the cart began to move. A single lamp hung off to the side, near the middle. Angelina walked to it and turned it on, and I noticed this one had no little person within. It swayed back and forth, and I took in my surroundings. There was a rich, red carpet on the floor, and a large bed near the front, drapes opened at the moment. A small bed-side table held another lamp, this one made of colourful glass. A quaint bookshelf held papers of all kinds, old and yellowed, in front of the bed. A tiny table with wooden chairs stood on the left, and to the right was a small cubicle, toward which Angelina pointed me now. I peered inside to see a handle from the roof, hanging from a chain, and a shower-head, directly above me. I closed the tent flap and decided to take a shower dressed. I didn't know when the next time I'd see a washing machine was, and I didn't care. I'd eventually dry off; no need to worry about wet clothes.

The water had a weird electric feeling to it as it splashed on me. Tingly, almost. I rubbed and brushed myself as best I could, splashing my face until no grey sludge came off anymore, all the while bumping side to side with the movement of the cart.

I let go of the water handle and a hand with a pale towel appeared through the drape.

"Thanks," I said, taking it and drying myself off as best I could.

Angelina sat at on the bed, shoes off, a little window open to the front of the cart, and she chatted with Toussaint, our driver.

"Where are we headed?" I asked.

"La ville sainte," our host replied, turning to look at me. "You look better, ma fille. You ever been to Prinz?" he said, smiling. Ahead, the enormous alligator half-slithered, half-pattered along at a good clip, much faster than I believed such a creature could have.

"Thank you, and no, I haven't," I said. "Is it nice?" Both Angelina and Toussaint burst out laughing, and I felt as if I'd said something stupid.

"Depends on who you pray to, love." Toussaint said. It turned out he was a wandering records-keeper, going from hamlet to hamlet, taking census of new arrivals and departures. He never stopped for long, and going by alligator-pulled cart meant travelling through the night, but it also guaranteed a certain safety from the things that might want to take a bite out of *him*. "Old Abner, he been around a time. He a good gator." He told us, and opened a small trap door near his bench. Something writhed and wiggled between his fingers, half-translucent, and he clucked once, the alligator's head perking up. He lobbed the thing over-handed, and the huge maw widened and clapped over whatever thing he'd fed it, crunching a few times.

The cart went a bit faster, and I swear I heard the alligator hum to itself in satisfaction. We closed the window and sat on the bed, Angelina's arms crossed, lips pinched in a dissatisfied pout.

"How bad is it?" I asked. She still hadn't told me why we shouldn't be here, but I'd rather know now than be caught unawares when some new danger came striking out of the darkness.

"Remember I told you I got punished for something I did? Well, the Baron Dimanche, one of the rulers of Wodun, is the guy I screwed over. Pretty sure it's not a coincidence we're here, either. I think Brock got the order to send us here," she said.

"But why would he, though? Couldn't he choose not to have done it?" I said, still very much pissed at him for his double-cross.

"Oh, honey. Brock's got his own secret sins to atone for. If I had been in his shoes, I probably would have done the same thing," she said, getting up from the bed and going to the back of the cart. Her casual attitude toward our ex-compadre's double-cross had me pumping acid blood. I hopped off as well, and noticed that I was entirely dry. The process had taken less than five minutes, and I had barely noticed.

"Does no one have any honour in the afterlife?" I cried after her, getting up myself. "That's it? He gets off scot-free? What kind of justice is there around here?" She turned around and came at me, grabbing me by the collar.

"You holier-than-thou little bitch. You think everything is black and white, don't you. Wait until you have to make some real choices in the afterlife, before going and judging me and everyone else as if there were a single yardstick," she said, and pushed me back. I fell, hard, my back against the library of records the older man kept by his bed, spilling some on the carpet. I felt a rising in my throat, but I wouldn't cry in front of this… this horrible woman. I wasn't allowed to believe in what I did, now? Who was she to make that decision for me? She stared at me, and her expression softened. She got down on her knees, and as I tried to pick up and put away the spilled documents, she came to help.

"You have no right to judge me. What Brock did was pretty bad, but look, we're still here, and we'll get him back. He still has to pay for what he did. I don't like it as much as you do, but right now, we have bigger problems. We have to find our way out of Wodun before the Loa find us," she said, and tried for a smile which might have looked more sincere on anyone else but her.

"What are the Loa?" I asked, putting the last of the files away and standing. She headed out the back door, and sat on the back porch as the cart bumped and ground on. I stayed standing in the small round doorframe, uncomfortable at watching the road slip away backwards.

"Godlings that answer to God. Intermediaries to a higher power. Or so they say. They're the monarchs of Wodun. Like I said, I took something that didn't belong to me, and now we're heading straight for their home-town," she said, dangling her feet over the edge and rubbing Barkley behind the ears. The light from the tiny spirit in the lamp extended a few feet from the cart, the darkness complete beyond.

No, you didn't tell me about theft, I thought. I sighed and asked:

"Can't we just, I dunno, head down the road in the opposite direction for starters?"

"There are several problems with that proposition. First of all, we're safe where we are. If we get off this thing, you have no idea what's hiding in the dark out there, just waiting for a chance to pounce on us," she said, extending her arm to show the expanse of forest that stretched out behind us. I no longer looked at what lay beyond with the same eyes. I wondered just how lucky we'd been to just walk out of the forest unscathed in the first place. I decided that the answer was: very.

"The second reason," she continued, "is that we would get caught anyhow. I have no idea how far we are from the coast, but if we just go traipsing about, they'll know we're here. As a matter of fact, they probably already do." She turned to me and gave a wry smile. Barkley lay on her lap and gave me a sideways glance.

"So what are you proposing, exactly? We go into town and find another ride out of it?"

"No exactly. I propose we go into town, sneak into the Baron's inner sanctum and take another of the objects I got from him in the first place, and that'll get us out of here."

"What? Of all the ridiculous… and how do you think robbing a god will help us? Isn't that what got you in trouble in the first place?" I said, a buzzing starting to develop in my brain, as if I couldn't quite wrap my mind around her proposal. I thought of Chloe and what would happen to her if we were caught red-handed trying to rob the most powerful beings in the land. Would she be turned into a dog as well? What about Angelina? How lenient would they be on a second-time offender? Obviously, she wasn't even supposed to be out, let alone wandering the countryside of the monarchs she'd offended. Whatever her punishment might be, it would reach epic proportions. After having been caught in the turmoil that were the Gardens of Lost Souls prisons, I knew that there was very little room for slaps on the wrists in this universe. And I was following her along for the ride.

Chloe, though, kept popping up in my head, ever since I'd woken up on the riverbank. I tried to push the image of her away, because if I didn't, I knew I'd be lost for good. All I could hope and pray for was that she was okay, wherever she was. That Brock, in his infinite wisdom, had decided to spare her. Because if he hadn't, she'd be God knows where, all alone, in the middle of the night, and I just… I just… I couldn't bear thinking of what might…

I wept, silently, my hand over my mouth, so Angelina would stay oblivious to the fact. I neither wanted her pity or condescension at this or any point.

"I've learnt from my mistakes, Olivia. We won't get caught. Trust me." I didn't dare look at her. My tears hadn't dried yet. That tone of hers knotted my stomach, though. How could she be so sure, anyhow? A whoosh in the trees caught my attention, and I threw a glance at the swaying behind us, beyond the circle of light. I ran a sleeve over my eyes, trying to get my composure.

Why me? I thought. Why us? I amended, once more thinking about Chloe, driven from me by that bastard Brock. What had we ever done to the Fates to deserve such treatment? If this was all written in the book of life, what kind of God had decided that this was the most appropriate course he could spare us? This wasn't "working in mysterious ways". This was "being so opaque as to be laughable".

Toussaint's voice came to us from over the creaking of the wooden wheels.

"Get inside, ladies. Ain't no time to get caught now." I glanced at Angelina, and she cocked her head. We both scrambled inside the caravan, shutting the door behind us. We hurried to the front, and only a slit allowed us to see through the window, Toussaint having slowed down his alligator to a trotting pace. A double-row of cowled figures walked before it, heading into the same direction as we were. Slender, with a slightly jaunty gait, there was a religious aura to their demeanor. I would've thought them priests and priestesses, had it not been for the machetes on their hips, hung loosely by leather lanyards. The only part I saw clearly of them were their long, clawed hands, swaying by their sides. Another quick glance revealed that those hands were semi-transparent. Greevers.

"Who are they?" I whispered harshly to Angelina, who clapped a hand over my mouth. She reached in and replied:

"Quiet! I don't know." The unending row of figures parted around the alligator, almost walking in the ditch. As Toussaint passed them by they turned and nodded in respect. Under each cowl, a grey face, emaciated and dry, bowed, glassy eyes sunken. I felt alarm and the urge to scream begging to come out, but Angelina had kept her hand over my mouth.

A long time later, Toussaint opened the window wider; the gaunt figures had gone.

"What were those greevers doing?" Angelina asked.

"Going to the Capital of Prinz, chère," the old man answered.

"That's not what I meant, and you know it. Why weren't we attacked? Since when are greevers organized, and not swarming in packs. They should've torn us apart. Why didn't they?" I understood her disbelief. In my brief experience, I hadn't known these creatures to be anything but dangerous and unpredictable. Of course, my experience was quite limited.

"They can be harnessed. The Barons know how to do it. It seem he found a use for them, eh?" Toussaint chuckled, and gave a quick whip of the reigns. The alligator's pace quickened.

"What kind of use? What would you ever want to do with those things?" I said, staring at the grizzled man's head.

"You want to get into Prinz, you'll need a disguise. The protection I can give you on the roads will evaporate soon as we get to the perimeter. Strong hoodoo there. Not to be messed with."

"How do we get in?" I said, my heart beating faster. Our driver turned to look around at us, giving a nod toward the road behind:

"You go wit' dem." Then he laughed, like someone who'd told a particularly good joke. Angelina's face told an entirely different story.

"We disguise ourselves. How?" she asked. Toussaint turned to us and grinned from ear to ear. His free hand shot out and touched each of us on the forehead, and a searing burn spread through my mind and body, as liquid fire filled my gut. The old man laughed, and I fell to my knees. Smoldering fire burnt its way along my arms, pain following. It was like watching a tree being consumed by a flame from within. Angelina clutched her sides, her face contorted and smoky. Skin turning to a grey husk, like mottled bark after a forest fire, revealed by whatever spell the old man had cast upon us. I tried to scream, but the only thing that came out of my mouth was an eruption of black smoke, choking me. I doubled over, the lava pumping inside threatening to disgorge itself.

As soon as it had begun, it felt as if it was over. A slight fever shook me, but apart from that, the pain had abated. I got up from the floor, expecting to see a ring of singed carpet underneath me, but it appeared only my body had suffered the transformation. I stumbled a bit and opened my eyes. I fell back, horrified, as an undead creature with a terrifying face lunged out at me. This time, nothing stopped me from raising my voice.

The monster, however, clapped its clawed hand over my face, frowning with a sinuous brow:

"Be quiet!" it said in Angelina's voice, save that it was cracked and breaking, as if crushed through the creaking bows of a tree. I opened my eyes and thought I recognized her, or whatever of her was left after the transformation. God but was she ugly. The only thing that truly remained was the colour of her eyes.

"You're hideous!" I said. And she was. Every inch of exposed skin had that grayish, curdled, past-due-date look, as if her corpse had been left to the elements for too long after having been soaked in some unholy preservative. This, I presumed, was the point.

"You're not too pretty yourself," she pointed out. "Toussaint, how long will this hold?"

"Day, maybe two," he said, his head oscillating from side to side. I looked at my arms in horror. So much for skin moisturizer. I might be up for Mummy of the Year Award with a body like this.

"Why are you...?" I croaked, and sputtered in surprise. It took me a moment to recognize my own voice. "Why are you doing this?"

"Because he's not a warmonger, are you, Toussaint," Angelina cut in.

Afterdeath

"I don't think what the Barons are doing be right. Not natural to use greevers for such. You ask me, there'll be Hell to pay for making them into soldiers. I heard about you, Angelina. You crossed Dimanche afore. You planning on crossing him again?" Toussaint looked her straight in the eye. There was as much hope as there was fear in that look, but Angelina never wavered. She smiled:

"Now that I'm here, might as well," and shrugged. Toussaint turned around and laughed wholeheartedly. "Cowls and weapons in the trunk by the door. When I tell you get out, you go. Be another patrol heading into the city not too long from here," nodding his head in the same direction the alligator trotted. Angelina turned away and shambled to the back of the cart, finding an old wooden chest in the recess by the door. Flipped the black metal clasp and pulled the heavy lid open. Inside were a cache of rusted, dented machetes and sack-cloth cowls. Angelina handed me one of each, and I slipped on my cowl, tying the machete to my side. Seeing the lot of them inside the box made me wonder: what was Toussaint's part in all this? I never got the chance to answer, because as Angelina put on her own sack-cloth, we heard Toussaint's voice loud and clear:

"Out!", and we scrambled out the door. Barkley jumped into Angelina's arms, and she hid him under her faded cloak.

***

The culvert was wet and dewy, but we kept our heads down until the cart had shambled out of view. The tall, stiff corpses that fell behind it never looked into our direction, just kept on walking toward the city, to whatever call its masters had sent out. As soon as the sound of the squeaking wheels had gone out of earshot, we scrambled to catch up to the last two in the row, imitating their slow, ambling footsteps, as if even their souls had desiccated, rendering walking difficult. I looked over occasionally at Angelina, but she stared straight ahead, and there was no way I could have told her apart from any other of these wraiths. She had the same, dull, stilted walk as they, and I tried as best I could to fit in.

Over in the distance, I could spy a lightening of the sky, and the darkness mutated into a dull grey. Along the ground, a thin mist circulated, slithering along at knee-height. The treetops stayed occulted by a dense fog as well, as if the clouds had decided they'd been spending too much time in the stratosphere, and needed some ground time. The occasional croak of toads in the underbrush reminded me of the wildlife that inhabited the woods. Off to the side of the road, I saw three figures approaching: just as gaunt and terrifying as those we followed, and as they climbed the embankment, coming into lockstep behind us, I remembered to keep my eyes riveted ahead. Over the course of the next few hours, more and more of these apparitions made their way into our ranks. I didn't keep count, and neither was I stupid enough to give ourselves away by turning around to take note.

Eventually, a dull orange disk rose to our left, above the treetops, failing to dissipate the thick fog that enveloped all. If anything, I was glad for it. Just one more thing to help us go unnoticed.

The knotted trees gave way to swampy patches, the dirt road zigzagging from solid mound to solid mound. Each tiny island covered in long reeds and scrofulous plants, still and unswaying in the humid morn. I did feel a chill. From the ambient weather or from my own fear, I couldn't tell. Perhaps both. The crooked path helped me spy the beginning of the row of soldiers, or at least, what I thought was the front. The chill gripped me tighter, as there were many. If ever we were discovered, we'd be torn to tiny bits. Well, I'd be ripped to shreds. Angelina would probably find a way to save her own skin, leaving me behind as bait or something equally heinous. What was I supposed to do when the only person I could trust would certainly be the one to betray me? If recent events were any indication, the afterlife was a free-for-all where no one could be trusted. Brock being a prime example. I was just going along, waiting for the other shoe to drop.

A haze, deeper than what covered the fen, unctuous, materialized water-like, and undulated in the air before us. Only a few hundred meters away, it hung, wavering, making whatever lay beyond it impossible to guess at. It was like watching a vertically flowing cutting across the marshlands. The army we had joined trudged on, mindlessly, directly into its flow. Panicking, I put a hand on my machete, its crusted skin closing on petrified wood. I walked on, the rush approaching. I felt my skin closing in on me, my head burning with a raw fire, but still I walked on, simply because I had no choice!

Then it was over. We had crossed. The scenery had changed in two important ways: the fog had evaporated entirely, for one, and secondly, and most importantly, there lay a city beyond a massive graveyard. The sun shone brightly above, and those dingy-looking weeds that had covered the moors glowed gold under the glorious star. A hundred weary paces beyond, the marsh ended, solid ground taking over. Small stone slabs filled the landscape in every direction. Grave markers of simple rock, crooked and bent, mossy and chewed up, ringed the outer walls of the citadel. This last was composed of an amalgam of stone, broken plaster walls and pastel-painted found building-materials. The entire massive ring gave the impression of a patchwork construction reclaimed from some massive disaster, uniform only in its schizophrenic bizarreness, jutting rebar, piled stone, skewed wood and all. An expanse of water could be spied in the furthest reaches beyond the city, on the left. The graves seemed to topple into the ocean at a snail's pace.

Onward the columns marched, as unsteadily as before, toward an archway in the wall beyond the stone graves. I glanced sidelong at the slabs closest to the dirt track, noticing the faded engravings of names long forgotten. I took a deep breath as we passed under the massive wall of the city, which I assumed was Prinz. The cities' inhabitants, for the most part tall, slim, African descendants, parted ways for the menacing-looking crew of which I was an unwitting participant. Among the throngs, men brought their wives and girlfriends a bit closer, and youths hid behind their mothers. Whatever they were witnessing was not part of their daily routine. I knew just how they felt. We had to get away from these things as fast as we could. Getting trapped in some sort of army barracks with a host of soul-suckers for a few days was the last thing I wanted. Especially if we were to revert to our original shape among them. Or worse, if we were sent off on some campaign of aggression. I had no intention of fighting against any sort of enemy.

Slant-roofed, two-story balconied houses were the norm. Most were wooden constructions, topped with wooden lattices and tiles. Multiple arched doorways stood open, out of which women wearing colourful head scarves peered in surprise. The main road along which we travelled, was the widest by far. All other avenues that led off from this one were tiny alleys in comparison, meandering away in no particular direction. Our march brought us on a steady course to the centre. A large, white brick building appeared in the distance, and as we approached, the road widened. It lay in the middle of the town, in an open space decorated with topiaries and shrubbery, marking a kind of hip-high maze of decorative greenery among the gorgeous stone-worked buildings at their center. Palms stood at regular intervals behind the high metal gates that surrounded it. The edifice itself, without being massive or imposing, had a majestic, turn of the century look to it; a dignity rarely found in modern construction. It bore a striking resemblance to the American White House, and may well have been modelled after it.

When the line stopped, I was caught off guard and stumbled a bit. Thankfully, I wasn't the only one. A man in black military uniform stood on a wooden dais at the front of our line, before the massive wrought-iron gates of that palace, barking orders to the wraiths within earshot. They began to walk again, turning left, down a perpendicular avenue. When we were about to pass before the imposing general on his podium, he raised a hand and called to halt. I bowed my head, being one corpse behind the front of the line. I had no idea if he had any way of identifying those who were truly a part of this group or not, but I didn't dare risk it. I peeked from under my cowl at the decorated general, whose black uniform harked to another era.

It reminded me of the kind used in the re-enactments Chloe and I used to go to with Grandma Rose. Those had been navy blue or grey, though. His fringes were gold-tasselled, and very stylish. He wore shiny black boots, but what struck me the most was the whiteness of his teeth, which matched perfectly that of his eyes. He had no pupils at all, only white, rimmed with the pale pink veins of ordinary eyes. I did not think for a moment that he was blind, though, because even though he lacked pupils, he glared about him like a man who sees beyond appearances. But God, please, not mine!

"You have been summoned," he began, in an earth-trembling voice, "to the court of the Barons. We will give you new purpose, soon. For now you may go rest in proper beds, such as you have not known. This, we give to you for your services. Choose that which suits you best." And he raised his left hand, pointing in the opposite direction from the previous column, and the Souls before me turned right, heading down another perpendicular avenue. Frightened people hustled out of our way as the column advanced, once again. I was glad that we were no threat to them. The next question was, of course, to whom were we? I was a complete stranger to afterlife politics, therefore had no idea how frequent raids and wars against neighbouring countries happened. I felt a sick knot in the pit of my stomach at the idea that this "life" was no better than the one I had been stolen from. At least in that one, I hadn't been a conscripted soldier off to some far-off theatre of war.

Another stone gate came nearer, and we exited the city. This time, though, the souls before me forewent the road and headed toward the marina, walking among the field grasses that half-covered the mossy gravestones, toward the left. Tall ships' masts jutted from behind the port cities' walls, round the bend from where we ambled. The swishing of grasses came loud as all those strangely departed behind me spread out, going the same general direction. Then those in front of me stopped. They knelt before newer looking stones close to the shoreline. I saw their knees begin to sink into the sand and weeds before the markers, and they bent down, as if in prayer, becoming absorbed by the grave itself.

I looked around, and saw who I assumed was Angelina, pointing at a marker close by. As horrible as she appeared, there was no mistaking the fact that she bore little likeness to the mannerisms of the other undead things that surrounded us. I searched around, found a fresh-looking marker, and gulped, as I knelt before it. A soft, comfortable sensation enveloped me as I began to sink into the sand and dirt before it. I turned toward the frightening apparition that was Angelina and she gave me a swift nod, then turned her face toward the ground, becoming one with the earthy loam herself. I held my breath and plunged my face into the dirt, and the soft, bedlike repose within.

Chapter 14

WHAT WE WERE

"You've returned, mistress!" the starling said, from the open window's sill. It cocked its head and looked at me more intently. The light purple sheen of its back shimmered in the light. The black of its face and beak contrasted sharply with the white of its belly.

"I'm sorry, did you just say something," I said, unconsciously cocking my head the same way it had.

"I was expressing happiness at your return, Mistress. We've been awaiting this moment for almost twenty years now, give or take." It tweeted, a curious little sound, then ruffled its wings. I sat down on the bed.

"What is this, a cartoon? How come animals can talk?" I said, neither believing nor comprehending what was going on.

"Anything that used to be human can speak. Or alter their shape. I did. I was able to escape Larunda that way."

"Are you telling me that any animal that was once human can speak?" I said, babbling.

"That's what I just said," the starling replied, hopping about the windowsill in annoyance. "We have much to do, mistress. The others are kept prisoner. If you would save your people, you must come and set them free!" It piped up.

I looked around the room, checking for some sort of normalcy. So far, there wasn't much to be found. The walls and bed were still there, at least.

"Why do you call me 'Mistress'? Do we know each other?" I said, curious.

"In your previous incarnation, you were our Mistress Antonia, of course. We sided with you against Larunda, and helped you escape her. You seem... diminished, somehow." Ah, yes, Antonia. The weird monster Olivia and I supposedly used to be. But *against* Larunda? That was new.

"What do you mean, you sided with me against Larunda?" The little bird hopped around nervously on the windowsill. It threw a glance outside the window.

"I can't stay here. I will be taken. Meet me in the garden, tonight, and I will explain." With that said, it flew off in a flurry of speckled wings.

I went to the window, but of course, it was nowhere to be seen. Sitting on the bed, I thought about what it'd told me. Did it tell the truth? Did I try to run away from Larunda? I mean, I didn't trust her now, so thinking she'd been a rival wasn't such a stretch. Then again, who took strange birds out of nowhere at their word?

There was a knock at the door, and I was greeted by Iuturna, smiling amicably.

"The Lady of the House would like you to join her for supper tonight," she said.

"Supper? I thought nobody ate around here?"

"Some people still do. Will you join?" I was curious to see what might be considered a proper meal, so I agreed.

"7 o'clock sharp, then. I will come to fetch you," she said, and I closed the door again.

***

I felt as if I'd only just fallen asleep. The soothing calm of the room had gotten to me. I'd left the window open in case my visitor decided to come back, but no such luck. I'd have to go traipsing about in the dark, looking for a talking bird. Fun. When the knock came, I shook my head, realizing that it had grown dark out, no moon visible beyond the trees. Crickets chirruped somewhere along the cottage wall and in the surrounding forest, the night sounds in full swing. The air had gotten chillier, but not uncomfortably so. I closed the window with a slight shiver, noticing shadows in the garden as I did. Joining Iuturna in the hallway, I followed her down the candlelit corridors. Previously sleeping guards stood at attention along the way, eyes wide open, but like those at Buckingham Palace, unflinching and immobile. Their bayoneted rifles held loosely, butt to the ground, in one hand, around the barrel. Along the way, gilt frames holding exotic paintings caught my eye, depicting dark battles between humans and things that only looked partially so. If I stared more than a second, the images began to move, much like a mirage, making me wonder if I was hallucinating.

Weird, dangerous predators "peopled" these oil canvases, rivalling camera snapshots in realism. It was as if someone had taken great pains in bringing the contents of mythology books to life, with extraordinary results. Save that these things weren't from any myth books I'd ever heard of. Even trying to describe them hurt my brain. A sudden, horrifying thought gripped me. If I (and Olivia) had been something as weird as everyone claimed we'd been, what were the odds that all these freaks of nature dancing in front of my eyes on canvas were just as real, lurking in a corner, unseen? The longer I looked, the more I could swear they crept to the edge of the canvas, seeing me, as if I were a passerby at the zoo, staring through their glass enclosure. Did one sit on its haunches, cocking its head, licking its lips while sizing me up? Like a pride of lions or a pack of wolves, myth come to life slunk closer and closer to the edge of the painting, huge and panting, attracted by the fine prey I represented. I could see the remains of carcasses, ribs jutting, naked and pointing at an unfair heaven. Still they came closer, and if I reached out with my hand –

"Are you coming?" I heard from beside me, and my head snapped back. My guide (and watchdog) looked at me. I peered around me in surprise, wondering where I was for a moment, realizing with horror I stood almost nose-to-canvass with that object of fascination.

"Yeah. Yeah, sure," I said, shaking my head. I gave the image a glance before moving on, seeing that its inhabitants had returned to their first positions, like actors in a play. Pretty sure that unlike the usual strutting on the stage that accompanied a performance, whatever came after they reached the audience would be painfully real. Did they begin to move again?

I hustled away before anything could happen that I'd regret. From then on, I avoided looking too closely at the gorgeous, gruesome paintings that adorned the walls of the "cottage", some basic inner instinct of preservation forcing me to avert my eyes whenever they began to wander.

"The Lady Larunda's menagerie is quite impressive, don't you think?" Iuturna asked me as we descended the plush-carpeted staircase. I shot a look at the last one at the top of the stairs, some elongated creatures, naked and claw-toothed, clinging to a tree where several people peered out of the foliage, looks of horror distorting their faces. The ensemble cast like a long-lost Hieronymus Bosch painting that by all accounts should have remained so.

"They're something, alright," I said, happy I hadn't eaten anytime recently. I was certain I couldn't have kept anything down if I had. "What the hell are those things, and why didn't I see them on the way in?"

"They are the Lady's nightmares. They weren't there when you arrived, if you were wondering. They only come out after the sun has set." She said, throwing me a knowing smile.

"Her nightmares. You mean, literally, or figuratively?" I paused on a stair, trying to wrap my head around the concept. It was one thing to have nightmares, but to stick them onto a canvas entirely another.

"Both. The Lady sometimes has... indigestion. It is necessary for her to externalize her thoughts. To balance her psyche. She—removes— her discomfort, then traps the imprint within the frames. It's a natural process," she said, like someone describing an artist's benign creative techniques, smirking at me and continuing her descent. I must have looked pretty stupid and slack-jawed, standing on the stairs, but I had no control over that at the moment. The red carpet muffled our steps, and I caressed the lacquered banister with a distracted hand.

The paintings were jails.

For a crazy queen's nightmares. Things didn't get any easier in this place, did they?

What if I'd come from that woman's fever-dreams as well? The painting, downstairs. The one that supposedly represented our former self. What was it, truly? The soft tick-tock of a clock could be heard from another room. We passed the front desk and turned down the hall.

Iuturna led, smiling. We turned corners I hadn't realized were there, and wondered if the house somehow expanded when it needed to, like a bellows, creating new rooms depending on what was in mind. Was it a creation of Larunda's as well, like the nightmares in the paintings? At this point, anything was possible. If a rabbit had run past holding a pocket watch and complaining of being very late for an important date, I wouldn't have been at all disturbed. It would just have been a drop in the big bucket of crazy that was my already insane week.

She pushed open a heavy set of powder-blue doors, all brass handles and white carved inlay, to let me into a dining room that would have been comfortable in the court of some French kings. Gold leaf ormolu framed mirror walls on one side, the other beset with tall doors to the courtyard, a cloudless, starry night glimmering above the tree-line beyond the garden, no moon to be seen. Larunda sat at the end of a table that could easily seat twenty, but for now was completely empty. She proffered a high-backed chair near herself, my footsteps making a hollow clacking sound all the way there. Iuturna came and sat on a silk pillow by her mistress, bowing her head until she was needed.

Larunda wore an extravagant blue dress, of what looked like satin brocade, poofy sleeves extending only as far as mid-bicep. When she lifted her hand once again to show me my seat, I saw fairly developed muscles, barely hidden beneath them.

"Sit, Antonia," she said through Iuturna, nodding towards the chair to her right. A butler in black livery stood two steps behind her throne-like chair, chin high, eyes closed. The kind of pose that told you that he might look relaxed, but would jump to action the moment it was required.

"Call me Chloe, please," I said. This past life business was way beyond me, and besides, if I ever had been this person, creature, whatever, I no longer *was*. I'd been Chloe for as long as I knew, and nothing would change that. I held my hands in front of me, not quite knowing what to do with them.

"Of course, you're right. Chloe." Iuturna spoke demurely, mulling the word about, as if savouring a wine she'd heard about, trying to decide if she liked it, herself.

I reached out and put my hand on the chair, but already the butler was behind it, pulling it slightly for me to get in. I turned to him and attempted a smile, but his head was still upturned, his half-lidded eyes complementing a neutral scowl. Perfect butler material.

"Thank you Barnard," Larunda said through Iuturna in the man's direction, and he nodded, ever-so-slightly, returning to his position behind his Lady. "How do you like your accommodations so far?" she asked. Never mind that I felt like a prisoner, that my sister was missing, and all the rest.

"They're... they're fine," I said, noticing the tools at her hand. No forks, or knives, or spoons. Not even a plate or bowl. There were three silver objects, as shiny as surgical knives: a long tube, which widened at one end, and came to a point like a syringe at the other. A small nail, and a tiny hammer.

"Have you heard anything about my sister? Or that woman she's with, Angelina?"

"Yes. Bad news, I'm afraid. They're deep in Wodun. Within the walls of the capital city, in fact. I cannot penetrate the forces that surround it. We must now rely on our turncoat friend. My powers have little strength outside my country, and even less inside the inner sanctum of another monarch," Iuturna said, Larunda's lips pursed.

"Why couldn't they just have walked out of there, or at least snuck out?" I said, thinking Angelina was stupider than I first thought.

"Because, my dear, Wodun is an island, far from the shore of the mainland. She and your other half could hardly have swum out, or even less snuck onto a ship without being detected. Wodun is a dangerous place, overrun with greevers. Angelina is not as crazy as she seems. The safest place would *have* to be under the Barons' noses," her servant said, she leaning her chin onto her hand and smiling.

"Who are the Barons?" I said. I noticed that the same instruments before Larunda, were also placed to my right. I picked up the nail and fiddled with it, never breaking eye contact with my host.

"Baron Dimanche, Baron Delatombe, Maman Margot. They are the main rulers of Wodun. I've had... dealings... with them in the past."

I nodded. In recesses of the room, more soldiers stood at attention, immobile. I hadn't noticed them until now, in fact. Still as marble statues, they reminded me of suits of armour found around European castles, save that these had moustached faces and lifelike features. Wax museums would've paid a ton to have these guys hang out for their customers. I glimpsed movement outside, once again.

I tried to push my chair back, but Barnard was there once again, holding it in place, stopping me from leaving. I gave up and sat down. Larunda gave him a tight nod and he returned to his position.

"Who are those people, outside?" I said, pointing out the window.

"The gardeners, dear."

"The gardeners," I said, nodding to myself, incredulous. "What are they doing, gardening at this hour?"

"I prefer the night. Daytime is... no good for me. I may be awake during the day, if business demands it, but I prefer to be active when darkness reigns. The gardeners, and all of my staff follow my schedule. So, to answer your question: the gardeners garden at this hour so that I can watch them—garden. Does that satisfy your curiosity?" Iuturna said, her master splaying her hands before her, giving me a toothy grin.

"May I...?" I started, pointing to one of the doors. At this point, going outside attracted me a whole lot more than staying in this oppressive environment.

"No, they really shouldn't be interrupted. The tiniest thing breaks their concentration," before I could even finish my sentence. I looked down at the nail that I was fiddling with, letting long silence lengthen. Larunda lifted a hand, and the until-then statue-like soldiers pulled the drapes along the windows closed, obscuring the "gardeners" and anything else happening outside. At the snap of her fingers, they left the room, boot-heels stomping on the finely polished tiles of the dining room.

Iuturna sighed.

"Chloe. You have no idea how hard it is to rule," she said, and Larunda shook her head sadly. "People depend on me. As much as I am a benevolent, loving mother, I must sometimes be cruel." A shiver ran through me. I felt very much alone in this enormous room, which echoed with Iuturna's voice, repeating Larunda's words. "You might not know this, but powerful people have enemies."

I wonder why, I thought.

"Now now, I understand that sounds hard to accept, but it's true. There are always those who seek to diminish your power. That's the way of it. A few months ago, I caught one of my servants collaborating with my enemies," Iuturna said, Larunda picking up the hammer on the table. Her cheeks reddened. My eyes darted reflexively to where potential exits might be.

Afterdeath

"Now, again, this is something that happens. This person, let us call him Gerold, could have chosen to redeem himself by revealing the location and the names of those who would try to harm me." She tapped the hammer with irritation on the edge of the table. I had put down the nail, and was holding the side of the table with both hands, my head spinning.

"But did he?" Iuturna said, Larunda staring straight at me, eyes bulging. The hammer kept tapping with a rhythmic pounding, echoing in the empty room with a boom. The muscles of her arm knotted and tensed. "Well?" she seethed.

"I— I don't..." I stammered.

"NO!" Iuturna howled, slamming the hammer on the edge of the table, chipping it. "He did *not*. And for that he had to be punished. Every single thing that was done to him, he deserved," bringing the hammer down on that table's edge, punctuating her every last word. Larunda pointed the hammer's head at me. "Now," Iuturna continued, "I need your help," putting down the hammer by her side, on the table, near the deep, raw wooden gashes she had gouged out of it.

"What do you need me for?" I asked, my thoughts swirling madly about my head, as if it had exploded from a severe blow, and now all my wits had escaped, terrified, sprinting here and there searching for that exit.

"I'm glad you asked," Iuturna said, Larunda winking at me. "I want to bring my kingdom to greatness, but I can't do it without my favourites. I know, I know, you're not the same without your sister, but that will soon be amended. I will tell you more when the time comes. Fret not." A wide grin spread across her features, and a hot silence, sauna-like in its discomfort, permeated the air.

"So, um, when do we eat?" I asked, clasping my hands together, trying to change the subject. Larunda smiled wider, and clapped her hands twice over her head. Soldiers turned towards the French doors and released the long, thick curtains, letting them fall along the entire hall with a whoosh of cloth. The door from which Iuturna and I had entered opened, and a long, cloth-covered cart topped with silver-lidded tray were trundled in by two men dressed in chef's whites. They pushed the cart silently all the way to the opposite side of the table. I stared, wide-eyed, wondering what giant meal could be hidden inside such an enormous dish. I looked up at Larunda, who had picked up her hammer and nail, rolling the hammer playfully, this way and that, while she stared at the dish. I looked down at my hand, reached for the nail again, and considered picking up my own hammer. The two men, neither of them betraying any emotions, each picked up their end of the dish with some effort, placing it in the middle of the table, lengthwise, closest to Larunda. She practically jubilated as they lifted the lid, steam pouring out from inside.

That was when I saw something moving. Something human, male. Something tied with nylon ropes like a pig about to be stuck on a shish kebab for slow roasting, right in front of me. Its features grotesque, a cloth filling its mouth, wriggling and jiggling, trying to get free of the bonds tying its feet to its hands, behind its back, but to no avail. Guttural growls came muffled and mumbled through the cloth, its eyeless holes darting from Larunda to me and back to her again, angry, feral. Hatred in that grey stare, palpable, making me push back on the table, my stomach bouncing in my throat with the same infernal rhythm as my beating heart. Its mottled skin moved over stretching muscles, using every ounce of energy to attempt freedom. I fell back away from it, tried to climb out of my chair. Barnard wouldn't have any of it. He clamped down his hands on my shoulders and sat me hard, my hip hitting the armrest.

"What the hell is that?" I screamed.

"You know very well who that is. Weren't you listening at all to what I said?" Iuturna said, Larunda giving me a curious look.

"Oh, how delightful. I love greever, don't you?" Larunda made Iuturna say, the way you would say 'beef' or 'pork', as the two "chefs" grabbed the thrashing thing on the table and held it head back, upside down to offer Larunda a better mark. Wide-open screaming mouth muffled by the rag inside, empty black sockets staring straight ahead into Larunda's leer. The tip of her silver nail, tracing lightly over its forehead as it tried to lash out, held down by two powerful sets of hands. Like a trapped eel, ready to fight until its end.

"What the hell? What's wrong with you?" I screamed, before a smelly hand came down over my mouth.

"It's been far too long for you, I fear. You used to love this so. Tastes change, isn't that so, Barnard?"

"Yes'm." came the reply, and I tried to bite him. I got a short slap to the ear for it. My hip hurt, and the whinging in my left ear stopped me from understanding the babbling she whispered so close to that creature's face. She looked as if she were giving a stern scolding to an unruly child.

"Now now, Barnard, no brutalizing the guests," Larunda admonished through Iuturna, pointing at her butler with the nail. She turned back to the thing in rags heaving on the table, (*her servant. Her own servant*, my mind screamed) and put the point of the nail to its forehead. I turned my head away, closing my eyes, but Barnard grabbed my hair and pulled it back, forcing my eyes open. The razor sharp end lay within the creature's first layer of skin, and her tongue stuck out just so, as she hit it with one short rap of the hammer. A soft ichor oozed out of the hole as she removed the nail, and she deliberately picked up the tube, putting the wider end to her mouth. She began to guzzle, and I felt sick to my stomach. Her slurping made me want to vomit, and the greever's sockets went grey. Its wiggling turned to spasms, suffering seizures like a fish dying in the bottom of a boat, and it stopped resisting a few moments later.

I couldn't move anymore. All the fight had left me. Barnard sensed that and took his hand off my face. He did not, however, leave his new post behind my chair.

Larunda was on her feet, the long tube protruding from the thing's forehead. She now stared directly into its dead eyes hungrily. The two "chefs" trundled the cart away, sure that the twitching thing on the table would no longer be a threat.

The nail went into the gaping hole on the man's forehead like a bottle stopper and she sat back down in her chair, putting a hand to her distended belly.

"Oh, but that's good. Bit spicy. Funny, you always expect more fight out of them," Iuturna said, as Larunda patted herself.

"You're a monster," I said.

"A monster? Haha! Pot, meet kettle. No, dear, I'm no monster. I do what I must to survive. What else am I supposed to do with these things when they threaten my rule," her hands dancing about, "Let them subvert my subjects?" She then let out a loud burp, her stomach regaining its normal composure. "It gives me the power I need to rule, that is all. I take its energies, and in return, get rid of a danger. If anything, I return balance to nature."

"You could have left it in a prison or something," I said, leaning forward.

"What good would it do me in prison? No, love, this is for the better. Pointless to ask you if you'll have any, is it," she said rhetorically. My angry face was the only response I deigned give this evil bitch. She shrugged and got up again. The thing on the table barely moved anymore. She plunged the tube back into the un-stoppered hole and slurped loudly. I saw the pitiful thing's shape contract, its skin growing darker, being emptied of all that composed its innards, until all that was left was a human-shaped sack, like a mottled paper bag. When Larunda removed the straw, the last of the human shape disintegrated into dust, and was no more.

"Delicious. Now, Chloe, I just want you to be aware that there are still dissenting elements about. I'm not stupid. I have eyes everywhere. I want you to know that they are always open. Watching," Iuturna said, Larunda leaning toward me, glaring, sitting back down and letting out a fat belch. "Goodness. That was a rough one." She rubbed her belly with one hand, putting a fist over her mouth and letting out more gas in little puffs, like hiccoughs. "Ooof," Iuturna said, her master stretching a bit and wincing, rubbing her stomach harder, as if something were macerating inside. "Don't disappoint me," she said, the other trying to smile, but only making a distorted grin. She got up and Barnard was not quick enough from stopping the tall chair from toppling over, hitting the ground with a resounding bang.

"Iuturna! Get up!" Iuturna yelled, and she lifted the young woman up by her ear. She held herself up by the table's edge, let go of Iuturna and gripped her belly. The young woman slipped under her arm to support her.

"Barnard, take her..." Iuturna said, Larunda's hand on Iuturna's head, then waving in the general direction of the far end of the room, without finishing her sentence. For the first time, Barnard looked like something might break through his perfect mask, a hint of frantic panic showing. He looked at both Larunda, then me, and pulled my chair back, gripping my arm and lifting me into an upright position. I watched as the soul-sucker left the dining room through a door a little ways behind her own chair, and Barnard led me back the way I came. I heard the doors at the end of the room slam, and hoped that whatever was wrong with her might be fatal.

The butler half-dragged me, stiff-legged, back up the corridors and hallways to my room. I once again avoided looking at the nightmares, concentrating on the pain in my upper arm. Barnard had me in a vice-like grip, thinking perhaps I might try to escape. I never once tried to, but that never registered with him. He was more automaton than man. Besides, if I wanted to avoid more slaps across the head, I knew better than try to go anywhere.

He opened the door to my room and threw me in. I picked myself up off the carpet, rubbing my sore arm, and lifted my sleeve to check the red bruise he'd left there. I inspected the redness on my hip, and took a look in the mirror at my ear. I hoped the great big fingerprints would go away soon enough. The pain was fading, but the impression remained. I went to the window and opened it an inch or two. Outside, the human shadows still moved among the bushes and trees.

Gardening.

In the middle of the night. For one woman's "pleasure".

Then the flood of horror descended upon me. Shockwaves rippled down my spine, from my scalp to my toes, as the fully-formed thought of her revenge crashed down into my consciousness. She was insane. Anyone getting on her bad side was a goner. Here I was tight-roping it.

I had a feeling I knew what I'd find, but I checked anyhow. Yes, the door was locked. My only avenue of escape was down through the window. I opened it wider, and no sooner had I pushed it all the way that the talking bird returned, landing as it had on the windowsill the first time.

"Where have you been?" I asked, still in shock from what I'd seen in the dining room.

"Avoiding her spies. I can't stay long. You have to wait a few hours. The best time to go will be right before dawn," it twittered.

"Do you have a name?" I said.

Afterdeath

"Apologies, yes! My name is Gassire," it said.

"Okay, Gassire, why do I have to wait that long?" I asked, hands on my hips.

"There are too many guards at the moment. Daybreak is when they all return to their rooms, since Larunda goes into hiding underground. I have to go now. Meet me in the garden, right by that line of trees. I'll lead the way once you get there," Gassire said, and before I could even ask it, or him how the heck I was supposed to get out of here, it flew off once more into the darkness.

Great, I thought, *I'm stuck in a psycho's house and the only way to get out is with the help of a talking bird. And now it's gone. I'm screwed.*

I spent the night thinking about my predicament, and then figured it wasn't so bad. Whatever Olivia, Angelina and Barkley were up to must be a hundred times worse. I was in a relatively safe place. The more I thought about it, the more I realized that what I'd witnessed was some sort of show of power. I was fairly certain that Larunda had no need to eat up a greever every day to survive, or even to maintain her power, so that had all been for my benefit. I hoped she was suffering from wild and unnameable cramps, excruciating stomach worms and terminal blockage. If she thought that that little display of freakishness was going to make me more manageable, she had another thing coming.

I had plenty of time, so I looked around my room. Nothing I could use to pick the lock, of course, but glancing at the sheets gave me an idea. It was like in those old kids' books: make a rope ladder out of bed-covers. I got busy tearing them off the bed and tying them together. My knotting skills were horrible, but I figured I didn't have far to fall if I did. What was a bruised bum on top of a sore arm, hip, and ear, after all?

Pretty soon I had something long enough to tie around the bed post that would reach down to the ground. At least it seemed so in my estimation. Just had to wait for the moment of truth to find out. I turned out the lights and pushed the bed up to the window, so that my weight wouldn't pull it over while I was rappelling. I then waited and watched, observing the people in the shadows down there, wondering who they might be.

I saw guards come out, rallying the shades. The soldiers were solid, as real as could be, but those others now forming a line remained insubstantial. A cry went up, marching orders, and the line began its slow trudge toward the forest, heading between trees, down a small path. I stayed low, waiting for something to happen. Ten minutes later, the soldiers returned, alone. They headed straight to the cottage, and went inside.

I heard footsteps outside my door, all marching in lock-step. Doors all along the corridor opened, then closed. I guessed that those were all the soldiers returning to their rooms for the day. I went to the window and threw my sheet-rope out. It hung almost all the way to the ground. Not bad for a first time.

I climbed down, putting one hand down, then the other, and sliding a bit more, careful not to make any noise. The "rope" pulled taut, as I passed my first knot in the sheets, going down ever-so-slowly. When my feet were a foot or two from the ground, the rope slipped, and I ended up lying down in the gravel by a window. I suppressed a groan and picked myself up. I hid behind a decorative cedar and inspected my failed "rope". The end tied to the bed had slipped off, cutting of my retreat. *Crap*, I though, picking gravel out of my elbow and arm.

What to do with my sheets? I wrapped them in a big ball and hid them behind the small decorative tree, hoping no one would find it until I could come and retrieve it. I crept across the yard, feeling exposed until I made it to the tree-line.

"Gassire!" I whispered. What a stupid name for a bird. Then again, it hadn't always been a bird, so I should probably think more in terms of 'he' instead of 'it'.

"I'm here," came the reply from a nearby tree. Around me, the ground was becoming clearer, as the sun rose. I might not have very much time before someone came to get me from my room.

"I can't go back to my room!" I said, harshly. "My rope... sheets... whatever—fell."

"Don't worry about that. Let's go," he said, and flew off into the forest. He'd fly off and land, from one branch to another, and from tree to tree, following the general path that I'd seen the 'gardeners' follow a little while before. The path was clean, and well-worn packed dirt. Tree roots criss-crossed over it, forcing me to watch my step if I didn't want to have a festival of tripping.

"You know that you were Antonia. Do you know who Antonia was, in relation to Larunda?" Gassire asked, ruffling his feathers.

"A weird kind of adopted daughter, I guess. That's what she told me, anyways," I said, pushing a branch out of my face.

"Yes, a very special one. You were her dobluth," he said, stopping long enough to see my reaction. I stared up in confusion.

"What you *were*, was the living embodiment of what monarchs use to cross over to the living world to capture and enslave spirits of the dead, influence events, speak to the living, in effect, the link that is crucial to hold and increase power in the afterlife," Gassire said, hopping along a branch.

I shook my head, holding my hands up to him.

"Wait wait wait. You're telling me that I'm... was... some sort of portal? To the living world?" Gassire skipped sideways and flew to a branch closer to me.

165

Afterdeath

"Not the portal. The key. A living key. Anyone who wants to wield power in this realm has to gain control over the souls of others. The best way is to get them while they're fresh. Some have different methods: Charon sends boats, Ran drowns people; others use their dobluth to get humans to pledge them their souls. That's what you are. You opened doors for Larunda. At least you did, until you quit," he said. He then looked at me, very intently.

I was speechless for a moment. What do you say to that, really? At least I knew now why Larunda kept me around.

"Why doesn't she get a new one?" I said.

"That seems like a fairly obvious question: because they aren't that easy to get, that's why. You were a fluke, born naturally, and not mined, as such things usually are. Well, when I say born…" I don't know how to describe an uncomfortable bird, but that's exactly what he looked like for a minute.

"I was a nightmare of Larunda's, wasn't I?" I said, voicing my suspicions.

"Yes, Mistress. But you developed into something much greater. Your followers are many. Ever since your rebellion, Larunda has kept us all, using us for menial tasks… as well as… sustenance. I've been awaiting your return for a long time." Gassire said, and twittered happily, flying to another branch, hanging sideways in glee. I couldn't help but smile at the display. It was nice to know that even as a monster, I had friends I could count on. It looked like not everyone judged others by appearances in this world.

We soon came to a cave, its entrance to the left of the path. I'd noticed that we'd gone steadily upward, but now a slab of grayish-brown rock jutted from the ground, wedged with another, creating an opening between them.

"They are all kept inside. A field keeps them trapped during the day, and the soldiers come to get them at night," Gassire said, jumping at the top of the entrance to the cave. I wondered why no one could leave, but as I stretched out my hand to feel around the entrance of the small cave, it was as if a cold wall stopped me.

"How am I supposed to get in, Gassire?" I asked, turning to look at him.

"I don't know, Mistress," he replied, tweeting sadly. "Someone is coming! Hide!" he cried, and flew into a tree. I looked around at the mossy ground cover, hearing footsteps nearing. I jumped behind a bush and lay down hoping that whoever it was wouldn't notice.

Then I recognized her.

Iuturna.

She approached the cave opening and whispered between her hands:

"Mother!" she said. From my hiding-place, I could see the cave entrance, and Iuturna hunched before it.

"Mother!" she whispered more harshly, and I thought I saw a shadow, more dense than the others, move inside the cave. I did not hear the conversation that was had between them, but as Iuturna rose to leave, I got up and yelled:

"What are you doing here?" She fell back, startled, and began to turn to run. I raced to where she was and held her arm. She struggled to get away, but I didn't let her. "Thought you said you never left the cottage?" as she pulled harder. "Stop it, I'm trying to help you," I said, and she quit tugging. "Your mother is in there? For real?"

She nodded. "She is a prisoner."

"Yeah, I got that. Where's Larunda right now?" I asked, peering around, wondering when I'd be attacked by sentient quicksand.

"Returned to the underground, nursing a terrible ulcer."

"Serves her right. She shouldn't gobble people up like that. This whole thing's been going on long enough, don't you think? Why don't you try to fight her?" I said.

"My father is inside the cottage. My mother is here. If I were to do anything against the Lady to help either one, both of them would suffer for my crimes! What am I to do, exactly?" she said, tears beginning to well up. I let go of her arm.

"Yeah, that is a pretty crappy deal. I'll help you, okay? We'll get both your parents out, somehow. She can't be everywhere at once. You have to get me back to my room, alright? I dropped my means of escape, and now I'm stuck. Can you do that for me so that I don't get caught?" I said, and she nodded. I looked back at the cave entrance and thought I saw thick shadows crowding the entrance. The sky was becoming more blue than black, and I had to get back before we both got caught.

Iuturna led the way, and we both ran as fast as we could. I grabbed my sheets and followed her to a side door near the back of the house.

Not only was the sky growing paler: Iuturna was dematerializing before my eyes. I could see through her more and more, as the sun shone down through the trees, and what had been a beautiful young woman now reminded me of an ethereal skeleton. She was a lot like that wedding-dress wearing corpse thing I'd seen at the wizard's shop in the Viking district of Necropolis. If anything unusual was going on, she didn't seem to notice.

"What's happening to you?" I cried. She looked at her bony fingers and turned around, her skull smiling.

"The same thing that happens to all of us in the sunlight or moonlight. This is one part of the Ghost Mother's curse. Now shush, we must not get caught." It was the strangest thing to have a see-through skeleton admonish me, but I kept quiet anyhow.

As we crept in, she returned to normal inside the cottage. She paused and put up her hand. I peered and saw Barnard and another servant walking away from us. Iuturna left me standing there and caught up to them, asking them how the Lady was,

Afterdeath

steering them down a side corridor. Before she rounded the corner, she turned to look at me, and I hurried down the hall, around the banister and up the stairs. I found my room and tried opening it, but it was locked, and of course, I didn't have the key. A few moments later, Iuturna arrived, took the key out of her pocket and opened the door for me. She then gave it to me and wished me good morning. I closed the door and locked it again, sliding down the door to the floor, exhaling relief. I put my head into my pile of blankets and thought for a moment.

Olivia and I were keys to the living world.

'Dobluth'.

We might have been able to get back on our own, had we only known. I sighed, thinking about how much could have been avoided had we been aware of the fact. Except I had no idea if I still had that power, and how it worked. Maybe only Larunda knew that. Question was, how to get it out of her without becoming her tool. Again.

I went to the window and watched the sunrise. Iridescent purples lit up the sky across vast marshmallow fields of nimbus clouds. It was a glorious morning to be alive. Too bad I wasn't. Whatever. I'd enjoy it anyhow. I closed the window and spread slightly dusty sheets back on my bed, after having pushed it back to its original position.

I then lay down again and fell more unconscious than asleep, grim mares of haunted wraiths shimmering behind my eyes. Reaching out for me. Pining to be free. Pleading.

Chapter 15

BREAK-IN

Warmth and comfort surrounded me. I bathed in warm dirt like it was a hot-spring or a duvet. I lay in the foetal position, hoping never to have to leave. This must be the blessing of eternal rest, the never ending bliss of one's own grave. Yet something disturbed my sleep. A hand, reaching in from above, groped me until it found my hair. Then it heaved. I thrust my head out of the ground with a yelp and saw a greever's arm, its hand gripping my hair firmly. It knelt before my grave, and whispered to my up-thrust head:

"Wakey wakey!" in a gravelly, beyond the grave voice. I knew it must have been Angelina, but the sight was fairly scary nonetheless. I pulled my hands out and imagined I must have looked like a zombie coming out of its tomb.

Outside, all was quiet. The sliver of a moon shone beyond the city, reflected off the silent waters. A bell tolled in the distance, echoing far and wide. I extricated myself, then got my bearings. The graveyard had shifted, somehow. We were a tad closer to the front gate than we had been before. Instead of going on to the side gate we had exited through before, Angelina led me in the direction of the moored ships.

"Where's Barkley?" I whispered, and she pointed at her tummy. I had a hard time believing she'd eaten her dog, so I let it slide. As we walked, the grave markers became cleaner, more defined. Fresher. On the water's edge, they stood, polished and shining.

"New ones keep coming out all the time," Angelina/ugly creature growled, and it was then that I understood: the markers weren't sinking into the water. They were emerging. With a trembling realization, I thought I saw a row of brand new stone tablets, clinging to slimy earth, moving to land. These virgin stones had no markings, no one they belonged to. That was the reason armies could take them as their homes: they were unoccupied until they arrived. The perfect homes for souls that had never known peaceful rest.

God, why did you send me to this savage, disgusting world? I would have given anything to have been transported back to my life at that moment; anything at all. The depressing part was that unless I got out of Wodun, it would never happen. I snuck nearer Angelina, and growl/whispered to her:

"Does it get better? Than this I mean?" she put her rotted index to her sliced lips, and gave me a sign to follow her. A pier stretched out along the water to our left, and we took stone steps to get down by the water. Overhead, criss-crossed beams supported a wooden marina that spanned the length of the city. She sat me down on one of the rotting supports. What ugly, terrible things we must have looked like. I'm glad there was just the two of us.

When she was sure that no one would interrupt us, she took my hands and looked me in the eye.

"What's your real question? Is there something better in the *next* next life? It really does depend on what your definition of the word 'better' is. In this one, you don't ever have to eat. You might even get away from sleep, if you work on it. Yeah, there's some pretty horrid dangers out there, too. So I guess what you want to know is: what do you have to do to get a hold of the 'good stuff', the crap all those dime prophets and liars promised you in the previous life so you'd do what they said. The 'real' heaven you were promised for being a good girl. You know what? I have no idea. No clue whatsoever. Here's the thing though: neither did they. Is this what you imagined the afterlife would be like? Well?" she said, her hands tensing.

"No, of course not!" I said, repressing my lip from trembling.

"Do you think this is what I was promised, too?" she said, sounding exasperated.

"I guess not," I said, looking to the grimy sand and algae at my feet.

"Let's be clear, then: no, it was not," she said, putting a hand on my chin and forcing me to look her in the face again, "So what can I do about it? Not a whole hell of a lot. Does that mean I have to sit down, give up and cry in my hands over the unfairness of the world?"

"But… you're stronger than I am!" I plead, feeling warmth travelling through my cheeks at the admission.

"Bull. The only reason you and I are different is that I don't accept this bullshit I'm handed as gospel truth. You can only go so far leading a life of fatalism. You want to see your sister again?"

"Of course I do! Who do you take me for?" I replied, indignant, trying to shake her hands off mine.

"That's the spirit. Now take that anger and transform it. Mold it into something that isn't 'woe-is-me'. Make it into armour. Live now, not for some far-off, uncertain reward."

"But I can't!" I almost screamed.

"Yes you can. It's all in there," she said, poking at my chest, emphasizing each word. "*Everything* you need to do *anything you want* is in there, right now. You just have to find it. So find it. Can you do that for me?"

I nodded, gritting my teeth.

"Good. Now come on, let's break into a presidential palace." That last one caught me off guard. She let go and I pressed my hands against my cheeks, rubbing the numbness out of them. She was climbing up the stairs, pausing to see if anyone was coming. I got up and followed, sending the warmth of my embarrassment to my heart, trying to make it glow with bravery.

Along the shadows we crept, keeping out of the lamp-lit areas, like the good monsters we were. Further, three greevers kept guard. Angelina stepped out of the dark, and my first reflex was to catch her hand, to stop her from going out into the light. One of the blank-eyed corpses spotted us, and turned to examine us. It grunted, getting the others' attention. The first one was average height, but bulky, its muscles lacerated with deep marks. I let go of her hand, and pushed the dread I felt into a tiny spot in my heart. My trembling steps could have been mistaken for some terrible undead disease, and I banked on that as we drew closer. The smaller wraith cocked its head at us, probably wondering what we were doing there.

Angelina grunted at them, lifting a limp arm, pointing at the dock entrance to the city. The third soul, a woman whose facial scarification resembled tribal tattoos, stepped in front of Angelina and I. The large one shrieked at the woman, and she turned to him and barked a guttural cry. This was no good. The woman was obviously the smartest of the three.

She'd put a knotted hand on her machete, and Angelina looked from one to the other. I was ready to bolt. Where to, I had no idea. The other side of the planet was a good start.

Angelina fell to her knees, clutching her upper chest, doubled over. She cried in pain, something pushing through in spasms. The three ghouls took a step back, their horrid faces frightened as to what might be ailing one of theirs. Angelina clawed her way forward, whatever it was that forced its way through her ribs becoming more frantic. A low, gurgling growl issued forth from under her clothes, and she lifted her face in agony to the now retreating souls. In an ecstatic push, she jumped to her feet and rushed our antagonists. All three stopped backing away and turned to run, shrieking as they did.

"Phew," Angelina said in her greever voice, as Barkley popped out from under her shirt. I had been on the verge of flight as well, but now all I wanted to do was laugh. Barkley ran around her legs, bouncing at his owner and licking her hand.

"How did you do that?" I said.

"I kept him inside me. It's a trick we learned a while ago. I can put him away without absorbing him. It came in handy when we were in the Lost Soul's Forest where you found us," she said, wiping her forehead.

"Does it hurt? When he..." and I made the motion of some beast coming out of my breast.

"Not at all. That was for their benefit. Come on, they'll be back with more soon. These souls are less stupid than the feral ones. They're almost human," she said, and had a faraway look in her poached eyes for a moment.

We walked on, the planks beneath our feet resonating like a creaky xylophone. The smell of brine filled the air, and the tall ships moored to the docks jutted jib booms over the quay. Lamps on posts lit the fore of the sailing vessels, and Barkley walked between us, claws clicking.

As the three we'd run into came into sight, we hid along a pier, between two close ships. The shadows they cast were enough to keep us hidden from the group that walked by now. It looked as though four more had been added to the search party, and we remained still until they were well away from us. We slunk back into the shadows below the wall of the city, avoiding the outthrust bits of junk that made up the defences. The guard post was empty, their men having joined the three we'd encountered in the search for us.

Angelina turned right down the first alleyway, then left. We hurried past homes with drawn drapes, staying off the main road to better hide our approach. What few patrols we encountered ignored us, thinking we were part of the guard.

When we did arrive at the Presidential Palace, only a few guards blocked our way in. Angelina whispered a word or two in Barkley's ear and I watched him shoot of into the distance, stopping in front of the guards, running between their legs, and into the courtyard. The confused soldiers turned and ran after him, and as they chased the little terrier around the furthest side of the Palace, we snuck in, climbing the marble stairs two-by-two. Angelina ran up to one of the lesser doors and gently clicked it open, allowing us passage into the foyer of the white-walled mansion. Directly before us were grey-and-gold marble stairs, leading to the second floor and basement. On the right and left were the main hallways that connected with board rooms and official meeting spaces. It was dark, and the main light came from what little moonlight slipped in through the windows. A particular smell to centuries-old buildings clung to the air, reminding me of museums and school trips.

Angelina, after hugging the left wall before the hallway, gave the all-clear, and we both dashed for the stairs leading to the second floor. The large, empty palace echoed with our steps. I felt an itch along my arm, and scratched. We ran in silence up the stairs, certain now that no guards were allowed within the administrative centre of the Barons. My neck felt as if it had developed a rash, and as hard as I tried, I couldn't stop myself from rubbing it. As we went up a bend in the stairs, I could see the marina in the distance, but when I focused on my reflection, I noticed that a gash was opening on the side of my neck. I checked Angelina, and noticed the same thing on her leg, as if some fabric were tearing off. She distractedly scratched her side.

"Pssst!" I called to her, and she turned around to look at me. Her eyes grew wide, and she made a gesture with her hand meaning "hurry up!" We both bounced up the stairs, rubbing our itchy skin as if fire ants had taken residency underneath. Angelina hung a right down the hall, and I ran, accompanied by Barkley, as fast as I could while the itch became a burn. Simple wooden doors on either side of the hall didn't interest Angelina. She headed for the second to last one on the right. She put her hand on the door, and the greever skin on her hand began to recede, up her arm, to her face and beyond. She looked on in horror, but her hand stayed stuck to the door like someone who's stuck a knife in a power outlet: letting go was beyond her will.

The evil disguise that had covered her sloughed off like snakeskin or falling leaves, coming down to the ground in fits and puffs and disintegrating. She let go of the round, metal doorknob and once again tried to turn it. This time it turned, with effort. She pushed it, whispering something under her breath, using all her might against something that wanted to keep her out and was failing. Her shoulder was into it, her legs pumping, and the door creaked in indignation. Barkley jumped around me, and I was wakened from what must have been a shaken state. I jumped through the door, and as I did, my disguise blew off. No soft moulting, just an explosion of rotted flesh, which started to smoke and disappear on the ground and walls where it had landed and stuck like fungus.

Angelina stepped out of the way of the door, and tried to catch its opposite doorknob, but failed, a giant boom exploding down the hall as it banged closed.

"Shit!" she swore under her breath.

Inside the room, many exhibits behind glass cases hung to the walls and on podiums adorning the floor. Two windows to the outside, on the far wall, let in meagre light. A light switch on the wall could have helped, but I assumed she wanted to avoid attention. Too bad about the door. We'd be getting visitors soon. There was no way that had gone unnoticed.

Afterdeath

"We don't have much time," she said, going from exhibit to exhibit, searching for something only she would have recognized.

"What are you looking for?" I asked.

"Something inconspicuous. It should be the last thing you'd expect to be an object of power." I started searching the displays, wondering what an object of power might look like, as well as its opposite.

"You—you don't know what it looks like?" I half-yelled.

"Of course not! They're all different! How could I know what the new one resembles? It's just quite probable that that oaf Dimanche left the new one among his collection of lesser do-dads and baubles." She said lifting the corner of a painting by a window.

"You don't even know?" I said, planted in the middle of the room.

"Look. Are you going to make yourself useful? When you touch it, you will know. It should have a kind of heavy charge. Touch things until you get the feeling that what you're holding has innate power. Let's try that, shall we love?" and she gave me a condescending smile. I began to pace the room, lifting things up and trying to get a sense of their inherent power. How was this thing even going to be used?

"But what does it do?" I said, looking at a small doll made of what looked like hair.

"It'll take us out of here." Her hands were on a glass case, her eyes roving over necklaces and bracelets. This room contained cultural properties, that much was clear. Why someone would hide their most treasured heirloom in this place was beyond me.

"Like a teleporter?" I said.

Then, a deep voice answered:

"No, like dobluth ember."

Two things happened at that moment. I screamed, and the lights came on. Out of the corners of the room stepped soldiers, not of the greever variety, but the very much lucid and angry-looking kind. The black man who had turned on the light was of average height and build, wore a tuxedo and a top hat, and had a beautiful face, like a famous actor. He was, for the moment, not smiling, quite unlike a famous actor.

The guards came closer and two grabbed Angelina and I.

"Dimanche," Angelina said, with a sneer.

The man knelt down and looked into Barkley's growling face. His eyes stretched unnaturally, and Barkley fell sideways, stunned.

"Angelina. I didn't think you'd be so foolish as to return, and you brought a friend along with you this time. I didn't realize you had any. Perhaps you can tell me where you put my power object?" he said, picking up the unconscious dog. He grabbed him under the forepaws and looked at his lolling head.

"And you, how do you like your punishment?" he said to the unconscious dog, then smiled and threw Barkley at another soldier who caught him and placed him under one arm.

"I lost it. Besides, it didn't work," she said, offhandedly.

The man's face contorted for a moment, after which he smiled.

"You lost it. The most precious thing one can possess. You lost it. Haha! Oh Angelina, you never seem to learn, do you?"

He opened the door and led the men out.

"As you can see, ma chère, I was having a bit of a soirée when you so rudely interrupted it. By the way, why would you think I'd be stupid enough to leave my most treasured possession in the same place it was stolen last time?"

"Because you're stupid?" she said, baiting him. The man shrugged it off without a sign of getting upset, and continued down the hall. The lights had all been turned on, the pretence of the Palace being empty now no longer useful. The men on each side of me pushed me ahead, stoic and hard-looking.

"I've known for a while of your escape. I'd sent a mess of people after you. Looks like the man in your midst was your undoing," he grinned. "Thank Bondye," he said, lifting his eyes and hands skyward.

"You hired some pretty crappy mercenaries, Dimanche. Boy scouts would have done a better job," Angelina taunted. The baron laughed.

"That may be true, but here you are nonetheless." We descended the grand staircase, went out the front door and were confronted with a throng of grim Lost Souls, armed greevers, amassed outside, at the base of the front steps. I strained against my captors, but their grip only became stronger. Everywhere I looked, all I could see were corpse faces sneering and growling at me. I never was this scared in my life as I was at this precise moment. I thought the Baron would toss us to the masses to be torn to bits. Every empty pair of eyes absorbed firelight, broken mouths gaping for our essence. Broken-nailed hands reached out to grab us, eager to shred us to bits.

"You see, chérie, I don't need that old bauble anymore: I have an army now. I can take whatever I want. Come, let me show you to a familiar place," he said, lifting a hand. He led the parade, the gibbering, spitting creatures parting before him, barely held back from attacking us. They lunged and sputtered, whatever controlled them having trouble containing their wildness. Even the soldiers who manhandled us shied away from their terrifying display. Only Dimanche walked diffidently through them, their heads bowing as he did so.

A small, dirty house is where he stopped. Passing a hand before the thick wooden door, it bled open in complaint. He raised a hand as if to say: "after you!" and the guards threw us into the darkened room. Barkley's lifeless form was tossed in after

Afterdeath

us, and the door slammed shut. It was decorated with a single barred window, through which the Baron now addressed us.

"You remember this place, right, Angelina? We had such good times together when last you betrayed me," he said, winking. As my eyes adjusted to the gloom, I saw strange instruments lumped around the dingy room. They looked almost like exercise machines. The more I inspected them, the more it dawned that they were definitely *not* exercise machines.

"I hope I'll see you bright and early tomorrow morning so that I may begin interrogations. Maybe we'll try with your young friend, here. I'd love to hear her pretty singing voice." He winked at me and left. I ran to the window and was instantly assailed by two greevers trying to reach in and get me. One grabbed my hair, and I pulled as hard as I could, scalp ripping in pain as an arm came through the window. Angelina jumped up and hit the offending arm with all her might, and I held onto my hair to avoid losing it. Finally, the thing let go and I fell back, almost hitting Angelina. She went to pick up Barkley from the ground, and stroked his back, her face in his fur.

I paced around the room, touching walls, trying to find an opening of some sort. The humid climate made the walls spongy and gross. I found no other opening, though, and sat down on a pointy pyramid-like object in the middle of the room.

"What is this stuff?" I asked, afraid of the answer, knowing, not wanting to, but having to nonetheless.

"Torture devices," Angelina said, her face still in her unfortunate companion's fur.

Lord have mercy, I thought.

I got up from my seat and looked at it more closely. Leather straps lay on the floor, attached to eyelets at the base of the pyramid. A wheel stood upright behind the pyramid, and the leather straps extended from the eyelets to the wheel. No one needed a degree in physics to know what would happen to someone tied to that thing, once the wheel began to turn.

I backed away from that as well, and avoided looking at the other miscellaneous objects scattered around.

"You two know each other," I said, matter-of-factly.

"Yes. He's the reason Barkley was turned into a dog. And the reason we ended up in prison," she said, holding Barkley close. I felt bad for her, of course. It must have been tough to lose her love, especially now that he was a dog. The thing I didn't understand was the first cause.

"Why did you steal from him?"

"I needed his power," she said, shrugging. I didn't think any line of questioning in the same vein would get me any further.

"But you lost it," I said, remembering the previous conversation with the Baron. She came within hand-span of my ear and whispered, almost sub-audibly.

"No, I didn't. I still have it. The problem is that it's out of power. I have no idea how to recharge it. No one ever explained that part to me," frowning.

"So where is it?" She put a finger to her lips, then pointed to Barkley. She had found a way to hide it inside him, just as she had found a way to hide *him* inside *her*. I had to give it to her, she was clever. The problem remained that we were stuck in a torture chamber at the very heart of her arch-enemies' stronghold. I was just as guilty of breaking and entering as she was, in the Baron's eyes, even though he's never met me before, and was therefore a brand new enemy to him. Bollocks.

"So we came to steal another, then. That's why we're in a filthy cell, waiting to be tortured." I looked up at the ceiling, maybe hoping an answer to our problems might drop down from there.

"Yes, except he doesn't have another one. At least I don't think so. He wants the one I stole from him, bad," she said.

"How do you know this?"

"By how angry he got when I told him I'd lost his. If he had another one, it wouldn't matter that I'd lost it. He needs it. Without it, he has almost no clout in his own country. None of the rulers do." Barkley's tail began to budge, and she smiled a bit. She let out a sigh when his eyes opened and his tongue lolled out at her.

"How rare are these things?" I wondered out loud.

"There are only a dozen or so on the planet at any given time. As soon as one is found, there's a scramble to harness its power. Wars are fought over them."

"Do you think that's why they've amassed this army of greevers?"

"I don't know. Maybe. This feels different, somehow." Barkley jumped down from her embrace and began to sniff his surroundings. He came back to Angelina and pressed against her leg, his tail wagging.

I looked outside the window and the crowd of foul creatures had gone, hopefully back to their brand-new graves. The vacant streets looked lonely and desolate, reflecting what I now felt inside my own heart. Stuck inside a stockade, waiting to be tortured in the morning for reasons beyond my control. I wanted to ask what the plan was. I wanted to, but I knew what she'd tell me. There was no plan. No plan, no hope, no way to reach my sister. I sat back down on the torture device I'd recently shirked away from, no longer caring.

"What... what are we..." I knew it was stupid, but how could I stop myself?

"How do I know?" she barked back. I buried my head in my hands. I once again held back the tears, a few managing to slip by, like drops in a cracked dam. Angelina went to the door and stared outside.

Afterdeath

"Why are these things so powerful, anyway? What makes them so special?" I wondered out loud. Anything that made you go insane for and kill for it to possess must have been mighty special, I reckoned.

"Let's put it this way," she started, turning toward me. "The place you come from, the living world, is made of atoms. Those are the basic building blocks. Here, in this world, the basic building block is death *itself*."

"Death's—"

"Don't interrupt. This Universe is constructed from the very fabric of death, you understand? Now, sometimes, there are some tiny, very concentrated bits that appear. We call that Death's Blood. It is extremely powerful, and can help any wielder control elements of the afterlife. That's what we call 'dobluth'. Death's blood. Dimanche called it dobluth ember, but it's all the same, really. Super-concentrated death."

So she had stolen this man's power. His Death's Blood. And she'd been punished severely for it. Now we'd come back to steal more. And were waiting for our punishment for being caught. I sighed.

She eventually sat back down, back against the wall. We both stayed silent for an eternity, the only sounds were that of some leak in the ceiling allowing a steady drip-drip-drip to fall on some dirty concrete part of the floor.

When the door opened, I was far from ready. Angelina pounced on it, dragging whoever was on the other side, in, Barkley growling. He stopped when he saw who it was.

"Toussaint!" I cried, running up to the old man and hugging him.

"You've recovered, mes belles," he said, smiling at us, while returning my embrace. "Not having much luck foiling the Baron's plans from in here, are you?" he joked. I saw an enormous shadow parked out front, and imagined the gargantuan jaw of his pet, resting on the wet pavement.

"How did you know we were here?" Angelina said. Barkley jumped happily around his leg.

"I just came back from a little party. Turns out the guest of honour is Hades," he said, sombrely.

"Hades. *The* Hades?" I said, vague memories of Roman mythology rising vapour-like to the top of my brain. Hades had been the ruler of the underworld in that particular historico-mythological world. Here he was just another monarch with a kingdom and too much time on his hands, I assumed.

"None other than, beauté. He's the one we have to thank for these wonderful cloaks: they spin some powerful whammy on them Lost Souls. I'm one of those unfortunate enough to have to make the distribution all over the country," Toussaint said.

"Wait. If he's lending them the cloaks, is he also providing the use of his dobluth to the Barons?" Angelina asked, eyes wide.

"I don't know, but it seems likely," Toussaint replied, frowning. So that's why he's helping us, I thought. Whatever he thought we could do, though, was predicated on the fact that Angelina still had and could use the one she'd stolen. So, even though she still had the thing, she had no idea how to refill it and use it properly.

"So are we supposed to steal Hades' power object?" I said. Both turned to look at me, but only Toussaint smiled.

"I s'pose that could help," he said.

"...in getting the entire country on our asses," Angelina added.

"Again," I added, for her benefit. "Well, what do you have to suggest?" I said, and she grabbed me by the elbow, turning to Toussaint:

"A moment please. My companion and I have to confer. Would you excuse us?" and she dragged me into the corner. "What are you doing?" she said to me in a whisper. Toussaint had gone outside to act as a lookout, and we were now alone with Barkley.

"I'm trying to help. What else are we supposed to do? How else do you want to leave this place?" I replied to her face.

"You know, I never intended to 'help out' as you say, in the first place. That man was a means to an end. He got us in. I told him what he needed to hear so that we could get close enough to find another ember. As you can see..." and she elongated the vowel, as if she were explaining to a child, "there is no dobluth ember to be had."

"Easily," I corrected.

"Same difference. We've been had. We have to convince him to sneak us out on a boat or some such. It's the only way." She then crossed her arms and looked at me sternly. I felt betrayed by this wretched woman. She lied literally to everyone, depending on what she wanted from them. It made me sick to even be near her.

"I see," I replied, all traces of emotion gone from my voice. Two could play at this game. I nodded in the affirmative, and she gave me a triumphant smile. I walked outside, where the enormous alligator rested, blocking most of the street. The cart lay behind it, pointing in the direction of the palace. Toussaint waited for us near his massive friend, petting it gingerly.

"We'll do whatever it takes to help out," I said, before Angelina could put a word in edgewise. I was acting out of spite, but at least gone was the mind-numbing fear that usually lived inside me. She'd managed to bring out the bitch in me, too, but in a way that would at least be a positive influence. Someday I'd get to thank her. Right now I'd only try to avoid her ocular knives, which I knew she must be tossing at my back at this moment.

Afterdeath

"Get in," Toussaint said, pointing to the back of the cart. I made a deferential move to allow my brand new enemy to go first. I knew that the coming ride would be a bumpy one.

Chapter 16

Return

It was the yelling that woke me up. Where was I? Ah. Yes. The cottage. Prisoner of Larunda. Outside my door, footfalls like thunder roared, and animated voices came, though muffled, to my ears. I hadn't slept long, so I felt a bit groggy, and the crash I heard next did nothing to make me feel better. Outside my window shone a radiant sun, completely out of the loop about what was going on inside. Then there was a roar. Iuturna came tumbling through the door, plaster dust sprinkled on her head and shoulders.

"You have to get out!"

If there was ever a time in my life where I wished I'd been dreaming, this was it. I got up, disoriented, a kind of buzzing in my ear. Around the edge of the wall, scores of guards ran down the hall, toward the right, in whatever direction the racket came from. It sounded like demolition. It was the kind of noise you associated with a building coming down after explosive charges had been detonated. Ten feet away from you. I crept to the doorway, and Iuturna grabbed my arm.

"Come on!" she yelled in my face, as another three guards brushed past, and one bumped into me. I finally snapped out of it, shaking my head as if it would clear out the loose bits. Over the banister looking down, I could see more soldiers running toward the front of the cottage. I followed them with my eyes, and then saw It.

Afterdeath

The enormous, grey-skinned stone giant we'd run away from a few days previous. Smashing its fists through the ceiling of the cottage, near the entrance. A look of pure hatred distorting its features, chunks of tile, timbers and dust raining down on the frightened guards below it. They kept out of its reach and fired single-shot weapons at it, retreating to reload.

The giant reached in, snapped up a soldier and threw it in the distance, its normal human features turning skeletal as it crossed the beam of sunlight that streamed in from the damaged roof. Over its shoulder the soldier went, then it resumed the pummelling, widening the hole. I was surprised at how resistant the house was: it should have crumbled at the first assault. Then again, should I have been surprised about something animated by Larunda's power?

I shrugged off Iuturna's grip, and stopped a guard about to run past me. He wheeled around, eyes wide, and I asked him where the armoury was, and he stammered,

"Down the hallway, downstairs. The passage is blocked, miss!" pointing at the obvious trouble I'd have going down the stairs. I let him go and he ran to his garrison preparing to fire at the beast.

I ran down the hallway, away from the fight, Iuturna in tow. I climbed over the banister and lowered myself slowly, one foot down the wall after the other.

"Where are you going?" she said, leaning over.

"To get a gun or knife or something."

"A what?" That was the last thing I heard, because I jumped. Now, if I'd been alive, the angle at which my ankle bent would be a clear indication that it was broken, that I'd need to go to the hospital immediately, and perhaps give up any hope of playing tennis for a few weeks. Or the rest of my life. This not being the case, I picked myself up and stretched out my foot and ankle, watching it go from that crazy, awkward angle to its normal position. I looked around, and saw that a bit further to my left, guards were exiting with what looked like a small cannon on spoked wheels. I ran into the room and looked around. There were halberds and rifles, pikes and cutlasses, although fewer now that the stores had been picked almost clean by the soldiers.

I chose a repeater rifle; a long gun with an ornate stock. It was light with a polished black barrel. I'd get it dirty soon enough. I just wished I knew what the hell I was doing.

Outside, the soldiers were massed directly down the hall. The giant had set foot inside the cottage, and looked wedged about the waist. It stretched as far as it could go with one arm, trying to snag more defenders. The ricocheting gunfire did nothing to stop it, only made it set about knocking down the rest of the roof so it could come in completely.

I took a deep breath. Then I started to run.

As I came nearer the guards, the booming of immense fists on the roof became the crash of the entire structure. Skeletal soldiers shrieked as the ceiling collapsed on those who'd been directly in front of the giant. Upraised hands disappeared under a hail of debris, flattened.

I did not stop, even when the thing peered into the cottage, sniffing and turning its head about, beady eyes roaming from the upper staircase where soldiers took a few precautionary steps back, to me charging toward it.

As I reached it, the ceiling above me imploded, wooden debris crashing down all around, stopping me in my tracks, blind. A cry rose among the soldiers behind me. As I stood there, wiping my face from all the dust that had followed the destruction, its enormous bare leg, as large as an oak tree, floated before my blurry eyes. The room was white with dust, and everything save the hole in the roof and this leg were visible.

Another volley of rifle shot came from above me, aimed at where its face should be, and I felt a rush of wind above my head, something immense swinging at the stairs, crashing into wood, breaking it like kindling. I heard cries of surprise and fear, and then silence. The dust began to settle.

I raised my weapon, my blood pumping madly, and a gigantic arm descended from above and swept away whatever few soldiers had been foolish enough to stay in its path, smashing one to the wall, and grabbing another.

It lifted the man, dragging him into the sunlight which turned him to a skeleton in uniform away from the cottage's protection. Squeezed him, popping him like a grape, then, wiped its fingers on the ground, leaving a long, wet streak in the dust and debris.

As the dust settled, turning everything to a chalky white, I saw an enormous and horrific head, furrowed brow and beady eyes, searching for something around the room. A booming voice came from the yellow-toothed orifice that was its mouth:

"MISTRESS?" it cried. I held my rifle shakily, unnerved by this beast with the appearance of a man. I shot and hit it in the shoulder, black ichor trickling down. Its giant head swivelled in my direction. I quickly reloaded, as I felt the piercing gaze of two barrel-sized eyes.

"MISTRESS!" it yelled, and its eyes seemed to fill with delight for a moment, before I fired upon it again, and hit slightly above its left eye. It yelled in pain and clutched the dripping wound. I took this opportunity to run like hell, up what was left of the stairs, on the left.

It was then that I saw Carson, who I'd thought dead, climbing down from the giant's back.

Afterdeath

"What the hell are you doing?" I yelled.

"I came to rescue you guys. I thought you could use the help." He said, climbing down the giant's knee. Whatever guards had survived had fled, leaving only Carson, the giant, me and...

"Who are you?" Iuturna yelled, from a safe place down the second-floor hallway.

"A friend of Chloe, Olivia, Brock, Angelina and Barkley. Who are you?"

"I am a servant of the lady Larunda." She answered, lifting her nose.

"Yeah, about that. You know the lady wants my friends for her own ends, don't you?"

"Carson, how the hell did you survive?" I asked, as he came toward me.

"Long story. Listen, we have to get out of here. Where are your sister and the others?" Looking around, perhaps thinking they were hidden.

"The lady! She comes!" Iuturna said, and hid behind an overturned dresser at the top of the stairs.

I looked about, as, at the feet of the giant, sand churned. It rose up from between the floor tiles, poured out from the walls, and began to run up its and Carson's legs. I reflexively took a step back.

"Crap," he said, trying to pull up his stuck leg, a shudder in the floor below him breaking into a large hole. Tiles snapped and jolted. Oozing sand began to flow like a geyser up the length of the giant's body, covering it. It pushed the sand off as best it could with both hands, brushing at it, but it kept crawling, right up to its head, covering the entirety of its body, like an army of beige ants too tiny and numerous to stop.

A disembodied voice yelled, filling the air: "Filthy creature. Destroying my house and ruining my sleep." The giant tried to yell, and opened its mouth wide. Sand flowed into it, and a moment later, it fell to its knees, barely missing crushing Carson. The sand rushed furiously about over its body, and it reminded me of a documentary I'd once seen about African ants, eating a carcass until there were only the bones left. The mass of sand looked like it was shrinking, but sick realization told me it was consuming the giant underneath it. Carson tried to move away, but his legs were stuck in the flowing sand. I ran down the stairs, and he yelled:

"What the hell is this stuff?"

A clump of slimy sand began to rise like a spire between Carson and I, changing into the shape of a woman, becoming more defined, until I recognized Larunda, her stomach distended and round. Some of the guards who'd run away during the fight came walking back from wherever it was they'd been ducking. Larunda grabbed Carson by the hair, and made him speak for her turning his head so that she stared directly into his eyes:

"Me. Tell me, cur, why I should let you go on existing?" Carson said, in that imperious tone I'd heard coming from Iuturna before.

Carson tried to stare at his own mouth, gaping like a fish.

"Because I'm a great harmonica player and I've been told I'm indigestible?" he said, gulping. His face changing to that of an angry queen's, spitting through clenched teeth:

"What were you hoping to achieve by destroying my home? Iuturna!" she screamed, and just then Iuturna jumped up from her hiding place, running and navigating the debris-strewn stairs as best she could, all the while tripping and falling.

"Yes my Lady! Here I am! So sorry my Queen!" she said, getting on her knees in the filth at the foot of Larunda, directly into a beam of sunlight. She was bleached bones and a simple dress, prostrate before her owner. I looked at her and felt a churning in my stomach, both disgusted at her behaviour and her treatment.

"Useless girl. I'll have to put you to gardening for a few years to show you proper respect!" she said through her slave, Iuturna's skull turning scornful.

"Yes, my Lady. A thousand pardons, my Lady," Iuturna's normal visage said. Then it was Larunda taking over Iuturna again, turning to poor trapped Carson:

"Well, speak!"

"Listen, I'd heard it was made of gingerbread. I was feeling hungry. You can't blame a guy for getting the munchies, can you?" he said, giving her an impish grin, splaying his hands.

"Silence! You dog! I've had enough of your lies! To the dungeons with you," she said through Iuturna, and snapped her fingers. The ground below him crackled and caved, and he fell straight down. I thought of backing away slowly, but where would I have gone?

Larunda then turned to me. I was halfway down the stairs, wondering what was going to happen now. Her scowl turned to a smile, though strained, and she asked:

"Do you know that man, dear?" much like a snake appears to be smiling when its mouth is half-opened, swaying side to side to hypnotize you.

"Yes, I do. I thought he was dead, though. He helped us escape the city when the bounty hunters came for us." A random piece of plaster fell from the side of a wall on the other end of the room.

"Won't you look at this mess," Larunda/Iuturna said, turning to look straight out the hole in the ceiling. Larunda put her hands together, fingers intertwined, indexes extended. A piece of rubble trembled by my foot, on the dirty red of the stair's carpeting. It shot straight up, followed by the timbers strewn around on the ground. Plaster, tiling and dust swarmed from the ground, turning like slow tornadoes in the air. Larunda's face reddened, a vein bulging softly from eyebrow to hairline. The tornado of detritus turned more rapidly, and rose to where it had been dislodged. The woman's face was now a deep crimson, and her clenched teeth shone white against the unsavoury tomato colour of her skin.

I looked around, and all that was left were the corpses of the soldiers on the floor around us and on the stairs. The hole in the ceiling patched, Iuturna had returned to a more human form.

Larunda exhaled, and her face regained its composure.

"That's better, isn't it?" One hand on Iuturna's head, she then lifted the other up over her head like a composer, but instead of a band striking up, it was the bodies of the soldiers that jumped up, by increments, marionettes on strings. Their heads lolled from side-to-side, as Larunda twiddled her fingers over her head. Their bodies bounced to a beat that Larunda alone could hear in her mind, and they crowded around her in a circle, slack, yet dancing for her. I could see her, over their heads, from where I stood. There must have been a hundred of them, all told, jiggling to her unheard tune, heads rolling back and forth on their chest, boots clomping in unison on the ground.

Larunda smiled at them, the same way a child might after opening a much-wanted gift. She took a deep breath, and held it for a moment, before exhaling in a circle around her, to all those gathered in her thrall. When she turned past me, I had to turn my nose away to avoid the smell of burned toast that emanated from her. Every last soldier she breathed upon came to life, their heads snapping up. After all of them stood still and at attention, Larunda put her dancing fingers down, and the soldier's heels touched the ground, in one, very loud clack.

Their eyes opened, not all at the same time, but within a few seconds, and they looked around them, first confusion, then joy spreading on their faces as they recognized their mistress.

"You may return to your posts, my boys. You've done a good job." The men saluted her and turned around, going up both staircases. Those that passed me didn't even look at me, as if I was invisible. I looked up the right side staircase and saw Iuturna approaching with careful steps.

For the first time I noticed that Larunda looked pained. I remembered the night before, after she'd ingested the greever. This looked far worse. Her face was greenish-grey, with colour draining fast. I'd been so busy watching all the weirdness that I hadn't noticed the change coming over her.

"Go back to your room. I'll have you sent for." Larunda/Iuturna said faintly, her form melting back to that of oily sand. I walked down the steps, crossed the entrance and nodded to Iuturna before going up the opposite staircase. Larunda was slipping into the cracks and hole in the ground, until, finally, a slab of stone popped up from below and sealed it. As I passed the paintings on the wall, I wondered what new nightmare she'd give birth to.

Barnard and some other manservant I hadn't been introduced to followed me, but made no attempts to direct or hold me. I walked diffidently to my room, glaring at both men as I pulled the door open and closed it behind me in one swift jerking motion. I walked, stiff-legged to my bed, and there, staring at the wall I collapsed. I didn't know whether to laugh or cry, my emotions tumbling out in a swirl. Carson was alive, and for that I was grateful, but for how much longer? Would Larunda be downstairs right now in her dungeon, extracting information through some onerous methods? No, the way she'd looked, she was probably laid up, trying to digest a giant. I hoped she would kick the bucket, or whatever it was monarchs suffered when they bit off more than they could chew. I had trouble imagining her birthing something worse than the giant as a nightmare, but then the rumbling started. My head jerked up. Was another giant attacking? Certainly not. The walls and floor shook for a moment, and then were still. Paintings on two of the walls wiggled and jerked comically, but I knew that whatever was happening in the bowels of the cottage was no laughing matter.

After the fourth tremor, Iuturna came into my room.

"What the hell is going on?" I asked.

"Larunda. She is sick beyond anything I've ever witnessed before. It was that giant she consumed. She writhes on the floor of her room like a garter snake trying to give birth to a watermelon. Some black thing is trying to escape her, and her manservants are having trouble containing it. No spelled frame is large enough to contain it," she said.

"What do you want to do?" I said. I just wanted to escape. Of course, with Carson in some prison in the basement, running away had ceased being an option.

"I want to save my mother and get away from here. I would like to take my father as well, but I'm afraid the spell on him is too powerful to break. Can you help me?"

"But how? There's some sort of force-field containing everyone inside! Can't we wait until tonight? Then we might have a chance, since they'll be free from their prison." I said.

She shook her head in negation, saying: "By that time, she'll have freed herself from the nightmare she's creating. It'll be too late. We have to act now, while she is distracted."

I would have given anything to help her, but I had no idea how to break into that cavern. Maybe Carson would know. His association with Brock and his father might have taught him how to use dobluth. We had to get him out first, then we might have a better chance.

Afterdeath

"We have to go down there and get Carson out." I said.

"No! The Mistress is down there! We'll certainly get caught! We'll be made to suffer just as much as he will!"

"What will she do to him?" I asked.

"If she finds no use for him as a hostage, she'll consume him." She said, matter-of-factly, and a bulging in my stomach sank two degrees.

"I'll only help you get your mother out if we get Carson first. I have no idea how to open that force-field. I'm not that *thing* I used to be. He's had experience with this sort of thing, so we need him to help us. Besides, we'll be better off three than just two. What do you say?" I said, looking her in the eye. She stopped to consider everything at play. She looked more resigned than accepting, but nodded in the affirmative anyhow. She extended her hand and pulled me out of bed. Around us, the walls still trembled at regular intervals. All guards had gone back to their rooms. That had been their orders, and that is what they'd done.

We crept downstairs, past the haunting nightmare paintings, and I wondered what would be the next. Worse than these? Hard to imagine. Down the red carpeted stairs to the tiny door on the first floor. The iron hinges cried when we pulled on the wooden door, and I cringed a moment, thinking we would be caught. But no, all available hands would be nurses and doctors at the delivery room, ready to catch the horror that would flail its way out of its mother.

We stepped, ever so carefully down stone steps that vibrated every so often. Small rivulets of dust dislodged and landed in my hair, caught in my throat. I repressed the need to sneeze, and advanced in the soft glow of candelabra in tiny alcoves along the tight space of the steps.

Thoom!

Walls shook. Candlelight wavered. Dust fell.

I couldn't say how far we'd gotten when I began to hear the screaming. It was an agonizing sound, as if someone were being torn limb from limb. I was not sure anymore if I wished even that on Larunda, but there was no way I could stop it from happening. Iuturna led me still, and once in a while, stopped to gaze at me with frightened eyes. I would bite my lip and nod my chin down the stairs, and our progress would resume.

Forever later, the basement door was reached, and we peaked though a crack. The hallway was empty, but the sounds of agony boomed down them like cannon fire, and I had to plug my ears for fear of going deaf.

The bellowing came from the right, and I was relieved that Iuturna took me into the opposite direction. The reek of a field of burning outhouses filled the corridor, foetid and nauseating. We hurried along the wall like raccoons incognito, the deep shadows cast by the sallow candles helping us along. No guards came around the corner to interrupt us, and she opened the fifth wooden door on our right with ease, a skeleton key in her hand and a smile on her face as she unlocked it with a "toc".

Carson lay on a straw-filled mat in a corner of the stone cell. His annoyed look was replaced by one of joy when he saw us peer into his holding place.

"What took you so long?" he said, getting up, and running to give me a hug.

"We had better things to do. Listen, your cousin betrayed us. I wanted to tell you before, but I never got the chance." I said. Carson's face became grim.

"Where is he?" he asked.

"Gone to get my sister back. Larunda needs her to make us "one" again. Long story. We have to go now."

"You will help us get my mother and father out, yes?" Iuturna said.

"Yeah, about that. I promised her we'd get her parents free. Larunda has her mom trapped in a cave with a lot of other people not far from here." I said.

"I don't think we have time for that." Carson said, wondering.

"We'll make the time." I said, firmly. "She's the one who helped me get you out."

Carson shrugged, "Right. We'll make the time, then. Can we get out of here before this whole place comes crashing down? Does either of you know what the heck is going on?" We all headed out the door and back where we'd come from, the booming screams almost knocking us sideways. Like an enormous wind, it raced down the tunnels and placated anything stupid enough to find itself in its path. Namely, us.

"The Lady has eaten that giant you were with. She is expelling the part she could not digest. All the evil within it is being born into a new form," Iuturna said.

"That's a whole lot of bad. You know, that thing was looking for you, Chloe, as well as your sister. It said you called to it. Not in any literal sense, mind you. It *felt* you. That might explain all the problems you've been having since you and your sister died, come to think of it. I knew there was something off about all those greevers showing up on our doorstep."

"Are you kidding me?" I said, opening the door to the staircase. A violent curse-storm slammed the door behind us as we piled onto the staircase.

"Not at all. It said it was one of your followers. Been surviving in the wild, eating greevers for years now. Like I said: whatever comes out of Larunda now will be tough to handle. Shame about that giant, though," Carson said, as we hurried up the steps.

We ran outside, and the sun was beginning its descent behind the trees. Purples and pinks danced on the last of the clouds strewn across the skies, and I paused for an instant to admire it. The tremors could barely be felt now, and the screaming had been muffled to silence by the thick rock that separated us from Larunda's room. I was thankful for that, at least.

Afterdeath

Iuturna ran down the path, half-skeleton, half-ghost, and I followed, with Carson close behind. We jumped over rocks and ducked under branches until we came to the tiny cave mouth that hid the entrance to the tunnel, where all the traitors to Larunda had been secreted away— followers of my sister and I. Could this even be happening?

"Carson, how can I get in? I'm supposed to have this power inside me, to go through dimensions, but I have no idea how to use it. I might be able to use it to break past this barrier. You knew Brock and his father, Charon. How did he cross over?" I said, looking at him expectantly.

"No idea," he answered, crossing his arms and looking at the open cave mouth with curiosity.

"He does not know? Why did we even bother to save him?" Iuturna yelled, waving her arm in Carson's direction.

"Relax. I said I didn't know. I didn't say I couldn't find out. You're a very excitable person," he said, still looking at the opening, but giving a calming motion with his hand behind him.

Iuturna crossed her arms and turned away.

"We don't have time for this. Soon the sun will set, and Larunda will have expunged her body of the Evil. Then it might be loosed upon is. We have to get them out before then!" she said.

"That goes without saying, but how?" I replied.

"Come here," Carson said.

I came nearer the entrance and knelt down beside him.

"Try to put your hand into the cave."

I did, and felt a buzzing where my hand should have gone straight in. An invisible force stopped me from doing so, as if a mildly electrified wall pushed back every time I tried to enter.

"No can do. It won't let me," I said, sitting down, and shaking off the buzz that had taken a hold of my hand.

"Okay, okay. No problem. Um," Carson said, and we all realized that the earth's trembling had stopped. The last of the sun's rays was slipping away, leaving darkness in its wake. "Try it again, but this time close your eyes."

Iuturna had turned toward us and was staring hard. She was now back to her human form. She was just as worried as we were, I could tell. Whatever was back at the cottage was now out, and we had no way of telling if it had been contained or if it would break loose at any moment. I took a deep breath and put my hand against the field, closing my eyes, just as he said. The mild electric shock ran to my elbows, unpleasantly, and I wondered how long I'd be able to hold on.

"Now, imagine there is no field. That you are through," he said. The buzz went through my arm, and up to my armpit. Then it was touching my neck and breasts, face, back of the neck, and I fell. I opened my eyes and saw the dirt I was lying on.

"I'm through!" I coughed, getting up on my hands. In the lack of light, I could only perceive silhouettes moving about. They were coming closer. One stood directly in front of me and I put up my hands protectively. It came for me anyhow, embraced me tenderly, and I smelled musty earth.

"Mistress, you've returned," it said, in a woman's voice. It then let me go, and passed by me. I sat on my haunches and turned around. Through the narrow opening, I could see shades passing, materializing as they stepped outside. I crawled on my hands and knees to the exit and stood. Outside, I could see the captives appearing, one after the other, becoming solid. They were emaciated, as if they hadn't been fed in a very long time, and my heart sank to see these poor souls.

Iuturna gripped her mother in her arms, and they both cried tears of joy. In all, I'd say about forty people were freed. All of them surrounded me, under Carson's bemused stare, and smiled weakly to have me be back. I felt ashamed for not remembering a single one. Their clothes hung shabby off their bony frames. They reminded me of horrible photographs I'd seen of prisoners during World War II, barely human at all.

It was at that moment that the purple starling Gassire landed on a branch above our heads and twittered: "You must all leave! A terrible thing has been unleashed! Run!"

But I knew it was too late, as the sound of the earth rending open came from the direction of the house, like bombs going off in a mine.

Chapter 17

MAMAN MARGOT

"Where are you taking us?" I felt that my voice carried a bit too far down the early-morning cobblestones, and I mentally clapped myself over the mouth to prevent another outburst.

"Voir la Maman," said Toussaint, into the slit I had opened between him and I, as Angelina and Barkley rested on his bed. She was giving me the evil eye every time I turned to her, so I eventually stopped looking in her direction. I took no pride in my betrayal, but I suspected she was more used to being the traitor, and did not even come to grips with the fact that what I'd done, she did fifty times a day.

"Maman Margot is one of the most powerful Loa," Toussaint said. "We can trust her to know what to do."

As homes trickled by, I kept half an eye on the greevers patrolling the streets. Not a one gave the man and his enormous companion a second glance, as its paws scritch-scratched on the cobblestones. Whether out of respect or fear, I would never get to know. We were at that point of the morning where the only thing stirring were mindless guards and puddles we'd cross with Toussaint's cart. Perhaps two hours past midnight, at the latest. Our absence had not yet been discovered, yet I knew it would not take long until it was, making us enemy number one. How fast would they make the connection between our absence and our present host? Were his allegiances already in doubt? If not, he'd take a fall, just like we would, and would quite possibly suffer the same fate. Was I even worried for his crocodile? I guess I was, a little.

It was hard for me to fathom how someone could shirk off their life debts so easily. I was scared, of course, but Toussaint had saved us. Letting an opportunity pass to repay him was wrong, no matter how dangerous an act had to be committed to even the plains of karma. How could Angelina not understand this? To me it was unconscionable.

A too-large moon hovered over the harbour waters, reminding me once again that I was far from home. Melancholy drifted like silk webs over me, and I rested my cheek on the sliding door between me and the outside world, even more alien now. I could tell when the Wraith guards sauntered by, the air turning acrid like chemical fire for a moment, before returning to a sweet chill.

My heart skipped a beat as we stopped by the city gates; one moment, two moments too long. Would we be discovered? Would Toussaint be suspect in this late exit from the city? The cart winced on its way, and we sighed in relief. The cobblestones gave way to dirt track, and the sound of wheels churning sand. The tiny window opened, allowing me a view of the extended cemetery by the ocean, with silent waves rolling in. We followed a winding coast to our left, the landscape going up, and on a promontory far off, I could see the black outlines of a squat, square shape, like an unadorned castle. From this distance, flickers of matches burned at intervals on its face, and only when we got close enough I recognized them as lit windows, tiny, vertical slits bathed in orange light.

The wind picked up, and the tall weeds on the edge of the cliffs bowed in our direction a moment. I rubbed my shoulders for warmth, and stared at the approaching structure. The pat, pat, patting of the Crocodile's gait was covered only by the sound of the creaking wheels of the cart. It was then I noticed that Toussaint had been humming something, and that his steed's head swayed this way and that. I could not tell if enormous crocodiles could smile, but I know I did. For the first time since I'd arrived, I felt safe. It was a fleeting feeling, I knew, and would dissipate as soon as I stepped out of the cart, like a dream state, but for now I let it take me: a mother's embrace.

Mother. Father. Sister. Grandmother. I was of two minds about their fate. Now that I knew they were somewhere, not gone forever, it gave me hope. But as I thought about the distance that separated us, my heart would dip again. I could not let despair take me again. I wanted to stay far from becoming one of those angry souls that wandered the Earth, trying to steal people's energies. It was so hard, though. So damned hard.

Sorry, Lord. I didn't mean that.

Angelina sat off the bed, resting her back against it. Barkley lay at her feet, his head on his paws. Whatever she was thinking might not bode well for me. I'd have to deal with that when the time came.

Afterdeath

When the cart came to a stop, I turned around. There was a gap between the building and the land. The stone building, a tall box, was built on a needle of rock that jutted from the ocean. I could see its crashing waves slam into the side of the cliffs on my left, as we were on the edge. The sheer drop gave me vertigo. I pulled my head back into the window, and watched as a drawbridge lowered, chains clinking through metal eyelets, until it thumped on the stone slab on our side of the divide.

"On sort, mes belles. Out you go, my lovelies," Toussaint said, sliding off his seat. We exited through the back door, and I went around the right side of the vehicle, not wanting to have to look all the way down to the slamming seas. A rush of cold wind made me lose my balance, and I sidestepped to regain it. Toussaint was running his hand along his beast, and it was putting its massive head down onto the beginning of the drawbridge, its eyes half-lit with a reptilian intelligence. Angelina and Barkley preceded me, and by her sauntering gait I could tell she would rather have been anywhere else. There was a patch of ground that surrounded the lookout tower, (or at least, that's how I'd describe the thing), and it ran around the building. Instead of going toward the medium-height front door, Toussaint walked to the left of the stone wall and rounded it.

The drop was so close I was afraid of falling every time a gust shouted from the depths. I turned around to see, in the extreme distance, the ring shape of the city we'd left, like a crown of thorns, volutes of smoke rising from lit chimneys, the pins of light like needle-point single-pixel dots, and the ship masts on the water's edge a forest of naked trees, standing in a semicircular row.

I went around the corner, and on the edge of the cliff sat a slim black woman, facing the sea. From behind, I could see her flowing, wavy brown hair under an orange headscarf. A beige shawl covered her shoulders, and when she got up, I was surprised to see her in a simple white blouse with frilled collar and orange plaid ankle-length skirt. I had surmised that this person Toussaint was bringing us to would be another deity or monarch or some such. What I was not expecting was such a humble woman. Her kindly face was not as aged as I thought she would have been, either. When someone is named "Maman", or, "Mother", you expect someone in the grandmotherly stages of her life, not the stunning person which was now judging us with her soft gaze.

"Maman Margot, I have brought you *les filles*," said Toussaint, kissing her hand, and she nodded, smiling at him.

"So you have, Toussaint. Merci," she answered, and her voice was music that trickled from heaven. Barkley approached her, tail tucked between his legs, head bowed, looking up to her with pleading eyes.

"Poor boy. You've suffered much, haven't you? Let's go inside," Maman said, and turned toward the building. I stared at her in wonder as she passed me, and she glanced at me before walking by, a trail of delicate flower smells following her. I blushed and turned away, shaking my head.

I thought I heard Angelina mutter to herself, but I was not sure what she said, and didn't think much about it.

We walked back to the front and she put her hand to the door, a loud clang sounding before it let us in. A soft glow of fire admitted us into the cozy first floor of the tower, a small fire pit blazing in the centre of the room, wood crackling every so often. Over it, a metal frame held a black iron kettle, roughened by age, from which floated a sweet smelling vapour. Around the fire-pit were five wooden chairs that reminded me of the kind used in schools, a long time ago. These had lost their varnish, and their bolts were blackened, the wood tarnished and grey. She went to the furthest one and sat, crossing her legs, leaning back with a creak. She indicated we should do the same, and I found myself going to sit on her right, while Toussaint sat on her left. Barkley took the chair next to Toussaint, and Angelina next to me.

Maman Margot turned to Angelina first:

"Why did you come back, child?" she said.

"Hey, I had no say in the matter. This one broke us out of jail," she said, sticking her thumb in my direction. I glared at her, and saw that she was glaring right back.

"You stole a ride from us! We had no idea where we were! You're such a liar!" I said, indignant.

"And who are you, ma petite?" Maman Margot said, her tone softening as she turned to me.

"I'm Olivia Borders. My twin sister Chloe and I died a few days ago in a car accident. I just want to get back to life! Angelina said she knew how to help us, but now I'm not so sure." I said, frowning.

"Did she, now," Maman said, turning to the source of my troubles. Angelina refused to look her in the eye. Barkley groaned. I felt a sinking feeling in the pit of my stomach. She'd lied to us. I knew it. Again. There was no going back. I bit back anger and the urge to hit her in the face.

"Has she told you the reason why she was put away, and her man turned to his present form, Olivia Borders?" she asked.

"Because she stole something from the Baron Something or Other?"

"Yes, but did she also tell you that her fate could have been much worse, and his as well?" Maman Margot said.

Afterdeath

"You didn't help at all! I was kept in that forest for ages, battling off the Vapours of Horror you so-called monarchs keep in there as pets!" Angelina fairly yelled, and she got up and prepared to storm off.

"Sit down!" Maman yelled, in a voice so cavernous that the buried dead for a thousand kilometres must have felt tremors rain down their desiccated spines. Angelina paused, then took her seat again. Her voice once again calm, she continued. "I was at her trial. If she were honest, she would tell you that I interceded in her favour. I was the one who convinced the other monarchs to let her continue in her present form, and that her punishment would be the reincarnation of her man. If they had had their way, you, Angelina," and she stared her deep into the eyes, "would have been absorbed until nothing was left of you."

"Might have well let them do it, for all I've gone through," Angelina sniffed. Barkley lay on his stomach, his head nodding in exasperation.

"Ungrateful woman," Maman said.

"But it doesn't matter! Baron Dimanche got another dobluth ember, obviously, since he's back to doing what he's always done! I lost the one I borrowed. I couldn't give it back if I wanted to!" I tried not to blush, but despite myself, my cheeks warmed. I just hoped Maman would not detect it as my knowing Angelina was lying between her teeth. As much as I detested her, she was my only link to Chloe, and giving her away might not be my best option, given the circumstances.

She did not look at me, but kept her eyes on Angelina. A silence grew, where their locked eyes became more than uncomfortable.

"The Baron does not have a new ember, you impertinent fool," Maman said, jutting her chin at Angelina, "he has one on loan, from that Prince of Evil, Hades."

I saw Toussaint's eyes widen, as if some unconfirmed suspicion had just been proven true.

"Why would he accept to take his?" he asked, perplexed.

"There is rumour of a deal," Maman said, and she extended her hand toward the lazily floating smoke that fluted from the kettle. The smoke took on a humanoid form, then resembled that of the Baron Dimanche.

"Without his ember, the baron is just a man. He cannot control the souls of the dead," Maman Brigitte said, and the smoke man raised his fists in fury. "After the trial, where Angelina was sent off to pay her penance, he was desperate to regain what he'd lost." The smoke Dimanche's back was bowed, looking dejected. Another figure appeared beside him. Larger, with squared shoulders. It wore a mask of iron, the only thing visible beyond it his roiling black eyes like pits.

"Hades. He appeared one day, many years après, and proposed a bargain. The use of his gem, if the Baron could gather an army of greevers for him. He even provided the weapons and cloaks to control them. But it would be Hades who would take control when the time came," she said, and the smoke became a field of death, covered in shambling Lost Souldiers, marching away from their new lord Hades.

"What does Hades want with an army? Why doesn't he make his own?" I asked.

"That, ma petite, is a very good question. I do not know. But I know how to get his ember. Take it, and he will no longer have the power to gather his army. Perhaps then we can stop whatever Hades is planning," Maman said.

Angelina burst out laughing.

"What is so funny?" Maman asked.

"You," Angelina replied, pointing a finger. "You would betray your man, after you condemned me to prison for doing the same thing you are now begging us to do. Hypocrites, the lot of you."

Maman rose to her feet, and the door behind Angelina flung open, cracking against the wall. Her expression slacked as she tried to get up, but something pushed her back down, pinning her to her chair. It slid on its hind legs out the door, and the door slammed shut.

"It's hard to have this conversation when we are so rudely interrupted all the time," Maman Margot said, one side of her mouth rising in a wry smile. I tried to smile, but I was too frightened by what I'd just seen. "Toussaint?" she said, and the old man rose from his chair, going towards the door, opening it gently and closing it behind him. I was left with Maman and Barkley, and once again, silence hung in the air like the vapours from the mysterious kettle.

Barkley looked back toward the door and then at the woman to my right.

"No, do stay a bit," she said. "Have you told her yet?" and I wondered what she meant by that. Barkley just nodded no in answer.

"Why not?" Maman said, and I stared intently at the dog, wondering where this conversation was going.

"I'm still angry with her," came the reply, in a deep voice, tinged with a hint of sadness. I felt my eyes widen beyond the scope of my skull, and I fell back against the chair. Barkley had talked. Not possible.

"Don't misunderstand, I love her with all my heart, but I'd rather she keep on thinking I'm just a dog," he said, and turned to me, with a pleading look.

"I won't tell," Maman said, turning to me. "Will you?"

"Baaaah..." is all the sound that came out of my mouth. I was too stunned to say anything coherent. I realized I was gripping the side of my chair with both hands, expecting to fall off, and let go, my fingers white-knuckled.

"Please?" Barkley said, looking at me. I just stared at him. Barkley the talking dog. I'd woken up in death a few days ago and had had to fend off greevers, ghosts and mercenaries. This was the thing that caught me off guard? I relaxed a bit while Barkley kept making a pitiful look at me to make me crack.

"No fair!" I said, "No using puppy-dog eyes! Fine. I'll keep it a secret," and crossed my arms. The things I had to put up with, I swear. Whatever slim chance I had of getting back to my old life again, I was certain I would not waste by telling anyone of the things I had gone through. That was a sure recipe for ending up in a psychiatric ward!

"Go to your mistress, Barkley. Secrets such as these should not be kept. She will be angrier than usual when she finds out your betrayal," Maman said, and Barkley replied:

"I know," and shrugged. Maman lifted a hand, and the door opened, Barkley hopping from his seat onto the stone floor, and past the threshold. Maman folded her hand, and the door closed with a sigh.

She turned to me and said: "Will you help me? I do not want whatever it is Hades is planning to come to fruition. Will you be my agent?" and I wondered why it was up to me to do this. Yes, I'd agreed to when Toussaint had asked, but it hadn't seemed real then. Like I was accepting to ride off into a dream to vanquish imaginary monsters. Now things had become concrete, and the stakes real. A goal and an outcome were imminent, and my survival as well. I tried to find that comfort zone I'd inhabited not so long ago, but it, of course, had evaporated. Now there lay before me a path, straight as a razor, which I had to walk very carefully upon if I wanted not to slip and fall. At the end of the path, cross-roads, where luck and skill would determine which one I, we, would take. Would we be successful, and steal the ember? Would we be caught, and made to suffer for our failure? My mind kept dwelling on failure, and the almost guarantee of its occurrence.

"What happens if... what happens when we get the dobluth ember? What do we do then?" I asked.

"Simple. Use it to take you back to wherever you want to go." A field with an ambulance flashed in smoke, a body on a stretcher beside it. "It has that power. Employ it," she replied.

"What does it look like?" I asked, and Maman extended her hand to the silky smoke before us. The Baron's shape appeared once more. He was surrounded by other dignitaries in a palatial home. He held a fluted glass with wisps of smoke within it, and his dinner jacket was stunningly ornamented with bulbous gold buttons. On each button, a tiny bone lay inlaid, like a jewel. The second from top was the one, I was sure.

"The one with the finger bone is the one you want. Take it from him, and wish yourself in another place, and there you shall appear," she said, and the Baron's shape dissipated.

"Can you show me my sister?" I asked, wondering what the smoke could produce.

"Let me see..." she answered, and her hand fluttered before her eyes for a moment, her sight going dim. The kettle began to shake, liquid popping and boiling out of the spout, and a vomit of smoke poured out of it, through the bouncing lid and spout, spreading throughout the room. Armed guards ran back and forth, fighting an enormous thing, its shape indiscernible and vast, taking up the middle of the room. Legs like a millipede covered its long body, writhing like waves in the air. Another group fought the soldiers, unarmed, and were being slaughtered left and right. They wore tattered rags and looked as if they had not been fed in months. Between the monster, the poor buggers and the military, Chloe was raising a sword in one hand, her mouth an "Ah!" of anger. I could practically smell the fear and chaos, the din of battle only in my head.

Then it all went away, and the vapours disintegrated. Maman Margot sat on her chair, her elbows on her knees, hands on her face.

"This only one possible future of many, but probabilities are great that it will happen. You have to go help her, and you have no time to waste," she said. "Go get the ember, and it will take you to her before all this happens. Go!"

I rose to my feet and ran to the door. My heart beat like a thousand war drums on automatic fire. The crocodile opened an eye as I flew past him, and I found Barkley, Toussaint and Angelina behind the cart, sitting down. Angelina's eyes were red, and Toussaint was patting her on the shoulder. Barkley looked up at me expectantly, and I frowned a bit before saying:

"We have to go, right now. My sister's in danger. We have to get that ember, thing, from the Baron. Get in," I cried. Toussaint looked at me with a curiosity, and Angelina as if she couldn't care less.

"What the hell are you waiting for?" I screamed. "You wanted me to help you, and I'll help you. But it has to be now. There isn't time to waste," I said angrily.

"What makes you think I want to help you," Angelina said with a sniffle.

"Look at me," I said, grabbing her by the front of her shirt, "You can go to hell for all I care," an inch away from her face, "I will do this alone if I have to. You've done enough damage to last a lifetime, and I won't include you in future plans. Step out of my way right now. You want to stay here? Fine. Stay. But *do* get off the cart, Angelina," and I threw her sideways onto the grass. She rolled once and pulled herself up. I expected her to be angry, but she looked piteous. Her hands balled into

Afterdeath

little fists, and I imagined myself staring off a six-year-old who might start to cry at any moment. Barkley went to her, putting his head against her leg.

"I don't blame you. You should be with her," I said. "Can we go, Toussaint? That party at the Baron's won't last until morning, will it?" I called to him, still staring down Angelina, who was a bit down the hill from me, some grass sticking to her hair. I turned to him, and he nodded slightly. I watched as he walked around the cart and tapped the crocodile on its flank, and it backed up, the cart turning down the hill, and then the crocodile turning back down the hill and stopping. Toussaint climbed up on his driver's seat, and I took the railing to the back door, then sat down, my legs dangling over the edge. Angelina just stood there, Barkley by her side, as the crocodile pattered away.

I burned, inside. I hadn't felt this way in... ever. Indescribable, how a surge of energy now flowed upward, making my body electric.

"Can we go any faster?" I called around the side of the cart, and with a cluck, the patter became a rumble, jerking me forward and almost off the ledge. I could still see her in the distance, now a tiny figure, insignificant. I sighed and pulled myself upward. I went into the cart and took off my shoes, climbing onto the bed. I knocked on the little door and Toussaint opened it.

"You brave, mam'selle," he said, turning a serious eye to me. An ageless face now peered at me, and I wondered if what he said was true. The crocodile cruised down the hill at speeds I hadn't imagine possible for such an animal, but there it was.

"I just want to help Chloe, Toussaint. My sister needs me," I said. He shrugged.

"Still, of all the paths you chose, it is this one the most difficult. Your sister is a lucky woman to have you." Ahead, the city loomed, and before any greevers could wonder what a speeding crocodile was doing heading straight for them, it slowed to a smooth walk.

Toussaint rummaged inside a bag by his side. He removed a pinch of something chalky and grey.

"Come here," he said, and I leaned forward. He started high on my forehead and brought his thumb between my eyebrows. Then, he began mid-forehead, on my left, and rubbed toward the right. If it was supposed to protect me, I felt no different.

"What does that do?" I asked.

"Makes you invisible to the eyes of Baron Dimanche. You are now completely uninteresting to the likes of him, like any other servant girl in his palace. Tu comprends?" and he gave me a knowing smile.

"Yeah, I think I understand," I said, and as I went to reflexively touch the chalk, he stopped my hand.

"Don't touch it or the spell is broken," he said, and let my hand go. "Now hide."

I closed the little door, stepping off the bed and putting my shoes back on.

The bumping of the wooden wheels on the stone pavement reminded me of a trip to Quebec City, a very long time ago, where horse-drawn carriages climbed the steep hills of the old city. I'd had a family then. Four-hundred year old buildings shrugged against each other like kindred spirits, all plaster, stones and timber. The metal roofs shone under July skies, and Chloe and I had run ahead of our parents to peer over the parapet that made up the defences of the walled city, along the wooden boardwalk. The plunging view of the Saint Lawrence River had been breathtaking in its breadth and scope. We'd eaten on a terrace on black table-cloths, and I remember thinking the silverware had been impossibly shiny, like frozen quicksilver. The shade of an oak tree almost made it to our table from the centre meridian in the street, where a roundabout caroused and the cars circled. The clippety-clop of hooves and clicking of the wheels on virgin-white carriages resounded as we'd eaten our meal. I could still see it when I closed my eyes.

Reality was different in the cool of the night. The mish-mash of houses reminded me of some sort of peculiar disaster. In science-fiction movies, sometimes things materialized together, and were fused. There was no clear demarcation of where one structure began and the other ended, only the patchwork of different materials straddling each other. A surrealist artist would have been hard-pressed to come up with a weirder sight.

Avenues ended abruptly, partially blocked by massive wreckage, an accidental maze, and Toussaint would avoid them, turning this way and that with the expertise of a man who knows his city by heart. I envied him. I'd lived in Oddawa all my life, and don't think I knew half of it. How could that be? Was it possible to be a part of something and not be entirely aware of what went on? That came as a sad shock. There was so much to know, I realized, but I went from place to place without ever taking the time to look around me. I never went strolling. There always had to be a purpose to where I went, and I never made the purpose just meandering. Why would I think about that now, though? Oh, right. I was heading in danger's maw. Maybe it was my regrets popping out of the woodwork, telling me I should have done things differently. Too late for that now.

I now wished Angelina was with me. Not that I liked her, out of the blue, but this whole ordeal would be easier to handle if she'd been by my side. Why had she let me toss her off so easily, anyhow? She wasn't the type of person who'd let anyone push her around, so why now?

I pushed the little window open a crack and checked the wobbly streets for Lost Souls patrolling. When I was satisfied they were out of earshot, I whispered:

"Toussaint. What did you and Angelina talk about, outside Maman Margot's house?"

Afterdeath

The old man was silent for a moment. Was he ignoring me? I knew he wasn't deaf, so his silence was a bit unnerving.

He turned, just a bit, and I saw the corner of his eye, judging mine.

"Angelina, she is ambitious, yes?" This was not a question. "No one is stupid enough to think that she has 'lost' the Baron's power item. I explained to her the misery she's caused to this land since her theft." He shook his head, his lips pursed. He grasped his chin in one hand and rubbed it.

"I don't understand," I said. I had no idea what the use or loss of these things meant. Objects of power, sure, but for what purpose? That much had never been made entirely clear to me.

"You see the city? It is a ruins. Dis ting happened because the Baron no longer has his power. Here's a little story for you, so you know just what kind of lady your Angelina is, chère. In the days after she took off with our Baron's power, there must have been a storm something fierce in the living world, because in one night, half of the buildings you see now appeared, and without his power to direct them, they landed on top of us. A lot of new, angry souls with them. There was carnage for years. People were trapped inside walls, greevers rampaged, draining the energies out of anyone they could find. It was a nightmare. All of that, preventable. My family was taken in that time. That is what I parlayed with the lady Angelina. I tried to get her to give us the power back," Toussaint said.

I felt dry-mouthed and brain-buzzed. I could hear my own breathing through my slack mouth. No words fell out. That was why she looked stricken. I had it in my power to help, though. Should I tell? Should I not? There were no longer buildings, only a forest, inside the city, like a park. The road had become a dirt track again. Crickets chirruped around us in the darkness beyond the lantern-lined road.

"What would he do if he did have it back? Would he stop this war he's planning?" I wondered aloud. In the distance, beyond the crocodile's massive head, a lavish residence was coming into view. Two stories tall, but with wide-set, metal-barred windows, and a flat roof covered in red convex tiles. Perhaps a Spanish Hacienda had bloomed here, and the Baron had taken possession? The pale, rough, plaster walls gave off an aura of noble dignity. The windows alight with candelabra and shadowed by people dancing in full dress regalia. Quite the party was underway. If I had to guess, I would have to say it was around one a.m., but then again, I had no certainty. Who knew how long this would go on until the revellers went home?

There was a tall, black metal gate that surrounded the property, with guards standing at attention at the entrance. Their dress was somewhat more antiquated, as if they were also dressed for the costume party. I assumed this was just some classic army uniform that had been chosen by the baron for his personal guards. Red coats with gold and black epaulets, as well as high black caps with a tassel running to one side. I think I'd seen something similar among uncle Philbert's collection of tin soldiers, but I couldn't be certain now.

I turned back to Toussaint, who was staring at me intently.

"No, je ne pense pas. I don't think so. He's gone too far with Hades to turn back now. He would only be doubly dangerous now." So that was my answer. Whether or not Toussaint would tell anyone if I told him didn't matter. The information could be gotten out of him somehow. I couldn't put Barkley in danger, or Toussaint either, so I might as well keep that knowledge to myself. What a mess.

"Should I hide?" I asked, when I saw we were coming nearer the Baron's home. I didn't think I would go very far as I appeared now, because, even though the vast majority of the population was black, the way I was dressed would get me noticed right quick.

"You don't have to worry. No one notice you. That mark I put on you makes you banal. You are beneath their attention. A house servant, unworthy of acknowledgement. There are some clothes you could put on, tough, in that trunk on the left," and he jerked his thumb backwards. I looked over and saw the wooden box beyond the bed. The same one that had contained the Greever uniforms when we'd first met him. Inside it, was a neat pile of clothing. On top of the pile, lay a white blouse and reddish skirt. The style was reminiscent of Maman Margot's, and I put them on. I found a headscarf, which I slid on, careful not to touch the mark on my forehead. As I put on the sandals, I felt confident that I could pull this off. I wondered if Angelina would have gone along with the idea of becoming a servant girl. It was one thing to agree to transforming into a monster, but another entirely to become someone's inferior. Ego might have played a big part in this whole endeavour, and I think it made me glad I was doing this on my own.

I crawled back to the window as Toussaint's crocodile arrived at the gates. He opened the window wide, and I fought the reflex to hide. Perhaps that made more credible my mummering as a lowly servant, wincing like someone expecting a beating. In any event, the broad-bearded night-skinned guard on the left of the carriage drew near Toussaint's seat, a long pike in one hand.

"Toussaint, ké tu fait là?" he said, pointing his chin at the cart, eyes suspicious. I looked down not wanting to see his angry face. "What are you doing here?" he repeated.

"J'amène une donzelle pour lé festivités. Une servante pour le Baron. You know, he always need more servants." For some reason, the way he said it creeped me out. I peered up with my eyes alone, making sure my head was bent forward in a gesture of submission, and saw the guard smiling at me.

Afterdeath

"'Ello, poussin," he said, cocking his head to peer into my eyes. "Amuses-toi bien ce soir. Have fun tonight," like you would say to a three-year-old.

It was not a nice smile. Muscles bulged under his uniform, and his pike came closer to my face. He smelled of dying fire, of oily charcoal. The leaf-shaped blade pressed against my cheek on its flat side, and I turned my face to look at the guard. I could feel the sharp sides digging slightly into my "flesh", and jerked my head so he wouldn't cut me.

"Don't leave marks, Wilguens, or you'll have to deal with your master's anger," Toussaint admonished. The man named Wilguens smiled even more broadly.

"She'll be a fine addition. Come in, Toussaint. Au revoir petit poussin. Chick-chick-chick!" he said, and retrieved his weapon, and the two men laughed. The other guard stepped back and pulled on the gates, opening them with a long wince. Toussaint's cart began to move again, and I had trouble keeping my heart from exploding out of my chest.

"I thought you said I wouldn't be noticed by anyone!"

"Guards are servants, too. They will notice you. Now remember, be silent unless spoken to," he said to me. "You have no rights here. Say yes to everything that is asked of you. You will be with me, so act like my servant. Don't worry, I am not so cruel as that man at the gate. Never find yourself alone with Wilguens. That is all I have to say," he said, then pressed his lips together in a taut line.

At least I did not have to go in on my own, I thought. My heart was still a mess after that encounter, but there was a hair-line fracture of relief at the thought that Toussaint would be by my side in the Baron's own home. We rounded the corner, and there were other carriages and carts, as well as cars dating back to the 1950's, all parked side by side. It was a jarring image of so many different eras all mingling together, and I had trouble wrapping my head around it. We passed a Ford Model A, then a coach pulled by four gorgeous horses, then a Studebaker, a Buick, and then what looked like a steam train on wheels. I'd never seen anything like it.

Toussaint pulled up next to it, and he unhooked Abner from the cart. He thumped off on his own, heading left into a field where torches had been planted, then further into a copse of trees. I watched him squeeze through, and the tops of the trees waggling dangerously, then he was gone.

"He can take care of himself," Toussaint said, sounding half worried. I smiled, thinking that a three-tonne crocodile could definitely take care of itself.

"Was Abner ever a human, before?" I asked.

"No, he was always a croc. Raised him from a little 'un. He got real big, that one," Toussaint said, with affection.

No doubt, I thought.

We began to walk toward the back of the house, and the servant's entrance, which was further to the left, past the parking lot. Gravel crunched underfoot, and I heard crickets chirping somewhere in the large home's dewy lawn. A few partiers chatted outside near French doors, holding cocktails and laughing politely. Just as Toussaint had said, not a one gave me a second glance. Their incredible dresses and tuxedos made my simple garb pale in comparison. I kept my eyes low, and stayed a few feet away from my "master", wondering what it would have been like to truly be someone's servant. Would I have enjoyed my life at all, if it had belonged to someone else? I thought not. What if every waking moment of every day of my life was dedicated to the happiness of someone else? How could I have been happy, then? Could I have tricked myself into thinking I had found fulfilment? Perhaps some people could. Yet, there had been so many people throughout history who had been forced into servitude to others. Would I have rebelled and died, punished for my insubordination, or would I have accepted my fate and suffered along with all the others around me. I know Angelina wouldn't have. She probably would have started an insurrection and burned down her master's house. I smiled.

"Stop that!" Toussaint hissed, looking at me with severity. I caught myself and stared down at my feet, returning my face to a more neutral pose. We went through a metal door on the side of the house, and a din jumped out from the busy kitchen. Chefs and servants hurried about. Steam rose from boiling cauldrons, and sizzling skillets wafted the scents of grilled meats. The servants carried silver trays of bits and bites on paper doilies from the kitchen to the main house, the door up a short set of stairs across the kitchen. Toussaint approached a large man in Chefs whites, a fine moustache on his pale brown face.

"Aimé, I want you to train this girl for service. She'll be working here tonight. I'll loan her to you," Toussaint said, touching the man on the arm. He nodded and peered over at me. I tried to look as demure as possible, and he nodded, trying to assess what they would need me for.

"Send her to Nadège, she'll train her," Aimé said, pointing his large knife over to a corner, where a woman in a black pleated dress and white cap and apron directed traffic in and out of the main house. The chef then went back to his work, oblivious to our presence.

"I thought the dead didn't need to eat," I said in a whisper to Toussaint.

"They don't need to, doesn't mean they don't. There's no better way to party than to pretend you are still alive," he said. "Now listen, you will do as Nadège says, and eventually you will be allowed to go in the common room. Take this knife," and he slipped a tiny object in my hand. I hid it up my sleeve, blade first. "When you come close enough to the baron, you will offer him some drink or tidbit from the tray. I

Afterdeath

will offer to hold it out to him, as a gesture of respect. While I do so, you will cut the button off from under the tray, and we will make our exit after that. Do you understand?" he said. It seemed simple enough. He just had to keep him distracted long enough for me to get the object and stash it. I was nervous, but confident.

Nadège was a nice enough woman. She started me off in the kitchen, where I fetched the raw ingredients for the chefs and sous-chefs to prepare the enticing foods the other servants kept bringing out to the guests. I worried that by the time I'd be allowed to leave the kitchen, the party would be over, but it did not take long before Nadège became confident in my abilities to put a tray on my arm for me to go out.

"Remember to smile," she said. "They won't care, but try to look like you're having a good time as well." She winked at me, and I gave her a shy smile. "Voila. You are ready, now go," she said, and gave my shoulder a gentle squeeze. I left the sweltering heat of the kitchen for the heavy-scented air of the corridor leading to the main ballroom. I passed other servant girls holding picked-at trays who averted their eyes when I crossed them. Golden, waxy light flickered in lanterns along the walls, from heavy electric globes. Hip-high Asian vases punctuated the walk on either side, filled with tall reeds and dried swamp flowers. I perused walls of coarse adobe with ornamental gold picture frames randomly hung and displaying well-dressed, serious-looking black men and women of ages past. Doors on either side of the hallway stayed closed as I walked past, and I wondered if any of them could have held sumptuous bedrooms with four-poster beds, the kind they portrayed in fantasy novels. I grinned. The relative quiet of the hallway made the stain-glassed doorway further along appear to hold back a stampede of voices, carried by a storm of merriment. I pressed my hand against the left door and took a deep breath. Pushed, and I was at the heart.

Even though the night was wearing on and on, guests milled around, the women in fabulous multicoloured dresses, and the men in somber tuxedos. Many wore colourful masks that covered only their eyes, and I saw a few top hats. Voices surged and dipped, exclamations of joy and concern, the slippery slide of alcohol greasing the wheels of exuberance and bubbling up in effervescence in a cacophony of mirth. Then I noticed the guards posted along the walls. I became nervous again, and a boy behind me had to nudge me along, since I'd stalled along the way. I began to move amongst the guests, as Nadège had instructed me, holding up the tray so they could sample canapés that had just been taken out of the oven. I hadn't been physically hungry since I'd died, but the smell coming off my tray gave me a kind of nostalgia, like the ghost of a hunger pang.

I couldn't stop staring at all the women's sumptuous dresses, come alive out of a different time period. Like a ball had transgressed time and space to be here from a hundred years ago. Feathered half-masks adorned smiling women's faces, and some of the men wore Pierrot or horned ones. The air was singing with the voices of merriment and laughter, and I couldn't help but be a bit jealous of not being one of the partiers. I bumped into a woman in a shimmering blue dress and bird's beak mask.

"I'm so sorry!" I said, and she frowned at me before walking away, stiff-necked. I felt my cheeks go red and continued to walk around, once in a while looking into one of the wall mirrors. I saw myself, but it was as if I was diminished. There was less substance to me, and I gulped a bit. No sign of the mark on my forehead, just a lack of presence.

I noted Toussaint's location in the crowd, and if he saw me, he made a point of not acknowledging it. I saw the large man with the empty eyes who'd greeted the newly-turned greevers into the city flirting with two gorgeous black women. I walked invisible among the fabulous and wealthy, never raising an eyebrow at my service. The servants were like the furniture, there to be used in due time, and I guessed, to be disposed of if they became a nuisance. I spotted the Baron chatting with three olive-skinned men. They wore military uniforms, and I assumed were part of Hades' retinue. The Baron looked serious as they spoke to him, and I decided to wait a bit before going to him. Soon my tray was empty, and I went back to the kitchen.

The corridor was barren, and I brought down my tray, flexing my aching arm. It's not that it was heavy, just that holding something over your shoulder for any length of time became tedious and even painful after a while. As I rotated my shoulder, a door on my left opened. A waft of charcoal smoke hit me before I saw him, but I knew: it was that guard, Wilguens. I accelerated, keeping my head down, bumping into him slightly as I passed.

"Hey! Watch where you going, girl!" an angry voice said. A terrible grip fell on my arm, and swung me around. "What do we have here?"

"Let me go!" I said, and a servant girl walked by, looking down and hurrying her steps, carrying a tray to the party. "Help!" I cried, and he clapped a hand over my mouth, dragging me into the room he'd just come out of, slamming the door. He swung me around, and I stared, wide-eyed, trying to find something or someone that could help me out of this situation. Memories— terrible ones, came rushing back to me.

Not again. Not again. Not again. Repeated endlessly like a skipping CD in my mind.

"Eh, poussin. Chick-chick!" he said roughly in my ear, as he kissed my neck, grappling me by my midriff. I could feel tears running down my cheeks onto his coarse hand still covering my mouth. I tried to bite, and he yelled.

"You want to play?" he said, and clutched my throat. It hurt. It hurt really bad. I felt as if the afterlife were being choked out of me, and I was going to dissipate here, never to see the ones I loved ever again, and it made me mad. This wasn't how it was supposed to end. His eyes bulged out at me as he grinned, holding me by my neck, and I got angry.

"Aaaaaaah!" I yelled, even as he held my throat in a pincer grip, my voice coming out mute and furious. His face changed from amusement to concern, and I saw red, my right hand lashing out at his throat, and I saw three deep, ragged gashes sliced out from below his chin, horizontally.

He let go of my throat to catch his, and we both fell to the ground. We lay on the ground for a moment, like prize fighters catching their breaths, but I got up on my elbows, coughing what felt like blood. He lay close by, taking shallow breaths, both his hands holding his torn throat, clear liquid flowing from the wounds. Wild eyes on me, he tried to kick himself backwards, ineffectually. I pounced on him, my hands ripping shreds of him, his face and neck through his hands, my claws (claws?) taking huge chunks out of him until he stopped moving, his head completely vanished.

I stopped, winded. I was sitting on his prostrate corpse.

It began to disintegrate, and I got up, looking at my hands. My long claws were turning back to the fingers I'd always known. Covered in that man's life essence. I got up, as he became nothing, and looked around the room. It was some sort of break room, most probably for the off-duty guards. There was a couple of sofas, and in the corner a row of cots.

I licked my fingers and looked at where Wilguens had been. On the floor were two silver coins, and I picked them up. Then I realized I'd been sucking my fingers, and took them out of my mouth, spitting.

What should I do? I couldn't stay here. I'd be discovered. I had a job to do. Oh God, I had to go back out there. My heart was beating out of control. I found my discarded tray and took a peak out the door. I took an enormous, shuddering breath and counted to ten. My fake smile waggled at the corners of my mouth as I went back into the kitchen. I was shaking from head to toe as I went down the steps.

Nadège patted me on the back and told me I was doing well, and I thanked her, my voice wavering, picking up a tray of drinks from a sommelier who was uncorking large, green bottles. I held my hand flat under the tray, but did not feel entirely certain about the long, fluted glasses that perched precariously on it. The head servant gave me a knowing, confident look, and I returned it with, perhaps, a lot less confidence.

I can do this, I told myself, as the slender glasses wobbled on my slippery tray. A sweat began to gather on my brow, but I ignored it, concentrating solely on keeping the thing steady. The bubbles in the glasses weaved this way and that as I tried to keep the whole thing steady. I walked up the steps, and almost walked on Toussaint's foot. He grabbed me under my arm, and started dragging me forward.

"Where have you been? We have to do it now. The Baron is leaving soon. Hades' generals have called some sort of emergency meeting. The whole party is abuzz with the implication. If we don't act, it'll be too late. Go to him!" And he pushed me, ever so gently, toward the man I was meant to betray. He went off to the side, approaching him from another direction, where he was speaking to a couple, but appeared to be saying goodbye. My tray began to shake, and I wiped my brow with the back of my hand, wiping some dirt that got on it on my skirt.

I had time to hear Toussaint say: "Baron! A moment of your time, please. You girl, come here," but as luck would have it, it was my legs who betrayed me, because as I walked toward them, staring at the tray so it would not keel over, I tripped, and fell forward, sending half my drinks falling to the floor, the other half directly onto the Baron's uniform.

He stared at his uniform first, horrified by my act. Anger bloomed on his face like a rising tidal wave. Then our eyes met.

"You!" He yelled, surprise and ferocity exploding onto his features, a volcano of emotions ready to devour me. I realized, then, with horror what I'd done. The smudge of dirt I'd wiped away was the protective sign Toussaint had put there to avoid precisely this. The Baron could see me as I truly was, and so could everyone else.

From out of nowhere, a streak of blue pushed him over and stood over his prone body for a moment, before getting up and turning around. It was the woman I'd knocked into earlier, and she was clutching a knife in one hand while her other one was balled in a fist. Panic rose higher and I tried to scramble away before who-knows-what could happen. She whipped off her mask.

Angelina!

"What are you doing here?" I yelled.

"Get up!" She replied, and put the knife away in the fold of her dress. She bent down to extend her arm, which I took, and she hoisted me up. Toussaint looked at her, dumbfounded, and she said: "You owe me for this. Out the back, quick. Maman told me about the escape plan. Let's get outside." Toussaint nodded, pointing at the kitchens.

"Guards! Grab her!" I peered around Angelina to see the Baron's outraged face, as he got up. The empty-eyed man was running toward us, and Angelina turned around and kicked Baron Dimanche down once again, and we all made a run for it.

Curious servants looked at me, wondering where I'd come from, not recognizing me from moments ago. Toussaint was right behind me, holding me up when I slipped, and pushing people out of the way. Behind us, the sound of boots hammering on lacquered floors was deafening over the awed silence and stammering consternation

Afterdeath

of the crowd. A glance showed me that Angelina had gotten rid of the blue dress, and had kept her regular clothes underneath. Servants and sous-chefs screamed as we bulldozed past them, heading out the back door. A knife bounced off the metal door, and I turned around quick enough to see Aimé's extended hand.

I had ruined everything. Now I had an entire household devoted to the Baron out to get me – us! Toussaint was no longer safe either. There was no time to think about that, though, as we made our way into the moonlit garden. Toussaint put his fingers to his lips and a loud whistle sounded in the night.

We kept running, of course, but before long, a crush and a roar came from the forest to the left, and I saw trees breaking further in, as if a bulldozer were careening wildly through it. I turned to see the military men pause for an instant, a look of fear crossing their eyes. They must have remembered who their boss was, because they started to chase again. That was when five huge trees came down on the grass, flattened like blades of grass, and Abner came rolling out of the forest like the devil on speed.

If it was at all possible, he was bigger than before. The men stopped dead in their tracks. Abner landed on his legs with an earth-shaking whomp, and glared at the gathered soldiers, a guttural roar escaping deep from within his cavernous bowels. He stomped up to them, and they backed off, shaking. Abner then turned away from them, and Toussaint helped me climb up on his back. Angelina jumped on as if she'd done this a thousand times before.

"What about your cart?" I asked, as he got on last.

"No time for that," he said. Abner began to stomp off into the forest he'd come from, and I heard a sick thump. My first thought was that another tree had fallen, and I turned around to try to spy it in the darkness of the undergrowth, but it was Toussaint. The point of a spear peered at me through his chest. He was clutching it, trying to pull it out. His face was writhing in pain, and there was nothing I could do to help.

"Hold on. He'll take you to safety," he said between clenched teeth, and Angelina and I tried to grip his body as it began to slide sideways, off his massive friend. We gripped his slipping form, but neither of us could quite grasp him and he fell, head-first, onto the forest floor. Still the giant beast careened through the trees, and we had no time to stop to pick up its fallen master.

I began to cry and held onto the crocodile with all my might. That night I abandoned my saviour to the wolves, and hated myself for it. Angelina held me down, and we kept as low a profile as we could.

I clung to the back of the animal as it crashed through the forest, jostling me up and down. A rough gurgle emanated from before me, as its jaws rose and fell. The trees became larger and larger until it dawned on me that it was Abner who was shrinking, and I had less trouble holding on. Within a minute or so, he no longer crashed through the trees, but went around them, taking an oblique path to our right. With the crashing halted, I could hear the noises around us, and the crocodile's breathing was a serpentine wheeze, low enough that it went almost undetected.

The trees still cruised by at high speeds, my hands almost touching the forest floor. It was then I heard the breaking of branches and footfalls of our pursuers. A torch shone off to our left, and voices cried out, echoing through the forest like a dream. Abner slowed down, but only just. His head swayed in the direction of the pursuers, and his eye gleamed, reflection from on an unseen light source. He clamped his jaws shut and picked up the pace again. We came to the wall that surrounded the city and began to follow alongside it, avoiding trees and low-hanging branched along the way.

I thought of Toussaint who'd given his afterlife for me. I thought of Maman Margot who'd counted on me. I thought of Chloe, who was in immortal danger, and I wouldn't get to see again if I didn't find a way back to her. Angelina and Barkley, who'd come too late. I thought of Abner, and what would he do without a master, now? Trees flitted by, offering no answers to my questions. My heart, which was of no use to me here, pounding like a hammer on anvil, at a thousand kilometres an hour, sending ghost blood to my jugular and temples. So strange to still feel the mechanics of living when I knew they were entirely obsolete. Just a living reflex to save me in case of crisis, perhaps.

The forest quit on us, and we found ourselves on a path that went straight through the wall on our right. Two surprised looking guards only had time to lower their pikes before the crocodile swivelled on his front legs, sending his hind quarters whipping in their direction. He grew to immense proportions as his body rotated, and we held on for dear death. The tail smashed them both in the mid-section, sending them both flying into the wall on either side of the door.

Abner paused for a moment, but seeing as the guards were out for the count, he became a bit smaller and went through the gate.

Outside, the cemetery fields bloomed, and Abner stayed carefully on the path to respect the sleep of the undead. He grew large again, stopping when he was the length of a school bus. He started to gallop once more, and I tried to imagine myself from a distance, perched on this immense creature, cruising at high speeds along the hills of Wodun by moonlight, Angelina behind me. There was something ridiculous and awe-inspiring in the whole exercise.

What we had gained in speed, we'd lost in secrecy. The military men would only have to break through the gate of the city to spot us and give chase. I wondered even now why they hadn't. Perhaps they'd be waiting for us somewhere down the way?

Afterdeath

"Where are you taking us?" I yelled into the rushing wind. I only got a gargling hiss for a response, so decided not to insist. Abner's hard spines bit into my back-side, and I was starting to look forward to a break in the race. I turned around, looking at Angelina with a frown, but she smiled meekly back, tapping me on the shoulder. A break in the landscape told me we were getting close to the edge of the island. Water rippled under the moon, when I squinted my eyes and looked right. The land sloped downward as well, and I figured we were parallel to the coast, wherever our final destination was.

I turned around and cursed, despite myself. Ancient Jeeps kicked up a cloud of dust coming out of the gate and down the dirt track we were following. They were fairly far away, but picking up speed now that they'd come out of the forest. They were still too small to pick out individual soldiers, but I was reasonably sure those trucks would be full to the brim with angry men ready to pick us off as soon as they had a clear shot.

"You're going to have to go faster, Abner. They're gaining on us!" I shouted into the wind, not certain he'd heard me at all, but hopeful he had a higher speed he could kick us into, before we were surrounded and attacked.

My throat was busy trying to keep my stomach down when I heard the first gunshot, like a crack of thunder. The bullet lodged itself into the dirt off to my left with a "thwip!", and the croc shot it a glance before his legs began to hammer the ground with renewed vigour. He zig-zagged from left to right, attempting to shrug off his easy target reputation. The crackle of rifles and the subsequent thumping of the lead on either side of us told me he was successful. For now.

The cemetery ended, as we bumped through an open field of muck and grasses. The track became even bumpier and pot-holed, and Angelina and I were jostled from side to side, up and down.

The first of the jeeps crept closer and closer to our left, and I kept my head ducked near Abner's body. I tried to slide over to the right, to offer less body space to shoot, but ended up almost falling off the beast. I held on with both arms as my legs kicked helplessly to try and climb back on. Angelina scrambled to hold on to me, gripping Abner with her own legs so as not to be knocked off. The men in the truck on the other side of the reptile's body found no humour in our predicament, and were getting up inside the truck, as if they were about to board a ship, pirate-style.

The croc went a bit further to their right, then changed course and slammed into the Jeep, with a bang, sending one soldier overboard, rolling over and over in the dirt, and the other three that had been standing up, sitting down, so as not to join their friend. The driver fought with the wheel for control, then began to close in on the reptile again. I'd finally been able to push myself to a prone position, my arms around the croc, my legs holding tight. Angelina held my back tight, her head almost resting on my spine. One of the men in the back of the Jeep tried to catch my leg, and I had to kick his hand away. He cursed when my foot connected with his forearm, but then Abner went even faster than I thought possible. I almost fell off again, and he passed the Jeep. When it was almost behind him, he raised his enormous tail to the right, then sent it flying to the left, catching the vehicle full-flank and sending it vaulting into the air sideways. I only caught a glimpse of all hands on deck landing sprawled and wheeling, before the truck landed overtop them.

I looked away. I'd never liked violence, and even though these men could not technically be "killed", my reflex was still to avert my gaze to any unpleasantness. I'd witnessed enough to last me a deathtime tonight already.

Two more trucks were arriving in the distance, and I could see the land dipping down to a beach in the distance. A wooden cabin lay twenty or so meters from the sand, and in the water, a small pier, with nothing attached to it.

"Where's the boat, Abner?" Angelina yelled. The croc let out a guttural cry, and a gripping, icy terror ran up and down my arms, then lodged itself in my belly when I saw the phalanx of men coming out of the cabin.

"Turn around!" Angelina yelled, and Abner veered off to the left, away from the coast.

"It's okay, I have something that'll help us," she said, and reached into her pocket. I looked over my shoulder to see her clutching something small, round, and golden. Hades' ember, the button the Baron Dimanche had worn. Angelina had swiped it during the confusion.

"I don't know if I can concentrate enough to get us out of here, but I guess I have no choice," she said. I prayed to God that she did. She let go of my side for a moment, and I turned around to clutch her shirt, so she wouldn't fall off during her incantation. She held the button with both hands, eyes closed tight. She mumbled a bit under her breath, then stopped, lips pressed together tight.

Her eyes popped open in terror.

"It's the wrong button!" she said.

"What?" I cried.

"I took the wrong one!" she said, and threw the thing as far as she could, almost falling off and taking me with her as she went. Abner was running far afield, heading back to the city. The two jeeps that had been far behind us, were now very, very close. Further to our left, more guards were coming as reinforcements. I felt my heart sink. There was no use fighting anymore. We'd get caught. I'd never get to see my sister again. This was all my fault.

Afterdeath

That was the moment we hit the first tombstone. Abner jumped up, as if he'd been electrified. Angelina and I were tossed right off, gliding through the air. She gripped my pants with one hand, and I had time to see we were going to land in front of a grave before we went right through the ground; straight down, for an eternity, like a couple of Alices in Underland.

Chapter 18

GETAWAY

I guess you could say I was frozen to the spot. I was surrounded by people who were weak, and in no condition to battle whatever was rending its way through the earth near the cottage.

Then that bird landed on a branch near my head.

"Go to the ruins, further in the forest. Larunda and her men will not dare venture there. If we hurry, we can make it before they come looking," it said.

"Can you all travel?" I said to the gathered group, most of them stooped and bow-backed in the moonlight. There came grunts of assent, and I motioned for the bird to lead us. It flitted from branch to branch, heading away from the cottage and the commotion that threatened to spill out from there. I stayed behind and made sure no one fell out of ranks. Iuturna held up her mother as they travelled up inclines and over knotted roots.

The half-moon transformed us all into shades. Long shadows pointed in the opposite direction of where it shone. Men and women moved in a hush, not speaking, their feet scraping along the forest floor.

At some point I had to pick up a rail-thin man who'd fallen over. He looked at me in gratitude, his raspy wheeze the only thanks he could muster, and I slipped my arm under his. We walked like that for twenty minutes, until the path widened, and I saw we were coming to a glade.

Afterdeath

Weeds grew short and stocky, not so much because they'd been mown. My impression was that the undercurrent that clung on the air was the source of their stuntedness. A kind of resentment that grew as we walked forward. Up a short incline, I saw where it must have emanated from: torn, cut-stone walls devoid of a roof. What must have been a small castle lay crumbled over the ridge. At some point, it would have been larger than Larunda's cottage, when once it had stood in one piece.

In the gaunt moonlight, its sable walls appeared almost romantic, but the awful feeling that emanated from it rendered it repulsive and dreary. Those ahead of me stopped, sensing perhaps the dread feeling as I did, unable to take another step toward something that wished them only ill.

The little bird landed on my shoulder.

"King Kosla-kuguza's stronghold. His destroyed spirit still resides in the walls," it said.

"I thought nothing could really die, in the afterlife," I said. It shifted, tilting its head.

"No. He is not dead. He is cursed. His spirit will forever inhabit the mansion in which he was obliterated. It is now hate. Hate for the woman who brought this upon him and his kingdom," it said, looking up at me.

I felt a lingering chill run through me, and I saw the ruins with a new eye.

"Larunda," I said. The others were sitting down, unsure as to how to proceed. We couldn't just turn back, of course, but our path was blocked by the essence of a man long gone. There was no way we could continue, either. I looked on the sad, sick faces of those who'd dared to go against the orders of their mistress, and felt shame. Even though I wasn't that creature they'd obeyed in a past life, I was responsible for their condition. I felt words and gestures bubbling inside me, and even though I had no idea where they came from, I felt compelled to act upon them.

I walked toward the broken stones, feeling a searing inside my heart. When I couldn't go any further, I got on my knees and faced the ancient castle. I could feel the others' stares on my back, making me feel uncomfortable for what I was about to do. It didn't matter. I bent my head down to the ground and called out, in the loudest voice I could:

"Oh King! We ask you your forgiveness and permission to enter your territory! We are pursued by Larunda and her cohorts! Would you not give us sanctuary for a time, so that we may be protected from her wrath?" the words felt odd, coming out of my mouth, but at the same time, right. There was no way I'd give disrespect to this old king who was only protecting what was left of his kingdom by using words that might anger him.

The heat I'd felt on my body wavered. I heard a sigh coming from behind me. Oh's of surprise followed, and then, the anger that had pushed forth from the ruins subsided, as if it had never been there. Like a gate opening, the way forward was made clear. I thanked the King with arms wide open, and got up, brushing off the excess dried grasses that clung to my pants. Carson and Iuturna were helping the others up, one after the other. Their slim bodies creaking upwards as if weighed down by incredible age. I returned to my position at the back of the line, and helped the last of the refugees into the safety of the ruins.

It felt cooler, within the confines of the rocks. Shadows had nothing to do with it, as I felt the same when I stepped into the light as in the shade. The ragged band rested on the dirt floor of the ruins, their back against what was left of the walls.

I saw Iuturna sitting with her mother and went to her. I knelt by her side, taking the old woman's other hand. It felt thin, as if she might disappear at any moment.

"She is so weak," Iuturna said, tears in her eyes. "Mama, what can I do for you?"

The old woman's lips moved, no sound coming out. Iuturna leaned in, and I saw her lips move again. Iuturna sobbed, and raised her arm to her mother's lips.

"What are you doing?" I said, pulling it away.

"She needs energy. They all do," she said. "They don't have long to exist if we don't feed them life-force!" I turned around, seeing those frail, trembling bodies, huddled like bags of sticks. Carson went from one to the other, assessing their needs like a triage nurse. I could tell by his face that he was as stumped as I was about how to give them what they needed.

"You'll run out of life force before they get better! Besides, Larunda's men will be coming to look for us, and we need you to have the energy to fight them off!" I said.

"They won't be able to get in. The king will make sure of that," Gassire said, surprising me. It was perched atop the broken wall Iuturna's mother was resting upon.

"Why not?" I said, standing up.

"The same reason that we couldn't get in earlier. The king protects his castle with all the might that is left inside him," it said.

"That's no excuse for Iuturna to give all her energy away. I need her. We need her," I said. "Don't do anything foolish, okay?" I said. "I'm just going to inspect this place, then I'll come back."

"Do you want me to come with you?" Carson asked.

"No, I'd rather go with this little guy, for now. He seems to know about this place. More than we do, anyhow. Come," I said, and walked off in the direction of what must have been the main castle. Piles of rocks and mortar blocked my way, and I stepped over them as expertly as I could. Gassire flew above and around me.

"What are you looking for?" it asked.

"Nothing. I just needed to think," I said, looking over the broken walls, into the forest beyond the fields behind the castle. Tall, dark, pine trees, slim and straight as arrows spiked the sky, no light shining through their branches. Would there be escape through there, if need be? Not if our new-found friends weren't fed something to get them healthy again. As I walked, my bird companion flitted from craggy wall to broken stone, keeping up with me in a flash of purple feathers.

I looked behind me and realized we must have been in a courtyard. I kept looking over my shoulder. The space was more open, the walls taller. I climbed now over mounds of stones, no discernible shape of tower or room to give away what had been there before. Just a pile of rubble, the kind you would never find in nature. The moon had reached a third of its climb in the sparsely clouded sky, and I guessed it must have been 11 o'clock at night. Without hunger, time felt even more relative than it was supposed to be.

Silence clung to the stones, except for those I made tumble, which tumbled as if underwater. I wasn't afraid of falling or even injuring myself, death no longer being an obstacle, but pain remained a factor, for reasons unexplained. You'd think that after losing your corporeal envelope, you would lose your pain receptors. So far, that had been a big, fat nope!

The pile of stones got smaller, and I found myself climbing downward. The base of several walls, in a rectangular formation, could be seen at the bottom of the heap. The closer I got, the more I felt a kind of reticence, mixed with pride. It took me a minute to come to grips with the fact that the latter were not my feelings, but those of the spirit that surrounded me in the walls.

When I stepped off the last stone, onto a dirt floor, I knew there was a presence there. It was diffuse, but it was there. Like walking through thin vapour, but instead of water, an emotion. Whatever this monarch had become, it was too spread out to communicate coherent thought, and expressed itself through emotion. There was a tinge of apprehension delicately floating about me. It was overpowered by the soft touch of patience on my shoulders, though.

"How did this happen. Do you know?"

"Yes, although this is much before my time. I learnt it from the birds. They taught me Kosla-kuguza's story," Gassire said.

"In ancient times, before the coming of Larunda, there was in this place the kingdom of Meath. The legend says that Kosla-kuguza was a kind, elder ruler, who looked after it with his Queen, Kosla-kuva. Their land was peaceful, and their subjects adoring. One day beautiful young woman came to them seeking refuge. She could not speak, but was educated, and so wrote them her story, explaining that other rulers wanted her dead, and that she had to hide from them. Because she could not tell a lie, her tongue had been cut out, for having revealed a monarch's cheating. Being the good king that he was, Kosla-kuguza could not deny protection of a defenceless girl. He allowed her to reside in his palace, and hid her from her pursuers. Even when a contingent of marauding soldiers came knocking at the gates of his castle, looking for her, Kosla-kuguza sent them away. He denied ever having helped Larunda. Eventually, the incursions and search parties ceased.

Larunda was adopted as a servant to the queen, and as her handmaiden had access to the castle, its staff and… the king. It was not long before the king took notice of this pure young girl. It was not long after that that his wife noticed his noticing. She flew into a rage and ordered him to get rid of her. But of course, he wouldn't. By then he was smitten. He sent away his wife instead, dispossessing her of her crown, titles and land. The stories do not say precisely what happened to her. The crows say that foul play was involved, and that her body was incinerated by the king's order. But that's crow-talk. The falcons say that she returned to her home in the mountains. None of the birds can agree as to the real history.

They do, however, agree to the fact that afterwards, the king began to groom his new love to be his queen. He taught her how to use his dobluth, and she became transfixed with its applications. She attracted souls from the living world to be her subjects, and soon the kingdom had new contingents of people loyal to the new queen, Larunda. She explained to her sovereign that they were there to protect the kingdom and her king.

The king became nervous. Then scared. He realized that a woman with this much power was a threat to his own. It had never been his intention to allow her so much control. He tried to take away the power object he'd entrusted her with. A battle ensued. The king's few loyal guards against Larunda's enormous new army.

You can see the result, here. The king was blasted apart by Larunda's ferocious power. By chance, his ember was destroyed with him, and so she was left without the ability to attract new souls to her cause for quite some time. But then she created you," Gassire said, and ruffled his feathers. I felt a heaving sadness seeping into the room, as if the stones themselves were attempting to cry.

"That's quite the story," I said. There was silence for a time as I sat on the floor and just allowed the sadness to take me. I returned gratitude to it, and consolation. Of course, I couldn't condone what the king had done, but neither could I begrudge him his all-too-human emotions. All I could do was comfort him and thank him for his help. The sadness subsided, and I felt the metallic taste of remorse in my mouth. He at least felt bad for what had transpired, and not only for having been punished, but for having sent his wife away. I could feel that on some deep level he'd loved her. That some lapse had entered his mind, and that he had thrown away a diamond to pick up a rock disguising itself as a precious stone.

Afterdeath

I felt bad for not being able to help him, but what exactly could I have done? I had twenty ailing souls waiting in the courtyard of his castle, with no way of making them well again, and Larunda's soldiers possibly on their way to surround us. Even if they couldn't come in to capture us, they could very well make sure we never left this place. If Larunda herself showed up, nothing said that she couldn't pull on us what she'd done to poor King Kosla-kuguza.

As I sat in the dust, taking in the king's emotional release, I saw Gassire hop about, then take to the air. He headed to where we'd come from. I got to my feet, and went to one of the walls, wanting to tell the king that all would be well, if I could make it. I put my hand on a rough, sand coloured rock, closing my eyes for a moment. I communicated peace to him, and the desire to help. I felt a stirring across the surface of the stone, like a slow undercurrent. I let go, and felt refreshed, ready to go back to the others.

As I nodded my head in goodbye to the room where the king had been vapourized, Gassire returned, landing close by.

"Larunda's guards! They've come!" it said.

"How far?" I said, my stomach knotting.

"A kilometre, maybe less."

"Go, and tell the others to stay hidden. I'm coming."

Its purple body bobbed a bit, and took wing again, flying high in the air.

I began my ascent over the rough rocks, unsure footing beneath me wavering a bit, stones sliding out of kilter. As I fell back, I remember thinking:

Well that was a stupid thing to do.

***

It was still dark when I woke, and I was alone, staring at the sky. Could the dead get concussions? I rubbed the back of my head, feeling a potato-sized welt.

Yes.

Night creatures had begun tuning their pipes, birds sending out mournful cries, most probably from somewhere in that dark forest I'd caught sight of earlier. My head felt upside down, and rattled from the hit. Some dark liquid had been spilt on the rock. Was that what I had for blood? Long shadows played on the ground, and I felt that chill from before, when we'd arrived at this place.

Why had no one come for me, I thought? Had the soldiers gotten inside, somehow, and eliminated everyone, while I was off in la-la land? If so, why hadn't they done me in, as well? That option made little sense. I shambled back from the stone pile, leaning against one of the broken walls for support. I felt a sick kind of rumbling in my stomach, and dry-retched with my hand on the wall. There was concern floating about, and fear.

As the moon dipped low, the contour of the ruins came into clear focus. It appeared as though they were covered in a clear coat of glass, though a millimetre thick. It was spotty, like dabs of paint had been flicked on them in great doses. Some coalesced. I drew closer to a small, clear pool, and put a finger on it. The feeling of concern grew greater, and I pulled my finger back. I looked around me, seeing for the first time the sheen like watery pools on so many of the walls, invisible in the daylight. The remnants of a man who would be king.

I felt less light-headed than a moment ago, and decided to climb the mound of stone again, like an unkempt pyramid left there by some bored giant. I was careful, this time, to stay close to the ground, and move only when the rocks remained stable. One hand, one foot, the other hand, and the other foot. That kept the pile from shifting. When I got close to the top, I noticed the orange firelight coming from the other side. I stayed in my prone position and inched forward so I could see over the ridge.

Four bonfires burned, outside the castle ruins, a short distance away. The shadows of soldiers wavered around each of them like skittish spider legs. Each fire had three, maybe four men around them.

I expected she'd have sent more, was the thought that came to my mind.

In all, there mustn't have been more than a dozen armed guards surrounding the keep. I looked inside the courtyard, and saw dark forms, huddled on the ground. None stirred, and I wondered what could have happened to them.

I clambered down the rock pile, careful not to slip or make a noise, aware that the light of the fires showed where I was. I couldn't go around the pile, as that would have brought me dangerously close to one of those guard posts, without cover. I slid down on my butt, putting one foot down, watching the stones shift a bit, my heart in my throat as I hoped they would not slide or make a sound.

I made it all the way down to the courtyard, and in the deeper shadows, saw that all my companions were fast asleep. Even Gassire had his head tucked under a wing, purple body expanding and contracting with every tiny breath. I found Iuturna, lying next to her mother and put my hand on her shoulder. I shook her a bit, but she did not budge. I found Carson a bit further, on his knees, with the front of his body resting against a stone wall, as if he'd been struck, fallen forward, and stayed there. I tried to wake him as well, but in my attempt, he slid sideways and fell with a resounding thump. That did it.

Afterdeath

"Who goes there?" I heard, from behind one of the broken walls. Fortunately, none of the men outside could see what was going on in here. That was just as well, since I was sure they'd have shot us if they'd had the chance.

"It's Chloe. What happened to my friends?" I said. I pulled Carson from his awkward position into a sitting one. He'd fallen with his leg bent under him. I didn't want for him to wake up that way, if he ever did.

"They've been put to sleep, Lady Chloe. This is the punishment for rebellion against our Mistress. Come out, and give yourself up. No harm will come to you," the man's voice said.

"Why don't you come in here and get us yourself, soldier?" I said. I peeked around the corner of one of the walls, and saw that seven guards were standing about twenty yards away, their guns in hand. The fires lit up the field of stunted weeds. I assumed that if I checked around the wall behind me, I'd see the rest of the contingent on high alert, ready to shoot, if they got the chance. For now, a silence had settled on the scene, only broken by the popping of the fire at irregular intervals.

"We will wait for you here, Lady Chloe. We have all the time in the world. Mistress Larunda will take what she needs from your friends, and then you will be left alone with old Kosla-kuguza. You know, he has a penchant for young ladies. I am certain you will get along," the man said, and there came laughter from the other soldiers.

I got mad. I knew for a fact the spirit-King would never hurt me.

"Oh, you poor little servants," I yelled at them, as coolly as I could, "too scared to come in here and get a single person. Not very brave for soldiers. I pity the woman who has cowards like you boys for bodyguards," I said, throwing a look around the corner again. I saw a pointed rifle and pulled back. A bang and fleck of rock cracked off from the wall next to my eye, and I covered my face. A warm feeling oozed from temple, and I put a hand to it, finding it covered in clear liquid.

"Missed, crack-shot. Anyone ever tell you you couldn't hit the broad side of a barn with a cannon? Because that would be an understatement." I kept my hand on my temple, and felt the wound closing up on its own. I crept to the side of another wall, throwing a sidelong glance around it. Whoever had fired was getting his gun taken away from him by another soldier. I came back to my original position. Gassire had told me that they wouldn't be able to get near us. The question now was, how did we get out of here?

"So what, we just wait it out? None of you boys have the guts to come in and get us?" I taunted.

I heard a bark of anger, and peered around the corner.

"You think this is funny?" the man who was saying this was not the same man I'd been talking to before. This one was the one who'd had his gun taken away. This one had anger issues. He was pointing a finger in my direction. I just felt like sticking my tongue out at him to see him steam. So I did.

He was mad. He was hopping mad. So much so that he was struggling against his companions' grasp to try and run at me. Whatever was holding the rest of them back was not enough to stop this fuming soldier from trying to barge in and choke me. I wondered if he'd succeed. He broke off from their grip and started running toward the wall where I was hiding. His teeth were bared, and he was raging.

He screamed as he ran at me, pulling a long dagger from a side-sheath. But as he came about halfway, he started to slow. He fell down on his knees. The anger was gone from his face. Now it was fear that glowed on him, making his face drip with sweat. But no, that wasn't sweat. It was coming down too hard. I could hear him gurgling, from ten feet away. His companions looked on, in horror, as his head dipped forward, caving in, his shoulders falling, literally, by his side. He looked like an accelerated video of a melting ice cream cone, all his features coming down in rivulets down his chin, onto his clothes, hitting the ground. Then he fell over, face down, and it was like he had turned into a water balloon, because as soon as he hit, he exploded.

The remaining men stared in shock at what was left of him, as did I. If I could have thrown up, you bet I would have. Not having eaten in several days precluded that idea from becoming reality.

"Wow," I whispered, under my breath, as I stared, wide-eyed, at the rapidly absorbed corpse of the soldier in the weeds.

"Don't think it's such a hot idea for you boys to come in after all. Just stay where you are. Better yet, go home to your mommy," I said.

"Lady Chloe, we are at an impasse. I have needs to speak to you. There is a pressing matter involved. Will you parlay with me?" the soldier who had originally spoken said.

"What's your name, soldier? I don't have much reason to trust you. You realize that, right?" I said, hoping I could come up with something. The prospect of going back to the cottage made me feel like crap, but so did the thought of having to stick around here for eternity.

"My name is Garcia Portillo. All I have to offer is the truth. Larunda is trapped inside her mansion," he said. Another man looked at him, wide-eyed and said:

"Be quiet, Portillo. She doesn't have to know that!"

"How are we supposed to get her out, huh? Just the eleven of us left, Alois. Do you think we'll be able to take down the nightmare on our own?" So that was it. Why had only eleven survived? Had all the others been destroyed? That would mean that whatever it was she had unleashed was incredibly powerful. What the heck was I supposed to be able to do against it?

Afterdeath

"I want guarantees. I want for these people under our care to go free. They can't stay prisoners to Larunda. My friends and I have to be let go as well, when this is all over," I said.

"There are no guarantees," the man named Alois said.

"Then you're not the person I should be speaking to, are you?" I said, peering around my wall. Garcia was looking at Alois with disdain, almost pushing him back. It seemed that whatever predicament Larunda was in right now, it affected the complete, blind obeisance of her troops. They seemed more human right now than they had been during the giant attack a few days ago; less like puppets, more like men.

Garcia spoke again: "It's true what Alois says, we cannot make those promises. I can pledge to speak on your behalf to my Mistress, but I can't say what the outcome will be," he said. I knew that to be honest, at least. This Garcia person at least seemed to be honest, something I needed in this situation. Who knew if any bargain would be respected by any of the other grunts if they decided to turn on me, though?

"You look like you're in charge, Garcia. Are you?" I said.

"I... I guess I might be?" he said, and shrugged. There was no formal command structure, then. Larunda usually called the shots and they obeyed. The others of his contingent looked uncomfortable with this arrangement but did not challenge his authority. I guessed that they had come this far under his impromptu orders. The puppets had had their strings cut, and now had to figure things out for themselves. The fires still crackled in the background, and some of the other soldiers had joined the group I was talking to, apparently no longer afraid we were going to try to escape. I wondered then how she'd been able to get all my friends to sleep if her power did not extend further than her cottage. It made no sense.

"Why do you want to take us back then? You're free, aren't you?" I said. I heard a chatter of voices. Some of them agreeing with me. I don't think they'd even considered this option before. Somewhere inside their programming a part of them yearned to be free, but couldn't come to grips with the reality of the possibility.

"My life debt to my Mistress forbids it," Garcia said, shaking his head. The others grumbled a bit, but appeared to be in accord with him.

"If I promise to help you guys get that woman out from her prison, can you promise not to hurt me if I come out there to talk to you? Remember, I've got a God-king watching over my shoulder, anything should happen to me. Just ask puddle-boy over there what'll happen to you," I said, pointing at the now dry grasses and dirt that had absorbed a soldier moments ago.

Garcia looked around to the others, who were shaking their heads in indecision. It was up to him.

"Deal," he said. He made a motion for the others to put down their weapons, and I stepped out from behind the broken wall, taking careful steps toward them. I hoped I wasn't angering the old King by helping his enemies, but at the same time, there was not much else I could do to get us out of this mess.

Fifteen yards away a man in antique uniform waited for me with arms crossed. I took a long last look at the unconscious crowd and started closing the gap between us.

Chapter 19

MIDDLE OF NOWHERE

There was some light in the kitchen, in the haze; something stolen out of time. The 1950's reclamation team must have been hard at work looking for this place. Off-white counters, sharp corners, tiny gold stars inlaid in the formica like tinsel stars on ratty fake Christmas trees. A silver-rimmed metal table off to one side, with three chairs 'round it. One of them was on its side, on the floor; all were gathering dust. The cupboards stood open, their contents on the ground, paint peeling. The shelves' green plastic flower-prints curled at the corners. Pale yellow tupperware and lids strewn around. A hand-cranked meat grinder pinned to the edge of the counter looked used and flecked with grit. There was no vegetable or animal matter to speak of, thankfully, and no flies, thankfully. A thin haze hung in the air and all was covered in fine beige dust. I ran a finger along the counter, picking up a trail of it, then saw Angelina's body on the ground in a corner and went to her.

Her hair looked as if she'd had an unfortunate run-in with a blender, but otherwise she was fine. Kneelin, I patted her on the head, and she answered with a groan. I got up and looked around a bit more. The origin of the light couldn't be found, as if it had no source. Nestled in the counter was a bulbous green fridge, with a long, silver door-handle. I pulled on it, and a stale smell wafted out. It hadn't worked in ages, and was room-temperature inside. No food here either, just empty containers, all of them clean. Weird.

A square-ish glass lamp hung overhead, the power out. I went to one of the wooden doors and pulled on the handle, but it stuck fast. Angelina shook her head and pushed herself up. While propped on her arms, she said something, quietly, and Barkley came out of her ribcage. He just slipped through, like a ghost. She left perfect handprints in the sand.

"Where are we now?" she said, standing up, dusting the thin coat off her arm with slender fingers and taking in the retro scenery as I had.

"Feels like an old house that stayed glued in my grandparent's time," I said. I walked over to another door and pried at it. The wood had swelled, catching on the faded linoleum floor. I could open it, but just a crack. On the other side was a hallway, with no way to enter without breaking the door down.

"Got anything on you to get this thing out of the way?" I asked Angelina. I coughed a bit, as the dry, particulate-laden air got into my throat and lungs. Whatever hung in it stung my eyes. I wished I had a mask, but this place didn't look like it carried such luxury items. I went to the sink beside the fridge and tried turning on the water, with little hope of getting any. When I turned the tap on, sand began to pour from it. I turned it off, not wanting more grit and dirt in here than was necessary.

Angelina was by the door, with a flat piece of metal in one hand, putting it to the hinges. Smart. Why hadn't I thought of that? She pushed it into the groove and gave her tool a good whack with the palm of her hand, pushing the pin up. She then got up and pulled it out. She did it once more, and for the final one at the top, she asked me to come and hold the door. As the pin popped up with a clang, I caught the door's weight, which was not very heavy, and set the thing against the other wall.

The crumbling corridor was dark. Walls ballooned inward. There were doors on either side of it, two on the right, and one on the left, not counting one directly in front of us, lying in shadows. I went to the furthest one, hoping to find an exit, but when I pulled the chain out of the way and rescinded the deadlock, the door opened onto a concrete wall. No, rather it was hard-pressed sand. I touched it and it felt solid enough, chipping a bit if I noodled around too much, but otherwise felt like a solid-packed wall of sand, almost stone. Impasse.

I went back into the kitchen, Angelina staying by the door and poking about a bit before coming back.

"Where the heck are we?" I asked. I pulled up one of the silver-coloured chairs and sat down, hard.

"I couldn't tell you love. There isn't much to go on," she said while walking around the kitchen, picking up plastic objects, turning them over, and discarding them.

"You wouldn't happen to know how we got here either, would you?" I persisted, one elbow on the gritty table, resting my cheek on my fist.

"See now, that's the interesting part," she said, and smiled. Barkley wagged his tail, and looked at me.

"Why's that?"

"You have a power," she answered, turning and looking at me intently. She rubbed her chin with the tips of her fingers, then went back to her explorations.

I turned to follow her meandering.

"What do you mean, I have a power? What power?"

"We fell into a grave. The only thing that should have happened was us bouncing on the ground. We didn't do that, though, did we?" she said, throwing me an inquiring glance.

"How should I know? I don't know the rules in this place Angelina. This is all new to me. So, what kind of 'power'? Why me?" I said, my voice straining to stay calm.

She walked around for a bit, still rubbing her chin. She turned around, pulled back one of the chairs, and sat next to me at the dusty table.

"We went through a *sepulcrum fores*, a grave door. That means that you have the power of a dobluth ember," she said, looking at me intently. I barked out laughing.

"What are you talking about? You have one, I don't! That gem you have probably started working again, and you just don't know how, that's all," I reasoned.

She got up from her seat, taking my assertion for cash. She walked around in the silty silence of the room for a bit. Barkley sat under the chair she'd just left, his tail flopping once in a while. The notion that I'd been the cause was so ridiculous that I chuckled a bit to myself.

"No," she finally said, "mine…"

"The one you stole," I corrected.

"The one I borrowed," she continued, "is definitely out of juice. I've tried many times to use it since the first time. It wouldn't have just gotten a charge, for no reason."

"But you don't know how to charge it," I said, "you said so yourself." She tilted her head left and right, her lips wavering from one side of her mouth to the other in deep thought.

"Right, but I would know if it *was* charged. My point is, there's no other logical explanation than it being you, Olivia. There's something about you that makes you special, I think." She came back to the table. Barkley shifted one paw over the other.

"So, where are we?" I asked. Back to square one.

"No idea," she said, glancing around at our tiny prison. For a moment I became intensely claustrophobic. Walls that had been several feet away now closed in, right next to me, making me choke on the dusty air. I felt a cold shiver play on my head, and I tried to regain control of my fear.

"Thanks for saving me," I said, looking at the table.

"Pleasure," she said, and I could practically hear the smile on her face as she did.

"How did you get there so quickly, anyhow?" I asked, wondering out loud as much as I was asking the question. It had been a fair distance from Maman Margot's stronghold to the Baron's mansion.

"Maman lent me a lift," she said, smiling from one side of her mouth. That sounded odd.

"I thought she hated you, and you her?" I said.

"Well, we worked things out. I think she realized the mission had a better chance of success if I was involved," she said, looking at me with a knowing smile. I'd sure botched it on my own. But then again, we'd missed our opportunity to get the real ember. "I promised to give her back the Baron's power object as soon as we'd taken Hades'. I guess that's not going to happen. He was wearing a fake. Someone must have warned him of Maman Margot's plans. Can't trust anyone, I guess," and she sighed. She put her chin on both her hands and stared at the wall.

"You were going to give back the gem?" I said. This streak of generosity surprised me from her. It was completely unexpected.

"Well, yeah. It's not like I can use it. The thing is dead. Without the instructions on how to activate it, might as well hand it back, right?" So much for that fleeting thought of her having any redeeming qualities.

"You are something, Angelina," I said, and she giggled, then became serious. "Why did you take it in the first place? Honestly. I just can't figure out why you'd go through all that trouble for such a thing. You could have lived out all your afterlife without all this trouble chasing after you, day in and day out. So tell me." And I splayed my hands in an inviting gesture.

"For the adventure," she said, eyes sparkling, and Barkley groaned under the table. There was something more to it than that, of course, but she wouldn't tell me, and I couldn't betray Barkley. Maybe I'd ask him later, if we could ever be alone. Angelina was, so far, the least forthcoming person I'd met in any life, either living or dead. No surprise that it would continue now.

I got up and went down the hall, trying every door. None of them budged, and their hinges were located inside the rooms. Disturbing the wall of sand made little sense, because it might mean flooding the room. No use in that. I wanted to go on for a while, not be discovered millions of years later as an afterlife fossil, if such a thing even existed. I inspected the various doors, doing what crazy people do, expecting a different result. I climbed on top of the counter, searching the upper shelves. The feeling of the room pressing in came back to me, pressure building up inside.

Afterdeath

In desperation, I looked inside the fridge again, and of course, there was still nothing of use.

I slammed the door. Hard.

Barkley let out a bark. I looked at him quizzically as he stared upward, over the appliance. I turned around, and saw a bit of dust dancing overtop the refrigerator.

I opened the door again wide, and swung it shut as hard as I could. It shut with a 'bang', and I kept an eye over top of it. Dust fluttered out from the top, but also a bit of extra light, for a second, as the thing rocked.

"Come and help me," I asked Angelina. She jumped over next to me took the right while I grabbed the left side, and we started to pull on the top of this massive thing. Barkley bounced out of the way as we pushed and pulled the fridge. This was the kind of activity they warned you never to do with a vending machine, if you didn't want to make it…

Topple! It fell down between us, crashing on the ground with a resounding boom. I felt sweat running down my arms from the effort, and I smiled at Angelina's wet, dust-covered face. I'm certain my own needed a good wash as well.

Behind the fallen refrigeration unit, was a square, paneless window. Outside, a clear blue sky, with barely a cloud in it, and desert everywhere. Whatever floated by was wispy, and as dry as this room felt. Looking down through the window was a most curious sight. This was not a house after all.

We were on what must have been the fourth or fifth floor of an apartment building, but it was caked in sand. One or two other windows poked out from the side of the wall, but it looked as if they were full of sand. Above us twenty other stories were stacked, and we stood in the shade of the edifice. Similar buildings could be spied in the distance but they were sparse, some of them looking as if they'd been cut down or had partially fallen sideways, like unwitting Towers of Pisa.

A thin wind blew across the desert, raising volutes of sand and making dunes against the apartment we were in. There was a two-storey drop from where we stood. I looked at Angelina. She shrugged. She called Barkley over and picked him up. She held him under one arm and put a leg over the windowsill. I held her elbow as she put her other leg over, and she jumped.

It looked like a long fall, but she landed in a forty-five degree wall of sand, then tumbled down to the base of the apartment block several more floors below. Once she stopped, she got up and let Barkley run around. *He* enjoyed it, at least. She gave me a hand signal to come down, and I started to put my leg over the hole in the wall. The distance down loomed large, and my stomach was jumping around in my throat, yelling at me not to jump because I was too young to die. I told it to be quiet, reminding it that I was already dead and it left me alone.

I put my other leg over the ledge and felt dizzy as a slice of wind rifled by. I teetered back and forth for a moment, then decided to go for it.

Freefall, and a mouthful of hammering heart.

I'd never expeienced bungie jumping or sky-diving, but I imagine jumping from a high distance would feel very similar.

I felt a slap as my legs hit the sand, sunk and buckled, sending me forward and sideways, tumbling down the dune, little geysers kicking up every time I spun. I rolled and rolled, until I stopped next to Angelina's feet. She gave me a hand up, and I patted off the extra sand on my clothes and in my hair. Why was I always getting so dirty?

I turned around to see where we'd been imprisoned, and it looked like a big, rectangular sand castle, with windows set into it. It also reminded me of those table mesas you saw in Arizona, like giant plugs coming out of the ground, except this one was incredibly tall. A hot wind picked up, and I coughed some of the accumulated particles out of my lungs.

"Where are we?" I croaked, when the coughing had abated.

"Desert," Angelina replied, putting her hand over her squinted eyes to scan the horizon. I closed my own and shook my head slowly. Why was I happy to have her there again?

"And then?"

"That's all I know. I'm not trying to be a bitch. I have no clue where we are. I've never been here before, wherever here is." Barkley came up to nudge her leg, and started barking in the direction behind us. I turned to look, and only saw dunes, wind, and the occasional apartment block. "Yep. Might as well start walking."

Like a deep sandbox. That's what it felt like to put one foot after the other, sinking a bit, and then pressing on. I'd seen deserts in National Geographic, of course. Everybody has; but those are pictures. They don't prepare you for the infinite vistas that go on for as long as the Earth is wide. That's what it felt like, at least. On the positive side, the beating sun made no difference. Heat was not a problem. It did get in my eyes, of course, but I didn't suffer from thirst, which in the living world would have been an excruciating ordeal. I occasionally looked back, and the building from which we'd departed got smaller and smaller, until all I could see was the top-most part of it. When we had overcome the crest of some tall dunes it was finally gone. There were others, of course, riddled along our way. Broken husks of construction that might have looked majestic and brand new, but now lay shattered and sand-filled for the desert to reclaim, like a slow digestion process.

Talking to Angelina was a futile exercise, so I didn't. I had a certainty that all my questions would get the same answers. - "I don't know." Barkley bounced about her

Afterdeath

legs with his usual enthusiasm, and I wondered if I could work up that kind of positive energy. I really wished I could.

Then I thought about going back to the living. Of course I'd find Chloe first, but what would happen when or if—better not think of it that way—we actually did get back to life? I mean, what would happen when we were going to die *again*? Living forever was not within the realm of any possibilities that I had heard of, so what would befall our immortal souls once we were good and ready to take a second trip down the Path with Ol' Death as our escort? What if I had an accident and came right back here? That was a mental groan right there. But what if I went on to something different? What would that be like? So many questions, and as always, no readily available answers.

Off in the distance, I saw movement, not any particular thing, though. It was as though the furthest reaches of the horizon were slipping toward the left. It was dizzying as a matter of fact; the closer we got, the weirder it seemed. Imagine coming to a riverbank to see a flowing stream, then realizing that the stream was entirely made of sand and moving lighting-fast. Well, that is exactly what we had before us. There was no way to tell how deep it was, but it extended further into the distance than we could gauge.

"Well that's interesting," Angelina said, staring off from left to right, watching the impossibly fast flow of sand rush by our feet. I came nearer the edge, and was about to dip my foot into the sand-river, when Angelina grabbed my arm. "Nuh-uh. That's danger, little girl. Don't think I could rightly catch you if you go tumbling in."

"What do we do now, then?"

"Thinking." She looked about us. I thought maybe we could build a raft, and I said so, and she laughed at me, telling me that that was all fine and dandy if I could gather enough massive logs to string together, and then we could maybe carve some paddles with our leftover wood. Except there was no wood, or string, or knives to carve, was there? I reddened, and she locked her gaze on the furthest horizon for the longest time. Maybe she was waiting for something. I was tired from all that walking, and sat down in the warm sand. This was honestly one of the only times I was grateful for being dead. If I'd been alive the heat would have killed me, I was sure. Thank God for small favours, really.

Wait.

Something was moving. Other than the sea of sand.

It was faint at first. Think of a flowing, light-beige background, cut horizontally in half by a pale blue line, and at their intersection, a few white dots. They were far away to our right and the only way I could see them was due to their movement ever so slowly, across the blue backdrop of the sky, over the dunes without end. Barkley looked up at Angelina in expectation, but she was busy staring at the approaching whatever-they-were.

As they came closer, we could see that the dots were little white cubes, perched with red buttons. We began to walk along the shore in the direction of the moving cubes realizing that if we didn't they might go by without noticing us.

"Hey, are we going to try to catch up to those things?" I said, counting five of them, all travelling in a row, but not toward where we stood.

"Do you want to stay lost in the desert?" she asked without stopping. Barkley danced around her legs sniffing the air. Even though I felt no thirst, my throat was still dry and sweat gathered on my brow. Perhaps I'd just become all desiccated like a mummy and start roaming the desert. Next I'd be looking for bandages to wrap myself in. I lifted my arms and made like a shambling mummy, moaning like they did in the movies.

"What are you doing?" Angelina said, giving me an irked look.

"Nothing," I replied sheepishly, yet uttering a last, tiny: "erg", before giving up.

The cubes were tents. I could see that now. We were heading toward an intercept course, aiming to catch them as they floated by. It was odd to see five white tents with red banners floating above them, drifting single file along the crest of a rapidly flowing dune. Then again, I should probably get used to all the weird things death was throwing at me if I wanted to make it back to the living world. Nothing would surprise me anymore, and I could live to whatever ripe old age possible, untroubled by all the irksome things a lifetime could lob in my direction. That was my plan, and I was sticking to it. I hoped to God Chloe was okay. I knew that the vision Maman Margot had shown me was one of the future, but how far ahead? Would I get there in time to help? Was it already too late?

I walked faster in the sand, my feet sinking a bit with every step. The tents were approaching the shore further ahead. At the front of the tents stood benches, facing forward. Sitting relaxed on the lead one, a red-skinned man read a book. When I say his skin was red, I mean it was blood-and-wine coloured. His jet-black hair was tied in a neat ponytail, which went all the way down his back in a braid. He wore a flowing robe of brilliant white with golden sleeve edges.

"Hey!" I yelled, and he looked up in astonishment. I stopped in my tracks, at the stare of his icy blue eyes.

"Whoa!" he commanded, and the tent slowed down near the shore. He took off his thin, round glasses as I came closer, and I realized suddenly that I'd left Angelina down the dune.

"What are you doing here little one?" The red man asked as he rose from his bench to greet me, while the carpet on holding his tent stopped at the edge of the shore.

233

Afterdeath

In turn, the other white tents came to a halt in formation with a gentle squelch. A dark blue, thicker set man, his earlobes stretched from large golden earring gauges, came striding toward us e from inside his tent,.

"What holds us, Iblis?" he said, before spying me.

"We have a visitor Maimun. Go tell the others we shall stop here for tea," he said, offering me a seat on the ground behind the bench. Throw pillows were arranged on a comfortable-looking carpet. He unrolled a flap of his tent, putting poles into holsters and making shade over the carpet. By that time, Angelina had arrived with Barkley.

"Hi, we don't mean to disturb you, we were just lost. My name is Angelina, this is my companion Olivia, and this is my dog Barkley. We were wondering if you could give us directions to the next city?" she said, as she stopped on the edge of the carpet. A snort came from a few feet in front of the bench, and twin eruptions of sand poofed out, like geysers.

I jumped back, and the man called Iblis smiled.

"You are a bit skittish. Never seen a ramil-sammak, I take it," he said.

"Never even heard of them," I said, my hand on my heart, staring at the spot where the sand was settling back.

"They are our mounts. You are on the back of one now. They are hard to tame, but once you have, they are invaluable for travel in this desert country," Iblis said, and smiled warmly. He made a gesture with his hand, inviting Angelina and Barkley to come and sit, which she did after a moment's hesitation. Iblis disappeared inside his tent, and came back out with a silver tray, populated by eight tiny glass cups with shining silver rims. Each cup was different, and etched in ornate designs, fine and dainty, the width of spider's silk.

He put the tray at the centre of the carpet, and Angelina bent forward to take one. Iblis smiled and wagged his finger 'no'. A few moments later, two other men, and two women came to join us. There was Maimun, the blue-skinned one, and we were introduced to yellow-skinned Barqan, as well as the slender and graceful females, green-skinned Adira, and black Kabira.

They all bowed and introduced themselves, before sitting down on the carpet next to us.

"How did you find yourself in our desert? You're obviously strangers to these parts, if you've never heard of ramil-sammak, our 'sand-mantas'," Iblis said, picking up a small cup in each hand and passing them to both Angelina and I. He then put one in front of Barkley, who sniffed it with curiosity.

"We..." I started, but was cut off.

"We were kidnapped and brought here," Angelina said, giving me a hard stare.

"I see," Iblis said, brow furrowed, as he put the tiny glass to his lips.

"We woke up in one of those apartments just now. We have no idea how we got there," she continued, pointing back the way we'd come.

"I see," Iblis said, his brow furrowing deeper, the corner of his mouth lifting in a smallish grin. "We are Jinn. We're heading to the city of Jubbah. It is a two day journey, as the ramil-sammak swims. If you care to join us, we'll be glad to take you there so you can go back to wherever you are from," he said, and bowed his head slightly.

"That's very kind of you, thank you," I said. I took a sip of the amber liquid in my glass, and felt a slight buzz. "Powerful stuff, not exactly tea, is it?"

"Not exactly. Amesainthe. It is quite potent," Kabira said, winking at me. She took a small sip and licked her lips.

"What's in it?" Angelina said, tilting her glass to make the liquid slosh gently around the rim.

"Herbs and spices only found in specific oases in the desert. And other things, of course." Maimun smiled, putting down his empty cup.

"Can I go lie down? I just feel tired right now. Please?" I said, and Iblis nodded slightly. My head had grown heavy, as if I'd lost all my energy. Iblis rose to his feet and opened the tent-flap near him. Angelina got up, helping me teeter to my feet, and put an arm around me as I went into this Jinn's inner sanctum. The sun shone through the cool white of the tent onto the ornate rugs that covered the ground. Still, it was cooler than in direct sunlight, and I could have just passed out on the floor. The floor had a slow, undulating movement, as if it were traversed endlessly by long waves.

Angelina held me up until we got to some mattresses pressed together, fine silk sheets of a cream colour covering them. The wooden chests around the room, the delicate decoration, it all danced before my swimming eyes. I melted away getting on the bed before I could be fully lain to rest. I remember thinking: "That smell... like chocolate..."

***

The room was strange when I woke. There was some sort of dulling sound, like wind rushing through a tube, save there was no wind. No tube either. The ground was hard under my shoulder, arms. I opened my eyes, and the view of the room was distorted as well. It was bigger than I remembered. I turned to find Angelina, pressed against a wall, frowning.

"Took you long enough," she said.

"What happened?"

Afterdeath

"You and I were drugged." So it was true. I then noticed the distortion was caused by a wall. I put my hand against it.

"We're in a jar, Olivia," she said, putting her head back, arms crossing. In a jar? Like a Mason jar? What were we? Canned fruit? I then came to the realization that the reason why everything looked so large was that, we, in fact, had been shrunk. We were presently displayed on a chest of drawers, a few feet above the ground. My breath started coming in quicker. The lid above us made me think we'd run out of air, and that only made me hyperventilate even more. The after-effects of the drug lingered, and I felt seasick. No. It wasn't that. We were moving.

"Relax, we just have to find a way out is all. Barkley was able to run away before he could be captured. We just have to wait for him to come back for us during the night." Where could he go? All around us was an ocean!

"But we're teeny tiny," I said, in a squeaky voice, suddenly feeling even more remorse for a caterpillar Chloe'd kept in a jar when we were kids.

"We were both zombies a few days ago, if I recall." That put things back into perspective. It just felt like this might be more permanent than the disguises we'd donned previously; like this was final. And all around us, there was that syphoning silence, like when you put your ear to a seashell to hear the ocean. That sort of sucking emptiness that reverberated in your skull until you let it go out of discomfort. However, this sound did not go away. This sound stayed. Constant. Whooshing.

Noises coming from outside told me that we'd have a guest soon, giving me the urge to run, but our prison prevented me from doing so. The tent flap waved aside, and Iblis walked in. He no longer looked the same. His skin was roiling, crawling, smokeless fire and he no longer looked entirely human. The horror in my face was reflected in his eyes glowing silver eyes when he bent down to look us over. Long canines, vampire-like, protruded above his lower lip uncovering a smile both frightening and devious.

Angelina stood facing him, staring him down.

"Good. You are awake. How are you feeling?" Iblis said.

"Where are you taking us? What have you done to us?" I wanted to yell, then caught myself. It wouldn't do to scream at him now that he stood ten times as large as we were, so I said it firmly, instead.

The Jinn put his elbows on the dresser, cupping his chin in his fists. His head was the same height as our bodies were tall, and I recoiled from fright.

"I told you: to the city of Jubbah. Fret not, I have only made you into a more... eh, handle-able size. That way I don't have to tie you to a tent-post and have to hear your infantile squalling all the way to our destination. It really is quite grating, if you've ever had to hear prisoners begging for mercy. Otherwise, are you comfortable?"

"What's your plan, red man?" asked Angelina, nonplussed.

"Sell you. Not often do we get foreign goods like you in our midst. I'm wondering how you taste. Amesainthe is usually made of sun-baked prisoners. I'm willing to bet you'll be softer to the palate." He walked away and brought a chair back, placing it a meter or so from where we stood. He took a seat, and crossed his arms and legs. He seemed to appraise us, like an antiques dealer who'd stumbled upon a rare find.

"I have to save my sister! I can't be here!" I cried, voicing my inner turmoil.

"Truly. Is she far away, this sister of yours?"

"Too far for you to get a hold of. You have to let us go!"

"No chance, little one. You are an opportunity too good to pass. We shall be at the city in a few days' time. Try to make yourself comfortable in the meantime. I'm sorry I don't have any tiny pillows for you," he said, and shrugged. He rose from the chair and walked out of the tent.

"Now what do we do?" I said, sliding down the glass wall, and sitting on the ground.

"Now we wait," Angelina said.

***

Before night, the movement of the tent stopped. Iblis the Jinn came in to fetch odds and ends for the setting up of camp, but did not address us. We watched him go about his business in silence. As the sun set, I saw the giant plate-like moon glowing above us, and wondered briefly where we might have landed. But, if Angelina didn't know, there was little chance I would either. I heard the laughing of the five outside the tent, and spied the dancing fire between them through the soft white fabric. Iblis came to bed later than I expected, lying down on his mattresses, in the semi darkness. The only light in the shadows then was that moon, immobile and silent, watching over us like a cold, white lens.

I spotted movement from under one of the piles of throw pillows in the corner, almost half an hour after the snoring of our captor had begun. It wasn't loud, but apparent enough that someone inside the tent would be aware of it.

We remained silent, but Barkley, sniffing the air and looking around, found us almost immediately. He put his front paws on the dresser, getting up on his hind legs. Still, he was too short to reach us. Angelina put both her arms in front of herself and made a silent "push" motion. From the back of the jar, we ran to the front and both extended our arms as we got to the opposite side. The jar slid forward, barely. Angelina looked at me, and we both returned to our original positions. We took a running leap at the opposite side and slammed into the wall of glass, bringing the jar half-way over the edge. I made the mistake of looking down and felt a tad queasy at the thought of falling again. Silly living people problems. We tried one last time, giving it all we had, and the jar came tumbling to the carpet underneath the dresser with a plop.

Barkley looked at us, then started nosing our prison toward the front of the tent. He stuck his head underneath the tent flap and lifted, while pushing us through with a paw. The night was sky and sand as far as the eye could see, and that moon, so big, behind and above us like a reluctant watchman. Barkley began to push again, but the jar was half his size, so he could be forgiven for the slowness at which we progressed. I still felt anxious to be far away, and so tried to roll the jar like a treadmill. Angelina followed suit, but as I said, sand is not the best of mediums to be doing this in, so our progress was slim to none.

I should have known this plan was doomed to fail. Some alarm bell should have rung in my head, telling me that this was plain stupidity. That there hadn't been was a failing on my part.

There was no wind to speak of. It was the stillest of nights, and yet, the lapping of the sand waves on the shore behind us grated and swashed. Iblis' tent began to shake. Nothing else on the desert floor moved, but our jailer's tent rocked and rolled as if a gale were lambasting it, right there on the beach. It was the sand-manta, though, of course. As soon as we'd dropped the jar from its perch, it had sensed it landing on its back. It had waited to find out what the problem was.

I turned to the front of the tent, and saw an eye-stalk poking out from the sand, riveted to us like a submarine's periscope, but sandy and grey. Angelina turned around, too, and let out a cry. The tent door vapourized, a hole burned through it by the charging Iblis. Teeth bared, skin roiling in furious fire, he came for us. A cry, so deafening I had to cover my ears, filled the Universe.

Then there was a tapping, and a tugging on my shoulder, and I opened my eyes. I was not in a jar. I was in the Jinn's bed. It was still night. Angelina was at my side, and I felt hot tears on my face.

"Are you okay?" she asked. I saw Iblis standing behind her, looking concerned. He frowned when I flinched away from him. "You've been out for a whole day, Olivia. You were screaming in your sleep." I rose on my elbows and felt my back to be sticky from my own sweat.

"I had a terrible nightmare," I started, but I remembered who was in the room and decided to go no further.

"I must present my most sincere apologies, child," the Jinn said, approaching only slightly. "Amesainthe is not for everyone."

"What's it made of?" I asked weakly.

"It is made of the concentrated essence of those who wish to share their power with the world. There are those souls who have lived for eons, and wish to take on new forms. Then there are those who no longer wish to *be*. Amesainthe is made of the latter. It is rare, and so that is why we offer it to special guests," he said. The admission gave me a shudder. The concept was alien to me.

"So... you don't kidnap people, to sell them, to make the stuff?"

"Why no! That would be horrid!" the Jinn replied, frowning. I took a deep breath and let out a sigh. I'd let my imagination get the better (or worst) of me. Never mind judging books by their covers: I'd been reading entirely different books!

Barkley waddled over to me and licked my face, and I embraced him. He eyed me concernedly, then walked away, his little tail flapping.

Angelina looked at me a bit before saying:

"I thought you were going to disappear. You convulsed for almost a day!"

"I can't describe to you what happened. I thought they were going to sell us to make that stuff we drank!" I closed my eyes and gulped.

"Figured that's what you were rambling about. You shouldn't be so paranoid about people."

"Me? You're the one who doesn't trust anyone, Angelina! You're the one who never tells anyone what's on your mind! I'm the one with the trust issues?" I almost yelled. I felt dizzy and lay back down. My stomach roiled, and I closed my eyes. When I opened them again, she was draining the liquid out of my cloth, dipping it into a bucket below my field of vision, and putting it back on my forehead.

"I'm careful," she whispered. "Not everyone can be trusted, in this world or any for that matter. Maybe especially this one, who knows? Back when Barkley and I were alive, we were lovers then, too. They burnt us at the stake. They called me a witch. Barkley's aunt found out we were together. She denounced us to the inquisition. My name wasn't Angelina then," she started.

"What was it?" I interrupted.

"I don't remember. Who cares?" she said, waving her hand. "Sorry. I'm sorry." She sighed. "They came to my hut. I lived alone in the woods. Barkley was with me that day. Twelve men broke down the door. Just busted it down. Pikes extended, swords drawn. The tall man in my courtyard, dressed in black said that he had orders from the Pape to find and destroy all heresy. I was not a Crosstian. Barkley's aunt had found out. I had a bit of money to my name. I made ointments and medications for the villagers out of forest herbs. Did you know you get a cut of the money when you denounce a witch?" she said, and leered ironically. I shook my head no. I hadn't studied that area of history. It was apparent there were large swaths of the human experience they avoided teaching in schools these days.

Afterdeath

"This man, in the mud in front of my own home, announced quite solemnly that I was to be "questioned" for witchcraft. He made it sound like a job interview! 'Are you a witch?' 'No sir!' 'Off you go, then'. No. That's not quite how it works, is it. When they want you to admit something, they do bad things to you until you admit it. When they've done enough bad things and you can't hold back anymore, you tell them what they want to hear. Barkley and I were burned alive. We both ended up in the afterlife together. So at least there's that. But you know, I've never quite forgiven his aunt. And so, I am careful." She said, and gave a tentative smile.

I nodded. Things like that stayed with you. "How do you remember all that? Chloe and I don't know how we died."

"We went to past death regression therapy. We relived it. Believe me when I tell you that you might be better off never finding out how you died. If you're here, it was probably nasty."

"Help me up."

I held out a hand, and she pulled me to a sitting position. She aided me in standing, and I let the swirling mist in my head twirl around for a few seconds before attempting to budge. The fog cleared, and I took a step.

"Strong drink, that stuff," I said, and laughed a bit. Angelina tittered, and held one of my arms. I felt somewhat recharged. As if the "rest" had filled my batteries to full capacity. By all accounts, I should be suffering. The feeling overcoming me now was one of power. I nodded to her and she let go of my arm. I walked to the front of the tent, getting used to the odd moving sensation below my feet, and pushed the tent flap open.

"Where are we?" I asked, wiping sweat off my brow. I tried to get up and felt a bit wobbly, but with Angelina's help, I was steady enough to walk to the front of the carpet.

"An oasis island named al-Iskandariyya, in the middle of the Sand Sea. We have come to harvest, if you care to join," Iblis said, with what I could tell he hoped was his most non-threatening smile. All five tents were lined up on the beach, side-by-side, and the other Jinn waited for Iblis. Sparse vegetation, but in the centre of the island was a tall, tower-like ruin of sharply cut stone, an arched bridge leading to it.

"Are you coming with us?" black-skinned Kabira asked. "It's entirely safe." She headed toward the wide, sand-covered bridge. There was no moon overhead, unlike in my dream. We walked in almost total darkness, with only the stars as guides, but oh how many there were! I don't remember ever having seen so many and I kept discovering new points of light as I walked on, following Maimun and Adira.

I felt a strong hand on my arm, and whirled around to see who had grabbed me.

"You should be careful," green-skinned Kabira said, one hand on my wrist, the other pointing toward the edge of the bridge where I had been heading—so much for total safety. She let go of my hand, and I rubbed my wrist, staring down into the abyss that yawned below us. I shivered, and walked on the middle of the bridge from that point on. The arched bridge was several hundred metres long, and I could see the ruin better as we got closer. The bridge went into its enormous base: a wide, tall carved-stone door. Whatever levels had been above the door had all collapsed save two, and their fallen rock mounds scattered through the doorway. The Jinn began to climb the large debris without hesitation, and I gazed up at the sky through the broken roof.

"Let me help you," Iblis said, and led me to the first step of cracked stone. He climbed up as skillfully as a billy-goat, and extended his hand. I hesitated and gave it to him. He pulled me up as if I were weightless, and put me down gently beside him. We kept climbing higher, and whenever a particularly large block loomed, he'd be there to pull me up.

It was not long before we reached a ledge that formed the outer perimeter of the structure.

"This used to be a beacon of light," Maimun said.

"What happened to it," I asked.

"Desperate people tend toward darkness," Adira answered, smiling wryly.

The parapet was two meters wide, and formed the outline of a square at the top of the building. Iblis recommended I sit down so that the wind would not push me off. I did as he said, watching the horizon of the Sand Sea with one hand over my eyes.

I marveled at the expanse of the desert. The utter, incomprehensible hugeness of the stars and Heavens, my being firmly planted on flat, dry stone. The indiscernible chill of night a kind of internal hum that tied all together. It was like being whole. With the Universe, yes, but also with myself.

The Jinn all stood along the same wall, staring out to sea, and began to speak at once, in soft, caressing voices. Angelina and Barkley sat toward the end of their row, next to Kabira, while I was in the middle. I don't know if I was meant to feel special, but I did.

"Souls of the dead,
Wandering the seas,
Rise from your resting places.
Souls of the damned,
Rending anger's flame,

Afterdeath

Rise from you haunts," but not in any language I could understand. This all happened in my head. These were the words they spoke:
Ey aawaaregaan daryaahaa
Az aaraamgaahe khod barkheezeed
Ey arwaahe nefreen shodegaan
Keh shekaafandehye shoelehye khashm hasteed
Az jaayegaahe khod barkheezeed

They carried on the wind, amplifying the further they went, until the Sand Sea echoed with the call. For a time, it was quiet, and I wondered what we were waiting for, but I did not have to wait for long. Glowing yellow sprites, like St. Elmo's fire, ephemeral and electric, began to lift from the sea. I turned around, and they came from everywhere, comets shooting toward the sky in slow motion. Floating above the waves toward the ruined tower. I was glad I was sitting at that moment, or I surely would have fallen off.

"I hope they make it in time," Maimun said, frowning. "They seem sluggish. Must be the phase," staring up at the sky.

"Why wouldn't— " I started, but then I saw: long, dark shapes rising from the sand dunes. As big as whales, maybe larger. Rows of sharp black teeth, obsidian knives, reflected in yellow light. Then, no more. The light behind which the shadow had been trailing extinguished, sharp fins cutting through the sand waves and slipping away.

"Sea Hunters, the black squalls," Adina said, gritting her teeth. I could see them, jumping out of the waters like great white sharks, catching the fragile lights, snuffing them, then sinking back under the sands with their prizes. Eventually, only a dozen amber lights remained, and climbed the walls to where we waited. Within the fizzing yellow lights were the frail forms of the dead. The Jinn communed with them silently. They removed empty glass flasks from their belts and held them up. Eight of the glowing spectres entered them, and the four or five that were left drifted away, each in their own direction. The Jinn stoppered the bottles, and we returned to the shore, my heart filled with a kind of dampened happiness for those that had made it. The tents and sleep waited for us, and we went to them.

***

I woke to the steady sway of the Sand Sea. Instead of making me feel sick, as it should have, I felt this comfort, as if I'd been taken home. Illusion, of course, but a warm kind of illusion. Well worth basking in while the goodness of it lasted.

"We are coming into view of the oasis that borders Jubbah. We should be there by mid-morning," Iblis said, sitting cross-legged, staring forward. The sand no longer flowed, and I saw that we had left the sea behind. We travelled on the crest of an enormous dune of reddish-gold sand. Below us, resting in the bowl of said desert, was a flowering oasis of squat palms and long-leaved, bushy plants, surrounding a clear blue lake. On the far bank, an amalgamation of brown-bricked one and two-story buildings had been haphazardly constructed. They, too, were crowded in by all the greenery. Caravaners could be seen driving their camels in from another direction to the right (I wasn't sure what my cardinal directions were). There was also a jeep kicking up dust from the furthest dune behind the city of Jubbah, heading away from it. By the banks of the oasis, men and women sunned themselves. I smiled, thinking of vacations in the South I'd never taken, and how, when my hellish ordeal was over, I would gladly come back to this place to more fully take advantage of its relaxed atmosphere. But there was Chloe to think about, and time was running out.

The ramil-sammak glided down the angled dune, circumventing the oasis from the left. I poked around the back and saw Iblis' companions following suit.

As we neared the blue-green water's edge, Iblis said: "Welcome to Jubbah. A most ancient and sacred city. Allow me to park my steed." He patted the ground, and the tent stopped near the bank. Iblis stepped off and said: "Wait for me here." A small plume of sand flew up in a chuff, and he smiled. "Please ladies, follow me," he said to us, and we disembarked from his mode of transportation. Barkley walked between us, and Angelina watched everything with a calculating eye. I have to admit, I just stared. Once we got through a small thicket of stubby palms, we found a packed dirt trail in cooling shade, headed straight for the city, with sweet smells wafting in the air.

"This city has been here for over seven-thousand years," Iblis said, raising his arms.

"It's beautiful," I said. It was true. I had no idea if the arrangement of homes, roads and plant life was intended to be this way, but it gave the whole place an entirely organic feel that I couldn't get over. The homes and businesses looked like big sand castles, with rounded edges and soft tones. In front of many, there were striped awnings of cream and red, or green and black, with men or women fanning themselves on cushions, just inside the entrance. Following the twittering of birds to their source in the trees, I was amazed by rainbows of plumage.

In this place you could buy baskets or lamps, or strange liquids in odd bottles. The latter reflected the sun's rays on their multi-coloured surfaces. The front of the shops stood open like wide garage doors, and the inside was cool and inviting. Men and women sat around tiny tables drinking from miniature cups. I wondered if it was Soul's Brew they imbibed, and my stomach giving a nervous reaction.

Afterdeath

All around stood thick palms no higher than twice my height. Stunted yet healthy, they provided shade wherever we went. The brouhaha of the city was a whisper, a soft laughter, a clink of glasses, or a chirruping of songbird. My heart warmed the further I walked. Iblis' naked feet made no sound on the dirt path. Only Angelina and I could be heard, feet crunching on little pebbles. Under the palms, bushes like cheerleader's pom-poms blossomed. Watermelon-sized, their long, arrow-shaped leaves all sprouted from one central source and curved back on themselves before touching the ground.

At the foot of the homes, cacti of a hundred and one variety grew; some flowering, giving the impression that the buildings might have been their progenitors.

"Where are the other Jinn?" Angelina asked, glancing back.

"Tending to their own business. Jinn are strange, in that we are solitary creatures, even though we may stay together for company. My friends and I have known each other for a very long time."

"I thought you lived in lamps," I said, jokingly.

"Only those unlucky enough to get caught." Iblis said, without turning around. Meandering paths brought us alongside a man-made canal, maybe two feet wide and half that in depth. Made of flat, interlocking stones, it flowed from the oasis to the rest of the settlement. Clear waters burbled down at a slight decline. It was on our left, then would run under the dirt path to reappear on our right.

Further to the right, beyond the line of short palms, a tall stone wall came into view. A bit further from the corner, an entrance gaped wide. Giant stone bulls with swan wings and the heads of bearded, crowned men guarded the entrance. I thought I'd seen similar carvings in National Geographic. They stood ten feet tall or more, and as Iblis raised a hand in greeting, one of them turned its head to follow our entrance.

"What the heck are those things?" I whispered to Angelina as we walked underneath their judgemental gaze.

"Guardians," she said, in a *Duh!* kind of way. It took all the strength I had not to crane my neck and stare at the enormous stone monoliths which were probably now considering whether or not we should be seen as meals or guests. I should have left my worries at the gate, of course. With a guide like Iblis, the odds were we could have been comfortable entering anywhere we pleased. Nevertheless, discomfort was my natural state, and I dared not stray too far from it too long. I turned again, and was struck with a vision of beauty.

A large garden came into view, bordering the inside walls, with much the same plants we'd encountered along the way, but arranged in such a way as to enhance the natural aesthetics of every genus found there.

The water ran into another larger basin. An enormous, multi-tiered fountain dominated the centre of the park, tiled in iridescent blues, with an unknown language in golden bits of metal, hammered in place along its rim.

The whole area looked like a checkerboard, with tiles missing. Trickles of pure water filled these holes and the fountain overflowed into its reservoir. I noticed other branches splaying out to the rest of the settlement, like life's nervous system. It was strange to me to have to parse where life ended and death began. As if all my notions of death were predicated on a clear separation that… didn't exist.

Around its circular base, statues of three men and three women sat in the waters, on thrones that were part of the fountain. The waters flowed over them. The parts of them that stuck out of the waters, such as their feet, knees and heads remained a copper colour, but everything submerged was either greenish or covered in algae and tiny marine life. The water which flowed was crystalline and pure. It made me want to take a long quaff, but I thought that might be rude, and held back.

Iblis walked to the first statue of an elderly man with dark tanned coppery skin like soft leather, the sun shining off his features. His beard was long enough to go from that gorgeous new penny colour to dip into the water and look corroded by the time it reached his stomach. He sat on a frayed-looking metal blanket with his back to the fountain, his balding head bowed to the flowing water all around him, eyes closed. I thought of him as a noble grandfather. I noticed a tiny crayfish swimming against the current around his lap, holding onto and using a wavering piece of spindly algae to propel itself forward.

"Wahy," Iblis said, standing before the elderly man's statue. "I have come for your help. Answer my prayer." He then proceeded to get on his knees and put his right fist on his heart and bow.

I keep getting surprised. It's beyond me. I keep getting dropped into shocking situations and have no control over my reactions. The statue opened its eyes and spoke and I reacted with a small cry, making a motion to hide behind Angelina. This time I caught myself—I did. You'd think the giant man-headed bull statues would have prepared me, wouldn't you? Well, no.

"You've returned from your travels Iblis. What have you found?" The elder man's voice was soothing, but at the same time, it was wind through a tunnel that extended back through time. It rang of an pseudo-instrument, as if it were one step away from becoming a trumpet, just not quite there yet.

"Nothing much changes in the desert. You must know this, Wahy," Iblis said with a smile.

"Ah, but change comes slowly, Jinn. And when it does, everything you once held dear is no more, save their memories. You've brought an agent of change with you,

Afterdeath

I see," the old man said, and I pointed to myself, my eyes wide. He smiled and raised an algae-encrusted arm.

"Not you young lady, but your companion. I'm afraid it is written all over her. She's a cross-road."

"What do you mean?" Angelina asked, fidgeting. Iblis had turned around, looking at her for the first time.

"We, the Wahy, are unconstrained by time and dimensions. We travel freely, yet try not to affect outcomes. We are watchers between the borders of life and death. You have come to the fountain that flows into life. I have seen the probabilities of your success," he said, staring not at but *into* Angelina, and I shuddered.

"And?" she said, with trepidation.

"That is all I can say. Another word and I will affect the outcome of your quest."

"Then why say anything at all!?" Angelina said, her temper flaring.

Iblis turned around, angered by her impertinence. The old man raised a hand to calm him.

"Because what would be the fun in keeping silent? Even in death, you take everything so seriously, so angrily. No matter. It helps and hinders. Always it helps and hinders." The elder man winked at Angelina, and she unclenched her fists.

"But you also have an important quest. Do you know what you are?" The Wahy said, looking at me, putting both hands on one knee.

I shook my head no. Angelina had said I had some special power, but nothing beyond that.

"You're an object of power. Half of one, really. But there is enough power in you to cross from here to there," and his hand waved to and fro as he said this. "If you were to be joined with your sister, then..." he squinted his eyes and leaned a bit forward. "you might very well be unstoppable." He sat back and smiled.

"But we used whatever power she had to get out of Wodun!" Angelina said. "She's, for want of a better word, empty!"

"I don't feel empty," I said. "I feel refreshed."

"Since when?" she said, incredulous.

"Since I woke up yesterday morning. You know... because of the..."

"Soul's Brew!" she said, cutting me off. "Is the way to refill the batteries of a dobluth to feed it soul energy?" she asked the Wahy. He tilted his head and smiled.

"Why didn't I think of that!? I'm such a bloody idiot!" she cried, clapping her head.

"I'm sorry, I have to get back to my sister. She's in grave danger. There's some sort of monster coming after her and if I don't help her, I think she'll get consumed!" I said, and the Wahy nodded solemnly.

"What you say is true. This is a possible outcome. We've seen it. What you describe has not come to pass yet. The fortune-teller can see futures, yet she knows not when they will arrive, or exactly how. It is like seeing the train coming into the station without knowing the timetable, or the proper platform. You must hurry, yes." The elderly man confirmed. A slight wind rose then, and I felt more chill than it could deliver. Chloe was safe for now perhaps, but not for long.

"How can we get back there, to Larunda's kingdom?" I asked, pleading.

"The fountain is a conduit to all possible worlds, but if you have no beacon, you will get lost. You must find another way, and quick."

"I can take them to the edge of the desert by ramil-sammak," Iblis said. The old man smiled and put his hands on his knees.

"You are a good Jinn, Iblis," the statue said, then closed his eyes. He looked as if he'd dozed off.

"Has he gone to sleep?" I asked, feeling foolish.

"No, he is gone," Iblis said, turning to walk away from the fountain.

"You mean, like, dead?" and I felt even more foolish, seeing as everything that resided in this world was dead.

"No. The Wahy have no body. They inhabit the source of life sometimes when we call, but their energy flows everywhere and everywhen. It takes a lot of concentration to remain in one place for that long, so I am told. He has just returned to his natural state, that's all."

I listened to the birds chirping in the palms for a second, pondering his words and all the different shapes that "life" as I knew it could take. Angelina looked perturbed by her experience. She said nothing and followed Iblis out of the gate. The man-headed bull statues did not give us a second glance, and I felt so relieved by what I had been told that I forgot to be scared for a moment. I'd be back in time to save Chloe!

We meandered back down the same dirt paths we'd taken to get to the Wahy, but this time, there seemed to be a hint of hurry, and I was glad for it. Iblis took our urgency seriously at least. I wondered briefly what it had meant about Angelina being a "crossroad," and how that might affect my sister and I in the future.

Back at the oasis, three of the other Jinns sunned themselves on the beach. Barqa, Adira and Kabira looked relaxed. Maimun was nowhere to be seen.

"Companions," Iblis began. They opened their eyes and propped themselves up.

"What is it Iblis?" Adira said, "You look too serious for such a gorgeous day."

"Come, Iblis, enjoy the sun by the water a bit," Barqan added, waving us over. Iblis shook his head.

247

Afterdeath

"I must leave right away. These little ones are in need of my help. I know this now. It's been too long since I've had a bit of adventure. I will take them to the edge of the desert and be back in three days' time. Wait for me."

"You would leave us behind and go adventuring on your own?" Barqan said, jumping up. His skin went from yellow to a deeper orange.

"Do you think we are unfit for this adventure?" Kabira said, smoky blackness roiling on her skin.

"Maybe our dear Iblis doesn't like us anymore," Adira said, crossing her arms and turning away, her chin in the air.

"Come now my dear friends. You know I would not leave you behind when you seem so keen on coming. We leave right away. Can you be ready?" Iblis said.

Adira whistled, and from nearby, Maimun popped his head out of one of the tents.

"So, are we going?" he asked.

"Turn your fish around, we depart this instant," Kabira said, smiling. Maimun winked and sat down at the head of his creature. It was then that Iblis realized he'd been had. He shook his head, smiling, and hopped onto his steed. He waved us over, and Angelina, Barkley and I got onto it as well. He walked into his tent and a second later, it collapsed, becoming a rolled package which he strapped down.

The others trotted over to where their own sand-mantas drank and relaxed, and did the same. They then sat at their heads.

Iblis sat near the front, his hands palms down on the ground.

"I recommend you hold on to something," he said, turning around. I looked around me, but all I could find was the corner of carpet's edges. That would have to do. I saw him tap the ground in front of him, and the ground began to shake.

I'd seen videos, long ago, of hovercraft flying across waters. I'd found it amazing how much water they kicked up, and the incredible speeds they could reach. This was even more awesome.

We skirted the oasis on the left, climbing the bowl at an angle. The higher we went, the faster it became. Soon it did feel as if we were flying through the desert, and I took a last look at the oasis, and thought I could recognize the bushy maze where we'd spoken to the Wahy of the fountain—then it was gone.

My heart rose sharply as we jumped over the lip of the bowl of sand, then levelled out. Sand kicked up all around us, and I saw the undulations of the mantas 'wings' all around us. If before it had been well-hidden under its natural element, it was now boring full-speed ahead at what must have been fifty or sixty kilometres an hour. This might not strike you as particularly fast. Remember, though, that we were sitting outside, with no protection from the winds or sand, and with no seat belts whatsoever. Believe me when I tell you that it was frighteningly fast.

I covered my eyes with one hand, and did as Angelina and Barkley did: lay down. That close to the ground, very little sand kicked up into their faces. I took a peek at Iblis, who navigated through the high-rise apartments which dotted the landscape. He'd put on a pair of aviator glasses, and just now noticed us crouching down. He made a kind of 'oops!' face and got up to rummage around in a bag. He came back with a few more pairs and handed them to us. Sadly, there were only two that fit, since he had no dog-sized ones. The sand that flew up from below made a sound as if it were being chewed up and spat out by a snow blower. I looked back and saw that the other four behind us followed in a "V" formation, to avoid being on the receiving end of the substantial plume of sand we all created. Anyone seeing us cruise through the desert might have wondered what kind of mad tornado was dashing through.

Day progressed, and then when the sun was dipping to the horizon, Iblis raised his hand. Our high-speed race through the desert began to slow, and he found the shade of one of the sand-covered apartment blocks in which we could stop. He got up and stretched, pulling his head from side to side. Truth be told, I felt pretty wracked from having stayed in the prone position all day as well.

I got up and bent my legs, extended one as far as I could go, then did the same for the other. Angelina had already walked off with Barkley and was touching the side of the crusted building with her own sand-covered hand. One thing I don't think I'd ever get over is how dirty the land of the dead was. With mud, and sand, and all the other things I'd been covered in, there was no way I'd start calling this place heaven; not by a long shot.

The others were "parking" their mounts, making a half-circle around the base of the sand-covered building. I watched as a chunk of sand fell off at Angelina's touch.

"Be wary of dislodging too much of the sand, girl," Kabira said.

"Why's that?" she said.

"Because then you might accidentally release what is still trapped inside," she replied, and went to help make a fire in the middle of the half-circle.

By this time, the sun had sunk so low it was a mere red bump on the horizon, and the desert cold was rising to take its place.

We sat around the fire, and the Jinns told us about what it was like to be near-immortal beings who could alter reality's parameters to ensure you could achieve those things you wanted most (wishes). *It only works in the living world, though*, had said Maimun, as a confidential aside.

Barqan complained that nowadays people didn't believe in the old religions, and that Jinns, like all the old Gods, had been set adrift in their own little world. Iblis shrugged. I think he had come to terms with all that, but I guessed it took others

249

Afterdeath

longer to wrap their heads around obsolescence. I mean as far as I knew, no one summoned Jinns back where we come from, and I imagine anyone trying it in the areas where they used to be popular might get stoned to death as heretics. I'd heard that some of the Worshippers of the Crescent didn't look too kindly on competition. Then again, neither did any of the other monotheistic religions. If only they knew. I sighed.

When I asked Adira what they did now she just made a face.

Maimun and Adira answered together and said: "exist," which to me wasn't much of an answer. Iblis said:

"We hold no purpose; we just are. We travel the confines of our kingdom relentlessly, looking."

"What for, though?" Angelina asked, curious.

"Purpose. It is the only thing worth going on for. Without purpose, there is no meaning. Meaning always follows purpose," Iblis said.

"Not true, not true," Adira said, waving a finger in the negatory. "Meaning is always there, whether there is purpose or not. It is the interpretation that binds meaning to purpose!"

"Is that why you are helping us?" I asked, feeling as if I'd touched something important.

"She's a smart one, this one," Kabira said.

"We do not know the meaning of your coming to our lands. But your quest gives us purpose. We are hoping to discover the meaning someday. For now, we are glad to interpret it as what is necessary to give us purpose, if only for a short time. Then we shall return to our wandering," Barqan said.

"What do you hope to get out of it?" I asked.

"A sense of accomplishment," Maimun said. "I know what it sounds like, but we've had a very long time to think about these things. We have also had a very long time to do absolutely nothing. Before that, we had an incredibly long time to do everything we could possibly want to do, with no negative repercussions. If you think about it, eating, sleeping, amassing treasures, coveting lovers, warring; all those things are just fine. But! When you concentrate solely on those, you lose sight of the interesting things you can accomplish as a thinking being. You accomplish nothing."

"But what if you had an enormous treasure? Couldn't you do a lot with that?" I replied.

Barqan smiled and said: "Sure you could! But most people don't! Dragons don't want to make anything with their treasures, they just want to keep them. All for themselves. They accomplish strictly nothing. It's what you do with what you have that counts as accomplishment, not what you hoard or obsess over."

"We've had a long time to explore all the avenues of thought that come with sentience Olivia. We've lost so many of our brothers and sisters to hatred, greed, and all the other selfish emotions you can be driven by. The five of us are left because we are driven by love," Kabira said, and she smiled so prettily that I felt a reddening in my cheeks.

Barqa reached behind him and took out a short flute, what might have been a recorder, but made out of a dried reed. He put it to his lips, like a delicate glass, and blew softly into the top aperture. The sound had a pacifying effect on my so-often troubled mind. For a moment, all anxiety retracted its tendrils from my body and went to sleep within my breast. The music rose in the night as the fire crackled merrily. It was enough to just hear it and not judge it. Happy or sad; it just was, and I let it *be*. Perhaps my trouble was that I constantly worried about purpose and inevitability. That I could never be here, and now. So I let myself, and I began to drift into the stars above.

***

On the second day, I thought Iblis was driving his manta even harder, if that was at all possible. It felt like mid-morning when a wall like a thin line blotted out the horizon. The faster we hammered the steeds, the larger that wall loomed, and then I saw the cliff-face for what it was. It stretched to both poles of the horizon, an unbroken line, thin at first, but growing taller as we neared. The surrounding apartment complexes had thinned out, and now we were left with sand, sky, sun and wall. But what a wall! At the very top was what I hoped was vegetation, but there would be no way to verify this until we'd climbed. This was, of course, the only way back, or so the Jinn had told us. No wonder their little world was so seldom disturbed. It had sunk into the sands of time, and now only the most obstinate could leave or enter. Thankfully this journey had made me more than that. Perhaps a few weeks ago I'd have looked up at this sheer cliff and thought of only impossibility. Now it was an obstacle, meant to be overcome.

I smiled inwardly at this.

All along the red-stoned cliff face, small shacks sprouted, from bottom, all the way to the top. They were connected to one another by ladders, from the roof of one to the bottom of the next one up. They reminded me of those little ice-fishing shacks that you could rent in certain frozen areas of Quebec during the winter. Like those, these were painted in various colours, but had had no upkeep whatsoever. Curled flakes fell from them like a molting, whenever a strong wind tried to disrupt them from their perch. Every house was a single, tiny room, with a hole at the bottom, and one or more at the top, where different types of ladders climbed even higher to the next one. From a distance, I could tell that not all of them made it to the rim of the cliff. Once we were close enough, I had no idea which would be the best ladder to take, as all I could see were the undersides of those tiny coloured shacks.

The sand manta slowed, and I got up, handing Iblis his goggles back. He put them away and looked up at the teetering ladders moving slightly to and fro with the shifting of the wind.

"You must choose the right one," he said, and soon the other four were gathered around us. Barkley wagged his tail nervously, throwing a glance to one ladder, then another, then up at his mistress.

"Little help in choosing, ladies and gentlemen?" she said, arching an eyebrow at our hosts.

"We have not left since the lands sank, eons ago," Barqan said.

"Who built these, then?" I asked. These contraptions couldn't be that old, I told myself.

"Those who could not stand the thought of remaining on a sinking world," replied Kadira. "That is why not all roads lead to the top. At one point, they did, but then they sank and other paths had to be built."

"Why so many?" I said. It was odd that so much had been constructed when a single, or a few would have sufficed.

"It was a mass exodus. There was fear that everyone would be swallowed up in the sinking sands, and therefore in the panic everyone began to build and build. The people followed; many escaped," Adira said.

"What happened to the rest?" I was almost afraid to ask.

"They were swallowed up by the civil war that raged here, so long ago. That is why we've stayed. We find those who still wander the sands and try to help them, if we can," Maimun added, and I remembered the yellow lights rising from the sand sea.

"And if you can't?" Angelina said.

"We give them the rest they deserve," Iblis said, frowning. Every country in Death had their mercenaries, those appointed to cut down marauding souls to keep the sane from harm. It turned my stomach to think about it, but I grew to appreciate its necessity.

I went to each Jinn in turn and thanked them for their help. Without their speed and diligence, there was no way we'd have gotten this far. I still felt ashamed for my dream, but the best recompense would be to judge from now on with an open heart, not a closed mind.

"So we get to choose," I said aloud, squinting at the noon sky, walking to a ladder whose solidity left to be desired. Had to start somewhere.

I put my hand out to the worn wood, and wiggled gently back and forth. As I was about to set foot on the lowest rung, which hung a foot or two above the sand, I heard a crack, and looked up. Sand and pebbles rained down from the adjoining shack, ten meters above me, and I jumped off the ladder, shouting:

"Run!"

A loud crack and boom sounded above as the shack let go of its moorings, tumbling slantwise, disintegrating from the cliff side. I saw Kabira and Adira grab Angelina and Barkley, and Iblis lurched for me as the other two Jinn forced the sand-mantas out of the way at top speed. Falling debris rained, a solid chunk of two-by-four impaling itself by my leg. Iblis carried me a bit further, and I turned around to look up at the domino effect of carnage caused by that simple act. Thankfully, no other cabin fell off, but it made me wonder if we'd be able to make it all the way to the top without being taken down by these decrepit things.

When the dust had settled we found each other safe, if a little shaken. The Jinn decided to test a few ladders for us before letting us get on by ourselves. Eventually, they did find one that promised not to fall apart in our hands, and we began the arduous climb to the top.

I'd asked them, if they wanted to come. I'd asked, and they'd said no, of course. As the last protectors of a dying land they could not simply follow us, as much as they might have wanted to. Is it because I wanted them around me to take care of me? In my old life, perhaps; now, not so much. Even though I understood the reason why they stayed, I thought they could have been much more successful in finding purpose in a place where things *happened*.

Still, it wasn't my call, and I had my own death to live.

Angelina had tucked Barkley away inside her again, and once in a while, I saw his head poke out. I led the way, so I looked down to see our progress. The Jinn became specks on the ground, then I saw the line of erected tents floating away toward the expanse of the desert.

Every once in a while, a rung would break off in my hand, so I'd made it a habit of holding onto the last rung just as tight before putting all my weight on the next. I also put my feet on the corners, to avoid any weak parts in the middle.

The fact that we hadn't fallen down already made me hang on to the belief that we might make it.

Progress was a healthy trot at first, as careful as we tried to be. After a few of those shacks though, we were getting tired. The sun was dipping down once again, and we thought we might have to take refuge in one of the cabins for the night. There were maybe ten or twenty meters between shacks, and I tried to take count of how many we went through. Sometimes we had to decide which exit we'd take out of the top, as there might be two ladders sticking to the inside of the naked cabins. We'd pop the trap to see where they lead.

At first we tried to be scientific about it. We'd check the angles, and see if there wasn't another connection further up. After a while that was a waste of time, and we turned it into a sweaty game of rock, paper, scissors. Whoever won decided on the next direction.

Every hovel was equipped with a dirty window facing the desert. It was hot in those things. The lack of air circulation reminded me of the apartment we'd been trapped in a few days ago, minus the dust particles dancing around in our throats. It was so hot we always kept going, not wanting to sauna our butts into dissolution. There was garbage on the floor, but nothing I recognized as candy wrappers or household detergent. Just rags and filth and broken clay bits.

We'd open the bottom trap, find out if there was a choice to make, then make our way to the next shack through the top of the last one.

I was tired. It's not like we ever got any real rest. My arms were shaking at one point and I thought I'd throw up, then just let go. Angelina also saw this, because she said:

"We're going to have to stop at the next one, whether we want to or not."

"It's so hot in those things though!"

"I don't care. We have to stop for a breather or one or both of us will fall back all the way down. Olivia, what do you say?" I was not going to refuse of course, but the thought of my sister's dangerous predicament always loomed large, and halting our advance for any amount of time meant that I might lose her forever.

"Just for a little while," I said.

"Just for a little while," and she wiped sweat off her forehead with the back of her hand. It was not far until the next building. The underside was brown and worn-looking, but the sides must have been a bright red at some point.

I pushed open the trap door and it fell back like all the previous ones, with a clack. A ruffle of dust kicked up because of our disturbance, but otherwise, it was identical to all the others before it. I crawled in, making my way away from the trap door, and Angelina climbed in as well. As I lay on the floor, feeling like I was dying all over again from exertion, she found the next trap door up. I lay there in a puddle of my own sweat, the hot floor pressed against the side of my head, as if they'd stick together should I stay there too long. Barkley popped out from her sternum and looked at me, tongue lolling. As Angelina began to climb again, a febrile panic took me.

"Where are you going?" I demanded.

"Relax, I just want to open the door and get some air circulation going on in here. You could melt in this heat." I felt a bit foolish for having thought she'd abandon me.

I came to the realization that whatever her flaws, she was not the kind of person who would just dump you on the side of the road—unlike me. The look on her face as I pushed her off the cart back at Maman Margot's came back to me vivid as a picture; the sadness and hurt I'd made her endure. She was a tough woman to love I think. Barkley's secret made me come to understand that she was also a tough person to deal with. I wondered if and when he'd reveal to her the fact he could speak. Would I let it slip by accident?

"I'm sorry," I said, as she came back down the ladder. She gave me a quizzical look.

"About what?" I got up on my elbows, trying to feel any potential breeze created by the opening of both ends of our hot box.

"When I tossed you off the cart. That was a rotten thing to do."

She stared at me wide-eyed, then began to laugh.

"What's so funny?" I asked. She had her hands on her knees, and looked like someone had just told her the funniest joke. I wasn't sure I should have apologized anymore.

"Oh Olivia. Pretty sure I might have done the same thing to you; maybe not, I don't know. You worry too much, you know that. I guess what I mean to say is, apology accepted."

I felt my cheeks redden, but whether from embarrassment or gratitude, I couldn't have said.

"You ever been so driven by something, that anything that gets in your way becomes collateral damage?" I thought about getting back to Chloe and nodded.

"I've been trying for so long to get what I wanted, that those who get in my way, for whatever reason, just get slaughtered. Believe me, it's been going on for a while."

"Angelina, what are you trying to accomplish? Even I don't know what that is. I'm hoping Barkley knows, but he's not saying, so do you think you could let a girl in on your little secret, huh?" I wondered if that had been a slip.

She stared at me. She stared and stared and stared until I hoped the shack would fall off the cliff side, just to get the tension out of the way. Angelina took a seat where I was leaning back. She crossed her legs and put her hands on her knees, chin on her fists.

"I'm looking for a sanctuary, Olivia. I want to build one. One for two," and she glanced at Barkley, who trundled over and sat between her knees. She fluffed the fur of his head and began to rub along his neck.

"I want to find a way to turn him back; maybe I can, maybe I can't. More than that, I want to create a place for us—just us: a country with our name on it, a kingdom for two." And she looked into my eyes with a stare so intense I thought it might border on madness.

Afterdeath

"Okay," I said.

She looked down smiling still rubbing Barkley's flank.

"She thinks I'm crazy, hon, just like all the others. Now you know why I don't talk to anyone about it." This last bit could have been for me or Barkley, I didn't know.

"I'm just not sure I follow, that's all. Why do you need a country? You could exist anywhere you wanted to. What's wrong with Necropolis City?" I noticed the sweat underneath me had evaporated, drank up by the fossilized planks.

"It's just Necropolis dear; adding city is redundant. But to answer your question, it's still under the rule of another, arbitrary rule at that. I'm not sure you noticed, but there is a dearth of safe places to be in this universe. They are not only scarce, they are inexistent. If you aren't fending for your survival in the wild open spaces, you're doing it with a whole set of new rules inside heavily fortified cities to protect you from the wildness on the outside. It's maddening, this so-called life."

"Where do you want to go? How do you want to make this place?" I got up, pacing a bit around the ladder that lead downward.

"I don't know anymore. Our first idea was to claim land and settle it, making it ours. Then we got the idea to steal a power object." Barkley barked. "Fine, *I* got the idea to steal a power object. In any event we both got caught and they decided to punish Barkley for it. We both ended up in that prison forest. The rest you know." She leaned back on her hands and stared upward at the ceiling.

"What was wrong with taking land and starting your own little place on your own?" I paused, thinking about the possibilities.

"Too hard. The only lands unclaimed are the Wylds. Nothing goes in there and survives. Impossible to do it just the two of us. Well, technically there's just me. Barkley isn't in a state where he can do much fighting. Sorry babe." Barkley grunted and sneezed. "Besides, as soon as we'd settle a place, you know there's an army commanded by one of the other rulers that'll come knocking at the door to take it over and get rid of whoever gets in the way." She smiled, but there was bitterness in it. I wondered how many years it took to become this hardened. Somehow, the afterlife was even tougher than I'd expected. Where were my fluffy clouds inhabited by angels and the souls of my loved ones? Was this place Hell? From what Angelina kept telling me, there was no such thing as a single afterlife, so what then? Keep struggling for what? What was the purpose of it all? Was there ever really an answer to anything, or just world after world, existence after existence?

"Why do you keep going?" I asked. Maybe her answer would give me reason to pursue as well.

"Adventure and the chance to destroy my enemies!" she said, waving an invisible sword about like some swashbuckling pirate. The little shack creaked a tad underfoot, and she became very still, putting her hands out as if to balance the shack.

"Oh cut the bull. I just wish you'd tell me the truth, from now on. Please?" I tilted my head at her sideways, taking in her slumped shoulders and companion lying on the floor, muzzle between paws.

She crept to the far wall, planks wincing quietly under her feet. She turned around and slid to the floor, back to the wall. She began to inspect her interlaced fingers, and refused to look at me.

"Mrm," is what I thought I heard her say.

"I'm sorry, I didn't catch that," I said.

Silence.

"Love," she said.

"You're serious."

"Why are you flying to your sister's rescue?" she said, her lips twisting with smugness.

"Good point." I got up from the floor, groaning from the muscle fatigue in my arms, and walked to the grimy window. I passed a shaking hand over the sandy residue, my prints clearly defined where my hand left the glass. A sift of dust fell to the floor, and I tapped my hand gently on my leg, red-beige powder falling to the floor. Beyond, the desert was still, and the sun was almost three-quarters done its travels until we would lose it again. Those apartment blocks dotting the landscape were unrecognizable as buildings, covered in the sands of forever. Tall sand castles, ready to crumble at a touch. That's how I felt, too.

If not for the things that animated me to movement, to action, I might as well disintegrate right here on the floor. But there was always a purpose, and a purpose, and a purpose. Because if there stopped being one, and a struggle to achieve it, there would be nothing. What then?

I thought I heard a silence louder than any other, but then a wind came from far away, lifting Angelina's hair as she sat staring at her tangled fingers, and Barkley lifted his nose, eyes wide.

Creak.

No good.

Crack.

No good at all.

Barkley started by barking, but it turned into his human voice in an instant:

"Bark, bark... have to go! We have to run, right now!" he said, and ran into Angelina, whose hands were now splayed before her in shock, knocked back by

Afterdeath

Barkley's sudden entrance. I would never get used to seeing a dog jump into someone's ribcage, I decided.

As Angelina rose in startled anger, my footing dropped by inches. The view outside tilted forward by as much, and the sound that came with it was a wrenching cruck.

Drop.

One foot tilt.

My heart lurched as my legs almost gave way under me, and the whole façade of the shack broke with a shriek, falling open like an old mailbox on a country road. But the hinge didn't hold, and it snapped off the base, tumbling down over the shacks we'd previously passed on our way up.

I lost my balance, leaning forward as the building continued to tilt downward at ticking intervals, and felt a hand on my belt as my head went overboard. I could see a kilometre to the bottom, where nothing but sand and the now breaking constructions were being taken out one after another.

I screamed. I must have. There was no way I could've stayed silent in this moment of sheer panic.

"Turn around!" I heard Angelina cry as the base of our building now sagged at an almost forty-five degree angle. I shot out my arm, and grabbed what must have been hers. I stared down into the emptiness, couldn't turn away, couldn't, couldn't, couldn't.

"Look at me!" she yelled, and I whipped around. She was holding the ladder with one hand, jutting out her body to hold onto me. I put one foot toward her, then the other, and grabbed her arm with both my hands.

She heaved, and my fingers slipped onto the ladder.

The platform screamed and dropped. It hit the side of the cliff, and made an attempt at a swan dive, but caught another jut and snapped to pieces, the ancient wood planks exploding as they banged against previous debris that hadn't been entirely destroyed by the falling front half of the shack.

My legs dangled in nothing. Angelina still held fast to my belt with one hand, the other one gripping the ladder.

"Are you secured?" she said, and I tightened my grip on the ladder. She gave my face a grimace of concern, and I could only assume I was grayish with fright, all blood rushed to my vice-grip fingers so that I wouldn't fall. "Climb up on me," she said, letting go of my belt and bringing her knees up. I pulled myself up and put a hand on the next rung of the ladder, while resting my foot on her knees.

I pushed, my heart racing, fingers trembling. I looked down and saw her wince. She was staring down at the path of destruction that went so far down that anything landing was unidentifiable.

"Go!" she said, noticing I no longer moved. I pressed harder, pushing down on her knee, and was able to lift myself up, then put a foot on the corner of the ladder. It was easier now. I began my ascent, making my way through the hole that was once a closed shack. Now only the side walls and ceiling remained—for how long?

I kept climbing, keeping my eyes on the next cabin, further up.

I felt a shudder, and risked looking down. Angelina was right above the roof of the death trap we'd just escaped, and was kicking the moorings that held the ladder to it. Every time she did, the ladder trembled and shook, and I felt it would come off completely, sending us straight down the hatch to join the rest of the debris in freefall. A churning crack, and she broke the ladder off.

She began to climb again, giving me a "go on!" gesture with her hand, and I came to, my daze fading as I remembered the immediate danger we were all in.

I think she said something to the effect of: "We have a lot to talk about," which may or may not have been meant for Barkley, but I was distracted by the sudden fall of the rest of the shack. It took a few tumbles, like a kite that had lost any pretence of wanting to fly, and just plummeted straight down.

I turned around and kept climbing, the blood I assumed I had in my veins pumping like a flood, my energy levels peaking like I was on something unnatural, never to run out.

I climbed.

One hand, one foot.

The other hand, the other foot.

And we stopped for nothing, not even the seagulls wheeling about near the summit, curious as to what we might be doing there as the sun slipped under the horizon.

Chapter 20

CHOICES

Morning was prowling through the dark forest when Gassire woke me. The previous night had been parlay and accords. We'd stayed up late deciding what should be done, as well as what our boundaries were. I was worried that they might try to rush us, but it appeared they were unsure as to how to proceed now that their mistress was being held captive by one of her own creations. The soft wet grass around me did not stay that way for long. My hair was covered in dew, and I felt a bit stiff from having slept against one of the broken walls of the stronghold.

Gassire chirped overtop the low wall, hopping in place.

"Rise and shine, milady!" he said.

"I wish I didn't have to do either," I said, putting my hand to my stiff neck. I turned it one way, then the other. Was I truly feeling this, or was it just the habit I'd dragged in from my living self? If there was one thing I wasn't sure of anymore, it was whether or not my body was supposed to feel all the aches and pains it had in life. The more I thought about it, the more it made sense that what I felt was what the clinicians called "ghost pain", the pain you felt at the loss of a limb, but thought you still felt. It made sense. After all, I was a ghost. What was this pain but the itchiness of a body I no longer had? The more I pondered it, the less I felt the pain in my neck—then gone.

Beside me on the grass lay Iuturna. I gave her a nudge, and her head poked up in a small cry.

"Goodness, I had a nightmare," she said. She wiped the sleep out of her eyes and looked around. "No, it would seem I am still in it."

"We have to tend to our friends," I said, and got up. Over the wall in the distance I saw the clumps of soldiers covered in blankets around charred fire pits. They would let us do our thing and wouldn't bother us. We had a deal. How long it would hold depended on how much we could help them, I supposed.

"Mother," I heard Iuturna say, and watched as she gently nudged the woman curled up on the ground a bit further away. The bodies of our friends and family lay against walls, and some of them were waking up. Those we'd rescued were acting odd, however. Iuturna's mother woke and turned to her daughter. I barely recognized the woman and my heart seized in my throat. She looked entirely different! This wasn't the shade of a person we'd dragged into the ruins the night previous. She stood rejuvenated and healthy, sunken eyes gone. She was beautiful. She smiled to Iuturna and said:

"My daughter. I have been brought back from the edge of the precipice."

"But how?" Iuturna said, her eyes watering.

"I know not, but I can only be thankful." She said, and opened her arms to hold her. I saw Iuturna's tears coming down and turned away, feeling like an intruder. It was odd somehow to see Iuturna holding her mother, now no longer a mere wraith. Tears that might have been years in the waiting flowed freely.

I walked away, waking up the rest of the group. Every one of them looked as if life had been restored to them. It was a minor miracle.

Carson came to me.

"What happened last night?" he asked.

I told him about my explorations and how I'd found everyone after I'd come back. Gassire landed on a low ledge near my hand.

"The old king has given you all his being," he said.

"What do you mean by that?" I asked.

"The aura of the king, Kozla-kuguza is no longer in the ruins: it is in you! You've been blessed by his essence," the little starling said.

"I don't get it. Why would he do that?" I said.

"Maybe you were worthy?" Carson said. "Maybe he was tired of leading a half-death. Maybe he wants you all to survive. Maybe we'll never know and we should just accept this gift of his." He winked. I remembered falling and hurting myself, then getting up again refreshed. It was the king's doing, I was sure now. I looked in the distance at the grey dawn where mists wisped through the black pines, eerie and silent. I shivered. A king had sacrificed his eternity for a band of nobodies.

"Are you crying?" Carson said, peering at me.

Afterdeath

"I'm fine," I said, and turned away running my sleeve over my face.

"Listen," I said, "We have a deal with the soldiers on the edge of the property. Thing is, if we now have the old king's energies I'm not sure what's to prevent them from just coming in and slaughtering us when we're done helping them, so we might want to keep that under our hats for now, okay?" A fine mist had begun to fall. It just clung in the air until it touched solids, and then clung to that, like droplets of liquid tension. The clouds were so thick the sun wasn't even visible as an orb, but a diffuse light turning the day greenish-grey.

Carson approved, and we rejoined the group. One after the other they'd woken to find themselves whole again. We pleaded for them to hold back their jubilation so that our temporary allies wouldn't wonder or question why this was. The tight-rope was set. We all had to walk it now.

It was decided that Carson and I would go with Garcia and the rest of the soldiers to see what had happened at the cottage. When we approached their camp, a few of them were already seated on tree stumps. Alois smoked a pipe, and Garcia gazed in the distance, toward his master's home.

"This mist is unusual," Alois said after having taken a puff. Garcia wiped some water off his face and shook his head.

"Our lady is losing control of her kingdom, I think," Garcia said.

"Don't you say that Portillo! Don't you dare say that! We will have our Queen out of this predicament in no time. Then she'll put everything aright," Alois retorted, staring at me evilly, arms crossed. Then he turned his back to us, and looked in the direction of the cottage, puffing at his pipe.

"You'll have to excuse Alois," Garcia said, "He's been out of sorts ever since this entire ordeal began. Our plan is to go back to the cottage and scout out this thing's weaknesses. We then have to formulate a plan as to how to best get rid of it." He put his hands on his hips and gave us a less than convincing smile.

"And what happens after that? What will we do once the monster is vanquished and the Evil Queen is once again ruling?" Carson said. Alois whirled around and sprang up, throwing down his pipe, drawing his sword. His face a contorted mask of anger, he lifted it above his head ready to strike. Quicker than him, though, Garcia had his own sword to protect Carson from the blow, which he deflected with a clang. He then hip-checked the man, who fell to the ground. The other soldiers gathered round to see what the commotion was about.

"We have an understanding Alois. You are not to harm them," Garcia said. He put out a hand for the other man to take but Alois only spat.

"Any man who can speak ill of my Lady that way should be put to death," Alois simmered. There was grumbling in the ranks.

"Any man who can so easily break a truce should rethink his loyalties to his uniform!" Garcia bellowed, and Alois frowned, getting up. "If any of you feel like a promise made is worth air, *you* are the traitors," Garcia said, turning around to look at all the soldiers in the eye, pointing at them with his sword. There were many nods of ascent, but at least three men only looked at him with fury in their eyes. Unanimity did not rule the day in this bunch. I tried to memorize the faces of those who sided with Alois; they would be the dangerous ones.

We made our way down the wet sand path, back into the forest we'd escaped the day before. Silence was broken only by muted footsteps. There was the insidious smell of rot on the wind; not vegetable, but animal. The kind you associated with greevers, but coming from far away. The odour equivalent of hearing a train whistle in the distance, and knowing it would be loud from close up. I could only imagine what we'd find attached to this vile stench.

I walked by Carson, and kept Alois in view up front. I wish I knew who was behind us, but I thought we'd be okay for now. I caught up to Garcia.

"Hey."

"Yes?" He said.

"Thanks for protecting my friend."

"I did it for honour, miss. Alois is a good man. Your friend shouldn't have insulted our Mistress. It was a bad move on his part. If we didn't need you, I'd have let him cut down that man." Then he gave me a sharp look. I stopped in my tracks. What a weird situation I'd gotten into. This felt like a grown-up version of High School. The enemies of my enemies are my temporary allies? Is that it? What would happen when the whole thing was resolved, and Larunda was free to destroy us as she pleased? Would Garcia spare us then? What was he doing here in the first place? All of us just victims of weird unusual circumstances, waiting for our opportunities to shine and not be straight-jacketed into one course of action or the other. That sounded like High School, too.

I caught up with Garcia again.

"What do you want from your, uh, afterlife?" I asked.

"I'm not sure what you mean," he said.

"Well, you know, what are your desires? What do you go on for?"

"I'm not sure I understand the question," he said, and we walked on in silence for a bit. Our shoes and boots made a squelching sound over the roots and mud of the track, and the gentle mist had changed to the patter of rain. Gentle for now, I wondered when it would turn to a flood. The tap-tap-tap of droplets repeated over millions of times throughout the forest was soothing, even as I was getting drenched. I felt only wet, not cold. I looked up through the foliage, watching bright green, healthy maple and oak leaves bouncing; the trunks darkened by the wet. A small stream had begun to snake its way along the path.

"How did you become one of Larunda's soldiers Garcia?" I asked, breaking the awkward silence that had wedged itself between us.

"That's rather a personal question, isn't it?" he said, taking a deep breath.

"How else am I going to get to know you?" I felt Carson's eyes on my back, as if he was wondering: *what are you playing at?* But this wasn't a game to me. I wanted to know his motivations. If I understood his past, then maybe I could figure out if we could have him as an ally later. This wasn't so much cold calculation as it was survival. Besides, he seemed like a nice, honourable guy. I was *also* curious to find out what made someone like that want to become a puppet to an evil woman.

"I was in the Rif War. I was part of the Spanish and French forces that were attempting to put down a rebellion in Northern Africa."

"Never heard of it. Sorry," I said, and instantly regretted it.

"No, it's not important. It's only the war in which I lost my life, after all." He sounded bitter, not proud. "I was at the battle of the landing of Al Hoceima, in Morocco. I was shot in the leg. Even though the wound was not mortal, it got infected. I lay in a hot field hospital tent for days, hallucinating. I wanted something, anything, to kill me. The fever made me see things that I was certain were not there. That is how she came to me, my queen, my Mistress of the Unending Dark. She would bring with her the soothing dampness of the grave and promised me eternal existence. How can one refuse such a gift? I'll tell you: you cannot. Such grace she had. Imagine for a moment that you are lying on a cot on the edge of a battlefield in the city. The sun bakes the streets, and the tent shielding you only does so reluctantly. It is stifling hot and dry, while your leg and body are afire. No amount of dressing and redressing can make the pain go away. Hell. I kid you not. Morphine for the pain, to dull it to a roar as they say, but the smell of putrefaction from your own flesh makes you nauseous. Terrible ordeal. But then night comes and you slumber. There is coolness and earth, like when you used to work on the farm, barefoot on the fresh-turned ground. Except it is night, and it feels like that ground is from your grave, save you've accepted that fact, and it is calling to you, soothing you in the moonlight. Pain is forgotten—for now. Then the lady is there, beckoning, smiling, promising. How many nights can one hold on to his duty as a soldier? How many days can one wake up to the sounds of cannons being horse-drawn down the streets and hear the moaning of the dying all around? The smell of death, filling your nostrils all the way into your soul until all you can think and want is that death? Me, it took me four days. That was when I broke, and knelt before my night-time apparition, begging for her to take me away into this world of night. I never looked back since. Do not ask me to betray the one who saved me."

Once again, I stopped in my tracks. My mouth was dry, hoping that was rain falling on my cheeks.

"You tried," Carson said, taking my elbow and getting me walking again. I continued in silence. What was the point of going on I thought, and realized I was taking the dark path my sister had almost fallen to. I missed Olivia so much in that moment. It was like the weight of love could only be measured in the absence it left. A void that when compared with its opposite showed you the height and breadth of your feelings. I took an enormous staggering breath and wondered where she was, and how she was doing. How long until we would be reunited? Would we? No, that was another turn down the dark path, and I course-corrected. I needed focus for what was to come.

When we reached the edge of the forest, I thought a vortex had taken the cottage. We lay down before the forest break. A slick, black shape surrounded it and clutched it. It was massive. Like a black millipede, coiling itself one time around the entire building, its head aimed at the sky, immobile. It protruded from a hole it had burrowed out of the ground, about ten yards away from us. I couldn't breathe. All were silent. We just stared at it for what felt like eternity—awestruck.

What do you do with such a thing? Its carapace looked thick and unyielding. Its segmented body sheened with the falling rain. Unmoving. Waiting. Dirty yellow legs strapped to the stone walls of the cottage, long as swords, thick as pipes, sharp as razors.

Its eyes were closed at least. We did not feel observed, thankfully. I would have freaked out and ran if that giant monster thing had had its monstrous beady eyes on us. I didn't like bugs. I wasn't afraid of them generally speaking, but when you were faced with something so massive, so monstrous, it didn't matter what your preconceived feelings were; this was dread incarnate. Bravo, Larunda. You'd outdone yourself this time.

The smell was almost intolerable. Mountains of burning tires didn't smell this bad. Covering your nose only mitigated it, and breathing through your mouth made you taste it. I wasn't sure what was worse.

"What do we do now?" Carson said. I was at a loss. What kind of plan could be formulated against such a creature? We barely had any guns, and I doubted very much that they would have helped. Swords? That was laughable. That carapace was impenetrable-looking.

Afterdeath

"Now we think. If we could free Larunda from this thing, she might be able to fight it off," I said. "What's the best way to get inside the cottage from here?" I said, trying to figure out how to evade the monster and get into the basement.

Garcia pointed straight at the thing. Not helpful. So we had to distract it, somehow, before we could get in. I got up and walked quietly around the entire house, making sure to keep my footsteps silent, and within the protective circle of trees. The rain helped, covering the crackling of the occasional twig. The monster never opened its eyes. It just kept its upper body stiff, straight, and directly toward the sky. Maybe it was meditating? Who knew?

I made my way across the road, then back onto the other side of the forest. Eventually, I met up with my party.

"There's good news and bad news." I said.

"Good news first," Carson said.

"Bad news first," Garcia said at the same time. I rolled my eyes.

"I'll start with the good news: There's a small opening at the front door. It's tiny, but someone could theoretically sneak in there."

"And the bad news?" Garcia said.

"The thing has a leg directly on the door handle. We'd have to get it to move somehow to be able to access it. I recommend we go back to the castle and think about our plan. This sucker doesn't look like it's going anywhere." I said, sticking a thumb in the insect's direction.

"We should attack now, while it is unawares!" a soldier said, from further away.

"Seriously? No. That thing will just gobble you up. We have to formulate a plan that doesn't entail getting us all eaten by a monster centipede," I said, frowning at the man.

"Will you allow this *girl* to dictate what we must or must not do, Garcia?" the man said, his descriptor sounding a lot like he was saying "trash".

Silence for a moment. Garcia looked at him. The rain sounded too loud at that moment, like it had decided to take up all the empty space.

"If you are so eager to run to your damnation, Stanislaw, I will not stop you. We require men with cool heads on this expedition. I do not expect you to survive," Garcia said, "but if you do, keep in mind that you may have ruined our chances of getting into the cottage. So take the knowledge of your dishonour with you to your doom. If, however, you truly wish to help our mistress, you will return with us to plot her release. The choice is yours."

The hush was palpable, heavy, under the tip-tapping of the rain. I got up first and started heading down the path. I had a bit of an idea, but I wanted to be far away from that thing to flesh it out. We also needed the help of the others to accomplish it. We'd be better off with twenty or more than half of that.

I hoped that the man named Stanislaw would make the right choice, but I knew I had to get moving to get things underway, whatever happened. In any case, what if he woke it up? I felt no compunction at not being there for it to chase us down if he did. Carson joined me.

"Hey. What are you thinking?" he said.

"Get all our people. Surround it. Sneak up to the door and everybody distract it while one or two of us take the front door."

"Risky. It'll move. What if it catches those getting in?"

"That's why it has to be us. We have to go down there and free Larunda. Maybe then she'll let us go," I said.

"Whoa, whoa, whoa!" Carson said, hands in the air. "Are you even listening to the words coming out of your mouth? We sneak in? What makes you say we won't get snapped in half by that thing as soon as it spots us?"

"Never figured you for a coward," I said, and kept walking.

"Ouch! And what makes you think we'll be able to do anything once we're inside?"

"Nothing. I believe in myself, that's all. We'll just have to burn that bridge when we get to it."

"And Larunda? The woman who wants to keep you as a pet so she can go back to her regular business of trapping mortals as her slaves. Did you forget that part? What makes you so sure she'll just let you go, huh?" Carson said, arms wide, stopping in the middle of the trail. Thankfully we were far enough away that his bellyaching couldn't be heard by our temporary allies or the creature.

"What else do you suggest, Carson? What else can we possibly do? Run away? To what? She's supposed to know how to get us back to life! That was the purpose of coming here in the first place. Maybe she *can* help us!"

No, she can't, I thought

"I want to get my sister back and end this. Back to our home, Carson. This isn't how I was supposed to end, was it? In the land of the dead, separated from my sister, fighting monsters *for* a monster? What kind of afterlife is this, anyway? This is bull crap!" I said, my voice raising an octave or two. "This is bull crap." I whispered.

Inevitability. It stomps in and breaks your dreams. Even the bad ones. You're trained to think, all your life, that the Universe is a certain way. Then you grow up and realize it's not. That's just interpretation. The Universe is nothing like the lens we view it through. It's rough and it hurts, and it doesn't care for you at all.

"It's okay, love," I hear, so close he is whispering in my ear, and I feel his arms around me.

Afterdeath

"Don't touch me!" I yell, and he backs off. I don't need his affection. I need time to think. He's not a bad guy, he just needs to know boundaries. "You need to ask permission before doing anything like that again, Carson."

"Boy, you modern girls are tough to handle," he said, in a sad little laugh. "I was just trying to help."

"I know. But you weren't. Not your fault. I just need you to respect my limits, please."

"Yes ma'am," he says, and salutes.

"Listen Carson, if we want to get away from here and find my sister, we have to free Larunda. If we don't, and she gets free herself, she'll send more mercs after us. Then what? If we let this nightmare thing take over, I won't feel good about it, and frankly, it's kind of our fault it exists in the first place." I start walking away toward the ruins, and he catches up.

"What do you mean by that?"

"You brought the giant here. That's why she absorbed it. You do the math."

"Wait, wait, wait, what? You're going to blame me for that… horrible monstrosity?" he said, pointing back at the path. "Do you happen to remember why I rode it into the Evil Sorceresses' lair? Oh right! To save you!"

"Correction: to save my sister," I said, throwing him a look of disdain.

"Right, yes, her too. But I did come back with the intent of getting you all out. That didn't work out so well, did it?" No, his cousin's betrayal had seen to that.

"Let's focus here. This isn't helping anyone. We need to take this step by step. First is getting into the cottage, second is getting that thing trapped in a painting somehow, third is dealing with the repercussions of one and two, and fourth is going after Olivia, Angelina and Barkley before Brock gets them. Sound easy enough?" I said, noticing the rain had abated a bit and the patter on the leaves lessened with every step.

"Aye aye, captain," Carson said, and I could hear the smile in his words. I turned around to see the guards were following us. Relief washed over me when I noticed one toward the back was Stanislaw. We really did need as many as we could keep, and who knows how many would have gone in half-cocked if that man had decided to do the "chivalrous" thing and sacrificed his death to attack that mountain of a beast?

Gassire came flittering in, landing on a wet branch beside my head.

"You have to hurry! We're under attack!" he said, and took off. I threw one glance at Carson and began to run. I yelled to the other men to do the same.

When we came to the field I heard screaming.

"Let's go!" I yelled, and sprinted faster. In the far distance, beyond the ruins, I could see a skirmish, but I had no idea how bad it was, or who it was, for that matter. Our allies were unarmed, so I couldn't imagine who they might be fighting. Then I realized that their enemies were unarmed as well. Greevers. About twenty of them, coming in from the treeline on the other side of the ruins.

Garcia caught up to me, drawing his sword.

"The forest, it neighbours The Wyld Lands. Our Lady's predicament must have loosened her hold on the borders!" he said.

Or the king's withdrawal from his Keep into my friends, I thought.

I ran as fast as my legs could carry me, but I had no weapon. I could see our friends fighting off the oddly malformed greevers with sticks and throwing rocks, but they too had nothing substantial to fend them off with. We veered away from the ruins, going straight for the pack of attackers. Two of them were latched onto one of our group, and I jump-kicked one of them, making it fall over. It got up, mad, and lunged for me. Empty pits for eyes gaped at me, an unhinged jaw clacking, spittle flying about. I punched it in the mouth, and watched it topple. I grabbed the other one by the hair, and it turned around, its mouth covered in the essence of its victim. It jumped on me, and I rolled on the ground, with this horrible humanoid thing trying to bite me, wherever it could get close enough. It got my arm, the one I was using to protect myself, and I felt its teeth dig in deep. I screamed.

Then its body was gone, but its head was still attached to my arm. Then the head melted away, and two coins fell to the ground.

I looked at my arm, and a coil of smoke oozed out of it like thick incense, as a greenish liquid suppurated down the length of my arm and elbow. I turned to the man that had just suffered the assault, lying on the ground in apparent pain. He grimaced and held his neck, which had a fair-sized bite mark. I knelt and tried to help him.

"You okay?" Garcia said, his sword still covered by what was left of my assailant.

"Yeah, just wish I had one of those, you know?" I said, holding up my arm and waiting for the holes to patch on their own. The nasty smelling smoke kept pouring out, and I felt like I was getting weaker. My wounds showed no signs of healing. The man on the ground struggled to get up, keeping pressure on his bitten neck. Tarry smoke bubbled from his wound as well, nasty smell filling the air.

"You got bit by one of them. Tie this around your arm for now," he said, and gave me a tissue he kept in his breast pocket. "As for weaponry," he unlatched a long dagger from his side and handed it to me. "You be careful with that," pointing at his present.

"What, you think a girl can't handle herself?" I said sarcastically.

"Not at all. That's a family heirloom. Do bring it back to me," he smiled, and ran off to help the others, locked in lively combat further down the field, near the edge of the forest. I looked at the tissue and put it around the man's neck, tightening it

Afterdeath

slightly so it wouldn't fall off. He groaned and mouthed the words *thank you*. The oily smoke sputtered from under the restraint, but otherwise looked uncontainable. He walked back to the ruins where some of the other wounded fighters were retreating.

Back toward the forest, Iuturna, Carson and the surviving soldiers hacked at the Greevers with intensity. I looked at the dagger in my hand and trotted toward the action. I felt a rush of adrenaline, but also a deep-seated fear, grasping me by the arm, spreading inside my body. I looked at my wound and saw greyness spreading from the bite outward, like the edges of a rank pool, getting larger. I slowed down a bit, as the adrenaline turned to loss, as if I'd just ran a marathon and was standing on my last legs. Another step, and my vision began to blur. It felt as if my mind keeled over, turning sideways, and then I was in lightheaded free-fall.

Thump!

I stared at the action in the distance with grass poking me in my right eye, I couldn't "feel" it, but just realized it was happening.

How strange, I thought, *to die again in such a short period of time.*

What would it be like this time around?

I closed my eyes, which were begging to find out.

Chapter 21

THE WYLDS

We'd slept near the forest edge, my head on gnarled roots, with my waking in the night several times with starts of fear. I had woken up exhausted to what otherwise was a beautiful day.

Now we sat, legs over the ledge, staring into the distance of the Land of Sands, with its dangerous buildings appearing out of nowhere to land on you if you weren't careful. Off in the distance, a sandstorm brewed. Black clouds smothered the sky, broken by the jagged strike of heat lightning bouncing at furious angles.

Angelina looked dejected, both hands planted behind her, staring straight ahead at the anger of the elements, a reflection of her own foul mood which I expected would erupt soon. Barkley was off by the edge of the forest at the foot of a tall, slim pine, staring at his mistress with the look of a being who was expecting a severe beating and knew no way of avoiding it. Here I was, somewhere in the middle trying to keep our little group from falling apart, and wondering if I could.

Doubtful.

"Maybe we should…" I started.

"No." Angelina said, not even turning to look at me. The air was dry on the edge of the precipice. The lightning storm so far away that not even the sound of thunder came to our ears; just the conflagrations of silver light, stabbing the ponderous clouds; swirling grit on the ground. I wondered about our Jinn friends.

Stillness.

Afterdeath

Maybe if a bird or wind, creature or branch had broken the silence. Maybe then I could have found a better "in". None of this happened though, and I stayed resolutely on the outside of her thoughts, locked out by her wall.

Somewhere far away, Chloe was fighting for her existence; or had; or was going to. I had no way of knowing which. My toes wanted to point in the direction where my legs would run. My head wanted to lean in and urge the rest of me into a dash that would not end until I had my sister before me. I got up and paced behind Angelina, throwing her a glance once in a while, and noticed Barkley's sad eyes at others. The line of the forest extending forever on one side and the other. No insect buzzed. No bird called.

I put my hands on my hips and stretched. Which way? The itch I felt to walk, to run, always pulling at the front of my mind. Which way?

I sat again next to Angelina and just stared at her blank face. She swung her legs a bit over the precipice, on the edge, and not caring. She looked at that black storm as if it were nothing, as if nothing around her mattered anymore.

I tapped my fingers on my knees, glancing back at the forest every little while. A black shape circled against the glare of the sun; primordial, hunting. A bird of prey of some sort; an eagle or hawk perhaps. I'd been a city girl all my life and couldn't tell the difference.

I would have given anything at that moment to trade places with it; to shoot off where I was needed and leave this pointless human drama where it stood, holding me back.

I could imagine myself looking down upon our three still shapes; so far we'd be tiny, swimming on air. The edge of the cliff dropping down, and in the distance, the blackness of raging elements; billowing, growing, metastasizing.

"Why didn't you tell her?" I said to Barkley. He just looked at me, his jaw over one leg, pathetic.

"Don't even try. We all know you can talk," I said, feeling silly in spite of myself. I'd never been one to talk to animals in the first place, and even though this case was special, it took nothing away from the weirdness of it. He groaned and closed his eyes. I watched him, then walked over, fists clenched, legs stiff.

"Barkley!" his eyes blinked open, his eyebrows arched. I bent down on one knee and he began to growl.

"Listen to me," I began, "Chloe is in danger. We can't stick around here forever waiting for things to fix themselves. You have to talk to her." I gave him my best pleading look, hoping something like pity would well up inside him.

"What do you want me to do?" he whispered, "She's mad right now. Madder than you would ever imagine. There's no way I can talk my way out of this one." He gave a short sigh and put his head down again.

"Then why did you stop in the first place?"

"Like you'd understand. I love Angelina, but sometimes she can be…"

"Driven?" I interrupted.

"Pig-headed," he replied. I smiled.

"So?"

"Well, we got punished for her crazy-ass plan. I'm the one who got turned into a dog though. At first I didn't realize I could talk. But when I did, I kept it to myself."

"Why, though?"

"Revenge." My eyes grew wide. "Yeah, I'm not proud of it either. But you know at the time, it felt like fair retribution for having been transformed into man's best friend. She did this to me. I do love her and I did then too, but I felt she needed it at the time. Not my finest hour, I have to admit."

"But you could have told her at any time. Why didn't you? Why wait until now?"

"Now was an accident. I would have kept on going if I could have. No, the thing is, once you get started it becomes impossible to stop. The longer you let the lie go, the worse you know things will be when the truth is discovered. That's why the lie has to go on." If it was possible for a dog to look miserable, Barkley had mastered it.

"That's horrible," I said, under my breath, not realizing it had come out. Angelina hadn't budged. Her hands lay palms flat on the half-grass, half-dirt edge of the cliff where we had so recently escaped with our souls intact. Up there in the sky the predator still circled and let out a shrill cry that finally rent the silence. I shivered.

It was hot on the upper side of the desert, and I was certain that the forest would be humidly so. I tried to peer nervously inside it, but knew I'd get nowhere without the assistance of my so-called friends.

I went back to the one who was ignoring us both, and sat next to her, observing the swirl that was turning into a massive tornado in the distance.

"I'll help you," I said.

"Do what." she said, her gaze never wavering. The question not sounding like a question at all but an automated response, almost robotic in nature.

"I'll help you build your country. I'll stay with you," I said, staring straight at her glazed right eye. She turned to face me, her lips wracked in anger.

"Why? Why would that help me now? Why would I even want to go through with it? For him?" she said, pointing her finger back at Barkley, who had turned his head the opposite way.

Afterdeath

"Yes. Yes, for him. And for all the others who might want to have a place to live free!" I said.

"Gods but you're naïve, aren't you?" Angelina said, throwing her head back. "How did I get saddled with a sad little Utopian like this one? Can you explain that to me?" she asked of no one in particular.

I felt my cheeks redden, my brow developing a cold sweat. I clenched and unclenched my jaw, holding back whatever wanted to escape from me and try to hurt Angelina.

"Right. Because it's a lot better to think that the world is pure evil out to get you, isn't it? Just because bad things happen, that's a great reason to become cynical and lock everything out? You want to know what I found out Angelina? The world doesn't care. It *has no emotions*. When people say 'Life is good', that's not a statement of fact, that's an opinion. The same goes with 'Life is shit'. Life simply does not care. I know Barkley hurt you. You know what though? You hurt him. I'm pretty certain that with your head shoved up your ass so far you've hurt a lot of people. Guess what? It goes both ways. Now that you've been hurt though, *now* is when the world falls apart? I call bullshit. Get over yourself! You dragged your boyfriend into something that got you both in trouble. Now is the time to fix it. I have to go save my sister if it's not already too late, and I need both of you to do it. So could you please get your shit together and talk to the man you love before I kick you over this cliff? Thank you!" I practically yelled, jumped up and stormed off. I felt as if I'd just ran the hundred meter dash in six seconds, and all my energy had been expunged in the process.

Still I walked on, like a balloon that's using up the last of the air inside it to shoot in strange directions before crashing unceremoniously to the ground. I didn't look where I went. The forest was on my right, and the Cliffside on my left. I'm fairly certain I muttered too, but what I might have said or thought made no coherent sense, just more steam to blow off from the pressure cooker.

"Olivia," I heard Angelina's voice calling behind me.

"What?" I screamed, turning halfway back.

"You're going the wrong way."

I stopped.

I wavered. Fingernails digging into my palms like razorblades. Hands so grey, they could camouflage as stones.

I dropped.

I did not roll. My knees dug into the weeds, pebbles and sand, and I sat on my ankles, my head hanging loosely. My mind felt that slow roll you get when you're dizzy. Like the world is immobile, but your brain keeps spinning sideways. Little sparklers burnt inside it, going off in various areas.

Have you ever had a moment in your life where you wondered if you were going to go crazy, and you were half afraid to do so, but the other half was whispering: "yessssss, do iiiiiit!"—that fear of total loss of control, but the manic pleasure that might come from it? Yeah, that's where I was in that moment. I almost relinquished full control to my personal demon, but even though it wanted to grab the levers I gently pushed it away, in the end. I'll never know if that was a good or bad decision, but on the whole I would say I was proud of myself. At the time though, my head buzzed and the outside world was shut out.

God but that woman could press the right buttons to make people go insane.

Her hand on my shoulder is what jolted me back to my senses.

"You were serious about what you said? About helping me?" I heard her say from above me. Flat voice, humourless. Good. I was in no mood to be laughed at. That demon was still lurking in my mind, trying to get the upper hand.

"Yes," I said, feeling my desperate energy running out.

"Get up. We have to go." I opened my eyes confused.

"Where are we going?" I said, the buzzing in my head so strong it was like an electric current. She laughed, but not meanly.

"To help your sister, you idiot." Yes, Chloe! My focus started coming back, and I took an enormous breath through my nose, then let it out from my mouth. The air was perfumed with salt and the petrichor smells of the forest beside us. Barkley was beside Angelina; not quite close enough to touch her, but near enough that I could tell the tension had dissipated. For now.

"You okay?" he said. Not sure how long it would take for me to get used to a talking dog. He sensed that I guess, and didn't ask again. Angelina was extending her hand and I took it, putting one shaky leg on the ground, then the other.

"You're right, you know. Life isn't one thing or another; it's just the way we view it that makes it so. If there's one thing I should have kept in mind, it's that we shape our reality, in this life and all the others. Just depends on how hard you're willing to fight to get to that point," Angelina said smiling.

"I'm ready."

"I see that. We better hurry. That storm over the desert is coming our way," she said throwing the roiling clouds a glance. She was right. They'd come a ways, and would overtake us sooner or later. I don't know if it was the ambient dryness or my imagination, but I smelled electricity in the air.

Afterdeath

"Where... where do we have to go?" I asked, regaining some perspective on the situation. She pointed her chin at the forest, which took on a few more degrees of darkness. I sighed.

**

We walked a ways before turning into the forest. A small path, almost hidden in the underbrush, was discovered by Barkley. I saw that even though they walked together their relationship had taken a hit. The camaraderie had evaporated a bit. I hoped it would mend. Until I'd met them, I'd never seen two people get along so well; or one person and one turned into an animal. Nope, I'd never get used to that part. My parents had been a bit like that, but my memory of them was vague. It was more feeling than visual. I pushed branches out of my face following Angelina, and Barkley led. I felt guilty for not having a better picture of them in my mind. Rose was a lot fresher and I missed her even more. I wondered where she'd gone; not here obviously. Would she have gotten the white cloud treatment and the daily chats over coffee and scones with a Savior or Saint? My experience was telling me this was doubtful. Wherever she was, I hoped my nana was doing better than Chloe and I. That's all you could hope for, wasn't it? That once the people you loved left you, they were safe and sound.

The loud buzzing of insects broke the silence that had been a staple of the edge of the cliff. Once in a while, a twitter or cry echoed through the air. The swish of the plants at our knees was the only other sound. I watched them part and twitch further away where Barkley would be ambling forth. I was surprised that he did not say anything more now. Wouldn't it have lifted the burden of his secret? Or was the shame still so intense that he dared not open his mouth to remind his love of that betrayal?

A weird thought came to mind, though: where did other people come from before they came to life? Some would say heaven, but that did not appear to be the way of things after all. Did we perhaps cross dimensions, retaining a part of our energy and memory, or were we mixed up with other people to make brand new beings? Would I be reincarnated as a tree or insect, a whale, or a coral reef? If so, would it be in the same dimension I'd come from? Would I know who I'd have been? Would it matter? Or was it all a part of the multiverse's obliviousness to rhyme or reason?

I thought to myself:

Is it some strange occurrence that we are a spark of life that appears one day, burns for the blinking of an eye, then, flashes back into the void? Even though I know now that that spark only transfers to another plane, it's not quite the same, and not quite different, either. At the base, is it all the same spark, from one singularity, shattered into a million, billion fragments so that it can witness itself? Pieces ignorant of the whole, cognizant only of conjecture and doubt, yet hoping to know itself some day when it finally extinguishes. I hope so. I think that's what Faith is.

It was hot in the woods just as I'd expected. The path we followed was grown over, in disuse for who knew how long. Low ferns made keeping upon it difficult, and we both relied on Barkley's senses to do so. It wound gently upward, the surrounding trees mostly coniferous: blue pines and jack pines (I may have grown up in the city, but grandma still took us to the park and taught us a thing or two). Their tall, slender forms touching the sky far up above. The forest itself lay cast in shadows; not so dark that it was impossible to see, but enough that it felt as if evening was settling in, even though it must have only been midday.

I heard thunder in the distance and felt my heart skip a beat. Then I remembered something.

"Didn't you say you'd never been here before?" I asked Angelina.

"Yeah, that's right," she said without turning around.

"Then how is it you knew I was going the wrong way?" I said, the now familiar heat starting to rise in my cheeks.

"I didn't. I said that to make you stop," she said, turning around and winking at me.

"I really despise you."

"Shhh, you have to be quiet love. This is the Wylds. There are things in here that no one should have to face without an army. I'm serious now. Keep it down," her index in front of her lips. I walked on, stiff-legged, imagining steam rising from my scalp in wafts. Not so far away, the thunder grumbled a reflection of my complaint. Torrid heat wafted from the ground, and if it wasn't for the insufferable humidity, I would have wondered if we'd left the desert at all.

The smell of decay was powerful, yet pleasant. I felt a patter on my shoulder, and looked up. The shadows on the ground had darkened further, and the clouds came over-top of us now. Several drops splashed around us, bouncing on the undergrowth and then a warm drizzle poured down. We were soon soaked, but we did not stop. We kept on slogging up that gentle hill until we reached the top. Under our feet, the slim path had become mud. I was reminded once again of our waking on the riverbank caked in grey mud. My shoes kept sticking into the track, and I eventually gave up and walked beside it. The sound of the rain was deafening, and we had difficulty seeing a few meters beyond.

We crossed a field of flowers pelted by the deluge; tall stalks that wavered in the attack. Dirty yellow flowers which must have been beautiful before rotted away into a black, oily ichor. As we walked by, they extended in our direction, foul black gunk covering them staining us on arms and legs, chest and thighs. I am only glad that they

Afterdeath

were not tall enough to slather us in the face. Their foetid stench was putrid and nauseating, like bed-pans and sick. If I could have, I would have gone around this whole area, but there was no way of avoiding it; the field extended through the forest in all directions.

We were going down now, and the way was steeper than before. The small path zig-zagged more sharply, and if the rain had let up I might have been able to see a valley of some sort.

Angelina was the first to notice the deep grooves in the trees and the disturbance in the air. When I heard the hoot, low and throaty, she was already on me, pinning me to the ground.

"What are...?" I began, but she clamped her hand over my mouth, her eyes wild. She put her other hand's index in front of her mouth, and then to punctuate her point, slid two fingers across the front of her throat.

I froze. I lay motionless in a mud bath, soaked to the bone with gummy flower sap slathered all over me, stinking me up to high heaven. The ferns I'd had at my knees now hid both of us from view. Angelina rolled off me, slowly, eyes squinted as if in deep concentration.

There was a crackle, like a tree getting ready for the long drop to the forest floor. It was not far off, maybe twenty steps ahead of where we hid.

A trembling.

The earth under my back thumped, and with it my heart started a wild cavalcade. I turned my head toward Angelina, whose face was almost touching the ground. Water dripped off the end of her nose in rivulets, and her hands were under her chest. She kept her head down, staring at the ground, without moving a centimetre.

Another crackle. Like a squeezing of trees, rubbing together.

Close.

Through the leaves, I saw a foot come down; gun-metal grey, long, taloned.

Shirking down the length of a tree, directly to my right.

Thump. I jumped a bit despite myself. My teeth wanted to chatter, and I put my hand over my mouth, promptly filling it with mud. I spat a bit and hoped that no sound would be heard, but now I gritted dirt and sand. The foot was connected to a muscular, grey-bluish leg, which was in turn connected to a whole naked humanoid body about eight feet tall, grey-blue from head to toe, incredibly strong-looking and hairless. Long brown claws seamlessly extended from the fingertips and toes. It was like the devils we'd been told about in Saturday school, but grey instead of red.

As I noticed the excruciating length of its claws, the thing ran its massive hand against the bark of the tree it had just descended, leaving deep grooves where it passed. The sound they made was a mix of branches breaking and the sighing of things too exhausted to scream. I shivered even harder.

When it turned its head in our direction, I clamped my hand back over my mouth. If a human being had started turning into an ant and stopped half-way, I think this is what they would have looked like. It had no eyes; not that they were hidden or very small. No, it had none to speak of at all. Where a person's mouth should have been, mandibles opened and closed, revealing a pinkish-black mouth full of row upon circular row of tiny, pointed teeth. When the mandibles, like two shoe-tips touching sideways, were closed, a pink spike-like tongue shot out from a small central orifice, wriggling upward, then down before retracting. It reminded me of a snake's tongue, the way they...

It was sniffing the air.

It would find us.

We were right next to it.

It took a step away from us, stopped, tasted the air. It turned.

I heard barking.

Its head whipped toward the direction in which we had been headed. It ducked to the ground, shrieked, and began to run—straight toward Barkley!

Chapter 22

NEW BEGINNING?

They don't tell you that when you die you spend as much time thinking about it as when you were alive; that when you're dying while *in* death, it gets even more confusing. Of course they don't. How could they? The most anyone thinks about it are one of three things: eternal life and happiness, eternal damnation and excruciating pain, and nothingness. I was one of those who thought about nothingness. Not because I liked the idea, but because it seemed the most plausible. I would never come along at someone else's funeral and pee on their parade of course. I would never tell anyone grieving for a loved one that that person was gone forever and there was no turning back.

I might be a realist, but there was such a thing as unnecessary cruelty.

I think it was also my way of accepting death.

I mean, if there's one thing we fear most when we're alive, isn't it not being so anymore?

I can tell you as I came in and out of consciousness, that I feared for whatever materials made me *me*. I would see Carson's face floating above mine, and sometimes Iuturna, but Garcia as well. They all had that "concerned yet pretending it was okay" look on their faces, telling me just how bad it was.

Whatever the poison was that coursed through me slowly, relentlessly, forced strange dreams into me. I was reminded of Garcia's story of how he'd died, and wondered if I'd get my own visitor from another realm. The thought made me chuckle, then cough, and made everyone come over to check on me, so I stopped thinking funny thoughts.

I'd be there for a while, and one of my friends would sponge my forehead, and then I'd slip out.

They were similar, the dreams, but never identical. And no, they weren't about otherworldly visitors come to entice me into bondage. Thank goodness. I think I would have kindly invited them to "F-off".

No, the dreams always started off in the back yard, at Grandma Rose's house. I was there, and so was Olivia. We were both around seven, so I guess we'd just gotten there. Since our parents... you know... passed away. Grandma Rose wasn't though, and I knew then that it was the dream, because she was always there when we were kids. She'd take us to the back yard to play. A flower garden bordered the hedge that separated her yard from the neighbour's; gorgeous lilies and fiery gazanias, bell-like lavender coloured foxglove on tall stalks, star-shaped purple petunias and so many more. Bumblebees droned all summer long, and we often spent hours watching them go from one flower to the next, legs overburdened with yellow pollen. We'd play in the treehouse that our uncle Philbert and our grandma must have played in when they were kids. The thing was ancient, might have been a midget haunted house but it kept us busy on those long summer days. Like a little Victorian castle, hoisted up in the giant willow tree in the corner of the yard, it was magical to all those who set eyes on it. Olivia and I had spent many nights telling ghost stories to each other, the door shut tight and a flashlight under our chins for effect. When a branch scraped the roof, we'd shriek and hide under our blankets. That was then.

In the dreams there was no grandma Rose. The flowers looked dull and colourless; the bees mere drones without agency. When I would approach one, I saw that whatever flower it touched began to smoke and burn with dark green fire, as if it'd been made of some odd, chemical-filled paper. Then it would fall off the stem and was added to the heap of charred remains below, on the ruddy-looking ground. This wasn't the garden of my youth and I knew it, but there was never any way of waking up. Olivia was always there, yes, but she never said a word, and when I tried to speak, it was as if I was trying to pull out my own throat. Eventually I stopped. She would look at me moving my mouth without facial expression. She would invite me to come up the steps into the treehouse, but I knew there was something wrong inside, the way you know you shouldn't ever, ever go down the steps into the basement of an abandoned house. But I walked anyhow against my will. Not because it was my sister, or that I had no choice... it just felt like I'd been programmed that way, and that whatever was in there, in the cool dark of the treehouse had to inevitably take me. And when it did, I would no longer be me but a part of the thing in the dark.

Afterdeath

So I'd walk slowly, with Olivia holding my hand, one foot going up a step, then the other, my toe banging against one of them, and it feeling so real, even though it was only a dream, then limping up one step, and the other, thinking: "where did the sun go?"

But as I drew nearer the top, and could feel the buzzing, bulging emptiness within, I felt more alive, and more resistant, and would pull on Olivia's hand. But she gripped my wrist like a manacle, and kept on dragging, closer and closer to the inside full of empty. She'd smile, and I'd try to scream, my throat on fire and ripping at my cry, and I'd come a step closer.

It wasn't Olivia that pulled me, though I always realized too late: just a thing that looked like her. A small part of that darkness that paraded around as her, but could never ever be her. How could she? My sister wouldn't have done any of those things to me, and even though I knew it was all a dream, I followed this thing up the steps like a robot. That's when you saw them—the flaws. The little things that told you it couldn't be your sibling. The little details in the hands that said whatever it was, it was ancient. The little details in the mouth that told you the smile was too cruel to be human. All the little details revealing that you were being dragged into something unfathomable by a nightmare creature that only wanted to see you destroyed.

Always I made it to the top step, and always it reached for the door to this decrepit version of our perfect little Victorian haunted mansion, complete with real danger. How many times had we pretended? Hadn't this been the first place we'd played with that Ouija board? Had we called the damned to stay with us? Had we made the thing *work,* in our youth and stupidity?

This, however, was no reason to hand myself over to them as food. This was a good reason to fight, and however wrong it was, I'd smack that thing that looked like my sister strong enough to knock it over and watch it revert to its true form; ugly and miserly like the petty theft of an invalid.

I'd then wake up to the still more concerned faces of my friends, inside the remains of the old king's castle. The grim green fog clung to everything. Despite the bleak cold, a burning heat filled my gut, extending to my head, my hands and fingertips, my legs and toes. I felt lost.

"You've been screaming," said Iuturna, eyeing the puffs of smoke coming from my spreading wound with apprehension.

"I'm sorry."

"That's not what I meant. We have to do something for you. The fever is getting worse."

"What'll happen to me? Will I turn into one of them?" This was one of my greatest fears, to become one of those mindless creatures, shambling about, looking for sustenance. Carson looked nervous, off to the side.

"No, uh—you return to the earth. You disintegrate." That was somehow even more dire than the thought of turning into a greever. Something got caught in my throat, and I croaked.

"Any... any way to stop it?"

Iuturna frowned:

"If we could get you to Larunda, she might be able to help you, but we don't have much time," she said.

"Then we need to get going," I said, struggling to get up, then falling back to the ground.

"Whoa, take it easy there champion. We need to organize our people. We have to make sure our plan of action is ready before we attempt any kind of assault," Carson said, putting a hand on my forehead.

"How long do I have?" I said, pulling his hand away.

"It varies—it depends on—there are many things—to consider. You'll be fine. You'll be—just fine," Iuturna said. Her face was paralysed into a short, sad smile that would have been funny if the situation had been otherwise. I lay my head down and closed my eyes. The darkness swam behind them, like an infinite whirlpool.

Shapes congealed, and I woke in the grey grass behind the house. The trees, bushes, flowers, house, playhouse, everything, including the sky had taken on that monochromatic hue. Colours had been stolen from my world. This was another side of death. It was the world of the forgotten. I knew that now. This is where I was headed. I would continue to exist perhaps, but only in the minds of those who'd known me, and then— no more.

No wind blew in the branches. The nasty-looking little bees went about their business destroying the memories I had of the flowers. Setting them aflame, one by one, and then falling to the ground themselves. I walked closer and noticed that every step I took turned the grass to ashes. That the bees I touched did the same.

I felt a movement, and whirled around.

Olivia.

Not Olivia.

Shade of Olivia.

She frowned and stepped forward, hand extended. I backed away from her shaking my head. I ran behind the willow where our little playhouse was perched, putting my arms around the bulk of the enormous trunk, feeling the roughness of its bark on

283

Afterdeath

my arms, but then a softening, powdery and smooth, where I had lay my arms upon it. I hugged it for dear life, wondering if that would help at all.

I felt my arms going through the tree, as solidity of it lost cohesion and became ash at my contact, spreading through the rest of it, changing the base into a charred remnant of a tree.

The stress became too great, and the weight of the thing, top-heavy with our little treehouse, dipped toward the bigger house. I stopped trying to hold onto the tree and held it back, but only made things accelerate. With a crack, the centuries-old tree mammoth began to fall, not in one burst, but in stutters, catching on the last bits that hadn't been turned to ash, then broke with a rending crash, falling all the way to the grass.

But it did not hit with a thud. It splashed down onto the ground and exploded like an urn full of dry powder, the tree whooshing into a cloud, flying into the air by the power of its own violent fall, and settled onto the area like nuclear winter. The grasses around caught the disease, and melted to the ground as well, a concentric circle of forgetfulness flowing outward unevenly, like a plague eating the countryside, transforming all in its path into dust-shapes of its original forms. Flowers, trees, grasses, hedges, all had the solidity sucked out of them, becoming like grey sand, falling apart.

Then the house.

I thought Shade Olivia had been hit by the tree, but I saw her getting up. She did not come closer to me. She just watched the destruction from where she stood. The destruction I'd unleashed from within the treehouse, the place where all flowed outward to absorb the memories and the existence of what I used to… that I was. Am. I am. Damnit!

How could I plug Pandora's Box? It had all come undone, and I just wanted to sit in the wilting grass and let the spread of the cancer continue unabated. Pointless to fight it.

Pointless.

Shadow Olivia smiled that very old smile, her ancient hands by her side, knowing that today was the day I would no longer exist. That when all the things that made me *me* would be gone, I'd be next. And that was fine. I wouldn't have to fight Shadow Olivia anymore.

Drop in the well.

So dry in here. No wind. All desiccate matter and disillusionment.

Drop in the well. One drop of water. I felt it.

Fresh.

Shade looking at me. Smile falling down. Black teeth showing as I lay cross-legged on the martyred ground.
Drop.
In the well.
Water.
Falling. On my face. I open my eyes and there is rain. The dead powdered things bubble and pop, changing colour. Shade is angry. She lashes out at the rain, falling from the sky. Helpless. She waves her arms about, but there is nothing she can do. It's pointless. The ground bulges and bops, splorts and fizzes. The grey melts, slick and sloppy, cacophony of plopping slops. Browns emerge, from the oily mass of grey, turning over the earth, making it new, making it fresh, making it live. Shade Olivia is sinking in the muck, in the rain, in life. She cannot stand it and silently screeches, but it is too late. The ground has eaten her up and she is gone: for now.

Green shoots flow upward from the brownish mulch, and before me, a thin wreath of a willow tree, but faster and faster it grows, magical, like dreams should be. The rain beats down on my face and I laugh, letting the water into my throat, it clears the pain away and my voice rings true and clear and loud. My laugh makes everything grow again, and the house stops its self-destruction, hesitating, but then its planks and floors and roof return, newer, fresher, like childhood memories ought to be.

I look up and the tree house has returned, and I don't feel the presence of the emptiness inside it. It too has departed, or become so small that I can't detect it. I know it is always there, but I prefer to think it no longer is. It's a choice we all make.

From around the corner comes—Grandma Rose? She's smiling and holding a tray of cookies. Her frizzly, frazzly white hair is almost see-through in the light of the sun that shines above now, and I notice that the rain has stopped.

"Are you girls hungry?" she says, and I look around. The window of the tree house pops open and Olivia's head comes out, smiling:

"Yes!" I feel something welling inside my heart that I haven't in a very long time, and I don't remember the name for it. I hear the little door clacking, its spring creaking and yawing, and my twin rushing down the stairs. I watch her run past me to the little white garden table near the house. Rose has placed the tray full of homemade cookies and glasses of milk on the wrought-iron table, and sat down with a tiny "oof" on one of the four matching chairs that surround it.

The day is gorgeous, and the nightmare is beginning to fade. Is this a new life for me? Have I died and continued on to the next plane? Is this my heaven, the one I didn't believe in? Oh, what if I could be put in one of my favourite memories for the rest of eternity? Is this what this was? I bit my lip and walked over to the table.

Afterdeath

As I sat down on the hard yet comfortable metal chair, I kept staring into the face of my beautiful grandmother, her little spectacles balanced on the tip of her nose, her smile wide and honest, and her fingers intertwined on the table before her. She was perfect.

But was she real?

"How come you're staring at me like that, child?" she said, while Olivia dipped a chocolate chip cookie into her glass. Even though we were both nineteen, she had that same look of glee she had when we were seven. Little girl in a big girl's body.

"I was wondering if this was real, grandma." The thing that stuck to my mind was breaking the spell. What if I said the wrong words?

"Of course it is, young lady," she said, putting a warm palm on top of my hand. I breathed a sigh of relief.

"It's all real... in your head," she said, picking up a cookie and inspecting it as if it were some expensive, yet not very attractive piece of crockery you'd find at a yard sale. Even though the dream continued, my heart deflated. She must have seen it on my face.

"Memories are a very special part of our lives, and they should be cherished. But you know, you shouldn't live there. You should visit them for comfort once in a while. Life is experiential. You have to go out and make new ones. That's what makes it worthwhile. Didn't I teach you that? I thought I had," she said, staring me in the eye for a bit, then deciding on the quality of her cookie, took a big bite out of it.

My mouth wanted to move, but no words worthy of the name wanted to take their first baby steps into the world. They'd all grown afraid of the light. They were afraid of being judged.

"It's safe in here, but not for long. You only got a reprieve, Chloe," Olivia told me, smiling sheepishly.

"It was the rain; the rain was sent for you, and for Olivia," Grandma said. I tried to understand. "It's still raining out there. It's keeping the wound at bay. It won't heal you, but it'll help you fight the emptiness that consumes you. You're not ready to be one with the world yet. You have many lives to live."

I stared hard and long at the treehouse, and the back yard, and the flowers in all their glorious radiance, and the sun shining down on my little slice of heaven, printing it forever on my mind.

"Wake up," Olivia said, tugging my arm. "Wake up, and go now. It's time."

"Wake up," Iuturna said, and I opened my eyes. "Wake up, we are ready to go. Please say something!" I nodded at her, and felt the rain drizzling on my body. The clouds rushed by in the sky, at speeds I'd never seen. It was warm, the wet notwithstanding, and I gave her my arm. I opened my mouth to let the rain in, and my dry throat relented, just as it had in the dream.

Rose.

Olivia.

Still there, etched as I'd photographed them. I looked at my wound, and the smoke from the scar sputtered and fizzled with rain getting in; cooling it, soothing the burn. My head was clearer, and the aches of my body felt relaxed; not gone, mind you, but bearable.

Our group and the soldiers milled around the camp, inside the ruins as well as out, picking up gear and making potential weapons; cudgels made of wood. I shook my head: that would never be enough.

"Help me up," I said to Iuturna, and she extended her hand. I let her pull me off the ground, and teetered against the rock wall for only a moment before regaining my footing. I knew this rejuvenation would not last, and that the only way out of this mess was to free Larunda by somehow fighting this thing she'd unleashed. Out of the frying pan, into the fire, then into the boiling lavas of Hell. Fun.

Carson was chatting with Garcia off to the entrance of the ruins, and I walked as confidently as I could toward them.

"Are you okay?" Carson said, coming toward me when he noticed my presence.

"Yeah, just a bit tired is all," I lied. The effort was taking its toll, but I wanted to be the strong one. No way I'd lie down and be a burden to this group.

"We are getting ready to go," Garcia said, sizing me up. I stiffened a bit, and he tried a corner smile for my efforts.

"Let's. The faster we get this over with, the quicker I can start looking for my sister," I said.

And that asshole Brock, I thought.

"You sure you can make it all the way back to the cottage?" Garcia said, frowning.

"Why? Do I look like an invalid?" I said, in my most *hell yeah* voice.

"We could carry you, you know," he said.

"No freaking way," I said. I'd make it all the way back on my own two feet or I'd dissolve trying. That was the end of it.

"Told you she wouldn't go for it," Carson said smiling, snapping his fingers.

"Guess you were right," Garcia said. The rest of the group, rescued prisoners and soldiers alike, had begun to gather around us.

"Sorry we made plans without you while you were otherwise indisposed," Garcia said, not a hint of sarcasm in his voice.

"You're forgiven soldier," I said, and managed a tight smile of my own.

Afterdeath

"Alright people," Carson said, raising his hands. "We're going to surround the creature. It would be pointless to attack it directly, since we are vastly underequipped to do so." I looked around, and saw the moue of disgust on a few of the soldier's faces, especially the brash Stanislaw, who quite clearly disagreed. The rest only nodded, looks of concern mingled with resolution.

"We'll try to get its attention, and break into the cottage. Either from the front door, or one of the first floor windows. Either way, our goal is to free our Lady Larunda so that she may capture this creature. That is our hope," Garcia said.

"What is the alternative plan?" someone asked from the front row.

"We don't..." Carson said, but Garcia interrupted.

"We'll discuss it in time, but only if that avenue has been exhausted. Believe in the plan, and we'll be victorious. That I can assure you," and he smiled. Carson put his hands on his hips and nibbled his lower lip, while nodding his head in agreement.

"Let's go," Carson said, raising his hand. I walked a bit, and felt the fatigue gaining on me. Whatever resolve I'd bluffed up was quickly leaking out of me with my energy, like the air out of a tiny hole in a bicycle tire. I kept glancing at my muddied arms, where the poison coursed through my being, holding it up to the rain to feel its refreshing feeling. I stopped for a moment against a birch, holding it with my good arm.

"Hey," Iuturna said, coming up behind me. She took my hand from the tree and held it. I gave her a questioning glance, and she nodded once. I sighed, and she put her hand under my arm, holding it up. I hated to be the weak one; always had. I should have shook her off. If Olivia had seen me like this, she would have laughed at me I'm sure.

To her credit, Iuturna didn't comment on my present state. She was content with holding up a part of my weight. She made it look like a gesture of friendship, not of one who was holding me up for dear life, and for that I was grateful. I tried not to hobble as best I could. I knew eyes were on my back, as well as Portillo's. Every time he turned around from in front of us, concern was clearly written on his features.

"Don't worry about them," Iuturna said, looking at me and smiling. The rain cooled the burning sensation on my arm, but it didn't negate the pain.

"It's just bad timing, you know?" I said, under my breath. She shrugged. I didn't want to tell her about my recent experience in my dreams. I wish I could have told someone but that person was nowhere near here. As soon as I could get better, I would go after her if Larunda would let me. It was starting to become clear that Death was made entirely of rocks and hard places. That as soon as you got clear of one set, you realized you were within another, like some sort of unending labyrinth. I sighed, and Iuturna must have heard.

Benoit Chartier

"What's wrong?" she said.

"Just feels pointless," I replied.

"How so?" as we navigated over slick tree root systems. The water dripping from glossy leaves and pitter-pattering onto wet ground.

"I've lost everything. I don't know what I should do now except give up." I felt her stiffen.

"That's the poison talking. You haven't lost *yourself*. Listen, I wondered a long time if I should give up as well. Mother was imprisoned after your disappearance. Father was always a soldier in her employ; a slave really. I knew I was fairly the same under Larunda, but I didn't give up."

"But they were still there though," I said.

"I was still virtually alone. I could rarely speak to mother, for fear of discovery and reprisal. Father was a stranger who did not recognize me in the Halls when I crossed his path. That was somehow worse than any dissolution really."

We walked on in silence for a moment, working our way around a great boulder that blocked the path.

"So why did you go on?" I finally said.

"Because no matter how painful it is, my life is my own to live. Any loss I may feel is tempered by the fact that I will gain something in the future. But only if I 'stick it out', as they say," she said, and flashed me a shy smile. Her hair was soaked, but there was a glitter in her eyes that caught me by surprise, as if I had just captured a moment of great truth.

"Life is experiential," I whispered, brought back to the dream.

"What was that?" she said.

"Life is experiential," I said, a bit louder, and she smiled wider. I thought of Rose's spirit shining down on me wherever she was, even if it was only in my memories.

"For good or ill, it is that, and so is death. And I imagine, all the other planes of existence. But we won't get to live those until we are ready."

"Right. I'm not ready to go on. Might as well live my death to the fullest."

She laughed out loud, which got us a few startled glances from the men in front of us. Portillo looked back with a frown, and Iuturna put her hand over her mouth, hiding her teeth.

"We're coming to the cottage," Carson said in a low voice. Through the trees, I could see the vast form of the black centipede, curled like a snail, head pointed at the angry sky. The rain ran slick over its segmented body, each part the size of a Volkswagen Beetle placed sideways. The dirty orange-yellow claws gripped the cottage and then itself, giving it the appearance of some nightmarish conch shell. Its coal black eyes stared blankly, and I could not tell whether we registered or not.

Afterdeath

All was still save the clatter of the rain.

Chapter 23

RESCUE EFFORT

I watched the things take off in the direction of the barking, and hoped to God he was running faster than he'd ever run before. Angelina had jumped to her feet and was yanking me as hard as she could.

"Come on!" she yelled, pulling on my arm. I began to stumble forward, but couldn't imagine what I'd do once I caught up to those monsters. There they were off in the distance, sprinting through the forest in the direction we'd been going in the first place. The skies had opened madly overhead, and their shapes were difficult to see except as rapid blurs in the distance. My heart was no longer in my throat after a while, it just fell out. There was no other way of describing it. I ran through bracken and ferns, slapped in the face by low-hanging tree branches, my eyes filled with the heavens' angry tears, but still I kept up with Angelina's furious running. We kept pace with the things, but still the question remained: what would we do, weaponless against such killers? Perhaps that was the question assailing Angelina's mind right this moment, and the reason we didn't dare catch up. Whatever happened, there was no way we'd let them get their claws on Barkley.

The driving rain and darkness shut us out of their vision, but also impeded ours. It came down so hard that I had trouble breathing at times, choking on what felt like a waterfall. The grey, rapid shapes ducked under leaves and branches like agile cats, while our efforts were clumsy and slipping, sliding ineptitude. The heavy rains covered all sound as well, and was almost as thunderous as cataracts—almost. If it had been, I would not have heard the thud. I would not have turned around. I would not have seen another of the creatures landing on the wet undergrowth behind us, putting down its head as it got ready to sprint.

My head began to spin and my wet body electrified. I caught up to Angelina and whispered harshly into her ear:

"There's one right behind us!"

"What?" she said, putting her hand to her ear. I grabbed her face and turned it around, still running, still dashing madly through the forest.

"Shit!"

"What do we do?" I could hear the thump of huge feet behind us, and dared not turn around. I didn't need to see its face.

"Run faster!" she said.

But the other two! I thought, not making any sense of her request, but not wanting to think too hard either. Complex plans were not in the cards right now. Fighting it was out of the question without weapons. Veering left or right would mean losing Barkley. Going faster and catching up to the others just sounded dumb. Stopping? No, I wasn't suicidal yet.

So we ran faster. The thing behind us kept pace, but didn't exactly overrun us, either. We were catching up to the other two. If I'd still been alive, I would have been exhausted and ready to keel over at any moment. I don't think I'd ever run so much or so hard in my life. The more I thought about it though, the more tired I got, so I stopped thinking and that seemed to help.

Angelina made a veering sign with her arm, first to the right, then coming back, then pointed at me. She wanted me to go around the two running creatures, to their right. We were close behind them now. Ten or twelve paces ahead, they bounded through the forest, intent on their prey. Suddenly she sped up. I thought she was already running as fast as she could, but apparently I'd been wrong. She ran at breakneck speeds between the two pursuing creatures, and I saw them both throw her a double-take, then open their maws full of teeth and try to jump her. I veered right.

I went right past them, and threw a glance behind me. The thing that had followed me had decided to go straight for Angelina as well. I ran faster than I believed was possible, and went around the carnage. I threw a look back and saw the three creatures piled up on each other. Oh no! They must have caught Angelina! They were furiously mauling her on the ground, and I saw claws flash and maws clamp. Their muscular bodies covered her, and all I saw was these horrid creatures attacking each other for a piece of her. I felt like screaming, but covered my mouth and kept running. I had to get Barkley!

Then I saw Angelina further ahead still running wildly. She hadn't been caught after all! I saw her scoop down and pick something up. I was now far behind, trying to catch up, but at least they were safe. I turned my head, saw the creatures picking themselves up from the fray, getting their bearings, and focusing – on me.

I ran harder. I ran faster. The rain pummelled down without mercy and filled my eyes, mouth, face and ears. Trees flashed by. Angelina had waited for me. Barkley must have been tucked away safely because he was nowhere to be seen.

The things ran again, and now they were three.

Even at the distance we were, we could feel the thumping of their feet on the forest floor. The rain washed away all smells, but I am certain theirs would have been horrifying. A steep incline began, and we clambered up it. Whatever abilities we'd had on flat ground were negated by the climb. Loose rocks and stones tumbled from underfoot, and our rapid progress was slowed to a crawl.

The creatures, however, did not have our trouble. They easily climbed and ran. Underbrush became thinner. We went over a hillock and kept on. Trees became scarcer and thinner. Before us stood a wall.

Not a wall, per se. A promontory, maybe fifteen feet high. High enough that we'd be dragged off it by the things intent on devouring us if we attempted to climb it. Angelina grabbed my hand and turned left, following its contours. Perhaps the higher and lower ground would come together again further that way?

"Are you sure it's this way?" I yelled, panting.

"No. I told you, nobody comes here because of things like *those*," she said, cocking her thumb behind her at our pursuers.

"Then why would you even…" I cried.

"Fifty-fifty chance, girl. Cross your heart and hope to…"

"Don't even say it. I'm getting tired of Death puns," I said, exasperated.

"Then you shouldn't have bit the big one, should you?" she responded, rolling her eyes.

Right, like I had a choice, I thought.

We ran alongside the rock wall, but the hill to the left of us and this natural formation to the right had formed a culvert, and the amount of rain that came down on us accumulated there like a pool. Knee-deep in water, the exercise was tiresome. Splashing about, I could hear the beasts coming closer. I heard a hiss from my left, and saw one on the hill, keeping pace with us easily.

I was tired. There was no more energy in me, I felt. Lifting one leg then the other to take another step required more effort than I was able to give. Angelina put her arm around me and dragged me. My breaths came in ragged. I turned to see where the other two creatures were, but there was only one other. Crap.

Afterdeath

I looked around, and saw it was following us from atop the ledge, on our right. Angelina fell in the water.

The monster above us pounced. High into the air, mouth wide open, talons wide, it came down like a missile. But then it twisted, and one of its arms reached around to grab something. I dragged Angelina, but it was on top of us, falling with a splash.

A half-dozen arrows protruded from its back, and as it lay overtop Angelina, it began to dissolve. She pushed the remains off of her in time for the one which had been following on our left to decide to take its turn. It flew at us from above, and stopped in the air dead as a volley of arrows stuck it like a pin cushion, right before our eyes. I turned around to see the third one turn tail and scamper off.

Above us, a dozen figures in brown leather capes and cowls peered over the scene.

"Who are you?" Angelina called out, picking herself up from the water.

"Don't you recognize friends?" A man called out.

That voice. It couldn't be. A stout man jumped from the ledge into the water. He pulled his cowl off.

"Aren't you going to thank me?" Brock said.

"Sure," Angelina said, and she cold-cocked him in the mouth.

Brock reeled back, falling on his ass into the waters. Bows raised above us, pointing at Angelina.

Brock raised his hand. He smiled. His face slowly regained its usual configuration.

"Had that coming. It's okay," he said, his hand still raised. He got up on his hands and knees saying: "You probably want to know..." and Angelina kneed him in the chin, sending him flat on his back underwater. I covered my mouth to hide a smile. He got up, spitting out dirty ditch water.

"Well that one was uncalled for," he said, rubbing his chin, while trying to regain his footing to stand up.

"You don't get to decide what is called for or uncalled for, you bastard traitor," I said. My cheeks ran blazing hot.

"Nice! What did you do with this one? She's got a fire in her now," he joked, waggling a finger toward me. Angelina took a threatening step toward him and he put up his guard, his smile gone.

"It's no coincidence you've come into the Wyldlands. You're here for us. Why?" Angelina said.

"A rescue. My father has sent me to retrieve you," he answered.

"A rescue? First you betray us, then you save us? What's the catch, Brock? Where's the next trap?" Angelina said.

"Don't you get it? I had no choice! It's not like I wanted to send a good friend to the hands of her tormentors. But because I got involved with said friend in the first place, I'm going to have to pay for it for a long time to come. Do you catch my meaning, Angel?" Brock said, pointing in Angelina's face.

"Yeah. Yeah, I get it," she said, seething.

"Where are you taking us?" I asked. By this time, the people who'd stood by on the cliff had climbed down into the water with us.

"Back to Necropolis, and to my father's. First we have to go back to Larunda's to get your sister out," he said, no trace of emotion on his face.

"What's so special about them?" Angelina said, suspiciously. Of course she knew, but did they?

"I've no idea, dear, just obeying orders. The plan is to get everybody back to the city before the fit hits the shan. Not sure you were made aware of this, but there's some heavy stuff that's about to go down," he said.

"How heavy?" I said.

"Invasion," he replied.

***

The rain continued unabated as we climbed back over the promontory and headed toward what I was hoping was a quick exit from the forest. There was still the risk we'd get attacked by one of the creatures that had made our life a nightmare a few hours ago, but surrounded by mercenaries I felt our chances were vastly improved. Nevertheless, we travelled as quietly as possible. There was no use in attracting much unwanted attention.

I wondered, as we traipsed down muddy trails, how many of those now escorting us might have been the same that had attacked us when we'd still been inside the city. Not that it mattered anyway. A mercenary didn't work for loyalty, but for money. How quickly a friend became an enemy when an assignment demanded it. How hard was it to return to previous relationships when trust had been broken? I hoped I'd never have to find out.

Darkness prevailed over the forest. The clouds swirling above in inky black masses blotted out the sun and any attempt it might have made to shed light on us. The one saving grace I could find in all this wetness was its warmth. I remembered when I was still alive, how torrential downpours like these might have been frigid. We'd lived through a few on our summer camping trips and those amazing nineteenth century re-enactments we loved so much. On those days we stayed inside our tents, snug under thick, scratchy blankets, a lamp above our heads, and grandma would tell us stories of when she was a little girl, her glasses on the end of her nose, and how her grandparents had come to Canada from the southern US. Chloe and I would listen

Afterdeath

raptly, sitting cross-legged, with only our faces poking out from our riding blankets. Outside, the re-enactment "soldiers" would go about their duties. Once in a while, we would hear the keening "ting!" sound of a hammer hitting anvil as the blacksmith would make a horseshoe, or of a concertina, accompanied by ribald songs that Rose said we shouldn't be listening to. Chloe and I giggled at the naughty words that accompanied the tiny accordion's music, under Grandma's fake glare. Eons wrapped in centuries dipped in eternities ago; another life.

We walked on, and the trees became thicker again; older forest, denser. Gnarled trees that had seen the dawn of time and would see the end, as well; single file, under the awnings of massive branches that almost managed to stop the rain from reaching us.

Almost.

Angelina and Brock and I walked near the front; Brock leading, Angelina after him, and I third. Angelina had let Barkley out and he ran through the brush beside us, no outward sign of happiness. I guessed he'd decided not to reveal his ability to talk to any others but us, because not a peep came out of him. Maybe this particular secret would turn out to be beneficial in the future?

As the day wore on, I wondered when the rain would abate. It just came down and down and down. I'd never seen anything like it. Fortunately we didn't run into any other monsters, which I was grateful for.

I don't know at what time we reached the clearing, but it must have been late afternoon. I was glad to see the ends of the forest, even if it meant being entirely exposed to the downpour which continued unabated.

There was a ruin before us, and Brock gave it a wide berth. We walked on, and I took in the broken walls, caved in roof and standing stones which must have been quite an impressive (if smallish) fortification back in the day. Brock kept looking at it as if something was wrong. We headed straight to the other side of the clearing, where another much less eerie-looking forest began. This one had the tameness of the woods you would find in your back-yard, not the silent, deadly attributes we'd just escaped.

On we went, until I heard the sound of fighting. Brock broke out into a trot, yelling: "Come on!" giving the go-forward gesture with his hand. I felt panic, wondering where we were and what we were supposed to do. The din became louder, and we broke out into another clearing. As I ran into the open space I stopped dead in my tracks.

Wrapped around a stone cottage was an enormous centipede; bigger than a bus, writhing in anger, its head coming down to smash people and soldiers that ran around its feet. The occasional sound of gunfire detonated, but otherwise they were attacking this behemoth with sticks!

I watched as one woman gave a heavily armoured segment a hit of her branch, and watched as black tendrils whipped out from the seemingly impenetrable armour, snatched her up, and dragged her screaming into its body, into silence and oblivion. I'd never seen anything so frightening in my life, or in all my nightmares.

Our companions unslung their bows and surrounded the centipede (if you could call it that). Still the rain came down, muddying the battleground. One man, who'd been attempting to slash at the base of the beast with a cutlass noticed us and came rushing up.

"Who are you?" he said.

"Brock. We've come to get Chloe. Any idea where she is?"

"Inside. This thing is of Larunda. If we can get her separated from it, we might be able to defeat it," he said. "I am Captain Garcia Portillo," he said.

Just then we all saw that the creature had stiffened and was preparing to slam down again. We scattered in all directions save the one in which it would fall. Like a giant redwood coming down in the forest, it slammed down onto the ground where our group had just stood, sending mud and water into the air. The force of the hit sent a few of us flying, to land unceremoniously a few meters further in a heap. I got up, my head spinning. Behind me I could see the enormous thing begin to rise again, preparing for another attack.

A purple bird landed in a branch near where I'd been sprawled.

"You are Olivia, are you not?" it said.

"Yeah, who are you?" I said.

"My name is Gassire. I was your servant before. The details are not important at this point. You must help your sister. She is ill," the little bird said.

"What? How?" I said.

"No time to explain. You must go down to the dungeons and help her," it said.

"How do I do that?"

"I will distract it. When you get a chance, go in through the door on the other side!" it cried, and flew up into the air. I watched it fly up to where the thing's head wavered, its burnt-orange legs waving angrily. I circumvented the house, and saw where the front door should have been. The din of battle made it hard to concentrate. People ran around, picking up rocks and throwing them at the monster. The little bird flitted about, high in the air, near the monster's face. It dove and weaved, hitting it in one eye, then flying higher, out of reach. Angered even further, the leviathan stretched and unwound taut against its bonds, which appeared to be the hole in the ground from which it protruded. The lower half of its body, covering the door, moved only

Afterdeath

slightly. I fidgeted, hoping that something would happen that would give me the opportunity I needed, but it barely budged.

Arrows flew now that we had joined the fight. This did nothing to harm it, but everything to send it into blind fury. It was like the valiant efforts of soap bubbles attacking a sky-scraper sized stack of pointed needles. I watched as they flew at its head, and bounced off without effect. Still the little bird attacked it, and ducked away in time. The beast stretched to the limit after one such attack, and I saw its body moving slightly upward from the base of the house. There, under its massive legs, an opening. I ran as fast as I could to it, looking one last time to the sky. Just in time to see the bird snapped up into the monster's maw. A pain clutched at my heart, but I kept running straight for that tiny entrance.

Someone hit me from the side, and I sprawled into the mud once again. I got up on my hands and knees, and a wild-eyed soldier covered in muck looked at me in anger.

"Goddamned kid!" he yelled, and fled to the rear of the house. I looked up and saw that the centipede was readying another ground attack. I looked toward the house, and saw legs shifting. I began to crawl on all fours, the legs beginning to cover the entrance. I sped up, launching myself at the last second, and went through the closing legs into the open door of the house.

Chapter 24

TRAPPING THE MONSTER

The fighting had been a blur once it had started. It had been Stanislaw who'd set off hostilities. My bet had been on Alois, but one instigator equalled another, in the Grand Schemelessness of things. Carson and I'd been planning an attack when the hothead decided he was in charge. Rushing into the clearing and firing one of our few guns at point blank range, the centipede had come to life. Tentacles had shot out from its carapace, as if the thing was made of them, ripped the gun out of the madman's hands and gripped him by the throat, snapping him back toward itself like a recoiling elastic band. He'd been engulfed into the thing's armour as if it had been a black hole, and we'd seen nothing of him since. Others had suffered the same fate.

By the time we thought we'd gotten some kind of defence going, it had started slamming into us with all its strength, sometimes sweeping across the clearing like a scythe.

A miracle: we'd been able to wedge its body out of the way long enough for Carson and myself to open the door and jump in. We'd found the stairs and gone into the dungeon. Now we stood before the twitching body of the monster's mother. Larunda lay on her back, on a magnificent poster bed, in an opulent room. Her pale fingers clutched the sheets around her, her neck tense and eyes closed. From her

Afterdeath

abdomen, where her bellybutton would have been, extended a thin rope, which, as it went upward toward the gaping hole in the ceiling, became larger and larger until it was the circumference of a wading pool.

Black, writhing.

Thin orange legs kicking at air.

Trying to escape its prison.

Carson and I stared at it with disgust, not knowing where to begin. Larunda hissed through clenched teeth. Not having her interpreter with her meant she could not communicate with us, and we were at a loss on how to proceed. Should we cut it out? Would that turn it loose or kill it? Or her?

I approached the bed carefully, biting my lip as I saw Larunda's trembling hands and the tears of pain slipping down her face and onto cream-coloured pillows. What would push someone to swallow so much evil just to have a bit more power? Clearly, I wasn't in her position, but it made me wonder nonetheless. Why go through so much pain if the reward was crippling agony? I was curious, and as much as I felt pity for the woman who lay before me, there was also the anger over what she had done to us and to so many others. How much of it was out of necessity, and how much of it was out of greed?

If Olivia and I'd been the thing that everyone claimed we were, it was obvious we'd made our decision on which side of the fence we stood, and even though we might have *been* some sort of nightmare, we'd been born with an idea of right and wrong and exercised it to escape the one who'd birthed us.

I extended my hand to touch the umbilical cord that was the centipede.

One finger, the length of its shiny black back.

Larunda screamed, and the thing pulled her up by the stomach. She hovered a foot or two above her bed still holding the sheets, but her mouth open, her piteous cries unbearable.

"Carson, give me a knife," I said, going back to my friend. We had to end this. I had no idea if there was any other way, but we had to deal with it now before other avenues were blocked.

"Are you sure?" he said, putting his palm on the hilt of a buck knife he carried.

"No. I'm not. I just know we have to put her out of her misery. I don't know what else to do. Usually she would put a thing like that in a frame, but I have no idea how to do that, and anybody who could help us isn't around, so..." I said, putting my hand forward.

"I don't think this is the best way to do it," he said.

"Carson. What's your better idea?" I said, looking him straight in the eye.

"I... I don't," he answered.

"Give me the knife, please," I said, then smiled.

He sighed and unlatched his blade, then gave it to me, hilt first. I went closer to the taut rope that was the centipede, and grasped it firmly in one hand, close to the base of Larunda's stomach. I saw her tense, and her eyes squint even more. One of her hands shot out, and she raised in the air a bit more. She grasped my wrist, the one holding the centipede, and her eyes opened, terror registering as she saw what I was about to do.

"Sorry," I mumbled, and put the knife to the centipede, right next to her bellybutton. She closed her eyes again and whimpered. I cut, with one strong, powerful pull away from my body. The knife went through with little resistance, spurting black goo from the wiggling black tail. As her body fell back to the bed, Olivia came through the door.

"Chloe!" she said, looking at the scene, watching as the centipede sped up the hole it had created for its escape. She came to me and we hugged, and I never wanted to let go of my sister ever again. Larunda stared at all three of us trying to mouth words soundlessly, and Olivia let go and went to her bedside, asking:

"What's wrong with her?" Before I could answer or tell her to stay away from the evil woman, Larunda grabbed Olivia and held her on the bed. She pulled her head down to her hand, and I saw the panic in Olivia's face. Carson took a step toward, but it was Larunda's voice that came out of Olivia's mouth next.

"You've let it go! I held it, and you let it go! It'll destroy everything!" Olivia's face reflected the fury that Larunda must have felt but was too weak to show.

"You're welcome, you bitch. I may have just saved you," I said, trying to get at my sister.

"Stop. I like you where you are. No, you didn't save me; you doomed everything else. It will consume everything in its path. You must stop it. There is no other way," my twin's face said, in a rictus of hate.

"How can we?" Carson said.

"Only Antonia could stop it," Larunda said through Olivia, and her face was cunning.

"We're not your pet anymore, Larunda. We won't become your slave because you say we can," I said.

"You must. Whoever is out there will become its next victims if you do not. Think quickly. Their time is numbered," she said. I thought of Iuturna and her family, and Gassire, Gassire and all the others. My arm was beginning to itch and burn again, since I'd been out of the soothing rain.

"How?"

Afterdeath

"Become one," she cried. "One soul, one mind. Become one." She let go of my sister, and Olivia tore away from her, batting at her hands.

"What the hell just happened there?" she said.

"Larunda. She took you. Olivia, all those people out there are in danger. I set that thing free. She told me… that… we used to be one and the same. We're her nightmare. Man those words sound like insanity when you say them out loud, don't they?" I said, turning to Carson for help. He just looked at me, his arms crossed.

"Shouldn't matter if it's the truth," he said.

"You and I. We are a split soul. If we join again, we can beat this thing. Thing is… I… I don't know how!" My twin looked at me and Larunda.

"Chlo, I've seen some crazy stuff in the past few days. I don't doubt you. I don't think you'd ever lie to me, but this is nuts," she said, and walked over to me. And something about Olivia wasn't the same. There was no fear in her. She touched my shoulder, and I'm the one who felt like I'd fall to pieces.

"We are one?" she said.

"We have to be," I answered. My arm felt as though it would melt off, and she lifted it to look at the wound. She placed her fingertips on the bite mark, and pressed, ever so gently. My heart caught in my throat, and fire engulfed my body, sun-tide ripping me apart.

The hole above us was clear of the creature. Rain was pouring down the gaping emptiness, creating a pool of light and rain. As soon as the deluge hit, I felt it, the transformation. My sister was no longer before me, and neither was she in me. We were each other and one. It was not as if I had one other person living within my body; it felt like I was whole again, and rising. My strength, like coils, unspooled on the floor, and I turned to Carson, whose mouth gaped at me as if he was about to be eaten. My head, like Alice in Wonderland's, kept rising as if I grew exponentially.

I looked down to see my body was massive rope, scaled and expanding. I turned to the sky, and wriggled my way into the opening that'd been created by my nemesis. As I rose, crushing stone and sand as I went, I began to hear wails of despair and screams of fear.

When my head finally protruded from the ground, I saw the centipede running rampant over the terrain, its many legs moving in waves, its body ducking this way and that, snatching people up as they ran, and eating them whole. The screaming intensified to a crescendo of horror and fear as I slithered out of the aperture, lifting my body into the sky. I let out a bellow that shook the heavens and made everything pause for an instant, even the rain.

The centipede turned.

It lifted its upper abdomen and whirled around to greet me. Legs danced wildly, and its maw opened in expectation of a wonderful, juicy meal.

It was then that I pounced. As people fled the scene into the forest, horrified to find that there were now not one but two monsters, I fell upon the foul insect and coiled myself around its body.

I squeezed.

Spikes shot out from its carapace, hitting me where I wrapped myself tightly around it. My snake's coils deflected most of the assault, but where they entered against the grain, I felt pain penetrating my massive body.

I squeezed harder and the centipede fell sideways to the ground, and I with it. We crashed among the trees behind the house with a resounding boom, felling them, crushing them flat, sending water, dirt and people flying.

The creature I held close snapped at my face, pincers attempting to grab my jugular. I ducked my head out of the way, but realized I could not do so for long. I stretched my spine, lifting up both our upper bodies, and slammed the thing down on the ground again. I smashed its head onto the wet, rocky soil over and over again, until its movements became slower, its attacks less powerful.

I then bit it as hard as I could, right where the segment between its head and neck began. I lifted our bodies once again, then coiled tightly, taking its head clean off.

Its body began to writhe in shock and I held on tight. It eventually stopped moving, and began to dissolve. Its head had become soft and gelatinous in my mouth, and I let it fall to the ground where it thudded once, before deliquescing into a pool and disappearing. I spat out the acrid taste it had left.

I felt weak.

I don't know how many meters tall I was, but my whole body hurt from the effort. I lay down on the ground panting. Someone, Iuturna's mother, came out of the forest and approached me like a supplicant.

"You've come back, Mistress," she said, smiling. I don't know if my body allowed me to smile, but that's what I felt it doing.

"I had to," I said, and a whirlwind came out of my maw, blowing the old woman's hair back, shaking nearby trees.

"Rest. We will take care of you," she said. I saw others coming out of the forest to see what had become of the fighters, but after that I closed my eyes, my breathing becoming slower because of the exertion. The pain was only a memory now, as healing had stripped it away.

Yet I felt so tired, and trusted all would be well if I slept.

Chapter 25

REBIRTH

Opening my eyes felt like lifting weights. My energy was depleted, even though I must have slept for days. The ceiling was white and stuccoed, and when I turned my head to the left, I saw a window, closed. Daylight spilled in, barely contained by sheer curtains. On a bed like the one I assumed I lay on, was— myself. Confusion swirled for a moment before I realized that it was Chloe. Having been one being had blurred the lines and delineations of who we were separately. This was the aftermath.

I strained to lift myself, my back sore. It was as if I'd been bitten repeatedly. In a sense, I had. I looked at the purple bruises on my arm, and sighed. Chloe stirred. She passed an arm over her eyes.

"Back in the cottage," she said, matter-of-factly.

I cleared my throat and she turned to me.

"Olivia!" she said, attempting to get up. She fumbled and fell by the bed. I tried to get up to help her, and only managed to roll over onto the floor beside her. She stared at me, and then we both began to laugh.

"Where were you this whole time?" she said.

"*That* is a story too long and tiring to tell now, I think," I said.

"Yeah, right," she sighed. She turned on her stomach and tried to push herself up. I grabbed the side of the bed and attempted the same.

"The part where we became a giant snake, was that true?" I said. It felt like a dream, or nightmare, or something in between.

"As far as I know, it's all true," Chloe said, inspecting her arm. Any bruises she had were identical to mine. The wound that I had touched before we'd joined was gone, and the colour on her face was that of fatigue, not terminal illness. Then a curious thing happened: flashes of memory, not my own, came in short bursts to the forefront of my mind. They felt like mine, but—

"Did you climb ladders on a cliff recently, by any chance?" I asked.

"Yeah— how did you— did you dream about Grandma Rose— and me?"

"That's too weird."

The door opened, and Angelina walked in.

"I see you two have recovered well. Can you walk?" I groaned, both hands on the bed to steady myself. Chloe stood up, took a tentative step, and promptly fell over again.

"I'll take that as a no. Carson!"

"Right here," said the blond man, walking through the door. He came to me, and I put my arms around his back.

"Hey," he said.

"Hey to you too," I replied. Chloe rolled her eyes, but smiled nonetheless.

"Okay you two, let's get a move on. Don't have all day," Angelina said, coldly. I saw Barkley poke his head through the door as well, while Angelina helped me up off the ground. Barkley's tongue lolled out.

"Jealousy," he said in Chloe's direction. Angelina snarled at him, and he backed away with his head down.

"Idiot," she said.

Carson helped me walk, one arm on my hip. I felt as if I'd been asleep for weeks, and this was my Sleeping Beauty moment. Like I was coming back from the deader-than-dead, and it was exhausting.

We walked down stairs and corridors and more stairs, heading into the depths of the cottage, where, Angelina said Larunda hid herself during the day. Soldiers at attention saluted us on the way down, and I looked at them numbly. Paintings hung along the corridors, but as soon as I peered into the details my sister turned my head away.

"You don't want to do that," she said. Instead of being insulted, I nodded. I felt as if her overbearing demeanour was something I could stand, for the time being. I was too happy to be reunited that there were many things I could forgive. Or maybe I should just accept the way she was; accept the fact she only wanted to protect me from demons and ghouls and dead things all around, just like she protected me from jerks and bullies while we were still alive. Or maybe…

Afterdeath

"I'll be fine. Stop worrying about me," I said to her and smiled, and she gave me the most curious look, and blushed.

Down spiral staircases underground.

Down halls made of stone, flickering torches lighting the way. I'd come here. This is where I'd come the first time. I recognized this place. Around the bend would be a wooden door, and there it was. Through it would be a ravaged room, but here ended the similarities.

Larunda's bedroom was as good as new. Whatever powers she had left, she'd used to make her living quarters resplendent again. She lay comfortably in her four-poster bed.

"Are you feeling better, Antonia?" she said through Iuturna. I gaped in surprise, and she refused to look at us; her eyes on the ground, her face a deep crimson.

"We're not her," Chloe said,

"And you know it," I answered. It felt like we were kids again, finishing each other's sentences.

"Nevertheless, you deserve my thanks, whomever you pretend to be," she said this coolly, off-handed, reaching for a cup of dark drink by the bed-stand. She took a sip.

"You are my guests, for as long as you like," she continued, "I've had rooms made up for you as soon as you'd recovered."

If we recovered, you mean, I thought, and threw a glance at Chloe at the same time she looked at me.

"We'd like to leave," Chloe said. "Right now." Larunda peered at her from over her cup, and tilted her head, as if she hadn't quite heard well enough.

"Leave? Oh no, no, no, you can't leave. I need you. If I can't have you, I won't let anyone else either. You must understand. It's a matter of security."

"You're keeping us prisoners? After what we did to save you? Don't you have any gratitude, you bitch?" I said, and Chloe did a double-take at my words. It almost felt like her words pouring out of my mouth like venom. When we'd become one, I knew what had happened to her during our separation, and she knew my misadventures. We'd melded into one being, and all those memories were now a part of me. They just took a while to surface, like bubbles rising and popping. I wouldn't easily forgive this vile woman what she'd done to my friends.

"My dear child, it's not personal, you know. It's just the way things have to be. You? Walking out that door? Leaving me powerless against the coming storm? Ridiculous. Not while I have something to say about it," Iuturna said, while Larunda stared at us long and hard, her lips barely suppressing a smile. Maybe she knew we were spent, and could not fight back. That we were indeed caught within her trap, unable to formulate anything other than idle threats. She took another sip of her drink, and I saw that little smile on the corner of her lips, the one that said: "I've got you. I've got you both, and I'm never letting you go." Iuturna *said* these words, but her *face* was sadness and pain.

I was furious, and it must have shown. Chloe put her hand on my arm, because I then noticed that I'd taken a step forward. What was I going to do? Attack? My mind was fuzzy with various intents. Fear was no longer there.

"Take them to the cave with the other prisoners," she said, and guards came through the door, grabbing my sister and I, Carson, Angelina, Brock and Barkley.

"How could you?" Chloe screamed at Iuturna, and as much as the poor girl tried to turn her head away, Larunda held it steady, forcing her to watch our shame through tearing eyes.

They dragged us up the stairs, kicking and yelling, Barkley trying to bite them. The same men with whom we'd fought the monster now returned to their previous master. I stopped fighting. What was the use? Eventually we all marched ourselves out the door, and into the garden. It was still a mess. Great swathes of trees had been broken like matchsticks under the weight of our battle, and the skeleton guards took us all past the carnage without skipping a beat. Of the giant beast, there was nothing left, of course; returned to the world like all nightmares, absorbed by the Great Nothing.

The trail was familiar, but it took me a while to realize that this was because of my shared memories with Chloe. There would be a boulder, then a turn, then a small cave opening. Yes. There it was.

One after the other, we were thrown into the entrance, lobbed without malice, but without restraint as well; just doing their jobs.

Inside, it was dark, and damp. Movement from the far wall told me that we were not the first, of course. The mercenaries in Brock's employ were here, weaponless and despondent. There were also the people Chloe had managed to save a few days earlier, and at that surfacing memory, I felt a great pride to have her as a sister. I wish I had her bravery but I very well could, if I wanted to. That was also a new thought. I could be the things I wanted to; if I did not let my fear of failure take over for me. Having that thought rise to the top made my resolve harden. A shadow came nearer.

"Hey there. I take it you refused the Queen's offer?" This man's name was Garcia. Garcia Portillo. He was a good man.

It's so weird having someone else's thoughts as your own, I thought.

"How did you end up in here?" Chloe asked him, clapping him on the shoulder, smiling.

"Same reason as you. I made my choice. Now I'll just have to suffer like the rest of you," he said.

Afterdeath

"My father will learn about this and send another contingent. We won't be here for long," Brock said, leaning against a wall. The cave was not tall enough to stand up, and I am not sure, but it might have been by design that we were meant to scurry like rats. Larunda had the type of personality that would love to abase someone, or a group of someones, until their spirits were broken.

"We'll just have to wait and see," I said.

I looked over in a corner to see Angelina scratching behind Barkley's ear. At least those two were getting along again, if only temporarily. My heart broke when I saw a woman in her fifties. I had a hard time realizing why at first, but then it came to me: this was the mother of the girl named Iuturna, who had gone back to her old mistress. Poor woman, I felt her pain. It must have been doubly hard for her: having lost her for so long, regained her, then lost her again. There was cruelty, even in death.

Chloe came and sat by me, and her voice was barely above a murmur. The dank earth smells filled my nostrils, but not in any unpleasant way. In a sense it reminded me of the gardening shed behind our house, where Grandma Rose kept all her tools and implements. There was a dull echo also, as voices tended to carry.

"How've you been?" she said, looking at her fingernails.

"You know," I said, making a mind-reading joke. She smiled shyly.

"I'm sorry I got us killed," she said, and I was taken aback by her apology.

"Could have been worse." She giggled, but it sounded like nerves more than anything.

"How? How could it have possibly been worse?" she said in a rough whisper.

I felt something rising in my throat. A dry lump, which caught and would not let got, making the words hard to pronounce, even as they wanted to fall out in a stream.

"I thought I'd never get to see you again." I said, and she looked me in the eye, tears streaming from hers. I hugged her, so hard, like she might disappear forever if I let her go.

"I... I know, but we're together. She can't split us up. Just wait until we're strong enough again, then we'll take her on," she said. I thought of it, but who would we consume to gather strength? How many soldiers would we have to fight to be free? I did not want to despair of course, but these points were valid, in my mind. As I thought them, I was sure she would think them as well. Should we wait for the cavalry, as Brock said it would come? How long would it take, and how many would they send, and how powerful a Larunda would they face? Those were also legitimate questions.

I let her go.

I got on all fours, and I crawled to the entrance, where the light made longer shadows on the floor, reaching the end of the small cave, where all concerned huddled.

Outside, two guards stood at attention, facing away from the cave. Like the first time, I tried to put my hand through but it came up against an invisible wall. This one did not want to give. It was solid, if completely transparent to the eye. Brock and Carson had been trying to break out through the small aperture as well, with the same result.

"They'll be coming soon. Anytime now," Brock said, and Carson shook his head.

As I looked outside at the sun lowering, four guards and one of Larunda's butlers came into view from the direction of the cottage, all six bleach-boned and uniformed. Barnard was his name.

He came to the mouth of the cave, but only stared straight ahead.

"Hilda," he said. "You've been chosen by the mistress. Come out now Hilda," he said, his jawbone clacking.

The woman I'd recognized as the translator's mother stirred in the corner. The twilight shone on the fear that filled her features. She tried to back-pedal into a further recess of the cave.

"Hilda," the butler said, honeyed words fairly oozing from his skinless teeth, "come out now. You wouldn't want your daughter to be the one that must give herself to the Mistress, do you? Or your husband?"

"Give herself? What does he mean?" I asked.

"Larunda will eat her," Chloe replied without a trace of emotion.

"Come, come now Hilda, you are making the Queen wait. You know she hates that. Your pain will only increase with the annoyance you cause. Be a good tribute and come out *now*." At these words, the man named Barnard extended his arms to the entrance of the cave, and the woman named Hilda fell to her knees. She tried pushing backwards with her hands, but some invisible force pushed her forward, skidding across the sand floor. Several people tried to grab her arms or body, but it was as if she was too slippery to hold. All the while, the woman screamed and screamed. As she passed me, I took my fingers out of my ears to grab a hold of her outstretched arms, but I too could not keep a grip on her. She slid out the door and into the waiting arms of the guards.

I heard her scream a long time, long after I could no longer hear her. She was still there, in my mind, screaming.

The sun set.

Barnard and those guards came back for four other people, their bones covered in a translucent layer of skin now that the moon had risen. They picked only from the group that Chloe had saved. All of them our old allies. There were very few left. Most of them had been consumed by her monster during the battle. The others had been taken by the guards.

There were about twenty of us left in the cave, and when the night was pitch dark, sparkling with the diamonds of stars, an even larger contingent of guards came.

"All of you," Barnard said. We crawled out of the cave, pushing off the guards' grabbing hands, and made our way back to the cottage.

Behind it stood Larunda, surrounded by her whole army, their faces floating over their sometimes fractured skulls. She looked as if she had regained all her power and more. Iuturna had the look of a beaten dog. The Ghost Queen held her firmly by a handful of her hair, crouched on the ground, like one would an animal that has displeased them.

"Welcome, slaves," Iuturna started, eyes to the ground, voice proud. "A new age is starting. With the power of the twins joined as one, I will be all-powerful again. As long as I have Antonia to do my bidding, our kingdom can only grow more prosperous," Larunda looked at her soldiers at these words, and cheers went up in the crowd. "I've gotten rid of all of those who would dare defy me; well, almost," she said, Larunda throwing a glance at those rebellious souls she had not yet consumed, "but that will be remedied soon enough. I will ask you one more time: will you join me willingly, or will you dwell forever in my forest dungeon until I need to feed on your bodies? The choice is yours. No pressure." I could have knocked the self-satisfied grin off her face with a shovel if I'd had one handy.

"I hope the indigestion destroys you. You're obviously not very swift on the uptake," I said. She stared at us wide-eyed.

"I— what's happening?" Iuturna said, consternation on Larunda's face.

A curious thing happened. A mist began to form on the ground around her. Except it wasn't around her, it flowed *from* her, like a vapour waterfall. But it was also coming from Iuturna and the other two survivors, as well as Chloe! It roiled and coiled, growing larger, pooling. It gathered around Larunda's body, and the surprised look on her face told us that this was in no way her doing. A voice, ethereal like the winds, rasped from her vicinity.

"It is my time to rule again, Larunda," it said.

"Who dares? Who are you?" she screeched through Iuturna, whirling with fright as the mist enveloped her, tightening around her body, seeping into it. She batted at it, and her soldiers crowded in, trying to disperse it. It was absorbed entirely into her body, and her eyes rolled back into her head as she choked.

All the soldiers fell to the ground, knocked backwards. All of those she'd commanded dropped.

"One of the many you betrayed," Larunda said, letting go of Iuturna's hair, and extending a hand to help her up.

"Koszla-kuguza," Iuturna said, in awe. The memory came to me, and I looked to see Larunda speaking, with what looked like a ghost tongue.

"Thank you for carrying me to her," he said "I am sorry I could not act earlier. I had to be whole. I apologize for your mother," he said to Iuturna, "and for all of the others she took into herself. I will not hold you here as she would have. You may go when you wish." Larunda's face and body were changing, becoming that of a white-bearded man.

Soldiers one by one came to, scratching their heads and wondering what to do next. They no longer looked like skeletons covered in a thin human skin. They were entirely human again. The king assured them they could do as they pleased, but that he would offer them employ if they wished to stay with him.

"Do you know how to get us back to life?" Chloe said, and the old king frowned.

"I'm sorry, I do not."

"How did you remain yourself all this time, and not get absorbed?" I asked.

"Even though Larunda attempted to destroy me and my home, I'd amassed enough power throughout my life to retain my consciousness. My psychic imprint remained stamped on the stones of my fortress. When I shared it with you, I was able to sustain it throughout, until I could strike back."

Iuturna rose unsteadily.

"So my mother, Hilda—"

"Is gone. I'm sorry," the king said softly.

He could have brought her back, I thought. *He could have brought them all back.* I shivered and fidgeted.

"We should go now," Brock said, "we don't have much time."

Why the hurry? I thought. Now that I'd been reunited with my sister, I just wanted to take it easy for a while. This, of course, was not to be.

"Alright, Brock, but first you have to remove these damned brands on our necks. I've felt like cattle ever since I woke up in Wodun," Angelina said, pointing at her neck. I felt a prickling on mine as she said this, and remembered my own mark. Carson gave him a harsh look and he stepped forward, passing a hand over the necks of Angelina, Barkley then me. It was as if I had become ten pounds lighter all of a sudden, and I might have floated away right then if Brock hadn't brought us to order.

"Now you come back with me. I'm serious when I say it isn't safe here."

We thanked the king, and headed toward the road that had brought us to the cottage in the first place. I saw Chloe talking to a soldier (His name was Garcia. This

I knew). They shook hands and hugged, and she joined us as we walked toward the front of the cottage.

Angelina, Carson, Brock, Barkley, Chloe and I, as well as the dozen mercenaries charged with our protection. We walked as fast as our legs could carry us. It wasn't long before we ran into…

"Bertha!" I said, overjoyed to see our boat of a car on the side of the road.

"Yeah, it crapped out on me pretty quick," Brock said, hands on his hips.

"Maybe we could fix the old girl?" Angelina said.

"Things like that aren't supposed to break down. That's weird," Carson said.

"Keys," I said, hand extended. No moon illuminated the road, but enough stars that I could see her outline. I ran my hand along the convertible top, and the locks all popped open.

"Looks like she's inviting us in," Angelina said. Chloe went to the other side, opening the door.

"You don't want to drive?" I asked.

"Nah, it your turn. You pick the music," she said, flashing me a smile. Brock gave me the keys, and went to open the rear door, but it locked on him.

"I think it doesn't like me," he said, frowning.

"No, *she* does *not*," I said. "Don't expect to be forgiven by everyone for your betrayal, mister."

"I guess not," he said. Carson went to get into the rear door, and the lock lifted.

"Sorry cousin," he said, and patted Brock on the shoulder before hopping in and closing the door. Angelina and Barkley got in on the other side, behind Chloe. I put the key in the contact and she roared to life.

"We'll meet you back in Necropolis at our place!" Brock said, but I was not listening. I was putting the pedal to the metal, watching the dust kick up behind us and the undulating trees parting for us in front.

Chapter 26

Going Home

I was proud of Olivia. She'd grown during my absence. I know that sounds condescending but it's true. I didn't feel like I had to be that "big sister" I'd been whenever I'd been around her before. She'd lit a fire, and I saw it burning brightly as she drove Bertha away from the dumbstruck group of mercenaries and Brock.

"Off to The City of the Dead, then?" I asked. "You know, we've been doing what everyone else wants us to do for the past little while. What do *we* want to do?" she said, keeping her eyes on the road. She drove fast enough that I saw the trees hurtling by, but not so much that the tires would squeal when we took the turns.

"Go back to the land of the living?" I said.

"Get to know a wonderful woman?" Carson said, looking at Olivia.

"Settle down and make a kingdom?" Angelina said, crossing her arms.

"Turn back into a human?" Barkley said, looking up at Angelina, who scratched him behind the ears.

"I am sorry, I am going to have to override most of you. Chloe and I were on a road trip, and we would like to end it," Olivia said. "Who do you know who's got access to the land of the living? I mean, I love you guys, but this is somewhat of our priority. Think hard." She kept her eyes on the road, and when a cross-roads appeared, she slowed down.

"Angelina, do you remember what the Baron Dimanche said when he caught us in the palace?" Olivia asked.

"No, why?"

"I'm paraphrasing a bit, but he said that we were betrayed by 'a man in our midst'."

Afterdeath

"So what?" I said.

"The double blind," Angelina said, looking a shade or two paler than she usually did. "The Baron couldn't have known who was working for him unless somebody told him."

"Somebody high up," Carson said.

"Charon," Barkley added.

"Right," Olivia said, grinning. "Where are we going now?" A cold chill coursed over my body. What if she hadn't caught that detail?

On the side of the road were two signs: Necropolis, straight ahead, and Kingdom of Sands, to the left. She turned the wheel and we headed toward the desert. Why, though? What would we find there that would help us in our journey? I did trust Olivia, but from the memories she had of that place, there wasn't much that would bring us closer to life, in my mind, in the eternal sand seas and deserts of the sunken lands.

"Why there?" I asked. I turned our memories over and over in my head, and couldn't figure it out.

"The Wahy. They have control over the waters of *life*. That means that the flow goes into the land of the living... and back. If anyone can help us get there, it's them." Olivia said, smiling.

She turned on the radio. The newest song by Kurt Cobain was playing, and even though I'd never heard it before, it had a wailing joyfulness to it that was infectious. It sounded as if he was happy now. I lay my head on the headrest and closed my eyes.

When I opened them, we were going down a spiral path, like the road in an underground parking lot, heading deeper and deeper. It dawned on me when I looked out the side window that we were in fact very high up, heading toward the ground below. Small shacks of various colours clung to the side of a cliff, and all around us climbed enormous vines, the kind you would find in fairy tales about giants living in cloud kingdoms. The ground was covered in tree-tall grasses, poking out of the ground. In the distance I could see buildings, like tilting apartment blocks, covered in greenery. Olivia had her hyper-concentrated look, and I didn't dare bother her. We got down to ground level, and I looked back to see the huge, spiralling vine that had brought us down from the upper reaches.

The Sunken Lands were nothing like in her memories, and I could see that in her face. She was just as puzzled as I was. Behind me, the others were still sleeping.

"What do you think happened here?" I said.

"Must have something to do with that storm. I can't see any other explanation." That made sense. If this place wasn't used to getting any rain, that torrential downpour would definitely have had an effect. However, this was pretty extreme.

She navigated the car around enormous vine stalks that grabbed at the sky like monoliths, twisting and turning all the way up. Buildings stuck out of the ground at odd angles, half-sand, half human construction, all covered in a fresh coat of vegetation. I knew Olivia had seen them before, or a version of them, but it was bizarre to see them in person. Like a Dahli painting come to life, after Van Gogh had gotten a hold of it.

We drove a while, grasses taller than cornstalk thwacking at the front of the car, not really knowing where we were going, but always managing to avoid the behemoth vines that towered above. They were so beautiful, in their awe-inspiring way. I wondered if they would last for very long. After an hour or so, our other companions woke, and we dropped the sun roof, letting the thick, heady aroma of wild plants into our cockpit. I felt sweat beading on my brow, and Barkley panted furiously on the back seat. It was a jungle out there, and by the smell of it, it was already decomposing. Nothing lasts forever.

Olivia stopped when the car burst out onto a dry creek bed. Whatever clay it was composed of had hardened and stopped plant growth, and seemed to point in the general direction we were headed.

We covered a lot of ground now. Our road was a cracked mess of dry mud, and we wobbled forward like a paint mixer on high. It felt like driving over a broken highway. On either side of us, the tall plants swayed in the morning wind. Then, the vegetation tapered off, until all that was left was a plain of dry mud, breaking off in heels three inches thick.

"Nice view," Carson said, and it was. The sunshine was barely coming over the side of the rim of the bowl we were in, far away in the distance. Light bounced over the ground, making the cracked mud appear to be flecked with gold. Behind us, we left a straight track with shallow grooves. Bertha's engine whined like a beast, and I thought I felt enjoyment coming off of her. We travelled for half a day, the sun shining bright and all of us pleased to be free. I thought I saw white tents with red pennant floating in the distance, but I assumed that was just my imagination.

When the sun started to dip and dive below the horizon, we saw lights in the distance, and drove toward them.

Chapter 27

THEATRE

Marquee lights buzzed and blinked from the cinema at the end of the deserted parking lot. The doors were rimmed in gold, just as the wraparound show announcements that advertised "This is Your Life", in black letters on white background. We crept up to a parking stall by the front, and I took the key out of the ignition. The two storey construction was the only thing visible in the desert now, and of that only the front end, as the back was wrapped in deepest shadows. Chloe looked at me and I raised my eyebrows.

"What do you think?" I said, to no one in particular.

"Looks creepy. I love it," Angelina said, grinning wildly. "Might as well stop here for the night. No sense in getting all tuckered out while driving through the desert. Although, I'm guessing this desert we're driving through is in fact the Sand Sea. Curious. Wonder if I should even step outside." Before anyone could stop her, she'd set foot on the hard tarmac of the parking lot. "Solid enough. Nice illusion. Wonder what's behind it." She was like a magic debunker, wondering where the strings were. She went up to the building, tapped it gently, gave it a swift kick, and then jumped around holding her broken foot. "It's real!" Her yell echoed between two swears. Maybe trying to scare out a shark using dripping red meat was a more apt description of what she was up to. I'd never understand that woman.

Benoit Chartier

Carson shook his head and stepped out of the car, followed by Barkley, Chloe and I. Carson stretched, and Barkley went up to the front doors and smelled them, peering inside at the red carpeting. A concession stand lay twenty or thirty steps beyond, with a few uniformed attendants talking to each other, like people do when they're bored at work. Otherwise, there did not seem to be any customers at all.

"This has got to be a trap," Chloe said.

"I agree," Carson replied.

"Don't go in, then," Angelina said. She winked at us and stepped into the building. Before closing the door, she waggled a finger at Barkley and ordered: "Stay." Blew him a kiss, and walked in. Barkley groaned and said: "Shouldn't have done that."

"Of all the stupid—" Carson said, hands extended into claws. He took a step forward toward the cinema, then thought better of it. Then took another step, shook his head, and stalked off to the other end of the parking lot, cursing under his breath.

"I don't want to go in there," I said, the shadow of my former self creeping up on me. "I mean, I would, but it is a suicidal idea, isn't it?" A subtle wind snuck in from the mottled desert to ruffle my hair, then tittered away.

"This place is too weird. Unreal, like. I'd rather wait in the car for her to come out," Chloe said. At least I wasn't the only one who sensed danger. Barkley sat on the stoop of the theatre, wagging his tail wanly as if expecting her to exit any time now.

Aaaany time.

Now.

No dice.

Chloe and I sat on the front seat of the car, the white leather groaning pleasantly. The only other sound was that of the blinking buzz of the lights on the marquee, on an ordinary-looking brown-brick building that nevertheless had the appearance of something conjured up from a horror movie. It was too ordinary. Or maybe it was the painted lines in the parking lot; all perfect and new. Come to think about it, so was the theatre itself. It was in a style that harked back to the 1940's, but had not aged a day. Then again, this was the afterlife. I didn't know what to think, obviously.

Barkley trotted up to the car and barked once, frightening us. I opened the driver's side door and he stepped in.

"How did it happen, Barkley? How did you and Angelina end up in that prison, and you into a dog? Give me the details," Chloe said. Maybe now that she wasn't here, we'd get a straight answer.

"I don't know if I should—" he said.

"Come on. She's not here, and no one will tell her. We want to know. Spill it, dog boy," I said. Olivia looked at me wide-eyed, and I shrugged.

Afterdeath

"Okay, okay. Well, you know that we wanted to build a country, right? A place to call our own. We'd known about dobluth embers for a long time, but we had no idea where we could get one. At the time, our little group of friends included Carson, Brock, Wilf and Sigurd. Carson had dropped out of the mercenary business—"

"Why?" I said.

"Tired of the slaughter," Carson said, making us jump and scream. He was standing beside the rear passenger-side door. He opened it and stepped inside, shutting the door with a clang.

"G-go on," Chloe said.

"Angelina got an idea one day. She thought if she could get close to the Baron, she might be able to uncover where he kept his power," Barkley said.

"Get close to, as in—" I said.

"Platonically. As a personal guard. The kingdom had fallen on dangerous times, and she offered her help as a trained bodyguard. Their greever problem was unmanageable, so they accepted. It took her three years before she was able to locate, plan to, and then steal his ember. She did though, and we were together again."

"How did you get caught?" I asked.

"Sheer bad luck. We didn't get far when we were jumped by a band of bounty hunters. Of course they'd put out a reward on us." It sounded to me like the plan hadn't been thought out very thoroughly.

"What happened then?" Chloe asked. A warm gust of desert wind had risen stronger than the last. Not enough to bring up the sand, but it force me to close my eyes.

"I was forced into reincarnation. They didn't choose, they just sent me back. I was somewhat lucky to have landed in a dog's body. Can you imagine if I'd come back as bacteria?" And his entire body shook.

"But then how did you land in prison?" I asked.

"That would be our fault," Carson answered.

"How so?" Chloe said.

"When Angelina lost Barkley, she was heart-broken. She came to Brock and I and begged us to help her get him back. Being a sucker for a good love story, I decided to give her a hand. You could call that our first mistake," Carson said wryly. "We took my boat to the land of the living, where we got in contact with a spiritualist. We explained the situation, and she helped us out. She killed Barkley in dog form, and we were able to retrieve him. Of course, we didn't know he was a dog at the time. Just had a general idea of what his soul looked like, not his physical appearance. Kind of glad he was a dog, really. Mortals don't look too kindly on wanton murder."

"That's horrible!" Chloe said.

"That's logical," I said, nodding my head. Chloe shot me a disgusted glance. "Although horrible, as well," I amended.

"That's where the happy part ends. Brock and I were caught using company property for illicit uses and were damned to Dis District for a good long time, while Barkley and Angelina were given perpetuity in the Garden of Lost Souls. unless they were absorbed by one of the creatures in it. But then you broke them out."

"So why didn't Charon try to stop us?" Chloe asked

"I think he knows a lot more than he's letting on, and he wanted to see where the chips fell before taking any actions that might be harmful to himself. He knew who we were, even at that first meeting. I'd be ready to bet real money on that," I said, remembering his words:

One day, you will know yourself. On that day, you will no longer wonder.

"We're not going to make it that easy for him though, are we," Chloe said. Barkley jumped over the side of the car door and began to pace in front of the theatre again, making little doggy worry noises. Carson stepped out as well, and planted himself in front of the doors, peering inside at the attendants who patently ignored him.

"Why did you promise Angelina you'd stay here with her?" Chloe asked me when we were alone. I knew the question was coming. It was only a matter of time. As soon as our memories had melted together, that one would come jarring its way through her brain.

"At first, it was because I wanted her to get up off her butt so we could go help you, stuck near the sunken lands as we were. Then I realized that that is what I honestly wanted to do. She is a lot of things. Maybe she *is* crazy. But the idea of building something bigger than one person for the benefit of all has an appeal to me that I won't find in the living," I answered. Chloe stared at me, hard. She was not smiling.

She got out of the car and slammed the door. She then headed straight for the theatre.

"Wait!" Carson yelled, and went after her. Barkley bolted for the crack in the closing door and slipped in as it shut tight. I just half-stood in the car, stunned. What had just happened? I felt sick to my stomach, and I would have emptied its contents if it had had any. I kept staring at those front doors, now alone in that big, black parking lot, the lights of the marquee mocking me from five meters away, taunting me, whispering to me that I was not brave enough to enter. Truth be told, I wasn't. I was baffled by what had just happened. Had I betrayed Chloe by telling her my feelings? Had what I said been so dire and detrimental to our friendship that she would rather throw herself headfirst into whatever waited for all of us in there than to allow me to live out my wishes? Typical selfish Chloe. I ran a hand over my face and glared at

Afterdeath

the dismissive theatre. If I had thought Angelina impulsive and brash, Chloe was being, well, an idiot. Did I really have to rescue them? God I hated being forced to be a Princess.

My legs wobbled as I stepped out of Bertha. I leaned back against her and stared, and stared, and stared. I thought of setting foot in there and my heart squeaked and thumped louder. I took a lunging step forward, and anger began to boil, like a thin coat of water at the base of my brain, simmering, hotter and hotter, until sparks flew. Who knew what horrors would snatch at me once I crossed the threshold? My vision blurred and I stomped toward the doors of the faux theatre, thinking:

Is this how I'll go, now? As I always did these days.

I put one sweaty hand on the vertical golden door handle and yanked it back, putting one hand over my eyes and stepping inside.

***

It was dark, so I opened my eyes. I was in bed. I got up and went to the bathroom. Chloe was already there, brushing her teeth.

"Don't forget we have volleyball practise today," she said, and I grunted.

"Hey, one more semester and High School is over."

"There's that at least," I said.

She left. I showered and dressed, and mom and dad were talking in the kitchen. Dad read the paper on his tablet, while mom made breakfast. Chloe was already munching on toast while looking into a social sciences book at her hand. I sat down and tried to eat, mostly playing with my toast.

I kissed mom and dad and felt weird for a moment, but Chloe and I left together to walk down the street to our bus stop. It was a sunny fall day, and only the cooler wind hinted at any changes to the temperature. The tree-lined boulevard was everything if not ordinary, and our backpacks bounced as they always did.

At the bus stop stood a pretty blonde woman and her dog, who reminded me of people I'd seen before. I still had that déjà vu feeling when the bus pulled in. It was one of those big old 1960s chrome-covered things. Not many of those left in the fleet. Strangely, it looked brand new, as if the maintenance crew had gone above and beyond to make sure it was kept top-shape. We got on, and Chloe and I went to sit toward the middle of the bus. The blonde woman kept on going to the back.

"I have physics today," Chloe said, with a face that said she would have rather eaten live cockroaches.

"It's the volleyball I'm not looking forward to," I replied. I'd never enjoyed wearing gym clothes. Something about those skin-tight short shorts irked me to the core of my being. Give me a nice long dress, sure. Shorts, though, belonged on the bonfire of bad taste.

A tall, muscular man got on the bus. He was kind of cute, in a bad boy sort of way, and a giant question mark materialized inside my head. Were those *my* thoughts? I crossed my legs and looked out the window.

"What do you really want to do after High School," Chloe said. Wow! Talk about lightning flash out of nowhere. We'd discussed tentative plans, but nothing serious, of course. It all seemed nebulous and open since we were kids, but now we were faced with our last semester, and real life beyond.

Chloe had taken out her phone and stretched out her arm and smiled, and I pulled in close to join her in taking an early-morning picture of ourselves on our way to school.

"You want to go hang out at Merivale Mall after school?" she asked me, and I answered

"Sure." Not really feeling as if there was anything too terribly important for us to do apart from that. I would get to look at that pair of shoes I had been coveting for the past two weeks. I might even get them.

I looked toward the front of the bus, and noticed that anything that was a few feet away from it, outside, looked blurry, unreal. I tilted my head and went to the front. Maybe my eyes were blurry, and I just needed to be closer to see what was going on further away. The odd blurriness did not abate the closer I got. I tried to see further, wondering what happened beyond a few feet, and for a moment, it became clearer, but then the bus driver, beside whom I was standing, told me:

"There's nothing to see beyond what is there."

It felt awkward, in my mind and in my heart. There was always something beyond what we could see and touch. It was then that I realized that I was on the wrong bus. That it was someone else's. I walked back to the seat where Chloe was waiting for me, giving me a quizzical look.

"What's wrong?" she said.

"Everything," I whispered, and she did not hear me, but kept texting on her phone. A bus that plowed blindly forward, full of people who asked no questions was wrong. I wanted to get off. Walk. Take a taxi. Anything that I could control, that afforded me a clear line of sight to where I was headed. This was all a bad dream. A dream meant to reassure you while you were heading who knew where. Lead by— whom, exactly?

It was like a bad scene out of a terribly boring movie, right before something atrocious happens. I looked at the corner of the bus, and thought I saw some blurring of the window. An off-green wavering that shouldn't have been there. My heart

Afterdeath

began to speed up. I always got anxiety attacks. Gosh darn it! I put my hands in my backpack's side pocket, and found nothing. My meds were at home. Double gosh darn it!

"Are you okay?" Chloe said, "You look grey."

"I'm fine," I said, louder, as I gripped the upper bar over the seat in front of me. I wasn't by far though. None of this was real. The wavering window in the corner now looked like a screen, with everything on it a sick, psychedelic mish-mash of transient colours, and then I bolted upright.

I was in a theatre. Looking at a screen whose projections were sickly greenish and purple, like hypnotizing lava lamps in an unending parade of ill feelings. On other red seats, Barkley, Angelina, Carson and Chloe stared, wide-eyed and slack jawed. There was no one else. I went to Chloe first and shook her, but she didn't move. A little bit of drool pooled on her chest, but she kept staring straight ahead.

The earth shook, with a dull, thumping sound. I shook Chloe and screamed: "Wake up!" over and over again until her eyes blinked twice, and she looked at me.

"Where am I?"

"No time for that, wake the others!" I said, as another shaking whomp rocked the building. She let go of the seat in front of her and went to wake Angelina and Barkley, while I knocked Carson around with little care for formalities. The far end of the building began to collapse, and we ran toward the exit at the top of the stairs.

Through the doors we found ourselves directly in front of Bertha, and the theatre dissolved before our eyes, the hard-packed earth underneath exploding out like a volcano. I jumped into the driver's seat. As the others ran for the car, a geyser of hard rock flew into the night sky, the theatre now only a bad memory.

A long mouth full of row upon row of black knife teeth, attached to a body like a whale made of darkness ripped through the opening where the theatre had been.

"Deep squall!" Angelina shrieked, and I punched the gas, heading toward our previous destination. The thing rose into the air, landing on the road behind us, breaking it like a nuclear jackhammer, and melted below the surface again.

I kept my foot to the mat, as I kept looking back. Multiple hills formed around us, and the car jolted from side to side as the hungry beasts tried to overturn us from beneath.

"Well at least now we know what that was all about!" Angelina yelled from the back seat over the roaring of the engine and booming of the hits coming from below.

Out in the distance, I saw them: flat shapes moving at incredible speeds over the desert. Five of them, as well as I could tell, coming our way in formation. A Squall rose on our right, tanking toward us, its enormous body like a roller, crushing everything in its path with a deafening boom, and I jerked the wheel to the left. It missed us by inches, lowering again into the sandy depths with a grinding sound.

The Jinn closed in on us, and kept on going past. For a second my heart sank, and I wondered if it meant we'd been abandoned, but no, they circled around behind us, and came parallel. Maimun rode his carpet low, and pointed straight ahead. Above the desert's crust and under his carpet, I could see the grey shape of his manta, floating. The other Jinn closed in on us, and as a compact mass of the enormous shark-like creatures erupted, they split into starburst, veering away from each other.

Maimun fell back, zigzagging on his much more handle-able sand manta. I looked back, and the Jinn had begun driving their beasts in one gigantic circle, the deep squalls pursuing them. With a shudder, the centre of the circle caved, and sand began to pour into the deepening hole. Sand mantas and riders rode faster and faster around the hole, and those behemoth whale-creatures unfortunate enough to find themselves on the rim were swallowed into the sand typhoon which was widening.

The Jinn split outward from the cave-in, and rejoined us in our hectic drive.

Maimun pulled up his mount and gave me the thumbs up and a wide grin.

Behind us, it was as if someone had pulled the plug on the desert, and the hard crust that had formed on the surface now broke up from the typhoon outward, fortunately not as fast as we could drive.

Drive I did. From night until morning, I kept my eyes forward and followed the leader of the Jinn's.

Chapter 28

THE WELL

As we topped a taller crescent, I saw the town down below. Olivia took Bertha to the edge of town and parked there. She closed the roof and tapped her twice in a friendly gesture. This reminded me of an old movie I'd watched when I was a kid, where the car was alive, and did all sorts of things for its owner. 'Bernie' or 'Hurly', or some such thing.

The town was deserted, the windows shuttered, the doors locked. Perhaps the inhabitants hid inside still. Mud caked the walls and had flattened a lot of the vegetation. Apart from that, the destruction looked minimal.

We walked to the centre of the tiny hamlet and made our way into a strange garden. Of course I'd seen it before, but like I said, it was my first time seeing it for myself. It did give me that sense of déjà vu though.

In the middle of the garden was a fountain, with statues of people. They sat in water, and Olivia led the way to the one of an old man with barnacles and sea life living in its beard.

"You have come back to us. The storm we sent was successful then." It said.

"That was you?" Olivia said, and I remembered the deluge that had followed them from the Kingdom of Sands and throughout their escape into the Wyld Lands.

"Of course. If we had not sent it, you would have easily been captured by the Emet, the forest sentinels. This way we hoped to make you invisible. Their sense of smell is attenuated by the rain. We also prayed it would help you with your injury," it said, staring at me.

"It did, thank you," I said. "How did you know?"

"That's a little more difficult to answer. We sense things. Let us leave it at that. You came to ask something of us."

Olivia stepped forward.

"Please send my sister back to the land of the living," she said.

"I'm not going back without you!" I said, whirling on her. I'd felt betrayed by her decision. I knew I'd been rash in abandoning her in the desert, but there was no way I would lose my sister, and if I couldn't be with her...

"You have to. You know I made a promise to Angelina. Besides, you have to go back and warn people of what is coming - this war. It's not a war among the dead; it's bigger than that. I've figured it out now."

"Is there a beacon?" the Wahy asked.

"Yes," Olivia replied.

"Step into the waters and it shall be granted," the Wahy said.

"I'm not giving you up, Olivia! I told you I'd never let you go, and I meant it," I said, and I grabbed her wrists.

"You're not. We'll always be together, Chlo. Trust me," she said this looking deep into my eyes, and it sent a shiver down my spine. Before I knew what was happening, she had twisted her wrists outward, bringing them back from a downward position, and was free of my hands. She pushed me, and I fell back, into the fountain. The last thing I saw was her hand held up in a gesture of goodbye.

Words flowed into my mind from above, perhaps from the gathered Wahy:

Dearly departed, we are gathered here today to send off our sister Chloe, to wish her well in her journey back to— and then they sounded like words spoken underwater, undecipherable save as ululations and vowel chants.

A surge, sucked deep into cold, black waters, pulled from my feet and stretched for kilometres, as if I'd been turned into an ever-expanding elastic. The rushing sound of water filled my ears, as if I bulleted down a waterslide filled to the brim, into a collapsing star. I sped faster and faster, my heart racing until it would explode, and opened my mouth to take a breath!

"I have a heartbeat!" I heard from above me. My whole body hurt, and I sputtered and coughed. My throat felt constricted, like it had been choking for who knows how long, and I couldn't move my body. I opened my eyes, and saw a black man's face, drenched. He had a white shirt on, with a black nametag that said his name was "Durban". A blonde woman appeared near him and flashed a light in my eyes, and I closed them in reaction. We were outside. It was raining.

"Miss, can you hear me?" I heard her say. All I heard was a groan as I tried to open my eyes.

Afterdeath

"Okay, let's move her," the man named Durban said. I felt myself rise, and then go down a bit, as the slab I was tied to "clicked" into place. I saw the flashing lights behind me of the ambulance as they pulled me inside it, and caught a glimpse of Olivia's car. It was a twisted wreck.

I was alive. Where was Olivia? Was she still in the land of the dead? I passed out again.

I woke in a hospital bed.

The steady beeping sound of the heart monitor comforted me somewhat. It meant I was truly alive. I looked around to see where they'd put Olivia, but couldn't turn my neck very far. It was painful to do so, and I must have been on pain medication, because everything was pretty woozy.

A nurse came in and I asked him: "Where's Olivia?" he looked uncomfortable and said:

"I'll get the doctor for you, okay?"

Those were the kind of words you said if you wanted someone to panic. Those were some "I've got some terrible news but I'm too chicken-shit to tell you" words.

"Hi, Olivia?" the Asian lady doctor said as she walked in.

"No, I'm Chloe," I said. "Where's my sister Olivia?" The doctor looked confused for a second and rifled through some paperwork she had under her arm.

"Um, my name is Doctor Yi. Can I sit down?" I tried to nod to the chair next to the bed, but barely moved my chin.

"Go ahead," I said.

"It's so strange. The ID we have for you must be wrong. Listen, I'm very sorry to have to tell you this, but your sister didn't make it. She—died in the crash. Is there anybody we can contact for you?" As soon as those words came out of her mouth, my mind plunged into a deep hole and refused to come out. I could hear myself bawling, but it was once removed, as if watching myself doing it, but having no control over it. I must have cried for hours.

Eventually, I got the identity issues fixed and called my foster parents, who came to visit me the next day.

"How are you holding up, champ?" my step-father Ted said. He was a big man, but right now he looked lost and small. He kept staring at me as if he didn't know me. It felt weird, like he was trying to pretend to be familiar with a complete stranger. My adoptive little sister, Shannon, came up to me and said: "I like your new hair."

"What new hair, sweetie?" I asked. By then, I was able to move a little, and touched my faux-hawk. Which wasn't there. I had long hair. Which wasn't my hair. Had someone put a wig on me? I tugged on it a little.

Then it dawned on me.

Benoit Chartier

This wasn't my body.
I'd come back in Olivia's.
Holy crap!

***

I left the hospital a week later, and my foster parents took me in. It took me a while to get used to Olivia's body, of course.

For a while, every time I walked down the street, it felt as if I stopped existing when I left the sidewalk. There's no other way I can explain it.

My foster parents didn't really understand, and I felt no obligation to explain to them what I thought I'd lived through. Would they have believed it, or would I have been sent back to the hospital for psychological evaluation? Tough call.

All her memories and thoughts were gone, but I still remembered sharing them when we'd been joined as... a... giant wolf-headed snake. Yeah. That happened. Did it?

My foster family was nice, of course, and was kind enough to let me stay for a month, but it was my decision to go back to an apartment I got in the city. I needed my space. In the meantime, I picked up everything from Olivia's apartment, and the landlady said how sad she was to hear of her passing, and how bizarrely identical we were. Yes, well we're identical twins, I explained, as best I could. How can you tell someone you're inhabiting the body of your dead sister?

I also found out that Olivia hadn't gotten time off from her job. She'd quit. She'd wanted to go on this road trip so badly that she had just given zero notice and left. I missed her all that much more.

I went to my body's funeral. That was weird. Not something I ever wish to repeat.

Over the next week, I kept hearing weird talk in the chat rooms about dead bodies coming back to life, but of course this always happened to strangers, so I took it as urban legend. It did make me wonder about Olivia. What she'd said before we parted.

The first few weeks live-side sped by in a blur; I'd been dead, after all, and come back as an almost entirely different person. I'd heard someone tell me once that that had been the best thing that could happen to him. Dying on an operating table did that to you. Don't know if I'd go that far, but it transformed *me*, for better or worse. Can't say I recommend the experience, if you can avoid it, but eventually, it does become a moot point. Too soon is too soon though, and I would rather live everything that's on offer before moving on.

Now I questioned myself, about everything: who I was, what I wanted, what truly mattered. Because I'd changed, the world around me had, as well. Like looking into

Afterdeath

the same house, but through a different window. The Universe had shifted, only a quarter of a degree, but it was enough to tell me: I mattered, in all things. That meant that whatever I did, mattered too, and that exhilarated and frightened me beyond anything I'd ever felt before.

I was angry at her for... a while. I'm not proud of that, but who wouldn't be? For the longest time I wondered how she could just push me out of the way, her own sister, to latch onto that crazy woman. Unkind thoughts, I know. Then I tried to understand her transformation. I don't think she "needed" Angelina the way she might have needed me at some point in time. She'd found that ineffable "something" that everybody looks for and not all find. That thing that makes your life worth living. That spark that she had never been able to light while she was alive. That made me jealous again for a time.

I came to accept it though. It made me wonder if *I* would find it. If I would know where to look.

I'd gone on a road trip with my sister to get to know her. We'd been split up almost immediately. In the end, I did get to know her, better than I would have if we'd both lived, perhaps. I'm proud of what she's become.

I got a part time job at a tattoo parlor and waited for University to start. I'd decided to study biochemistry, but I took a minor in World Religions, just for kicks. As if my busy schedule wasn't packed enough, I volunteered once a week at St. Stephan's, the shelter near my sister's apartment. It just felt right.

At some point you have to accept other people's decisions and go on with your life. Part of it is letting go and being okay with it. The other part is honoring their memory by loving every moment of your life, the bad and the good, and trying to do Good. Because it counts for something. Maybe I still didn't think there was a Grand Scheme of Things. Not in any cosmic sense. But there was a tangible result to my actions. That counted more than any made-up story, in my mind.

And then one night, when I was leaving the shelter, I got into my car and sat staring long and hard at the passing cars, gripping the wheel as if my little beater was a tank, and put my hand to the shifter. There was a tiny bag, right next to it. A clear, cellophane bag with a cheap red plastic bow on it. It was filled with candy.

I picked it up, and looked at it, and craned my neck around to see if someone was hiding, playing a joke on me, but there was no one; no one at all. Still I couldn't hold back a giggle.

When I got home, I went through our stuff, and I found the musty old Ouija board: the same one we'd used to try to get a hold of Grandma. Yeah, I was scared at first, but I had to try. I wanted to confirm my suspicions, present weirdness notwithstanding.

I placed the candles around my messy apartment, not caring if I turned it into a firetrap. I lit them, and turned out the lights. Cold moonlight from a living world shone through the window, and I felt a strange trepidation as I asked:

"Are you there, 'Liv?"

And my hand moved on its own. First to H, then to E, slowly to L, away a bit, then back to L, and then finally, O.

Afterdeath

Dear reader, this book exists because of you, and I thank you. You've trusted me to tell you a tale, and I hope I did not disappoint. If perchance you would trust me a hairsbreadth more, would you be so kind as to grant me a favor? If you could visit www.goodreads.com or Amazon.ca to leave this book the appropriate amount of stars you believe it deserves, which in turn will help my works be known, this will increase my chances of being able to bring you more. If this is one hairsbreadth too much, I thank you for having had the patience to follow my meandering mind this far. Have a wonderful day and may love be with you always.